Praise for *The Fr...*

"Lochner's prose is as sensory-rich and delicious as the settings and twists and turns of her story. This is a book to savor in a quiet corner in low light, with a glass of something rich and no other humans in sight."

- Susanna Daniel, PEN/Bingham Prize Winning Author of *Stilstville*

"Lochner's debut novel is in the vein of Tonya French's *The Likeness* and Donna Tart's *The Secret History* with a trippy *Alice in Wonderland* twist for grown-ups."

- Amelia Dellos, Author *Delilah Recovered*

"An inventive, sharply written thriller that explores the world of simulation, *The French House* will make you question what's actually real—and what isn't."

-Sandra A. Miller, author of *Wednesdays at One*

"A thesis on culture and memory; *The French House* is one to discuss at the dinner table, you won't forget this one."

-Kelsey Ramsden, internationally bestselling author of *Success Hangover*

"Atmospheric and haunting, *The French House* will leave you questioning your memories, and wanting to discuss its twists long after reading."

-Gregory Lee Renz, author of the International Award-winning novel *Beneath the Flames*

"Spellbinding. This novel is an important thesis on segregation, mind control, and our existential need to fit in. An absolutely stunning debut."

-Jean-Christophe Born, French film and opera star

"*The French House* is an intriguing read with richly colorful scenes and characters. Intrigue and suspense keeps you on the edge of your seat."

– Caroline Brookfield, Author of The Reluctant Creative

The French House

Minneapolis

First Edition September 2022

This is a work of fiction. All of the characters, names, incidents, organizations, and dialogue are either the products of the author's imagination or are used fictitiously.

Printed in the United States of America.
10 9 8 7 6 5 4 3 2 1

ISBN: 978-1-950743-95-7

Cover and book design by Gary Lindberg
Cover photo by Ian Graham Leask

The French House

A Novel

Courtney Lochner

Minneapolis

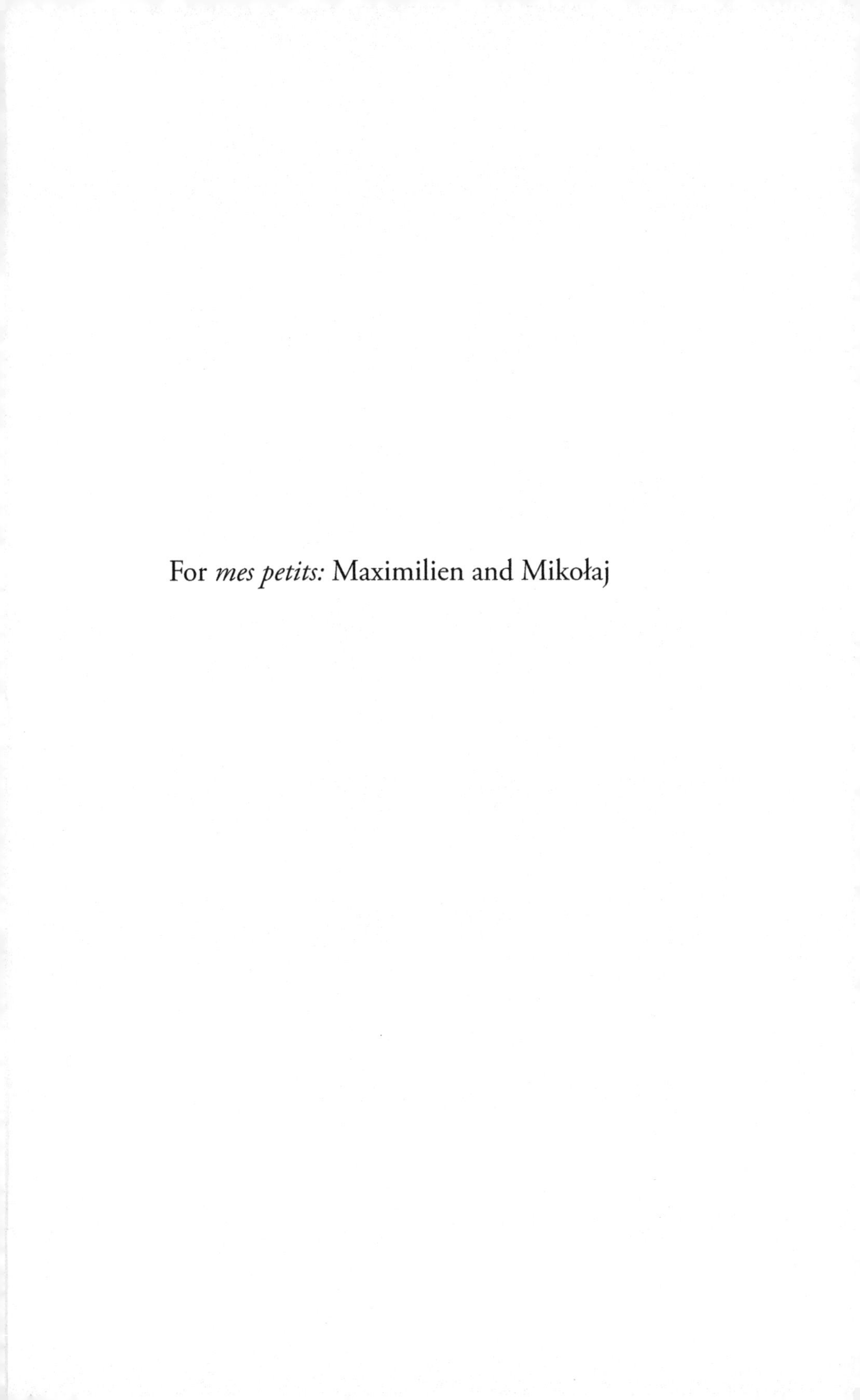

For *mes petits:* Maximilien and Mikołaj

Book I

Les Liaisons Dangereuses

Chapter 1
Day of the Dead

November 1, 2022

They said Alice in Wonderland represented an opium trance. That a man once peeled off his skin during an LSD trip. I'd heard all sorts of things *they* said and yet I didn't know who *they* were.

They were druggies, I guess. Problem people. Outsiders. Me? I was clean. An upstanding citizen.

Until I wasn't.

And so, I suppose there were a few good reasons the police would want to speak with me. There was Professor of course. The type of woman they probably waited their whole lives to question. Whatever she might have done, my name would surface being I was her favorite. But then there was Camille, someone I'd worried about for a long time, never knowing how far she'd take her games. Finally, looming over all of us was The French House. Not just a residence hall; this was the university's simulation of a study abroad program. It was designed to make us feel as if we were all living in France and let's just say it provided an experience far more profound than chocolate croissants in the morning and Balzac by night.

"Did they say why?" I shouted to Papa down the hill.

He paused next to his black truck and lowered his head. Jesus, it was serious. That the police had tracked me down here—*chez Papa*—and on a Sunday.

He cleared his throat. "Someone from The French House died."

The sense of *l'appel du vide* drifted up the hill with his words, a cool wind like a slap to the face. I shivered. The call of the void. Run, jump, or hide? By now Papa was halfway in the truck saying he wanted to drive me into Madison himself, that we should get going, that I should grab my passport to prove I was a citizen. The thought hadn't occurred to me. We'd lived in the States since I was six and my accent wasn't noticeable, or so I *thought*.

I rubbed the arrowhead I wore on a rope around my neck. Just two months into my freshman year. A new life, new friends, new love—and someone, possibly Charlie—*died.*

Papa stuck his head out the window. "*Dépeche-toi!*"

"*J'arrive!*"

I made my way downhill weaving between vineyard rows to buy time. Harvest was long since over and the interlacing vines spindled against their wires looked dead from the cold. Wisconsin winters hit early and managed to catch you by surprise every year.

Once out of the vineyard I felt exposed, as if the sun was a spotlight: *you're on.* The surrounding bluffs stood like proud soldiers at this early hour, but by three they'd hover over the valley like old ladies and shadow everything in their path.

Blue exhaust was smoking out of the truck and quickly dissipating into the morning fog. Papa had one arm bear hugged over the wheel, and circled the other to beckon me in. On the passenger seat his aluminum Thermos dribbled coffee onto piles of unopened mail. He swiped them onto the floor mat, and I got in.

"You've never looked so interested in vines in your life."

I buckled my seatbelt. "What are you talking about?"

"You were stalling out there."

"No, I'm just," I shifted, "I'm confused. Who died? Did they say?"

Papa jerked the gear into reverse and made a half-circle until we faced our long gravel driveway head on. He sped to the end and pulled a farmer stop, nothing more than a pause, then pressed on the gas until we were on the highway hurtling toward town at a roaring eighty miles per hour.

Fog thickened as we descended the valley, rising from the riverbed like steam from a roast.

"I didn't hear you come in last night. Should I assume you slept in the forest—" he cocked his head to the side—"like you did as a girl?"

"I guess," I said, moving the seatbelt strap behind my shoulder. Had I slept in the forest? I didn't remember. Why did I come to Papa's in the first place? Or leave The French House? "Did they say who died?"

He didn't respond. Pain pulsed in my temples: I rubbed them, but it got worse. I grabbed a water bottle from the drink holder, there was only a drop, but I drank it.

In town Papa slowed to forty-five in a twenty-five zone. We coasted down Main Street, a strip of mom-and-pop shops and burly oaks that snaked alongside the cliff above the river's edge. We passed the single-screen movie theater and its bulb-lined marquis advertising some superhero remake, the perpetually busy pancake diner, Lizzie's Knot So Fast knitting shop, Lichten's Photography Studio boasting the same toothy grinned senior in the window since the day we moved here, and finally Schneller's Hardware, the town's portal into 1954, and the only store on Main I'd bothered to venture into. Past Main was nothing more than blocks of ranch and Victorian homes, a school, hospital, and a fire station, all the community necessities packed into neat grids until the town abruptly ended as if the cornfields had drawn a border and told it to *stop right there.*

Papa slammed the brakes, and I lurched forward. We were an arm's length from a Ford Fiesta in the middle of the four-way stop next to Gaertner's Funeral Parlor. The guy in the Ford honked, retroactively, like he just now realized we nearly rammed him.

"Les cons," Papa muttered as he pulled ahead, ignoring the other car at the four-way stop, which likely had been there before us. We crossed the bridge, the fog so thick it masked the river. Canoes drifted below in empty space, black silhouettes paddling through smoke.

And finally, we were on Highway 12 toward Madison.

"Are we going to police station or The French House?" I said, rubbing my arrowhead so hard my finger hurt. I waited a beat, cleared my throat. "And did they say who died?"

But Papa was hitting the dashboard. After a harsh blow the gas gauge ticked back to life. The truck was half full.

"Papa?"

He flapped the visor down, tapped his fingers on the wheel.

"Papa! Who died?"

His eyelashes fluttered. "They didn't say."

I exhaled a puff of warm air. Ignorance by default. A world where all of us were fine, Professor, Reine, even Camille, but especially Charlie, at least until Papa and I arrived at The French House, and I risked learning otherwise. Anyone but Charlie, I prayed, a monstrous thought, but losing him was unfathomable, and yet I knew the world was cruel enough to do it. It had already stolen my mother. I rolled the window down and unfocused my eyes, a way to transform the green alfalfa fields and golden hay bales into a Monet.

What happened last night? Why'd I drive to Papa's? Why'd I sleep in the forest—like I did right after Maman died. My darkest period.

I relaxed against the headrest, pinched my eyes shut—concentrated.

Then, an image.

I jerked—startling Papa. Our truck veered over the highway line and the border grooves honked like an oncoming semi.

"What the *hell*, Simone?"

"Nothing," I said.

I couldn't tell him I remembered blood on my hands.

Chapter 2

September 6, 2022

Three weeks prior to my first day at the university I received a peculiar letter. The first few lines were innocent enough, a greeting from the French Lit teaching assistant, but it took a sharp turn in the second paragraph.

> *Beware, you'll be entering a class designed by the devil herself. Over the years, Professor Anne Boucher has driven many students to madness.*

The letter's sinister tone didn't bother me at first. I was too caught on the name Anne Boucher. Sure, it was a common one, but it was more than that, the name held real estate in my mind. But I needed a reminder why.

The letter went on it in a more self-serving direction:

> *But why be a silent observer? If you choose so, you may take part in this adventure. I have an exciting theory about the professor, and the goal of my thesis is to prove it.*

Camille, the TA, must have some issues, I thought. Not that I was a psychologist, but I'd spoken to one enough in the past to know. Whatever the case I decided to take her words as a challenge and vowed to impress the so-called devil, Anne Boucher. I started by quitting my prescription—cold turkey. Eleven years swallowing all those little yellow pills (twice-daily, preferably-with-a-meal) and I just stopped. Call it an experiment or maybe just hope. A woman known for driving people to madness (probably because she was freaky-smart) would surely find my prescription a weakness. And I still had three weeks left to prepare, three weeks to rediscover the pre-pills version of myself, the Technicolor Simone. The one I scarcely remembered.

Those weeks passed quickly; harvest season didn't afford me another thought about the matter. But arriving on campus now, fluttery stomach and all, I risked destroying any chance of making a decent first impression on Anne Boucher: there wasn't a parking spot in sight. When you grow up in the country you don't allow extra time for finding parking or getting stuck at stop signs as hordes of people cross. You just pull your truck onto a patch of grass and leave your keys in the ignition. "Shit, shit, shit." I punched the steering wheel, horrified at the thought of walking in mid-lecture. The heads turning. Anne Boucher frowning. My name tarnished from the get-go.

Then, from a dead-end street against Lake Mendota, a bronze Aphrodite statue caught my eye—how could she not? She was as great as the Venus de Milo herself, sunlight gleaming off her green skin. Better equipped for the Louvre than for campus, her arms fell to her side with grace, one hand gripping a book. She was dressed in a Greek robe, waves of hair rolling down her strong back, and her profile facing what must have been the only legal parking spot within a five-mile radius. I had to claim it before someone else did. I pulled around the car in front of me the way Papa would and parked next to the glorious statue. "*Merci, Madame*," I saluted then took off in a jog.

"Hey, wait!" a girl called. "You gotta rub the statue or she'll curse you."

Curse me? I stopped and turned around. A blonde girl was leaning against the statue's enormous bronze base, smiling and pointing up. *Okay then*. I rubbed the bronze woman's foot which oddly felt warm as a light bulb.

Statues had always intrigued me. Maman's library had a section devoted them. She'd bought an enormous book about the hidden meanings of statues at the Louvre gift shop after visiting the Susa collection where she fell in love with Queen Napir Asu's statue. I don't remember this, I was only four, but Papa snapped a photo of her standing by the giant bronze, head dropped back in admiration. She was wearing a purple wrap dress with mustard-colored heels, her long black hair pulled in a loose twist. I keep that photo in that book's Susa chapter, specifically at the page with Napir Asu's inscription translation: *whoever destroys this plaque will be cursed, his name erased, his life barren.*

Maman had a few statue-related novels too, like the one by Prosper Merrimé about a giant bronze of Venus that curses an entire village and murders someone to boot. *Allegedly.*

I searched this statue's base for an inscription but there was only a jagged section where one must have once been. How did it break, British pillagers? Frat guys? Maybe that explained the curse.

"It's been damaged for a while," said the girl rubbing her hand along the chipped piece. "It's The French House's statue." She pointed to a dark brick mansion at the end of a cobblestone walkway behind her. Intricate as a gingerbread house, it had a turret on its right side, and dormer windows from the third floor.

"The French House?"

"Yeah, a residence hall, but like only for French majors and stuff."

The House pulled into sharper focus. So sharp everything else reduced to background noise and I was suddenly woozy from the attention shift. Of all places to end up this morning, *The French House.* I rubbed my arrowhead and shook my head. Something sent me here. *Was it you, Maman?*

"Pretty snooty place. They all keep to themselves. Which is fine, the place is eerie as hell—bad things have happened there, like *really* bad."

Poof: spell broken. "Like what?"

The girl was reading something off her phone, smiling. "Anyway," she hauled a blue Jansport bag over her shoulder, "now you should have good luck."

"Yeah, let's hope so." I looked into the statue's vacant eyes above. A cloud edged away then, sending a spear of light into her patina sockets and giving them a flicker of life.

* * *

Rushing to the French department I found the University of Wisconsin campus exactly as I'd imagined. Like a snow globe outfitted for fall. Cranberry colored leaves scattering across the clear sky, settling over the gothic buildings and students like confetti. I was accustomed to not recognizing a soul. I'd survived four years of high school invisibly, always on the outskirts, never at the football games, the prom, the play. But here was a perfect place for a new start. Aside from wanting to impress the revered Anne Boucher, I was determined to ace her course too: Fundamentals of French Literature's Euphemisms for Society. The class was extremely competitive to get into; Camille's letter said most people tried for years to test in, and I credited Maman's library as to why I made it on my first try.

I jogged the rest of my way to the romance languages department, a limestone building striped by white columns, and checked the number: 717. This was it; I'd made it on time.

Carrera marble floors and walls filled in as my eyes adjusted to the light inside. There was a directory near a wide staircase, and I rushed to it.

Boucher. Boucher. Boucher. Where are you?

"May I help you find what you search?" said a man with a thick Italian accent. He must have been pushing eighty, with jowls like stirrups, and nobly sporting a three-piece brown houndstooth suit. When I told him my course's name, he tapped his tortoiseshell cane against the marble and leaned in, coffee and cream on his breath.

"Fundamentals of French Literature's Euphemisms for Society, is that so?"

I nodded.

"Very well. You'll find it, or shall I say—*her*, in room 203."

"Thank you, sir." I said then hurried to the staircase prepared to take two steps at a time when he called for me.

"*Signorina—er, Mademoiselle?*"

I twisted around. He was leaning against his cane with the Tower of Pisa's angle.

"*Oui?*"

"Hold your head high, speak like you mean it—and as we say in Italian, *in bocca al lupo.*"

"To the wolf's mouth," I said.

He mocked tipping a hat.

"To the wolf's mouth," I muttered as I ran up the stairs then down the corridor. I felt sweaty and lightheaded, and paused just outside room 203's door to catch my breath and shake out my hands. But this was no time to doddle; I pushed the door open expecting a small classroom setting, only to find a surprisingly large lecture hall with tiered theater-style seating.

And there she was.

Professor Anne Boucher stood before us like a hologram wavering in and out of the light. She wore a tweed pencil skirt, slim fitting white blouse and suede boots, her mahogany hair draped in a chignon. She was beautiful in the way I thought her glasses were an act, a purposeful distraction from her voluptuous figure, green eyes and full lips. They hung from her neck as an accouterment, a prop. The message clear, she was an academic, not a doll.

On the dusty green chalkboard she'd written three titles.

Les Liaisons Dangereuses
L'étranger
La Vénus d'Ille

Below the titles:

What is the theme that connects these works?

I couldn't help but think—nothing. I'd read each of the books many times over and they were entirely different in style, voice, and theme. But I'd have to come up a theory. It was evidently the way to win her over and to become the best in class.

If you solve this, come see me.

Was this what had driven others to madness? Her riddle? Or was it her detachment? She paid no attention as students filed in, didn't acknowledge the loud girls holding Colectivo coffees and complaining about their schedules, didn't turn toward the guy having a coughing fit on the far end. I observed her as if from the other side of a double mirror and she didn't know we were here. She half sat against the wooden desk on her side of the room and slowly moved the palm of her hand along its length. Her fingers and open palm glided over the wood as though she were stroking it.

I pulled out my notebook and it was this of all things that caught her attention. She looked up, the rafter lights making her chatoyant eyes glow blankly like the statue's. And just as the cloud had shed light on the bronze's gaze, hers shifted and met mine.

"Why are you sitting in the back row?" Her voice was rich as syrup. "Move in."

She had a point. I was the only one in the back, laughably distanced. I grabbed my bag and claimed a seat ten rows in, next to a girl in a hijab hunched over her notepad like it was a fire in the cold. I resituated and clicked my pencil ready to take notes. The girl handed me a syllabus, which I skimmed; in addition to the three books written on the board, there was an endless list of French novels assigned.

"*Professor—*" said a guy from the front row, "Charles Derosiers." He walked to the center of the room and every girl perked up, me included. He was tall and slim, dressed in brown corduroys and a white shirt, unbuttoned just enough to reveal a touch of his chest, his sleeves rolled up his forearms. He ran his fingers through his thick brown hair and smirked at Anne Boucher. "But you're welcome to call me Charlie."

She arched an eyebrow and crossed her arms.

"*Pour vivre heureux, vivons caché*," he went on ignoring her. The quote I knew: to live happy, live hidden.

"Did you write that one yourself," teased the girl he'd been sitting with moments ago.

"*Oh là là* come on, now! You were supposed to respond with the corresponding quote." Despite his arrogant tone there was a delicious layer underneath it, warm and spicy as cinnamon, or was it clove? "You should have known that quote, Reine. You live in The French House and it's etched above the front door."

There it was again, *The French House*.

"How about another?" he went on. Behind him Professor's eyelids dropped half-mast. She was either amused or too proud to protest. "And let me say," he held up his pointer finger, "I'll forever worship the person to find a smart quote in response to this one."

Again, all the girls in the room leaned in.

"'Those who can make you believe absurdities, can make you commit atrocities.'"

I don't know how else to explain it other than to say the perfect answer simply sprouted effortlessly in my mind, the same way math problems did for my brother. Without thinking further, I quoted: "'the regularity of a habit is generally in proportion to its absurdity.'"

Charlie looked up, the girls sitting in the row ahead of me turned around, and the coughing guy had another bout.

"Who said that?" Charlie scanned the room.

After a moment, I raised my hand in the air and waved once.

"Ah," he said meeting my eyes and instantly I was hot in a moment of rapture, tugging my shirt's neckline to cool my neck. "Proust, from *The Remembrance of Things Past.* That was it. The perfect response—I'm not sure I would have even come up with it myself. But can you name mine?"

I nodded. "Voltaire of course. From *Questions Sur Les Miracles.*"

He slowly walked across the room watching me. I refrained from smiling, though in my head the champagne was popping. This was exactly the inspiration I wanted from my studies, the erudite dialogue and the beautiful cultured people I had longed for during my years at Country Bumpkin High.

"What's your name, and how'd you pull that off?"

I'd already sent my bio to the teaching assistant Camille, who wanted to know a little more about all of us, since she would be missing the first week of class. But this was different. I wasn't prepared to share my story with the entire class, nor to lose the position I briefly held with Charlie Derosiers.

Ouch.

I'd rubbed my arrowhead's tip so much I drew blood.

"*Mademoiselle?*"

"Are you okay?" The girl in the red hijab next to me whispered.

I wiped my bleeding finger on the class syllabus. "I'm Simone Duchamps."

"And?"

"My mother read me all of the greatest French novels before bed and now I have to read them myself—to keep her voice alive."

Professor tilted her head and smiled at me with a Cheshire cat grin.

* * *

When class was over I paused on my way out to study Professor's image one more time, sorry we hadn't heard more from her. Charlie pretended he was the professor the entire hour and had gone on to ask each person to introduce themselves and share their reasons for loving French literature.

Professor Boucher gave a delicate nod and exited stage left, draining the room of all energy as though she'd never been there to begin with. She'd left something on the table though—a book, sitting alone on her desk. The lecture hall was already empty so I walked over and picked it up. It was hers. She wrote it, and I recognized its title: *The Power of Suggestion: A Woman's Guide to Empowerment.* That's why her name rang so familiar. My mother used to read this book. It was no longer in her library; I was sure as I'd reread all those books many times over. But I could hear Maman's voice saying this title so clearly that I knew my memory was right. I turned it over, the cover was worn and felt waxy, the corners rounded. I pictured Maman's hand enclosed around it.

"Hey—"

I dropped the book then quickly set it back onto the table. Charlie Derosiers stood at the same door Professor had just exited. "I'm sorry, I didn't mean to scare you." He smiled differently from the megawatt version he'd given the group and I sensed this was his natural state. He put one hand in his pocket and let his hazel eyes roam the room for a moment like he knew I'd wait for him to go on. And he did. "Looks like I'm the winner."

"I'm sorry?"

"The book. Boucher's book. It's not part of the course material, obviously. Mimi—I mean *Camille* asked me to plant it there to see if you would grab it. I bet you would, she wasn't so sure."

I wanted to say a lot of things then. How bizarre a test that was, and above all, why me?

"I liked what you said about your mother. She must have been an incredible woman to read you such great works when you were only a child."

"Yes." I rubbed my palm along the wooden desk the way Professor had done earlier. "My memories of her are disjointed without them, clear for a second before the images and sounds fizzle away, replaced by something . . . *else*."

My memory was like listening to the radio while driving through the hills. One moment a great song was on, then static took over, followed by strange—sometimes horrifying voices.

Charlie cupped his jaw as though suddenly aware of his five o'clock shadow. "In a way, books revive the dead." He took two steps backward and paused at the door. "I'm sorry, Simone but I have to run. I'll see you later, *n'est-ce pas?*"

"Yeah, see you," I said, but he'd taken off. Already I knew I'd replay this scene over and again in my mind all night, weighing alternate things to say, places we might have gone in between classes. I again picked the book off the desk and held it tightly in my hands, glancing around the lecture hall and imagining Camille the TA observing me from some campus security camera, watching her test unfold, her bait claimed. But when I opened the cover, I saw the reason why she felt the book had been intended for me.

My name was already handwritten on the first page—in my mother's handwriting.

Chapter 3

After class I drove to the vineyard craving a glass of our *Philtre de Courage* wine. Supposedly Anne Boucher had driven many to madness, and God help me if I was already headed that route. Maman always wrote my name in books she felt best for me, Bertrand's in those for him, and kept them in her library. So how did Camille get Maman's copy of Boucher's book?

I pulled into the vineyard around five-thirty and parked by the winery's main building. It was the size of a football field and designed with European flair, white-shuttered windows and a red tile roof. It housed our tasting area, a gigantic fermentation room, Papa's lab, wine storage, and offices. It connected to a charming old carriage house turned gift shop where we sold wine, cheese and charcuterie, as well as the full spectrum of oenophile gifts from vineyard paintings and grape earrings, to the more unfortunate kitschy goods our manager Carol insisted on, shirts that said *It's Wine O'Clock!* and *Wine a Little, You'll Feel Better.*

By now the guests were already gone. Only minutes after closing time at five, the vineyard emptied. Walking through the suddenly silent halls, standing in the gravel driveway and looking into the immensity of the vineyard inspired loneliness. And then of course, there were those synaptic snaps that shot across my visual horizon. Terrifying scenes that passed so quickly that I couldn't hold them and they slipped away. Were they just innate anxieties? Like every child fearing the basement? For a time, my angst was so bad my teachers had told Papa that, "We had to see someone about this." All I ever wanted to know was, what was "this?" I still don't know the answer to that, so I strive to find security in the stillness that comes with quarter past five and beyond. Telling myself that at the very least I can expect it at the same time every day. Clockwork.

The silence was all the better for Papa who hated crowds, he was the vintner behind the wine's magic and preferred roaming the hills alone over anything to do with marketing. A journalist for *Food and Wine* described him capable of improving grapes by simply touching them. That's not to say success for our vineyard happened overnight. In a place where most people prefer beer it was my mother's idea to make the vineyard a tourist attraction and publicize it. "It's not Disney World," she'd said in an interview with *Saveur*, "but Dionysius World." They'd put a full-page photo of her standing in the middle of the vineyard smiling coyly, her long black hair flowing in the wind, and her eyes soft-lit, like she'd just woken from a lustrous dream. Her top lip protruded slightly more than the bottom to give her a pensive look and Papa used to say she looked like Juliette Binoche. I however was the unfulfilled version. While I shared most of her features my nose was longer, my figure more boyish, and I lacked her stylish savoir-faire. I never experimented with make-up or coiffure, and unlike her sophisticated ensembles, I only ever wore blue jeans with a plain, or mariner style t-shirt. A penchant for stripes marked the extent of my range because I didn't dare touch her clothes or go into her closet. I left her things alone.

Smoke donuts puffed from the house chimney, but I had a feeling Papa was still in his lab. I wanted to tell him I was home, and what was for dinner.

Entering the main building's atrium was like going into an enormous old-world apothecary. Wine bottles lined the dark walnut shelves as if they were tonics and medicines, each one with sweeping calligraphy on its label. Filling the remaining space were tasting tables, old world scales, half-melted candlesticks, marble bowls with wooden pestles, and an assortment of stools and armchairs. The largest tasting bar served our most popular wine, *Philtre d'Amour*. There, classic French romance novels were piled on one end, and a tiered silver platter topped with chocolates and *petits fours* on the other. This counter was our most popular check-in point on social media, not that I partook in any social platforms, but our PR director frequently referenced it.

Carol came from out of her office holding a broom. "Hey, doll. Have you seen your dad?" I shook my head. "He's a phantom." She deposited the broom in a storage closet. "I gave *twenty* tours today, that's gotta be a record for a Monday, right?" She slipped on a North Face jacket, zipped it and tugged her long grey hair out the back. "I gotta run, will you tell him one of the toilets in the women's bathroom is acting up? I don't have a clue what to do and Jim's on vacation."

"Sure," I said following her out the main door. "Have a nice night."

She got in her red Jeep and took off, gravel dust in her wake. I walked through its cloud and uphill to my house, the only building the tourists couldn't enter. It was high enough on the hill to remain immersed in light, and as the wind blew, the vines that grew from the ground to the shingles shimmered like scales of a mermaid tail.

Inside, my brother was sitting in his usual spot, in the chair facing the west living room window to absorb the last bit of sun. His face flickered as I walked into the room. I felt guilty for starting at the university, leaving him behind. Still two years until he graduated high school, and now instead of my hand guiding him, he had to navigate the halls with his seeing cane. Bertrand had lost more than just Maman the day they crashed; he lost his eyesight too. I wasn't in the car. I'd unwittingly signed the devil's half-priced, guilt-loaded deal.

"So how was it?" Bertrand asked.

"It was just how I'd pictured it would be, aside from—" I knew he'd say that I should be cautious around these people, Charlie and the TA Camille, if I told him everything.

"Aside from what?"

"That I missed you," I said. "How was your day?"

"Tap, tap, tap." He nodded toward his stick.

Instinctively I closed my eyes to imagine what it felt like for Bertrand. When we were younger, he loved to challenge me; we'd tie a bandana around my eyes and send me on a challenging route around the house. When I banged into the dinner table or tripped over the doorstop like a clumsy newborn calf, Bertrand tried to teach me to elevate my other senses. "They'll help you see the way I do." And so I tried to smell what was in my way and where it wafted from, to hear where he was and gather what direction he was moving based on the slithering sound of his footsteps and the floor's predictable creaks. But no matter how hard I tried I always ended up with bruises on my shins.

Though it was normal for the blind to develop heightened senses, Bertrand was diagnosed with synesthesia by the time he was eight, which meant he comingled taste with sound, numbers with feelings. For him, math problems solved themselves by way of color-codes and shapes. According to him these color-mixing forms were more amorphous than any traditional tag would allow and moved like a three-dimensional Rubik's Cube that clicked and swished until forming a visual solution, making him a mathematical prodigy. It wasn't just numbers. Days of the week, places, and even people he associated with shades of the rainbow and emotions.

"Can you feel how people are?" I'd asked my brother once.

"Are you talking about auras?" Bertrand said, feeling around for a tray of apples, and I'd said yes, having years ago learned to stop nodding or shaking my head. "Everyone has an aura and I suppose I see it. Or, I feel it." He bit into a small, red apple and told me that my aura was rosy pink. "Your aura is like…toast—warm toast with honeycomb, and the light finally breaking the black. Morning is the most optimistic time of day."

Those words stuck with me, they will forever. There are weeks when I think of them every day, every morning. The most optimistic time of day.

"You always led me around school because I let you, Simone," he said. "I know my way around so well I hardly need the stick. And of course," he faced me, his mouth curled into a sweet smile. "I still have the Misfits."

The Misfits. My dear, dear Misfits. Sam, a girl with Down's Syndrome, Kip with cerebral palsy, and my blind brother. These were the kids dismissed from gym class (bullied to bruises by the cool crowd: people who thought making fart noises with their armpits was comedic genius and drinking cheap beer in cornfields was the ultimate Friday night.) Seeing Sam, Kip, and my brother forced to sit on the sidelines drove me nuts so I'd volunteered to create a P.E. class for them. Since I graduated they came over on Sundays to stroll the vineyard, and sometimes stay for dinner. Sam lived close enough to walk over and some days we would call out to each other, our echoing voices boomeranging through the grassy valley.

"I should fix dinner," I said to Bertrand. A nightly ritual I hadn't missed since God knew when. I went downstairs and into the kitchen. Beyond the white farmhouse sink, a large framed window we left open most of the year welcomed the breeze, singsong of birds, and the view of the vineyard hills. Above the butcher block island hung a half dozen heirloom copper pots that only I used. Now that I'd be preparing dinner already past five however, I planned to rely on slow cookers, and on the island sat one I'd filled in the morning with beef, potatoes, carrots, celery, garlic, and, of course, wine.

I grabbed a wine glass from the shelf and noticed my bright orange pill bottle on the counter below. The pills I hadn't taken since reading the letter about Anne Boucher. I set it next to the sink, so I'd remember to hide it upstairs.

"Catch," Papa said. He stepped inside leaving a trail of muddy footprints. He had a rare smile as he held up a tan arrowhead and tossed it to me, the screen door closing with a squawk in his trail. I caught and surveyed the old stone with my fingertips. Its edges were less jagged than most; it had dulled over the years, or maybe it had never been finished. There were so many arrowheads in the soil, and each of them different.

"Nice try but I'll keep mine." I placed it in the vase by the sink amongst fifty some others. I opened a bottle of *Philtre de Courage* and poured myself a small glass.

"What's this?" Papa grabbed my pills. Shame on me for leaving them out. He scrutinized the white label covering the container. "There's too many here given the last time you refilled. You're taking them twice a day, *n'est-ce pas?*"

"*Mais bien sûr,*" I said, turning from him and lifting the wine halfway to my lips. He remained still until I grinned at him and offered him a glass. He shook his head and went upstairs.

My pills changed me, I had no doubt about that. They changed my entire landscape too, into bland nothingness. As such, I categorized my life in a trio of tapestries. My youth: a Renoir. The period after

Maman's death: a Pollock. Everything thereafter (thanks to my pills): an Agnes Martin, one of her grey incoherent canvases, nearly blank. What I needed was to get back to that Renoir, the color and gentle brushstrokes, the perfect beauty. My memories lived there I knew, the memories of Maman. *Et oui*, I realized that returning to my Renoir might require passage through the chaotic Pollock, like Odysseus into Hades.

* * *

Papa and Bertrand enjoyed my stories about school, from the students walking in the middle of the street to the hippies drumming under the sun. Sitting at the barn door dining-table, we slurped our way through second bowls of my stew, drank our wine, and talked in the candlelight.

"Who's your French Lit professor?" Papa asked. "Someone I might know?"

"*Bof*, I doubt it," I said, setting my fork down. "Just some woman from a teeny town."

"Which one?"

"You know a lot of Professors from small towns in France?"

He wiped his napkin across his face and finished chewing. "I'm only trying to make conversation."

"Sorry, you just don't usually ask for details."

"Tis true," Bertrand said breaking from our spoken French into English, and even adding an exaggerated British accent. He rubbed hands along the table, picked up his glass and sipped.

"She's from Pont Saint Esprit."

"Seriously?" Bertrand protruded his lips. "Where there was that mass poisoning?"

"A mass *poisoning*?"

"She's from Pont Saint Esprit?" Papa interrupted. "*T'es absolument sûre?*"

"The CIA covered it up. It was very suspect."

"Since when did you become such a conspiracy theorist?"

"I didn't say I believed it."

"What's her name?" Papa asked.

"Anyway, I'm also enrolled in psychology, calculus, and a business development course this semester. *Voilà*. So, Bertrand, how was *your* day?" I didn't want Papa to know she was also the author of one of Maman's beloved books. I wanted to keep Professor Anne Boucher to myself.

There was no bio in the French Lit syllabus but I knew from her book's jacket cover this minute detail: Anne Boucher was born in Pont Saint Esprit. Of course, I had considered looking her up online or gossiping about her with my classmates, but I preferred to peel her oniony layers myself. I knew she had something to offer me if I proved I was worthy. Then again, if she really were the devil, what would that something be?

* * *

Later that night, long after Papa had fallen asleep on his worn leather chair downstairs, a brandy at his side, I sat in Bertrand's room in the silent darkness. Even the crickets must have packed up and left with summer.

"Want to hear something weird?" I said.

"Of course."

"We're supposed find a common theme across three books for our final paper in French Lit." I told him the titles.

"Sounds like Duchamps family recommended reading for six-year-olds."

I laughed. "I feel like it's a trick question given the TA's warning about the Professor. I told you about that, right?"

"Yeah," Bertrand said scooting across his bed to lean against the wall. "I've never read *La Vénus d'Ille*."

"Ah, it's a short piece about a Parisian archaeologist who visits the small town Ille. The townspeople show him their enormous bronze Venus statue hoping he can transcribe its inscription. They say it curses them, and sometimes comes to life. Obviously, the Parisian thinks they're crazy and writes them off as superstitious country folk. But during his stay he's invited to a wedding, and the groom gets killed the night of the ceremony. They find gigantic footprints around the scene of the crime, the same size as Venus's enormous, bronzed feet, and claim she came to life, seduced and killed him, leaving his poor new bride alone and widowed."

"Okay so you've got love triangles in *Les Liaisons Dangereuses*—loads of sex and backstabbing, then in *L'étranger* you've got an existentialist outsider who murders an Arab, and in this last one, an unsolved murder. That's an awful lot of focus on death. It's got to be an allegory, like the death of childhood. The theme, maybe a rite of passage?"

"Oh, I like that." I stood and brushed the transparent curtains aside. The vineyard rows were illumined in moonlight. "That might be too simple though."

"You callin' me a s-s-simpleton?" he said in a drunken hillbilly accent.

"What's the square root of one thousand four hundred and eighty-nine?"

"Thirty-eight point five, eight . . . how many decimals you want M'am?"

"Just as I suspected, he's an idiot!"

We both laughed.

I let go of the curtains and rubbed my arrowhead, allowed my mind to return to Charlie. Where did he live? What did he eat for dinner? How well did he know Camille—what had he called, her, Mimi?

Outside, the wind picked up. Our tire swing squeaked back and forth. After Maman died I spent hours in that thing, skidding my toes back and forth in the sandy dirt. I'd study the tourists, mainly the women. The flick of hair, the giggle into a cupped palm, the swirl of a wine glass.

"Simone?"

"*Oui?*"

From the moonlight I noticed Bertrand simultaneously finishing a sentence in his braille book. When we were younger, I thought he was a superhero because he read in the dark.

"You—you look different."

"My aura? What's different?"

"Are you stressed?"

"We've been sitting here laughing and you think I'm stressed?"

"On a deeper level, yes."

I sat back down. The full aftermath of quitting my prescription was not yet obvious to me but I couldn't put anything past Bertrand, if anyone would see the edges of my new energy emerging, it would be him.

"Remember when Papa would make us calming tea? After Maman died and we suffered nightmares."

"Yeah," I said. "I'd forgotten about that. But he left me one this morning."

"No, I made you the tea."

"You did? No wonder it was delicious! Papa's always tasted awful. What's in it anyway, valerian root or something?"

"I'm not sure, I felt his old mason jars until I recognized the glass bubbling on one that was familiar. I remembered holding it while he prepared our calming tea. So I made it for you this morning but dumped a bunch of raspberry syrup in it so it wouldn't taste so bitter. I wish Papa still made them."

"He probably figured we grew up and now we're fine," I said, thinking I needed to make the calming tea again; it must have been why I'd felt so bold in class. "Bertrand, did Papa know you were in his lab?"

"No, I went in there when he left for the bathroom."

"He gets so weird about his stuff," I said lying down on his bed. "Why'd you make me the tea?"

"I don't know, you were so nervous for your first day that I wanted to help you."

"What's my aura giving off?"

Bertrand paused and fingered along his book. "I'm not sure yet."

Chapter 4

Before heading to campus, I stopped in Papa's lab. He wasn't there and the door was locked. What was so precious? He didn't bother locking our house at night.

I flipped on the lights and immediately saw the containers. Bertrand's words about my changed aura had tormented me all night. Come morning my eyes were red, even my blood tired. But he also reminded me about Papa's calming tea, and this morning I knew I would need more of it to stay calm without my prescription.

The shelves were lined with countless jars, each filled with tealeaves and herbs. I could hardly remember anything from when we made herbal concoctions with my father but decided that the memories would come back to me. I fingered through one after the other until I discovered a container labeled "L" hoping it stood for Lisette, my mother's name. But one whiff told me it was rancid. Of course, it was. It had been twelve years since Maman was here to have tea. Ignoring my tightening throat, I returned the jar where it would continue to go unused.

There was more than just jars of herbs. I noticed a giant beautifully bound book, brown with a threaded gold and patina pattern on the top shelf. I went on my tiptoes and pulled it out but as I did two little books fell from a shelf behind the jars, a worn moleskin journal and a unicorn notepad. I grabbed the unicorn pad feeling a stinging familiarity and flicked open the first page—wham! The winery's main door opened and closed. Footsteps echoed in the hall. *Papa.* I froze.

The footsteps got closer. I looked at the moleskin notebook and held my breath to determine how close he was. He was outside the door. I stuffed it back in the alcove and noticed hundreds of stacked yellow college ruled papers. *I'm looking for some paperwork.* I heard Maman's voice in my mind, something that only ever happened when I read books she once read aloud. Was the memory real?

I stepped forward and reached for the papers.

The doorknob turned. I stepped back, put my unicorn notebook in my backpack, and stood lamely in the middle of the room.

He startled upon seeing me. "*Qu'est-ce que tu fous là?*"

I blinked a few times. "Looking for you."

"*Never* come in here without me again."

"*Je m'excuse, Papa.*" I walked past him toward the door then turned around to clear the weird air. "I just wanted to say bye before I left."

His eyes bore into mine and his upper lip twitched. "Goodbye."

* * *

Bertrand was standing in the roundabout when I came out, ready for school. He laughed when I told him what happened with Papa. "Leave the man alone, those herbs are all he has." He pulled a small tincture bottle from his green messenger bag. "Here, this is the tincture I used to make your tea yesterday. There wasn't much left, so I soaked what remained in the raspberry syrup and put it in this dropper bottle. Take it, you need it."

"In other words I look like a wreck," I said grabbing it. Maybe quitting my meds had been a bad idea. "I don't know why my aura appears so troubled. I love it there—at the university. So far that is."

"Tell me more later," Bertrand said. "Kip's mom's here."

Seconds later I heard Mary's sedan pull up our gravel drive. "Alright, Bertrand, give my love to Sam and Kip, and try not to embarrass your math teacher."

"Just another day in paradise."

* * *

Once again the statue held my parking spot on campus. I nodded my thanks to her, rubbed her bronze foot and studied The French House at the end of the path she guarded. I pulled the tincture bottle from my backpack's side pocket and released several drops into my water bottle. The purplish liquid plumed into the clear water and I took a long sip. *My potion.*

A dark-skinned girl came out of The French House then, her rhinestone hairclip glinting in the sun. I recognized her as the one who'd teased Charlie in class yesterday and failed to recognize his quote. She wore a luxurious black fur bolero over a drop waist ivory dress, black tights with ivory polka dots and oxford heels. She stepped onto campus as if from a different era. She held no phone. Her posture was ballerina straight, and she ignored her surroundings with a level of meditative calm you'd expect from a model in an antidepressant brochure. A stark comparison to the girls in Bucky Badger sweatpants or ripped jeans and tacky knee-high boots on the sidewalk nearby, all of them on their phones, and if their voice's decibel was any indicator, speaking to hard of hearing grandparents.

The girl from The French House rubbed the statue, grinned at me and walked on.

I watched her trail off for some time before I too went on my way, to the math building for calculus, but just before going inside I changed course. As if Professor Anne Boucher had sent out a siren song luring me to her. Besides, I needed to ask her about the book, and if she knew how Camille had gotten my mother's copy.

There were many offices in the romance language department, none of them with name plaques, but I located Boucher's from a paper taped on her closed door: Fundamentals of French Literature's Euphemisms for Society: open hours Tuesdays & Thursdays 10 a.m. – noon. It was nearly ten so I lingered outside.

The light underneath the door shifted and footsteps shuffled over the marble. I straightened my posture. The door opened and the girl in the hijab from class hurried out, bumping me. She was crying, but quickly looked down and muttered an apology. I was about to ask her if she was okay but Charlie Derosiers came out of the office and I stepped back.

"Hessa, *attends-moi*! Wait!" Charlie chased after her, a sheet of paper fluttered off a bulletin board in his stream. He stopped at the main building doors, shoved them open with an echoing thrust, looked both ways and heaved a sigh I heard halfway down the hall. I toyed with the idea of calling to him, but he rushed out, instantly swallowed by the blaze of sunlight. I snatched the fallen paper off the ground: *The French House's Anne Boucher Scholarship*.

"Simone." Professor's molasses voice came from behind. I turned around. She stood tall and statuesque in a Tartan blazer and black dress, long legs, and black ankle booties. The hair I'd taken for russet under the classroom lights now looked golden.

"Have you come to see me before class?" She stepped toward me with two clip-clops of her boots. I fidgeted with my backpack zipper while her eyes focused, tuning me like a mandolin.

"Well?"

I nodded, mute as Philomela.

"Then come in." She stepped into her office fluidly, moving like she had studied with geishas. She motioned toward a chair across from her desk and folded her long hands together atop a pile of papers. She appeared as a silhouette, a tall window behind her partitioned into diamonds. Even through the embossed glass I saw the weather was turning, that cloudless blue sky engulfed by a growing storm. I remembered how Papa had said this autumn was going to be "one for the books" according to his Farmer's Almanac. An "unruly and wicked season" is how I think he'd put it. Thinking of his thick almanac my eyes traveled up the rows of dark walnut shelves filled with what looked like first edition French books, so beautiful and delicate, I wanted to run my fingers through their thin pages the way I did with those in Maman's library.

Her office was timeless. Dark wood. High ceiling. Dim lighting. Books everywhere. Old craftsman furniture perfect to fall asleep on, horsehair stuffed cushions, the air redolent of mahogany and lemon. Even so, there was an odd sense of order to it all and I had a feeling that if I so much as moved the butterfly glass paperweight on her desk an inch, she'd notice. I was about to ask her about my name in the book when she spoke.

"Which book comes to mind first? When you remember your mother?"

"*En fait—*" I paused, feeling the herbal tincture fully kick in. My thoughts were flowing like the ice cream from the soft-serve machine I'd marveled over the first time we went for cones in the States. But I knew the answer to her question. Ironically, it was one from her assigned list. "*L'étranger.*"

She inhaled deeply through her nose and leaned in toward her desk, toward me. The smell of burnt sugar came with the shift, crème brûlée actually. Without my anti-anxiety prescription, my olfactory senses were reactivating, in fact all of my senses were.

"Do you think it's because of the first line, or because she read it so often?"

No longer able to hold her dazzling blue-green eyes, I looked back at the books. I wasn't sure I knew the answer to her question: psychology 101, was the memory planted there because my mother's voice, or because the first line of Albert Camus' *L'étranger* sticks out so: *Aujourd'hui, maman est morte.* Today, mama died.

"Only a French mother would read her child such an intense book before bed," Professor said, perhaps realizing I was too flustered to respond. She didn't smile, didn't look away, just kept watching me, her sculpted features motionless. "Your mother was French?"

"Yes. Both of my parents," I said, settling further into the chair, feeling a spring coil under me.

"Did you cry at your mother's funeral?"

At first I didn't believe she'd asked me such a thing, but then I realized what she'd meant. It was a joke, and in a sick way, a good one. She was referencing Meursault, the protagonist in *L'étranger*, the man who didn't cry at his mother's funeral, the man so freed in his mind that he felt no guilt.

"I thought you were French given your accent," she went on. "*Alors*, it looks as though you have a head start on the reading assignment. But as to the theme of all three works, I'll ask you to give it some real thought."

"I will, Professor. But let me ask you," I said, pulling her book, *The Power of Suggestion: A Woman's Guide to Empowerment* from my bag. I showed her my name written on the first page. "My mother wrote this. She had your book."

"Many people do."

"Yes, but how did your teaching assistant Camille get my mother's copy?"

"You'll have to ask her."

"Professor,"

"Call me Anne."

"Did you know my mother?"

Raindrops started to beat against the embossed windows then, swishing across the glass like shooting stars. I followed one fat drop as it zigzagged down the window just like the leaves outside.

"Simone," she said—oozed was probably a better word.

"Yes?" I asked, edging up my seat.

"I must make a phone call before class, so if you'll excuse me."

"Of course." I tried to hide my disappointment as I stood when her hand landed on mine.

"Come see me after class later this afternoon, I have something else I want to tell you. It could be," her eyebrows lifted slightly, "life changing."

* * *

Professor Anne Boucher waited for me after lecture, serene as a cat in the middle of the classroom. When I reached her, she said, "Walk with me." I did, down a long dim corridor the opposite way I'd come in. Bulletin boards covered the walls, all of them tacked with papers slit at the bottom for phone number takeaways: *Tutor Needed! Tutor Available. Wanted: French/Italian Speaking Roommate. Misc. Services, Call Irena.*

I saw through the building door window that the weather had turned. We stepped outside, protected by the building's overhang from the plump drops of cool rain. The air smelled tangy and thunder crashed.

"Have you got an umbrella?" she asked.

I realized, foolishly, that I did not. Papa told me the forecast each morning and yet I'd dressed for the sunshine that day: a thin t-shirt, jeans, red flats.

"*Tant pis*," she said with a shrug. Apparently, she didn't either. "Follow me."

Professor and I walked exhaustively close to one another, our shoulders bumping as if we were sharing the umbrella, we wished we had. We crossed streets with crawling vehicles, their speedy wipers *ree-raw, ree-rawing* back and forth, and headlights on to navigate the stormy dark. We maneuvered around pond-sized puddles, rushing down Frances Street toward the lake and I worried with each step that I'd step on her black leather boot. Students sluiced about from every which way, screeching girls in Bucky Badger sweatshirts holding notebooks over their heads as they ran, and a few gothic types purposefully slowing their pace to give in to the sheets of rain. My feet were soaked, my hands so cold they burned, and clouds puffed from my mouth with each breath. The rain had turned horizontal, smacking against my face harsh as hail.

Professor linked her arm in mine as a car's bluish headlights beamed in our way and I imagined what we looked like to onlookers. Best friends? Mother and daughter? An idea warm as soup and cozy as pajamas. I had no women in my life.

It was when we arrived at the imposing bronze statue I'd rubbed for luck, that Boucher veered onto a walkway and to the dark brick mansion beyond.

The French House.

It was even more extraordinary than yesterday, and stood triumphantly singular, bucolic even, despite the cramped row houses lining the blocks leading to it, segregated by perfectly clipped hedgerow. Menacing gargoyles leered from their perch over a patina roof gutter and two maple trees framed the stairs leading to its grand entry. And while the giant maples were littering red leaves into the wind, remarkably, not one landed on the home's green checkerboard mowed lawn.

"*Bienvenue*," Professor said, and I realized that the only language we'd spoken together was French and it made me feel like I was already home. She stood underneath the entryway's gas lamp. Etched into the brick above the door was the quote Charlie asked us to recognize: *to live happy, live hidden.*

"Go on, open it," Professor Boucher said.

I twisted the intricately engraved knob and stepped inside.

Chapter 5

"This is The French House," Professor said matter-of-factly. "It's a residence hall for French exchange students and French majors."

The foyer was painted black and illumed by a giant lantern hanging from twenty feet above. Colors played at the edge of my vision: pink chrysanthemums sprouting from a crystal vase on a round onyx table, a mustard-tinted Chesterfield fainting chaise, and hanging over it, a Modigliani nude oil on canvas so perfectly lit the brunette's skin looked wet.

A red carpet lined staircase worked its way up three levels. Polish reflected from the banister, sure to capture the fingerprints of anyone who touched it.

Beyond the dark foyer was a labyrinth of rooms with wainscoted walls each painted a different color, all of them united by the herringbone flooring, thick red Turkish rugs, and intimate sconce lighting. The main salon was off the left, with baby blue walls and museum-lit oil paintings, impressionist seascapes and Lautrec's Moulin Rouge. There were green velvet sofas and linen wingback chairs arranged around an inglenook complete with crackling fireplace. An arched passage led to the turret room which served as a library. It had a cathedral dome ceiling from which hung a giant iron candelabra. Its rounded brick walls were lined with books from the ground to ceiling, and there was even a ladder on a tracking system to travel the room's half circle and reach the second level's Juliet balcony.

There was no question. The house was exquisite.

As if reading my mind Professor said, "*C'est charmant, non*? It is an island on campus. Walking inside that door is like entering a new world."

She stepped in swift and elegant movements toward the dining room and I noticed another room, a solarium no less, from which humidity seeped like morning fog. Inside palm trees were lit from below to create shadows akin to skeleton fingers.

At the dining room's windows, I saw how choppy the lake had become from the storm. I patted my wet hair, wiped my face with my scarf, surprised she didn't tell me to go to the restroom and dry off. But no, she told me to sit.

There were ten white linen covered tables in the dining room, each with two crystal decanters filled with burgundy wine. Professor told me to pour myself a glass saying that she had too much to do later to enjoy one for herself. "Relax, make yourself at home." We were the only two in the room, but their dinner must have been scheduled soon for the scent of root vegetables and meat filled the air, the meat not strong enough for steak though certainly not chicken or pork. Aha. Veal.

"*Tchin tchin.*" She motioned toward my glass and I raised it, eager to sip from it as though its essence would officially transform me into a French House guest. The wine had blackberries on the nose and a harmonious balance of minerals and velvet.

"Simone, I brought you here today because I have a proposal for you. I want you to live here. Complete my equation, my mission." She unclipped her hair. It fell down in a tumbling cascade worthy of a shampoo commercial. I swallowed and looked around. How I wanted to live there: a view of the lake, like-minded students—Charlie Derosiers? Yes, there he was entering the salon and making himself comfortable in one of the wingbacks. He crossed his leg and flipped open a book. I knew from the book jacket it was Baudelaire's *The Flowers of Evil.*

"Is it coed?" I asked, hoping I didn't sound painfully juvenile.

"*Mais oui.*" She replied, her eyes following to where mine had landed. "Charlie Derosiers. The object of every girl's desire." She flashed that Cheshire cat grin again. "Simone, the reason I want you to live here, is that we've got a bit of a predicament this year. Normally we have far more French exchange students living in the home, providing native level language immersion that helps the non-native residents improve. And this year is our Centennial Fête."

My mind caught on *Centennial Fête.* It was at my father's family winery's Centennial Fête where our fate was determined. Where Maman had done something so horrible that Papa lost his inheritance and hence, we moved to the States. Whatever it was she did, I still didn't know.

"It will be held November first," Professor went on. "We'll have very prestigious guests and to be honest, they'll question why we have so few French and Francophone residents."

"Who are the other natives?" I asked, glancing quickly once again at Charlie.

"*Bon*, there's Camille of course. And you'll surely understand," she paused and looked around the room, "why I'm concerned about her." Professor's voice was lower now. She moved her hands into her hair, tying it into a silky knot. "Surely you read her pre-course letter, the thesis she mentioned? How's she intent to prove something about me?"

Again I nodded.

"You should live here, Simone," Professor said. "Go on the journey—and," she nodded conspiratorially, "help me keep an eye on Camille."

I folded my hands together noticing dirt in my nails. I couldn't live in The French House. Not only could we not afford it but who would care for Papa and Bertrand, cook dinner, clean the house?

"I'll arrange for a full room and board scholarship for you, one in my name in fact," she said, solving my first dilemma. "We normally have enough for six native speakers so clearly we have more than enough to cover your entire fee. Why don't you stay for dinner? Mingle, drink, make yourself at home."

"*D'accord*."

"I'll need to know by Friday though. The scholarship's funds need to be allocated by then or else they'll be reconciled for next year." She wrapped a muslin scarf around her long neck, tying it with that quintessential Parisian flair, loose and billowing. "Sunday is the kick-off banquet dinner for all of the donors and the board. A chance for them to meet the young students carrying on the torch of their beloved house this year." She reached my shoulder and squeezed it. Then leaned down, as her red lips nearly grazed my earlobe and caused my left side to tingle and goose bumps to rise, "Talk to Charlie, *ma chérie*."

With that she was off. I took a deep breath and then another sip of wine because yes, I did want to talk to Charlie.

* * *

Before I knew it I'd drained my glass. Soon Papa would enter the house expecting rich scents of *fricassee de poulet à l'ancienne* and discover that both his daughter and his dinner were missing.

As I stood the alcohol hit me. The room spun like a Merry-go-Round.

"Mademoiselle?" said a man wearing a tall white chef's hat. I had never seen anyone wearing one in real life before. "You don't have any allergies that I should take in account, do you?" he said.

"No, I don't." I gripped the table.

"I assume you're here for dinner. More allergies sprout each year, new names, new definitions, and new restrictions. Gluten-free, sugar free, peanut free, soy free, fat free, cage free, food free, you name it, somebody proclaims the need for it." He laughed. "But nothing bothers you then—Mademoiselle—"

"Duchamps. Her name's Simone Duchamps."

I gasped. Jackie Kaiser, from my little town. The same girl who tormented me from the first day I'd stepped into class and was introduced, my name mispronounced. From that moment on she'd picked me apart like carrion.

"Jackie. You live here?" I asked, hoping I sounded neutral. She gave a half-committed shrug as if there was a small chance that she did not. This was a girl who'd used my French nationality as the butt of her jokes for years. If I remembered correctly, she'd studied German in high school. What place did she have in The French House?

"*Vous vous connaissez! Super, allez*, have a seat together." The chef motioned toward an empty table.

"Ah—but we're from different sides of the cultural tracks, aren't we?" She tilted her head toward the chef. Even now, invited here by Professor, I was apparently an outsider.

The chef drummed his fingers together. "I see you've got the scholarship information." He nodded toward the sheet of paper I'd grabbed off the floor in the corridor earlier, soggy from the rain. "Please, please, apply—"

"Yes, please do." Jackie was smiling obnoxiously. "We need more native French speakers, Simone. Our Centennial Fête is coming up and all eyes are on us." She'd kept her eyes on the chef as she said this, imitating his gestures and voice as though she'd heard him utter the same words far too many times. "Heaven forbid they figure out what's *really* going on here."

Neither the chef nor I responded to this and Jackie sauntered off, flourishing a backhanded wave.

He wiped his hands on his apron and sighed. "Never mind Jackie. Maybe you should sit by Charlie and Reine, stick with the natives tonight. I'm Henri, The French House's official chef and guardian." With that he held his hands up in the air and took a step back. "No kisses, no handshakes, I'm greasy–the dacquoise's buttercream. Hope you like it."

I thanked him and sat. My body heavy and my mind unfocused, it hit me how hungry I was. In the salon Charlie laboriously stood from the wingback and stretched his arms high. His white undershirt came untucked from his navy corduroy pants and showcased his tight stomach. He caught me looking and made a grimace I wasn't able to define. Embarrassed as I was, I didn't look away, and as he walked my way I noticed he had a sort of gimp to his gait I hadn't seen in class, and which I couldn't help but stare at until I realized just how shameful that was. Just how immature and thoughtless. It was the same way people stared at my brother's malfunctioning eyes, at Kip's shaky twitch, at Sam's random groans, and to think of myself in the same category as those folks made me cringe.

"I shattered my knee in a ski accident," he said stopping at my chair. I stood from my chair as if addressing the king. I hadn't been nearly as close to him in the grainy auditorium as now. His face was sharp like a Lempicka.

"He was this close to skiing in the Olympics for France." It was the girl with the fur bolero I'd admired earlier. She caught up from behind, no longer in the bolero but the same ivory drop waist dress and a long art deco necklace. She pulled out a chair next to me and smiled. She had an overbite, teeth too big for her mouth but just the right amount to be charming. Her eyes were wide and slate colored. "I'm Reine by the way." She had a syncopated accent from the islands, Africa maybe. She must have noticed my analysis as she then added, "I'm from Gabon."

"I appreciate your flattering intro, Reine." Charlie said. "But the knee accident happened a week before qualifiers, we'll never know if I'd have made the team or not." He had the kind of exaggerated Parisian accent that I loved and my father loathed. The accent and its accompanying pout and shrug, which Papa would scoff at as he, Bertrand, and I watched Jeunet's films after dinner, Bertrand telling him to shush so he could hear.

"I love that you already grabbed a glass." Reine nodded toward the wine in my hand. I considered telling her that it had been Professor to offer it, but stopped. I remembered what being teacher's pet had done for me in grade school. Charlie kept his eyes on me as he pulled out a chair and sat opposite. He picked up the empty wine glass from his place and rubbed his thumb against it in circles. Reine filled it for him and I suppressed a smile, the thrilling sensation of *What is yet to come*? tickling my nerves. I'd once been taught to meet that feeling with an extra pill to calm myself down. A sobering thought which, returned my mind to Papa and Bertrand waiting for me at home, no sound of my pickup crunching up the gravel drive, no squeak of the door, no drop of my bag, no honey I'm home.

I pulled my phone from my bag but it was dead. I never remembered to charge the thing, Papa only gave it to me a couple of weeks ago, worried about my constant commute.

"Oh, I'm sorry," Reine said, her face crumpling like she was about to break my heart, "but there's no cell phone, tablet, or technology use of any kind allowed on the first floor. You can only use them in bedrooms or the study rooms upstairs."

"No problem, the thing's dead anyway. I just wanted to call my father, tell him I won't be home."

"I'd lend you mine but naturally—it's upstairs. There's a public one near the office down the hall; you can't miss it. It's an old English phone booth. Bright red."

In the booth I lifted the phone from its hook then saw a note that only local calls were allowed. My stone house on the hill, perched high above the Wisconsin River and sprawling vineyard of purple and green grapes, was just out of zone. I missed Bertrand and Papa, but they were a world away. Here I was among peers. Friends, maybe. I gripped my arrowhead, my talisman, and looked for a sign. The phone beeped a series of flat tones, and I hung it up. As good a sign as any. I'm sorry, Papa. The House wins.

I unfolded the phone booth's accordion door and walked back to the table, my empty place awaiting me still, next to Reine, and across from Charlie. In high school I always sat at the Misfit's table.

In the short time I'd been away, many of the other chairs had been filled and the dining room was humming with French conversation. I spotted Jackie's overly highlighted hair and gaudy gold hoop earrings, she sat at the middle of one table, commanding the attention of her group. I knew she sensed me when she raised her voice and adjusted her leopard print cardigan.

"There you are," Reine said with a smile, "We thought you'd left, that we'd scared you off, or perhaps that the House had. I know it looks perfect but . . ."

"Reine," Charlie said in a low tone.

"Hey, I love your necklace," I said to Reine. She looked down like she'd forgotten she was wearing one, lifted it and said *merci*. "And thanks for saving my seat."

"There was no need to," she said, then took a sip of wine and planted her glass firmly on the table. "No one ever dares sit by us. Now that you have, let's see what happens."

Chapter 6

"What do you mean no one wants sits by you?" I asked, looking at Charlie despite responding to Reine's comment. He was swirling his wine, eyes glazed over. I assumed the reason had to do with what Jackie said earlier.

"They're intimidated," Charlie said, his glass stopping midtilt.

"Oh please, that's the safe answer," Reine said. Charlie's eyes worked the room, landing on what I assumed was one person. I turned to see who it was but stopped myself halfway. I'd do it later without him knowing.

"I'll give you the G-rated version, Simone, and save the story about Anne-Marie Fisker for another night," said Reine.

Whatever the story about this Anne-Marie Fisker girl was, I was more interested in Reine's suggestion that there would be another time to tell me, that I'd be back here again—with them.

"We're native speakers and they're not," Charlie said. "That's the divide."

"But that's what they've come here for, native speakers, so they can speak like one. Maybe you've given them reason to feel intimidated," I said before thinking better of it. It was just the type of comment Bertrand would have made had he been here. But I pushed Bertrand out of my thoughts.

"That's interesting, Simone," Charlie said. I wanted to bathe in his voice until I was soaked to the bone. "Maybe we have and we don't know it. But I think the answer is simply human nature. There's a barrier between us."

"What barrier?" I shook my head. "We all speak French, and we're all interested in the language and its culture."

"Ah," he tapped his finger onto the table. "It should seem that way, shouldn't it? And yet we segregate based on something as minute as fluency level. It reminds me of that Jane Elliott experiment where she convinced educated, brown-eyed people to distrust the blue-eyed people-—and it worked. Quite disturbing." He yanked off a hunk of the crusty baguette that lay between us, and popped a piece into his mouth.

"'The phony must die said the Catcher in the Rye.'"

"Okay, Reine maybe not *that* disturbing." Charlie dipped his head.

"I've read about that, it was a simulation for racism." I said. "But there was an instigator. First they gave the brown-eyed people a reason—however untrue or pathetic, to consider the blue-eyed people inferior. So what's the instigator for fluency level segregation here?"

"Maybe it was a bad example." He rubbed his thumb across the spotless plate as he'd done to the wine glass earlier. It hummed, the way I was sure to do were he to touch me.

"I brought it up because it was a simulation and so is this House," he went on, tearing another piece of the baguette between us. "Maybe we should be asking what the true purpose of a simulation is."

"Some argue that life on earth is a simulation," Reine said, adjusting her rhinestone hairclip.

"*Ouf*, don't blow my mind, Reine, not until I've had more to drink."

"We might be living in someone's game now. An alien's science project."

"Then please tell the alien to relocate me to the Renaissance. I don't like the world today, too many blips and beeps, constant push notifications. Anyway, what was I saying? Ah yes, a simulation of studying abroad, can this House really mimic that?" he said chewing the bread, even stopping one point to remove a piece of it from between his teeth. I'd have found it crass had anyone else done it. "What I do know is that once you move abroad you'll never return as the person you were pre-departure. It's like prisoners released to the real world after a long sentence. You've encountered *hiraeth*, that Welsh word I love. Or *saudade* in Portuguese, *adoro essa palavra também*."

"What time's intermission?" Reine pursed her lips.

"*Mon dieu*, you're right." Charlie placed both hands flat on the table. "We rarely have a new audience *et oui*, I'm totally overdoing it."

"I don't mind a show," I said.

"Good," he said lifting his wine glass to ding against mine.

I scooted my chair closer to the table. "And I know what you're trying to say. You're talking about *dépaysement*, the loss of nationality."

"Yes, exactly," said Charlie, "when you leave your country long enough you change faster than the rate of those you left behind like . . ."

"Time dilation."

"*Quoi*?" Reine laughed.

"Or maybe Gibbs Paradox," I mumbled thinking of a concept Bertrand once explained. Entropy is the reason we have the arrow of time. When entropy decreases, as in Gibbs Paradox, in theory we would be going back in time. But would it be the same as it was?

"Okay you win," Charlie said. "You lost me."

"I'm *euh*—" I laughed. "I didn't mean to sound like a *petit malin*, for a second I thought I was making sense. I must be drunk if I'm quoting the stuff my brother listens to. He's blind, and constantly tuning in to podcasts about quantum physics. The point is, yes, once you go abroad for a long time, you change faster than you would at home and that in itself changes your concept of home."

"Simone, you're—what are you," he straightened his back, "unstoppable."

I gulped an ungraceful slug of wine. "*Merci*."

Charlie brushed the crumbs from his hands onto the table and started again, "Maybe it's possible to be a foreigner anywhere, even within your own family. We're all susceptible to choosing sides, and I'm afraid everyone here has chosen to keep off ours." He sighed. "Every scale has a tipping point, and I fear this House is nearing one."

I broke off a piece of bread to keep my hands busy, Charlie sat back apparently satisfied with his speech, and Reine sipped her wine. Maybe it was the optimist in me but I refused to believe what they said. Considering what I'd heard about the teaching assistant Camille, perhaps she was the reason for the barrier in the House. I was about to ask, when Charlie spoke again. "Where are you from, Simone?"

I swallowed my bread and sipped my wine. "A small town you'd never know, thirty or so minutes from here along the river. The same town Jackie, the girl over there is from." I looked around. All the other students, thirty or so of them, sat together quite separated from us. Thinking about what Professor had said earlier, that this house was an island on campus, I supposed that made us an island within an island. As I scanned the room I saw one more outsider though. One table over, Hessa, the girl I'd sat next to in French Lit sat distanced from anyone else. I remembered how Charlie had been chasing her from Professor's office this morning. Today her hijab was the color of wood violets. She squeezed a lime into her water-filled wine glass, and smiled at me. I returned the favor, understanding a little how she must feel—a Muslim in a house of drinking free-spirited language students. *Another Misfit.*

"You're from Wisconsin? I thought you were French," Reine said, breaking into my thoughts, her nose scrunching. "Camille told us about you."

"She did?" I asked, flattered over how much energy the mysterious Camille had apparently put into me. How much I had existed before I officially arrived. "Actually, I wanted to ask you about the book Camille had you leave in the lecture hall, Charlie. By Boucher, *The Power of Suggestion: A Woman's Guide to Empowerment.*"

"Oh la vache, she had you do that again?" Reine asked.

"Wait, *again*?"

"She's done this before."

"But it was my mother's copy of the book."

"I just mean she's left Boucher's book out before. To see who would grab it. And if someone doesn't, she finds someone to give it to."

"What do you mean it was your mother's book?" Charlie said.

"I think she targeted you." Reine said over Charlie. "She was talking about you for a while."

"Targeted?"

"Look, she was just charmed by what you wrote in your introduction I'm sure," Charlie said quickly, his eyes pinging to Reine's. She nodded back. "So where in France are you from?"

I frowned for a moment, feeling lost. *Don't overthink it.* "We're from a little town in Bordeaux, we moved here when I was six."

"*C'est fou*, why?" Charlie gave a classic French pout. "To Wisconsin of all places! What were your parents trying to escape?"

Though he winked, his question was unsettling. Instinctively, I defended my family. "My father originally came here to fulfill an internship. He worked on a small Wisconsin vineyard for a year and when he returned to France…" I tripped on my words here, questioning again what Maman had done to cause Papa to lose his part of the family winery in Bordeaux. "Until my grandfather decided to leave the entire vineyard to my uncle instead of splitting it between both sons. We had nowhere to go. But as fate would have it, the proprietor of the vineyard Papa interned with here in Wisconsin, died shortly after so Papa bought it and we moved here."

"*Oh là là*, are you saying that your father is the man behind Duchamps Winery?" Charlie asked, shifting his silverware forward.

"You know it?"

"Oh come on, a Frenchman will seek the nearest winery on day one, *n'est-ce pas*?" He laughed. "Your winery is doing very well. I read an article not long ago about the *Philtre d'Amour* beating out some big-name California wines." He twirled his glass again and then abruptly stopped and took a sip, his eyes meeting mine.

"It did." I nosed into my wineglass.

"What's with the wine's name?" Reine asked.

I lowered my glass. "That was my mother's idea. A marketing campaign to entice people to drink wine in the land of beer. Each of our blends is a different philtre, or potion for a different desire. *Philtre d'Amour* is our biggest seller. It's a fruity wine, mainly Marechal Foch grapes with a touch of Millot. You could say its taste mimics love."

Charlie raised one eyebrow. "How's that?"

My face flushed warm and prickly. I was not an expert on love but I did know wine. "Because the taste is both bitter and sweet." Charlie's eyes softened. He looked about to say something but Reine beat him to it.

"*C'est adorable*, I want some; this stuff is doing nothing for me." She held her glass of wine, shrugged, and drank anyway.

"Yes, well they had to figure out a cheeky way to draw attention to their wines. People didn't want to take wine from Wisconsin seriously so my mother came up with that." I purposefully changed the topic. "I should ask you both what you are doing in Wisconsin?"

"Ah yes." Charlie backed out his chair and patted his bad knee. "This is why. I wanted to get as far away from France as possible because," he paused causing two lines to sprout between his brows. "I was fed up with the pity. My ski accident left everyone perpetually apologizing to me for what could have been. And they were so desperate for French people at The French House I'm afraid I was lured in. I loved feeling needed again."

"Oh look," Reine interrupted with a contrived smile, "it's our turn." She stood abruptly and padded toward the buffet table. Dizzy, I too rose and followed her, conscious of the way everyone looked at us.

Just as I had begun to scoop salad onto my plate at the buffet Jackie leaned over my shoulder. "Don't get me wrong, Simone, I want you to live here, too. Purely for the entertainment of it, watching you gush all over Professor Charlie over there," she said, mocking him for conducting class the other day. "But you should ask yourself why they really want you here. Spend the night—maybe you'll figure it out."

Chapter 7
Le Passé

September 2006

Jackie Kaiser was the first person I saw in the elementary school's entryway when we arrived for Open House night. Maman and Papa there with me to see Bertrand's and my work and meet our teachers. Jackie paused when she saw me, and her mother scowled in our direction before she stomped down the hall into a nearby classroom. Under her breath Maman said, "That was awfully rude." And it was. Jackie's mother worked for us after all, at the cashier stand in the vineyard shop. She was always calling me *tutz*, whatever that meant, chomping on her gum and watching everyone from the corner of her eye. Before following her mother, Jackie waved at me as though we were best friends, but I knew better. I was thankful I wouldn't have to join her in the room and suffer her usual ridicule. She was in third grade and had a different teacher.

"See Maman, I told you the school smells like old cheese," I said as we walked down the cubby-lined hallway. I tugged on her hand, impatient to show her my drawing of a lavender field in the art room, the tambourine I rattled in the music room, and the cafeteria where they served soggy noodles and bright green Jell-O blobs on plates with square compartments. Maman laughed and told me that sometimes it was a good thing other people didn't understand French.

My teacher Miss Kemp was busy talking to the other mothers and fathers when we stepped into my homeroom, but everyone quieted and turned to look at us. It was always like that. Maman said that if you're different, you get noticed. But it was more than us just being French. Maman looked nothing like the other mothers, who were either big ladies wearing silly jeans, the kind Papa wore when working in the vineyard, or skinny chain-smoking ladies with bleached hair like Jackie's mother. Maman was tall, her hair was dark and smooth, she wore flowing dresses and the heeled shoes I loved trying on in her closet. Papa looked different too. Although he didn't dress up or even say much, he had the looks of a movie star compared to the rest of the men in town. Whenever he did open his mouth to speak, the women at the grocery shop or gas station always gushed the same thing, "I love your accent!"

"These are the books you're reading?" Maman paged through some of the big-lettered books with bright accompanying pictures from the yellow shelf by our desks. Bertrand sat on an orange bean bag.

"*Oui*, Maman. It's very simple, *non*? But that's okay. English is still difficult. But they really are boring when I compare them to what you read to me. They're not about existentialism or seduction. They have no theme."

Maman's red lips expanded into a smile, her hand shooting up to cover her mouth as she chuckled.

"What's so funny?" I hissed.

"Nothing, I don't mean to laugh. You surprise me that's all." Her eyes crinkled like a cat's. She ran her hand down my cheek and said, "*T'es si intelligente*. I'm so proud of you for searching out the theme. Find it and you solve the game." She stood tall again, capturing everyone's eyes. But they would never truly know her—she was mine, mine and Bertrand's, and that meant we'd be okay here in America. In this stinky school, reading picture books and getting told to go back to France, a place Bertrand and I sometimes had trouble picturing now that we'd been away half a year. We relied on Maman's stories to keep our home country alive in our minds. On good nights, she'd pull out her favorite book of Renoir prints and describe our old home to us, painting the scene with her words as he had done with his brush.

"I'm sorry about the hard time the kids are having with the others," Miss Kemp said to Maman. "This town, what can I say? Doesn't deal well with change. And everyone loved Hal Green—the man who ran the vineyard before you," she paused to nod toward Papa. "He was a foreigner too, though. Moved here from Washington D.C. of all places. Didn't he work for the government? Rumor had it he had some big job, not the FBI but the other one, what's it called? CIA! Anyway, he gave a lot of money to the town, you know, to the parks, the schools, basically everything benefitted from Hal and people still miss him."

"Are you suggesting we buy our social acceptance?" Maman asked.

"No, no, gosh, that came off wrong. I'm just giving you the backstory." Miss Kemp shifted her weight. "Listen, all of the children and their parents are going to Becker's for brats and custard shakes tonight, you should come, and bring Simone and Bertrand—besides, there will be beer for the adults—oh wait, do you drink beer? Or only wine?"

"Oh, we like to try it all and that sounds very nice, but we already made Quiche Lorraine." Maman nudged me because I'd helped her make it.

"Well," Miss Kemp said, "I have no idea what that is—but I'm sure it's delicious."

I wasn't surprised Miss Kemp didn't know about Quiche Lorraine. No one in town grasped why we sold croissants without frosting. Last weekend Maman and I baked hundreds of them. We wrapped them in her favorite Jacquard linens, placed them in baskets, and brought them to the Saturday farmer's market in the park by the river. They were still hot. We sat at a picnic table with the clapboard sign I'd help her make: *French Croissants*! Maman looked extra pretty but we only sold about five or six to people who pronounced them croy-sahnts. Most people mingled at the cheese curd stand, run by the Gaertners. Their sign read *Fresh Squeaky Curds!* I asked Maman why curd would be squeaky. She said she hadn't a clue. I figured I'd ask Sheila Gaertner from my class but when I waved at her she looked the other way like she hadn't seen me, even though I knew she had.

"I hate it here," I mumbled.

Maman, sniffling, put her hand on my shoulder. She pinched her eyes shut for a second then pressed along her dress like she was ironing it. "We'll be okay," she whispered lifting her chin. She smiled but her cheeks were trembling.

I'd have done anything to take her back to France. *Home.* Mamie and Grandpère. My best friends Benoît and Julie. Baguette the dog. My native language, anything for that sense of belonging again.

When we returned home from the farmer's market, Maman and Papa got into another argument about Papa keeping to himself in the lab while Maman ran the show. Maman claimed Papa used his poor English skills as reason to ignore mail, avoid paying bills, or pick up the *damn* phone. She fell into one of her fits, hurling anything she found across the room, pounding her fists like a toddler, and throwing herself in the corner to cry until Papa served her a calming tea, soothed her with his words, and she disappeared within herself.

* * *

In my classroom now, Maman was still calmly talking to Miss Kemp, so I excused myself to go to the bathroom. Jackie was there, washing her hands at the pink porcelain basin. My stomach knotted into a sharp pretzel and I considered darting out, but it was too late. She saw my reflection in the mirror and squeaked the faucet off. The last time I'd run into her here she'd snatched my arrowhead necklace and thrown it into the toilet, watched me splash around to get it back, and told everyone later that I smelled like pee.

"Just who I was waiting for," she said stepping toward me. She flicked her wet hands in the air, droplets hit my face. She got right in front of me, so close I smelled her blueberry-candied mouth, and squeezed my cheeks the way my old relatives used to do in France, though much harder.

"Listen to me, Frenchie. I want you to tell your daddy to stop fucking my mom. My own dad found out about it. Beats her up. He's gonna leave us. You understand?" Her voice vibrated around the bathroom like a jumpy wind-up toy but I didn't understand what she meant. She crossed her arms, that scary smile dominating her wide cheeks once again. "Do-you-understand? Or do you need to get your lil' dictionary?"

The bathroom door opened and Jackie took a quick step back.

"There you are!" Jackie said to her homely sidekick Alli Bischoff.

"I can't get that song from chorus out of my head," Alli said. "*Have you seen the ghost of John? Long white bones and the skin all gone!*" She sang in a low, creepy tone.

Jackie joined in, singing one round behind, "*Wouldn't it be chilly with no skin on*?"

They snickered. Jackie lifted herself backwards so her butt sat in the sink. "Alli says your dad is having sex with her mom, too. Just can't keep his dick in his pants, can he?"

"Having sex?" I said. This I understood very clearly. I sucked in a breath that smelled like toilet cleaner. "No, he's not."

"Yep," Alli nodded, "My Ma went to interview at your wine yard—"

"Vineyard," Jackie corrected her with a nasty laugh.

"Shut up same diff, anyway she thought she'd give tours or whatever, and during the interview he took her to some back room, dropped his pants. You guys are sick you know that? Everything about you and your Frenchie-French ways—God only knows what you do in your sick French house."

We were not sick and I didn't believe what they were saying. Papa loved Maman. Papa didn't even talk to anyone but her.

"Consider this your warning French Fry." Jackie hopped off the sink.

* * *

After Open House when we were back home having dinner, Maman noticed I hadn't eaten one bite of ratatouille. She told me it tasted extra delicious, that the warm fall had sweetened our tomatoes. I shrugged. Papa and Bertrand didn't notice my attitude, they just kept on slurping away, but Maman knew better.

"Simone, *mon amour*, what's wrong?"

I knew what I was doing when I turned to look at Papa, hunched over his bowl like a caveman, and said, "Papa, you have to stop fucking the women who work on the vineyard or I'm going to get beat up at school."

Silverware halted mid-air and all eyes turned to me.

"What did you just say?" Maman's face was red, her forehead lined. I had switched to English when I used my new word.

"The girls at school say Papa is having sex—"

"Enough!" Papa slammed his fist onto the table. "Go to your room."

In my room I laid in bed listening to Maman and Papa argue for so long I had seen the stars shift from one side of the window to the other like a planetarium. Glass shattered in the living room.

"How can you do this to me?"

"Lisette, *calme-toi*. I didn't sleep with her. I interviewed her friend—I didn't give her the job because she looked like trash. They made up this story to save face."

"Where was I during all of this? I told you I wanted to interview anyone leading tours or working in the shop—"

"Probably off reading your damned—"

"My damned books?"

"How many times can you read Camus?"

"It helps me deal with my new reality! Banished to this country—"

"Banished? That was your own doing, Lisette. I'm the one who lost my birthright because of you!"

"And that gives you the excuse to humiliate me over and over?"

More plates shattered, books thrown to the floor. The two sides of Maman.

"Lisette." Papa adopted a gentle voice. "I'll make your tea, you need to relax, please, *please*."

The usual routine. Our new normal. Maman was less and less the Maman I once knew, taken over as Papa explained to us, by her mental sickness, meanwhile Papa was having sex with other women. I hated both of them. I told myself to never bring up troubles from school. I would rather face Jackie and Alli myself. I closed my eyes and covered my ears with my hands and sang. *Have you seen the ghost of John? Long white bones with the skin all gone. Wouldn't it be chilly with no skin on.*

Chapter 8

Wine, so much wine, Charlie's beautiful eyes, Reine's infectious laugh, the candlelit intimacy. Hours spent on veal and salads and pommes dauphine, and dacquoise and espresso. If that weren't enough, Charlie filled three crystal goblets with *poire eau de vie*, and we emptied them quickly. I was relieved when Reine suggested we move to the salon. I sank into a sofa's green velvet cushions, eyes glazed with liquor and pleasure.

In between the fire's crackling I listened to them finish one another's sentences, pulling information from their acerbic banter. Reine was a junior majoring in Movement Theory, intent on designing a therapeutic dance program for emotionally scarred and physically abused women. She was combining her classical dance training with traditional Gabonese tribal music. What else? She was known for her impeccable style, for walking with her toes turned out "all those damn ballet lessons," and falling asleep mid-sentence on the sofa, a habit she blamed on Charlie, "that bore" and the eccentric articles he sometimes read aloud in the wee hours of the night. "Articles his Maman sends in care packages complete with chocolate biscuits for her darling Oedipus."

"It's true," Charlie concurred sleepily. "Er, minus the Oedipus bit—but my mother is the one to have written the articles, and furthermore I only bring those packages because of the way you and Camille devour said biscuits."

Reine referred to Camille several times as a genius. Camille had finished her undergraduate at the Sorbonne in record time, and despite being the TA was only twenty-five, a few years older than Reine.

"She returns next week," Reine said to me, but quickly looked at Charlie to share another lucid moment I was unable to translate.

It wasn't Camille I was interested in though; it was Charlie. Aside from his mother's care packages and his ski accident I knew nothing, so I asked him his major and to this he shook his head with a laugh, and told me I truly was a peculiar girl, but that this was not a bad thing. Running his fingers through his hair he took a double take at me, realizing I still expected an answer, then laconically added that he had no concept of time; that one lives more freely this way. He sat back again, relaxing enough to go on and offer a few details of his life back in Paris as an only child, what it was like growing up in his parents' posh flat in Le Sentier neighborhood, going to the hip clubs as a fifteen-year-old, vacationing in Corsica, and ski training in the Alps since he was five only to have his dream disintegrate in a second. He'd known Camille much earlier as their families were friends. "*En fait*, I used to babysit her," he said with a wink.

Weird. I'd assumed he was Reine's age—twenty-two-ish. Reine leaned in and whispered that at one point, Charlie and Camille had had "a thing." *Aha.* She'd meant it as a euphemism, one fit for *Les Liaisons Dangereuses.* Camille must have been childish and needy in their relationship.

"Now it's my turn to ask you a question," Reine said. "If you're going to consider this home, I must know your thoughts on Anne Boucher—the woman, the legend, the devil."

"Well," I paused to clear my throat. "I don't know." The truth was I didn't want to discuss Professor with anyone else. I didn't want anyone to know that she was the one to invite me here. Didn't want anyone to think I was getting treated specially, and most certainly didn't want to let anyone know she'd tasked me to keep my eye on Camille.

"We live like this because of her. She donated a couple hundred thousand dollars to the House, you know. She wanted to rid herself of her fortune so she wouldn't do it again."

"Do what?" I asked.

"Reine, stop already."

"They say she has a hold on us all, that she controls our actions."

"Well, she doesn't have a hold of me," Charlie said with a mischievous smile, his legs thrown over the end of the sofa. I'd seen him departing her office earlier however, and I had to question what they'd been discussing after just one lecture—or what Hessa had been doing with them. "In fact I like to think I throw her power off its course."

"I wouldn't say you succeeded in that," Reine said, tossing a pillow his way.

He caught the pillow mid-air. "Wait and watch." He lifted his head to meet my eyes. A cold tingle ran the length of my body despite the fire two feet away. I always got a bad feeling from proclamations like these. He may as well have called out to Fortuna, begged her to strike.

* * *

I woke on the green sofa alone. A ray of light poured through the salon creating prisms through the chandelier. I sat up and finger brushed my hair. God, Charlie had seen me sleeping, hopefully I'd been somewhat of a beauty. There were a few people eating breakfast in the dining room, while others sipped coffee on the lake-facing terrace, books at hand.

I needed to freshen up, but first I peeked around the only wall obscuring part of the dining room to see if Charlie and Reine were there. There were plenty of people eating but Charlie and Reine were not among them. The breakfast buffet was incredible. Flaky croissants brimmed from a woven basket, prosciutto, salami, and rillettes were lined atop a wooden chopping block, Roquefort, brie, Mimolette, and goat cheese on a marble cheese tray, apples, pears and bananas filled a crystal bowl next to hard-boiled eggs in a metal container, yogurt in a ceramic ivory bowl, and finally—there was a small silver dish of cornichons.

"*Bonjour,* Simone!" Reine bounded down the red carpet lined staircase. Already showered, she smelled like jasmine and vetiver. She again wore a drop waist style dress, this one navy, and with a long strand of pearls.

"Henri shouldn't have bothered getting the cornichons out, Camille's the only one who eats them," she said putting her pearl earrings in. "I'm glad you're still here. You were so peaceful on the sofa I didn't want to bother you. You can shower upstairs if you like—or even take a bath, we have a beautiful claw foot tub."

"Thanks, I'll be alright." We had a claw foot at home on the vineyard as well, but I hated baths and hadn't used it since I was six or seven.

"Well, I'm happy to lend something to wear if you don't have time to drive all the way to the vineyard."

"Oh, thanks." I smiled at the idea of wearing one of her beautiful twenties-era dresses and string pearls to class. "I'm alright, I mean I'll just wear this again—that'll officially make me a college student, *non?*"

She giggled a cheerful trill, then invited me for breakfast.

"I really should go. I have class soon."

"See you soon then?"

"Yes," I said, thinking I'd sit by her in the next French Lit class.

* * *

It was five by the time I made it back to the vineyard. The whole ride home I'd practiced ways of asking Papa to allow me to apply for the Anne Boucher scholarship and move into The French House. I was surprised to see him when I walked into the kitchen. He stood at the farmhouse sink holding a white colander filled with knotty red potatoes.

"*You're* cooking?" I opened a drawer in the island and took out a potato peeler. "Here."

He dropped the colander into the sink and walked past me, and outside. I'd have much preferred a screaming quarrel over the silent treatment, for that said it all. But he returned a minute later, thrusting the door open, his eyes deranged. He grabbed my wrist with his right hand then pulled an arrowhead from his pocket and pierced it into my forearm.

"Does this hurt?"

"Papa, *arrête*!"

Pinch—drag—bleed. He ran the arrowhead down my arm. My back contorted.

"Why are you doing this?" It was like the blood was fake—this wasn't happening.

"To show you how much you hurt me by not coming home." He pulled the arrowhead out and tossed it onto the counter. I applied pressure to the wound and watched him dumbfounded as he went back outside as if nothing had happened. Yet I knew better than to chase him. I knew better than to brood. But I had to release my anger—an anger I hadn't experienced in ages, one that would have been impossible under my pill's foggy control. I picked up the arrowhead and threw it like a dart toward the window. I wished the window had broken because that may have satisfied me. But it didn't, so I picked up a frying pan and whacked it against the butcher block so hard it dented. *That's better.* I swallowed my remaining fury. Closed my eyes. Reset.

I decided to make Quiche Lorraine, my mother's favorite. I tried to center myself, to recall what she looked like when she made it. What type of clothes she wore and how her voice sounded as she listed out the ingredients. I chopped bits of lardon from Papa's cured pork belly. He'd left me a roll of it yesterday morning, knowing I refused to go into his curing chamber where dead animal parts hung, their putrid odors permeating the cedar lined walls and ceiling. Of the few childhood memories I clearly recalled was when I'd seen Papa's bloody hands carving animals. His bare hands bound the bodies with string so tightly they oozed. He then hung them, salted, and rubbed them with garlic and herbs, and left them to dry so that months later we'd be able to eat their salty-sweet fat in our pastas, quiches, and stews. I'd been so overwhelmed by all the death in that room that room that I never again returned.

Hearing my clatter, Bertrand found his way down the steps and pulled out a rickety stool at the island. He ironed his hand along the grooves of the ancient butcher block, like an archaeologist deciphering our eating habits. I didn't want to tell him what Papa did, I didn't want to worry him. I understood I was wrong not coming home, but cutting me? It was unacceptable. I would give Papa this, and only this one out.

Instead of whipping the eggs I opened a bottle of wine and let it breathe.

"Are you hungry?"

"We thought we'd have to fend for ourselves again," Bertrand said, scraping at something on the island with his fingernail.

"Don't be that way. I cook for you both because I enjoy it, it's not my job." I poured him a glass of our table red and put it in front of him, tapping my finger twice on the glass. He lifted his head and reached for it. We both knew what I said wasn't true. After Maman died I'd taken over her role to my best ability. I assumed if I didn't, we'd be left with microwave dinners and take-out. Seeing Papa with the potatoes indicated I may have been wrong.

I picked a few downy feathers off the ochre-colored eggs and cracked them.

"Those are Sir Clucks-a-Lot's eggs," Bertrand said. I laughed, the tension releasing. We got all our eggs from my Misfit Sam's farm. She named her chickens, hens and roosters alike, and always told us whose eggs we were getting when we picked them up. When I'd told her that only female chickens—the hens, laid eggs, she'd nodded seriously and told me that Sir Clucks-a-Lot was gender confused.

"Bertrand, do you remember if Maman was looking for something in Papa's lab?"

"Are you kidding? I was four years old. And even if I did remember, our memories are not to be trusted, Simone. We suffered *post-traumatic stress disorder, as you well know*," he imitated Dr. Landau, our school psychologist's raspy voice.

"I know, but I swear. I had a real memory when I went in Papa's lab. I think it's actually working."

"What's working?"

"Well," I set my glass down, "don't tell Papa, but I quit taking my pills. They make me so out of it, so I thought it would help me remember things—and I think it's actually working. I think I recall Maman looking for paperwork in Papa's lab."

"She was probably looking for a bunch of bills he hadn't opened."

Papa came back inside then and looked at my arm. I hadn't bothered to wash or dress the cut. I stopped whipping the eggs, expecting an apology but he rubbed his nose and sat at the dinner table. Waiting to be served.

* * *

I made my plea after Papa had finished half his quiche. "*Ecoutes*, I got the invitation of a lifetime. A scholarship application to move into a campus house for French majors."

Papa finished chewing. "Simone, with your state of mind I'm not sure you can handle being on your own—or that it's right to leave your brother alone in this house."

"My state of mind?" I asked, at the same time as to Bertrand said, "Don't make this about me!" Bertrand exploded out of his seat and pounded thunderous steps toward the staircase. "She can do whatever she wants. I'm fine on my own. I swear to God I can see more than the two of you put together!"

"You're not living at The French House, Simone. Now both of you sit down and eat," Papa said calmly. Bertrand and I both sat with a dramatic thump and ate our Quiche Lorraine in silence.

I decided there was no way I would let him stop me. I would attend the banquet on Sunday, I would apply for the scholarship, and I would move into The French House. I had a bargaining chip after all. About a month ago, Papa agreed to attend a wine expo in Paris over Thanksgiving weekend, and he was relying on me to prepare for it.

By now the candles had melted to a puddle. Papa finished his last bite with sloppy wet sounds and Bertrand sighed. Under the table I tapped my foot into Bertrand's shin and he grinned. Papa set his silverware onto his empty plate and backed out of his chair.

"I'm sorry it didn't taste as good as Maman's," I said.

He pulled a handkerchief from his plaid flannel shirt pocket and blew his nose with a honking sound that again prompted Bertrand's agitated sigh. Still in his work boots Papa walked to the drink cupboard in the living room. He opened and closed a cabinet, pounded a snifter onto the table, and poured brandy with a glugging sound.

"You know," he paused to sip then turned around, "your mother never once made Quiche Lorraine."

* * *

After dinner I lay in bed pinching my eyes shut until I gave up on sleep. Downstairs, Papa snored in his armchair, the room glossed over in deep evening light.

"You're ruining my life!" I shouted louder than intended. The sound echoed in the cold silence, waking Papa with a startle. "This is the one thing I've ever wanted, ever asked for—you cannot take it away from me." I pounded my fist onto the wall. Two oil paintings we'd brought from Bordeaux rattled to a diagonal.

"Don't you ever talk to me that way again, Lisette!" Papa pushed himself out of his chair. He outstretched his arm and slapped my bare cheek.

"Lisette?" I whispered lifting my hand to my cheek, his handprint there like bas-relief.

* * *

I went upstairs and peeked in Bertrand's room. In the soft blue light from his computer I saw him curled up asleep, a podcast still playing.

I returned to my room and switched on my bedside lamp. I took Boucher's book, *The Power of Suggestion: A Guide to Female Empowerment* from my backpack and traced my finger across my name on the first page. "Where'd you leave this book, Maman? And how did it find its way back to me?"

I put a few drops of herbal tincture into my tea and read, channeling my mother's voice.

The power of suggestion is infinite. That is to say a woman can get exactly what she wants with a suggestion alone. Used and disguised properly, a suggestion is a spell, a sword, a seduction. Women have been conditioned to spend most of their lives cleaning, apologizing, following up, reminding, asking, begging, pleading, chasing, and crying. All of those ugly verbs lead to the loss of self and as such, the woman herself becomes ugly. She begins to despise herself. Unable to articulate what she actually wants and worst of all, she has lost sight of what that is.

This book is designed to help women claim the gift they have been granted, a power so entrancing, so dominant, so persuasive that when used properly, is unstoppable. Finally, this book is intended to help women identify what or whom is standing in their way, followed by instruction on how to eliminate it or him.

Chapter 9

Maman set her book on the bed. It was the third night in a row she'd come to sleep in my bed. We took up the entire space of the mattress and her feet dangled off the end when she didn't curl up. I loved it. I slept in her arms like a newborn baby.

She dabbed her La Roche-Posay cream onto a cotton ball, swiped it over her clear olive face, then gently dabbed the area under her left eye.

"Maman, what happened to your eye?"

"I fell down the stairs," she said setting the cotton ball on my nightstand, her face constricted.

"You didn't fall down the stairs."

"No, I didn't." Maman wiped her hand across her forehead. "I don't understand it, Simone. All I can say is that something happened when your father first came to the States. He hasn't been the same since. I should have known that by coming here, as a family, he'd only get worse."

"Worse how? Maman forgive me. You're the one struggling here, while he's—"

"With other women," she said, immediately shuddering. "And it's not just the women, there's something else about him, my God look at me, I do this all day. I dissect everything he's doing, I work myself up with sick ideas and by the time he comes back from the vineyard I'm ready to strangle him. He said I'm paranoid and that's where he's right, I'm going insane here, I mean look at me, I shouldn't be telling you any of this." Tears streamed down her face and I wiped them away. She squeezed my hands in hers. "Simone, did you find the papers I asked you to look for—

you know, in Papa's lab?"

"I did but I didn't take them, he was with me the whole time."

"What were they about? Was Hal Green's name on them?"

"I don't remember. I read them as fast as possible when Papa had his back to me, mixing tea. Something about The French House like you said. And about a girl named Anne-Marie."

Chapter 10

The French House stood welcoming and warm despite the lake's chilly winds. Above the main entrance a banner flapped and swayed. It read: *The French House Centennial Fête - November 1st.*

All Saints Day. *Day of the Dead.*

Papa had said I couldn't live here, but I refused to stay away. I rubbed the bronze woman's foot and walked to the end of the sidewalk to see if anyone was on the terrace. I risked missing my business development class if I stayed too long, and when I saw it was Charlie Derosiers there I knew that I would. He sat facing the lake and upon noticing me motioned toward the weaved bistro chair across from him.

"It suits you," he said, poker-faced, his eyes on my lips. I'd donned a traffic stopping red lipstick for the first time in my life, which I'd bought on a whim from a pharmacy a couple blocks away. I was feeling edgy and knew this color would get attention.

"What does?"

"You know." His eyes glinted and the song of suggestion zipped through the air. "Red lips. Black hair." He widened his eyes. "Lovely."

I easily might have fainted but managed to hold his eyes as I sat across from him. "*Merci.*"

"Macaron?" Charlie nodded toward a tray filled with colorful dainty cookies: pistachio, raspberry, cappuccino. "Henri's intern made them last night and they're delicious."

I reached for a pistachio macaron and placed the delicate cookie into my mouth, biting into its creamy middle, hoping to maintain elegance—and my lipstick.

Charlie sank his teeth into a raspberry macaron with a smile, saying with his mouth full, "No more career on the slopes, may as well live off pastry."

We sat in silence for a while and I didn't feel obligated to fill it, rather I relaxed into the chair. I watched the lake's waves sparkle under the sun and attuned my ears to the wind's whistle and rattling leaves. In the far distance, I heard the marching band practicing, smelled bratwurst grilling on frat row.

"This arrived today," Charlie said, digging in his sweater pocket. He leaned over to hand me a piece of thickly folded stationary and I caught a whiff of his raspberry breath. "She sends everything express." He laughed as if the answer were obvious. "Camille."

"Oh," I said. The letter felt heavy in my hands. That she'd written him a letter reminded me of *Les Liasions Dangereuses*, an epistolary novel. I decided I was Cécile, the novel's ingénue character recently released from a convent and looking for love.

"Please, skip to the last paragraph," Charlie insisted.

I unfolded Camille's letter to find five pages of inky swirling script, palimpsest in nature. I'd never be able to skim the rest without him noticing.

> *For Simone: I truly look forward to meeting you. It is not often that someone new charms our group and therefore, I expect to be as delighted by you as Charlie and Reine seem to be. Great Expectations—as they say in English. How might you possibly live up? You're destined to disappoint me. Oh ma coquine, don't overthink my words!*
>
> *Prove me wrong and I'm yours, Camille*

Reluctantly, I pressed the letter back into its trifold and he grabbed it.

"Since the beginning of summer she's sent letter after letter, as if we'll forget her. But there are some people you can't forget." He paused and licked his lips, giving me a sideways glance. I turned away, touched my cold hand against my hot cheek. "What I miss though, is her violin, she plays it out here. And Reine will sometimes do interpretive dance to the music and, needless to say, the others think we're crazy, but I find it beautiful. With this view, the violin's haunting melody, and Reine's movement—you might fall asleep and never wake up. It feels like," his voice drifted, "like things are normal."

I wanted to ask him to explain, but it was as if I'd lost my voice. Why weren't things normal? What was normal? Certainly not me, with my dead mother and blind brother, my splotchy memories, Misfit friends, and Camus as my bedtime reading. Instead, I tried to picture what Camille looked like. Surely, she was beautiful. I didn't want to be jealous, didn't want to ruin the friendship beginning to sprout with immature daydreams of Charlie and me, but it was there, lingering in the back of my mind. The girl I was destined to disappoint. *Don't overthink my words.*

"What did she write that you didn't want me to see?"

He took another bite of macaron. "Nothing."

"Oh, well then Charlie, I've got to go," I said, standing. "I've got so much to do today."

"I'm sorry," he said quickly, wiping his mouth. "It's silly. It's about her thesis."

"Ah, the famous thesis. What is it she's trying to prove about Boucher?"

"*Euh*...actually it has more to do with a girl who used to live in the House."

I frowned. "There's enough about one girl to write a whole grad thesis? Wait, is this the girl Reine brought up at dinner, Anne-Marie something?"

"Fisker, yeah." Charlie sighed, setting his macaron onto the plate on his lap. "Anne-Marie Fisker—née Maria Fisker—she murdered the group of native French speaking residents living in the House, then killed herself that same night; 1982 I think."

"Oh my God." I covered my mouth. It was true what the girl had said my first day. Bad things happened here. "How many people died?"

Charlie looked down. "Seven—eight if you include her. It was all over the American news from what I understand. International too, I don't personally remember reading about it in France at the time, but I looked up the articles after I moved here."

"How can the House still exist after something like that?"

"They shut it down for a year, refurbished, re—*structured*."

A gust of wind shook the oak branches overhead then, sending a flutter of yellow leaves onto the terrace.

"Why'd she do it?"

Charlie finished chewing and brushed crumbs from his hands. "Supposedly she was obsessed with Boucher's book. She wanted to be her—she wanted to be French. She changed her name to Anne-Marie and started pretending she was, even speaking English with a French accent. The French people ridiculed her. And then…she snapped."

Boucher's book inspired this girl to kill? I thought of the end of her book's introduction:

> *This book is intended to help women identify what or whom is standing in their way, followed by instruction on how to eliminate it or him.*

"So there's a deeper reason for the split between native speakers and the others," I said. "Just like Jane Elliott's experiment, there *was* an instigator—Boucher's book. You and Reine made it seem like it was just a cultural divide."

"Would this have been better, 'Nice to meet you, Simone, did you hear about the mass murder in this house?'" He lifted one eyebrow.

"Touché." I smiled for the first time. It faded as I moved my attention to the House looming behind him. It looked darker than it had a minute ago, the bloated gargoyles leering. "How'd she do it?"

"Stabbed them in their sleep."

I closed my eyes. On the other side of my lids I saw fluorescent splatters and black dots, like when you've looked at the sun too long. Except inside those dots I saw the slain victims sprawled about The French House. I opened my eyes and focused on the pistachio macaron in my palm.

"Camille's playing with the devil by bringing this story back up. As if we haven't been through enough."

"The devil as in Boucher?"

"Look, there have been other concerns since Fisker. The board is under pressure to shut us down. Some of the members come to dinner from time to time, check to see how we're doing."

I'd noticed a man and woman I'd placed in their sixties arrive in the middle of that magical first dinner, and figured they were someone's parents—someone's very rich parents, dressed in perfectly tailored silk.

"Besides, we're strapped for cash. Fewer and fewer French students are coming and despite Boucher's donation, funds are dwindling. Henri—I love him, but he's not exactly helping with the exuberant buffets. I'm sure he makes an exorbitant amount and anything else he spends on new curtains and tablecloths."

"Sounds a bit Madame Bovary."

Charlie broke into a beautiful laugh and reached his hand toward mine, stopping just short of touching me as if it would cross a border. He retracted, holding my eyes. And somehow, I felt the absence of his touch, a sort of buzzing, vibrating energy between us.

He cleared his throat. "That's why they opened our Centennial Fête to the public—to earn money and donations. Henri's desperate to find ways for money or savings. In fact, he wants to ask you if your father will donate wine for the fête."

A flock of seagulls cawed overhead, half of them fluttered to the terrace railing.

"I think the fête may be our last hurrah, Simone. If we pull it off, the House lives on. But if something—*anything* goes wrong. It's the end of The French House."

* * *

Sunday came, the day of the banquet. I had a few hours left to convince Papa to let me move into The French House and thus attend. My application had already been accepted. After sitting with Charlie on the terrace I had found and assured Henri that Duchamps Winery would donate the wine for the Centennial Fête, and he insisted I fill out the form right then and there to "push it through before the big day." Now I just had to convince Papa it was a good idea.

All weekend I'd been thinking of Charlie and Reine, talking incessantly about them to Bertrand and my Misfits, Sam and Kip. Then, much to my extreme pleasure, they showed up at the vineyard shop, just before I was about to give the tourists a vineyard tour. They stuck out like roses in a field of dead dandelions, Reine in a brown flapper style dress and cloche hat, and Charlie with a felted beret that would have been preposterous on anyone else. I smelled cinnamon and clove on Charlie's breath as he kissed my cheeks. The slightest head shift would have touched my lips to his.

I asked them what they were doing all the way out here—at our vineyard. Had Professor sent them to work some magic? I had gone to her office on Friday to tell her Papa wouldn't allow me to move in. She'd simply responded, "Nonsense."

"*Parce-que*," Reine said with a shrug, facing the shop's glass shelves, "we have to pick Camille up from the airport later and thought it was a perfect day to visit a vineyard." She ran her fingers over a packet of wine glass markers and smiled at me. "This place is incredible, Simone."

"Who are your friends?" Charlie eyed the Misfits who were standing behind me. I don't think any of us believed Papa when he said there were people waiting in the shop to see me.

"These are," I paused and considered my words. "These are my best friends, Sam, Kip, and my brother Bertrand."

Sam bounded into Charlie with an aggressive hug and moved immediately thereafter to Reine, going on about how beautiful they were. Kip hesitantly staggered over with his crutches and shook their hands. Bertrand remained in place and waved.

"The Blind Man and the Lame," Charlie said.

"*Charlie*," Reine whispered low, chewing her thumbnail.

"'A blind man carried a lame man on his back, lending him his feet and borrowing his eyes,'" Charlie went on, flipping his palms up. "Oh come on, someone say they recognize Plato." He poked Reine's arm. "You should shop less."

"You should talk," she scoffed, giving him a lighthearted push. "My father's personal shopper sends me all of my clothes. And anyway, I'm not studying Plato at the moment."

Charlie placed his hand on Bertrand's shoulder and gave it an affectionate squeeze. "I am the Lame in this story. I shattered my knee and because of it, I sometimes walk with a gimp. But anyway, we came for a vineyard tour so where's our tour guide?"

"You're looking at her," I said. "Carol usually does them but she called in sick. Let me grab a coffee and we'll get started in five."

I went outside to calm down. I'd need the herbal tincture to get through this—to give the entire tour to Charlie.

"Simone!" He'd followed me outside; he grabbed my arm and spun me around with the dexterity of a dancer.

"Charlie—"

"You are more fascinating to me with every encounter." He gripped my elbows. "I haven't been able to stop thinking about you since you visited me on the terrace."

I looked at my feet, my red flats. "Why is that?"

He tipped my chin back up with his hand then brought his steepled fingers to his lips. "Because you always leave me wanting more."

"Do I?" Surely there was a smarter response. A suggestion to architect my desired outcome. I had finished Professor's book during the bottomless night. Boucher's lessons had sold me. While I had set off reading the book to find what Maman may have liked, and which part inspired Anne-Marie Fisker to kill, I instead found it empowering for my own devices, like winning Charlie. I scribbled endless thoughts in the book's margins—and again, most of them were about Charlie. All weekend I did everything with him in mind to the point in which I found myself practicing our future conversations and acting out my hopefully elegant movements as if he might manifest before me at any moment: while I prepared breakfast, walked in the vineyard, or in the damn bathroom—like a bad song, he was stuck in my head. And here he was, I successfully conjured him—and the right response.

"There's more of me to discover, Charlie. A *lot* more."

He ran his fingers over my cheek. They were warm as freshly baked bread. I parted my lips and, tilted my head.

"Most girls, most women, how do I say this? They shut out anyone who's different. But not you, you may be the last good person on earth,

Simone." His fingers moved into my hair, his nails lightly running along my scalp. "The truth is we're here because I begged Reine to come. She was at the dance studio this morning but I didn't want to show up alone—and I had to see you, and make sure you'd come tonight." He pulled away from my hair and gave me a slap on the back. I shuffled slightly forward, confused. Then I noticed Reine in the foreground, beckoning us to come back. Charlie held up his pointer finger and faced me, motioning his head toward the stone-lined cave burrowed into the hill at our side, and asked me what it was. I told him it was the Old-World way of storing wine, where wine matured and improved, and that any self-respecting Frenchman ought to know that. I did not mention it was also where we'd put Maman's ashes.

"How far back does it go?"

"Honestly, I don't know. I don't go inside anymore, and I've always been afraid I'd fall into it. Supposedly the Count who first started our winery also built manholes to enter it from the top of the bluff. But hey," I smiled, "this is stuff you're supposed to be learning with the tour group."

"Does that mean I'm getting the private tour right now?"

I again channeled Anne Boucher with my reply. "That *is* what you want, *non?*"

We held each other's eyes for a moment, my nerve endings building a beautiful storm I wanted him to set off.

"*Bon,*" he said, "go get your coffee, I'll be with the public tour—for now, that is." He jogged back to Reine, and they disappeared behind the door to the tour room. I looked into the deep, dark cave and rubbed my arrowhead necklace.

* * *

The tour started with a video and I was thankful. I needed a moment to reflect on what had happened. The tour guests, there were five asides from Charlie and Reine, watched from the salvaged church pews while the film chimed about our vineyard's history, the Hungarian Count who'd incorporated our small village and planted the first grapes, about Hal Green, the man from D.C. who moved here to give winemaking a shot, and then how my parents reinvigorated the winery with their

French savoir-faire. Throughout I focused on Charlie's face, his olive skin changing with the rise and fall of the screen's glowing light. Reine sat to his left, and a pretty blonde woman in her mid-twenties on his right. She was digging inside her giant black leather purse like a squirrel burrowing nuts. Charlie watched her with a frown then whispered something into Reine's ear and the two of them scooted over.

After the video I led the group to the vineyard and walked them up and down rows, and explained the grape varietals we used, those that best survived the cold Wisconsin winters, and the distinguishing aspects of our terroir: the chalky-tasting, highly fertile soil the Wisconsin glacier left behind.

A woman in a black cardigan with Halloween inspired macramé patches (a witch, jack-o-lantern, green goblin, and *BOO!)* asked me what kind of work we did in the summer. I told her I'd spent most of my days desuckering vines, removing the shoots without grapes, then trellised them so they'd get maximum sunlight.

"Hence the reason you're so *bronzée*," Charlie said, holding his hand over his eyes to block the sun. "You must have been out here all day."

"I was, and would be all winter too if it weren't for class. After harvest we still have to remove about eighty percent of the shoots because they won't produce fruit anymore. When it comes to the shoots, it's the younger the better."

"Well, if that ain't telling," the woman said. "Sounds like my ex-husband."

"Pity he didn't realize the end product tastes much better with age," I said.

She held up her right hand. "High five."

I stepped forward to give her a light slap. Behind her Charlie mouthed, *Boo!* and I held my breath to keep from laughing.

Next on the tour was the fermentation room, big as a school gymnasium and filled with fifteen-foot tall gleaming silver fermentation tanks breeding wine, the smell of baby alcohols so pungent and sweet. After my spiel a hulking man in a Canadian tux raised his hand like it was a classroom.

"The guy who used to run this winery, Hal Green."

"Yes, what about him?"

"Wasn't he in the CIA?"

"I highly doubt it," I said.

He scratched his head, and the movement caused his denim shirt's last button to unhook and reveal a triangle shaped view of his hairy belly. I rubbed my eyes to keep from seeing it.

"That's what I heard anyway. My neighbor used to be a big wig at the university's psych department. He got piss drunk one night and told me about some covert work he used to do there with a former CIA guy named Hal."

"*Covert?*"

"Really?" said his wife. She had feathered eighties hair and was chewing a wad of mint green gum. "Now *that* sounds interesting."

And my tour wasn't?

"Sure does," Halloween cardigan agreed.

"Covert as in questionable research," the guy went on. "I'll ask your dad, he's the owner, right? He'd probably know."

"That might be a good selling point." It was the first thing the pretty woman with the big purse said all day. She had one hand inside the thing now, digging and digging and digging until she removed a tube of lip-gloss. After a quick swipe she rubbed her lips together so fast I expected a flame to spark. "People love the mafia tours we have back home in Chic*aaa*go."

"Well, I don't know anything about it," I said, "And my father doesn't like talking to tourists."

The denim guy tucked in his shirt and I thought I heard him mutter, "French people."

* * *

The end of the tour brought us to the atrium apothecary tasting room where I sent the guests to the five different counters to try our best *philtre* labels. The apothecarist-clad workers showed them how to swirl their glasses for proper aeration, and for those interested in testing their noses, Bertrand had made a scent kit which held glass tubes of scents native to the Wisconsin bluffs, and which consequently fertilized the beginnings of the wine's character. Charlie was the first to try it. He dipped his nose into a tube, closing his eyes, and pulling in a deep breath. "You've stumped me on my very first try, Bertrand, and I've got to prove to myself I can do this."

His mouth opened and closed a few times, accentuating his plush lips as if he wanted me to see them. "It's earthy and I want to say—moldy, but in a good way."

Bertrand would identify which tube Charlie was inhaling simply from the vague description. His synesthesia helped him navigate the kit uncannily fast, numbers appearing with each scent and offering him instant answers.

"Is it mushrooms? Hopefully not the poisonous kind!" Charlie said with a full smile, reaching to touch Bertrand ever so slightly to alert him to where he stood.

Bertrand moved his hand up Charlie's arm to locate the tube to lean in and smell to be sure. "It is," he concurred, "Very good. And no, those are not the toxic variety, though we have plenty on our property."

"Like what?" asked Reine.

"*Psilocybin cubenis, amanita muscaria*…you name it, it grows here," said Bertrand feeling around for the empty spot in his scent kit to return the mushroom tube.

"*Psilocybin* like 'magic mushrooms?'"

"*Oui, exactement.*"

"We have something like it back home in Gabon. A hallucinogenic root that grows in the rainforest. We call it *iboga*. The Bwiti followers use it during their rite of passage, they say it helps them see the future and speak to the dead."

"Maybe I should try some," said Bertrand.

Reine was working her fingers around her pearl strand. "More and more tourists are coming from France to do just that. Anything to get high."

The rest of the tourists were watching our group, all except the purse lady who was texting. The lady in the ghoulish sweater said she didn't understand a word we said but *boy*, weren't we charming and *gosh*, didn't it feel like they were in France instead of Wisconsin?

I had that sensation of being watched and sure enough I was right. Just like Bertrand always said, there's a lot we can trust from our instincts without seeing a thing. It was Papa. He caught us all in the act of laughing and having fun and I hoped he wouldn't think that I was no longer hurting. That he'd made the right choice.

Reine noticed my change in demeanor and apologized, saying they'd have to go. It was time to pick up Camille from the airport and get ready for the big banquet dinner.

"Camille will require our full attention of course, she'll be desperate to hear what she's missed while on vacation, and she'll have plenty of questions about you. Will we see you there?" Her wide slate eyes were hopeful.

"No, you won't." I looked at Papa, who was now within earshot, so he'd see my grin transform into a scowl. Apparently unaffected he grabbed my arm in a tight grip, the kind that made it awkward for anyone watching and naturally, everyone was. I was the tour guide, he was the winemaker, and this was a spectacle.

"Can I talk to you outside?" Papa said in English. He only ever spoke English to guests. Again I made a face and wiped my hands on my jeans. He dragged me to the door. Charlie and Reine watched.

"Did Hal Green used to work in the CIA?" I asked as our feet hit the gravel and the tour room door closed. Birds peppered the sky, a few clouds scurried low.

"What kind of question is that?"

"A tourist's."

"Oh, well there you have it. Don't be silly." He cleared his throat. "Now, this whole thing with your—*friends.* It was nice…seeing you happy, laughing with people your own age, people other than your—your Misfits."

I reminded myself not to resort to begging. Professor had written: You mustn't beg or ask for anything more than once. If a request is repeated, its effect is lost and consequently, so too is your power. Lose your power and you can no longer summon what you wish to happen.

"It's because of that residence hall," I said casually. "It's the first time I've been with French people—aside from you and Bertrand of course. I feel calm there."

He perked up upon hearing this word, *calm*. I knew he would. "If I were you Papa, I would simply allow me to move into The French House for a short period. Nothing determinate, nothing serious."

"Nothing serious?"

"Right. Just a trial."

"Oh, Simone," he said, his features lightening.

"If I can't handle it, I'll come home."

He rubbed his forehead leaving behind a dirty black smudge.

"And with more time on campus, I'll have more access to my business development professor, who I can tap into to help me prepare for the wine expo."

"The expo," Papa said tasting the word like it was wine.

There it was. My bargaining chip. Our winery was one of the few invited to a prestigious expo to be held at the Centre Pompidou. Because my uncle Guillaume's vineyard—the family's chateau, was also invited, Papa initially said we wouldn't go. He didn't want to see his brother "that vengeful liar" and he didn't want to return to France. Additionally, the expo would host a contest for the unveiling of a new branding concept, specifying that the judging would have nothing to do with the actual wine, which Papa found a disgrace—*c'est insupportable*!

At first it was a weird concept to me as well, until I realized the challenge was designed to show what creative labeling did for the industry. Our invitation letter had praised us a "leader in innovative marketing" and hoped our participation would inspire traditional houses. Reading between the lines I understood it was their way to get old school French houses to up their ante against the creative branding popping up around the States, Australia, and South Africa–wines that were reaping elevated profits due to labeling alone. I'd told Papa that we shouldn't turn the offer down. That we'd do it for Maman, as a tribute to her, for it was her creativity that had placed us on the map. She had been one of the pioneers in winery branding strategy. She'd lost his winery in France for reasons I might never know, but she'd saved our winery here. Alas, what could he say? He let me fill out the paperwork and enter, so long as I promised to avoid my Uncle Guillaume while there.

"You may move into The French House for one semester and if it works you can stay another. If it doesn't, you move back home."

I leaned into him, forcing a hug. "*Merci*, Papa."

After a moment he wrapped his arms around me and I closed my eyes, moved with his deep rocking breaths. His skin smelled like fresh air and fermenting grapes. But I didn't have time to relish my victory; there was a banquet to prepare for—and Camille to finally meet.

Chapter 11

"Who are you going to meet, Maman?" I asked. We'd been in the car forever. But I was excited to see Madison; we rarely visited.

"Someone from home," she said distractedly, "from France." She pulled along the side of the road and parked. "You two stay here," she said looking in the mirror and finger combing her hair. "I'll be back soon." She locked the doors and walked off and into a beautiful home with a giant green statue in front. But she came back immediately.

"What's wrong?" Bertrand asked.

She sighed. "The person I wanted to see wasn't there."

"Maman, what's this all about?"

She started the car and we drove off. "It's about the paperwork I've been after in Papa's lab. I don't know, maybe I'm losing my mind, Lord knows your father thinks I am."

At a red light I peered out my window and admired the capitol building.

"*Merde,*" Maman said. "I forgot my book there! I set it on the table in the foyer and left it."

"Which book, Maman?"

"Never mind, it must have been meant to be."

The light turned green and we drove off. When we got home Maman sent me to Papa's lab for the papers. I asked her again what it was all about.

"When we first moved here and we were unpacking, I remember seeing all this paperwork, I didn't read much, just scanned it and left it.

But I learned about some things—some bad things that happened nearby and some of the names and places correlate to the papers."

"What does correlate mean, Maman?"

"Just go check the lab and come back, would you please?"

I did as she asked. But Papa wasn't there and the door was locked. I returned to Maman in the kitchen, she was mixing cake batter. "I'll help you," I said putting on my matching apron.

"You know Simone, unlike the universe, art is not infinite. A great painter will have only three masterpieces in a lifetime, no more."

"Ok-*ay*," I said. She'd been doing this more and more. Responding with things that made no sense. And while she tended to reduce things to threes, lately she did so with everything, from the spiders she spotted in the house, to the amount of times she locked the door.

"I'm sorry I didn't get the papers," I told her.

She shrugged as if she no longer cared about them. "You only get three chances to seduce the outcome of life in your favor. I only have one remaining." She was rolling dough on the island, her pink apron covered with flour, a few specks on her face. I copied her movements, in this way we made two of everything and she said one day I'd be cooking for her. That when you repeated an act enough it commits to your muscle memory, your body remembers for you, not your head.

"One more chance for what?" I asked.

"To save us."

This was this type of talk Papa worried about. Maman was falling off the edge, he said. At dinner she'd veer into tangents from the book she sometimes read to me in bed. Words about eliminating anyone who stood in the way of finding your inner power. When Papa asked her what she was talking about she'd quickly change the subject to *L'étranger*. "When you're The Outsider," she'd say, "you're bound to snap." On her most fiery nights she spat words about Uncle Guillaume and Papa's wretched father. That's when Papa and I would put Bertrand to bed early and prepare Maman's tisane. With a clattering tray in hand, Papa led her to bed and sat by her side telling her everything would be fine, as he served her the calming tea. Some evenings I was allowed to follow and snuggle with Maman, on the worst of them I was not. The last few nights had been particularly bad. I think she broke every candleholder, photo frame, and decorative plate we owned. She hurled these items at Papa and when he successfully dodged out of the way, she tried to punch him. He grabbed her thin arms and she writhed within them until he slowly calmed her down.

Now she set the rolling pin down and brushed the side of her face with the heel of her hand. "You know what? I'm going to make my move tonight."

Chapter 12

I had only an hour to prepare for the banquet—fifteen minutes considering the drive time. I owned nothing suitable for such an event and had no choice but to go try Maman's closet. I flipped on the light and it was as if the room's walls shook. *Breathe.* I dipped my head to my knees to get blood flowing. Try again. Maman would want me to wear one of her dresses.

But everything smelled like mothballs. I shuffled through the remainder, hoping to find at least one dress in protective covering. Instead, I saw a letter jutting out of a knit pink sweater. I grabbed it.

> *Vi,*
>
> *The children and I will see you in Paris soon—I have nearly everything set. I can't call you again as he's monitoring the long-distance charges—so this is it, our last correspondence until we meet in person! I will be whole again in France I know it. Here, I am sick in the head. Have you any news of Guillaume? I'm sure you would have told me if you did. I cannot stop myself from thinking we'll find our way back to one another despite it all. I love him still. And so, even if you haven't, please talk to Guillaume. Ask him if he kept my work.*

I have a feeling he did and I'm going to do everything I can to get it back. It would save us, and the sooner I know the better.

Your loving sister, Lisette

I wanted to crumple the letter and throw it in the trash, but I didn't. It was a memento of Maman. She had touched it. It was her handwriting, and I should treasure anything so intimate. But the letter was disturbing—she was in love with Uncle Guillaume? Papa was monitoring her long-distance calls? Did he know she loved his brother? I knew Papa hadn't been faithful. A few years after Maman died I remembered when a kid at recess shouted to his friend to *Stop fucking around!* I suddenly pictured Jackie telling me in the pink tiled girl's bathroom that her mom was *fucking* my dad. I asked Papa if it was true and he admitted it was, just the one time and he felt awful. He said I had no idea how hard it was for him to live with Maman's mental illness and he had looked for comfort elsewhere, something he'd never forgive himself for. I left it at that, not bothering to remind him that I *did* live with her, because I didn't want to imagine the specifics. But for months I spat in his dinner plate just before serving him.

I didn't know if Maman knew about the affair or not. My Pollack era had obscured reality. I needed to talk to Bertrand and ultimately, to my uncle Guillaume when we got to France. What did she think he kept of hers and was it true, when in this letter she admitted to her mental instability? Would it have anything to do with the papers she was searching for in Papa's lab—if that memory was right? There was no time to think it out now. I had to leave for the banquet, and my white blouse, mariner striped mid-calf tube skirt, and red flats would have to do. I looked at myself in the mirror ashamed, imagining the glamorous gown Camille would be wearing.

I may be underdressed but at least I would be calm. I quickly made myself an herbal tincture loaded tea and got in the car.

* * *

Professor spotted me the moment I walked into The French House. She slithered her way toward me, gently weaving among the other guests, all of whom were sporting cocktail attire and holding bubbling flutes of champagne, happily chirping away over the sound of a pianist's fluttering melody. People filled the salon, the turret's library, the solarium, yet no one had ventured into the dining room. Maybe we needed permission.

"Does this mean what I think it does?" Professor asked.

She was stunning. A long shimmering dress of gold and ivory sparkles hugged her hourglass body, reminding me of Grace Kelly's Piper Heidsieck ad. I was more laughably underdressed than I'd feared I would be. Everyone and everything was so glossy and perfect and colorful, like the tropical room in Madison's botanical gardens we once visited in high school, and I wanted so badly to belong in the scene.

"Come, we have enough time." She wrapped her arm around my ribs to lead me upstairs where I hadn't yet been. Then led me down a long cream-colored hallway with golden-lit sconces. My shadow rose and fell as I walked, like I'd awakened a ghost in the wall. Professor entered a bedroom at the end of the hall and closed the door behind us.

"I was going to wear this." She pulled a gown out of the closet, putting a hand on her hip to accentuate the dip below her ribs. "Well go ahead, try it on." She stood before me, holding the gown to her side. It drooped down in elegant wisps from the wooden hanger like an ultimatum. I laughed. The dress was black as my hair yet completely translucent.

"Professor, forgive me but I don't think I should wear a see-through gown on my first introduction to the board."

She waved her hand dismissively. "There's a little slip for it underneath, and Simone," she said, running her hand down my arm. "This is The French House not the Catholic Society. As for impressing the board don't worry about it. I'm the most important, with the money I donate, and you already have my approval."

"*D'accord,*" I mumbled. She began unbuttoning my blouse. Button by button slipped out of its hole, her long fingers working their way down. I hated that I didn't know if this was normal or not. The last person to help me undress had been Maman but she passed away well before I woke up a confused and hormonally charged teenager.

Professor unhooked the last button. "Charlie's going to like this dress, Simone," she said. "And Camille will not. You must keep your eye on her as we discussed. Keep her calm."

"Professor—"

"Call me Anne," she said as she slid the blouse off my shoulders. "He's a handsome young man, you'd be silly not to vie for his attention." She handed me the translucent dress, the scent of crème brûlée so strong it was Pavlovian, my mouth watering.

"I'll help you."

I wasn't sure if she meant she'd help me dress or help me vie for Charlie's attention, but I took the slip from her hands and put it over my shoulders when she made a quick no-no sound and shook her head.

"That bra will show, take it off."

I swallowed and the sound echoed within my head, the latest rumor I'd heard about her, this one from Jerry in my business development class circumvented my mind like a storm, *The French Lit Professor got caught sleeping with students—almost got fired.* I had shrugged it off at the time but now it wasn't so farfetched.

"Take it off, Simone."

At the border of the Holy Roman Empire and the Kingdom of France, Marie-Antoinette was stripped of her clothes and belongings. Ritual required this shedding of her heritage to create a clean slate for her future as the French Dauphine. I did what I was told.

Chapter 13

How quickly would she make her move, whatever it was? At dinner, Maman wouldn't stop talking, asking Bertrand and I questions she knew the answers to, until she finally set her silverware down and looked at Papa with her chin held high.

"My sister's doing quite well. She has a show coming up in Paris. I'd like to go see it—and her."

Papa sighed and leaned into his chair. "Who else do you want to see?"

"Just her."

Papa rubbed his face into his palm. "You're not going anywhere. You can't handle it."

"I can handle anything. Stop telling me otherwise."

"Lisette," Papa pleaded, "you've struggled here. You're forgetful—unpredictable, you've become mentally unstable—"

Maman lifted her steak knife and dove across the table toward him. The table shifted to the side. A wine bottle and my dinner plate fell to the ground. Red wine spread across the wood and oozed over the transparent fish bones scattered from my plate.

Papa gripped Maman's wrists. She was screaming and contorting like an animal, the knife in her hand.

Chapter 14

Professor reapplied her bright red lipstick in front of the bedroom's mirror and met my eyes in the reflection. "You look fabulous, Simone. Go downstairs and find him. I'll be down shortly."

The heels she gave me were too big and I walked downstairs slowly, though I doubted anyone would be looking at my shoes given my transparent dress. Charlie and Reine were in the salon holding champagne flutes with who I presumed was Camille. She wasn't what I'd envisioned her. She had thick auburn hair that swooped into a plump bun perfectly centered atop her head. She wore heavy black glasses and had the kind of obvious freckles that implied she'd dotted them in herself exactly where she'd wanted them, her cheekbones so high and symmetrical they reminded me of a Slavic princess, and her mouth insouciant, resisting a smile. She was *jolie laide* in that she demanded further inquiry, the mind curious as to whether to determine her beautiful or not. She whispered into Charlie's ear without removing her close-set eyes from mine, eyes that were simultaneously bored and sorrowful.

"Smashing dress, Simone," Reine said with a warm smile, her eyes zipping to Camille. I searched for Camille's reaction but saw nothing. She eyed me intensely but stoically. Professor had said she wouldn't approve of my dress, but was that because it wasn't the right designer, or because it was too revealing?

"*Merci*, you're a vision yourself." I turned to Reine. She wore a purple sheath and sequin cap; she'd joked that the Jazz Age had been incomplete without her. I grabbed a flute and downed a glass, hoping to relax. I knew Camille was the group's gatekeeper and I wanted her to like me. She was hard to read, her eyelids heavy as if she were half asleep yet her hazel glare remained fixed on my chest, the black transparence barely concealing me, confirming Professor's intuition.

"Simone, this is Camille," Charlie said as if he'd been waiting for the perfect moment to formally introduce the two of us. He quickly nosed into his champagne and stepped back as Camille kissed my cheeks.

"*Ma minette*, finally we meet," she whispered as she planted her second kiss. Her voice emotionless, and her words cold as a glacier.

* * *

A white-haired woman wearing a chiffon purple gown announced that we may be seated. I followed Camille. Unlike Professor who walked fluidly but directly toward her target, Camille meandered as though she had no destination and was intent on the longest possible route. At one point I stopped walking to watch her crisscross the room and run her hand along everything she passed: the piano, a walnut buffet table, the staircase banister, as though she were contemplating it all for estate redecoration. It was amusing albeit frustrating and I ultimately moved passed her to claim the chair next to Reine, and across from Charlie, surprised we hadn't been assigned seats. The white-haired woman joined our table and introduced herself as Hélène. Her face was shiny as a store-bought apple and her skin pulled back so tightly her lips stayed in a constant state of *eek*. She wore enormous diamonds on her frail fingers, perhaps the reason for their arthritic curvature.

"Mademoiselle Cloutier," she said hoarsely, "sit already."

And finally, Camille sat.

* * *

"Reine you aren't touching your food," said Charlie eyeing her steak.

"Check me into rehab, for I have a pumpkin addiction," Reine declared dramatically. "And Camille told me I'm looking much pudgier than before she left for vacation." She pouted.

"Well you are," Camille said, holding her wine glass above the table like she was ready to give a speech. "I know I once told you that you'd look better with a few pounds on you, but I'm afraid you've gone too far."

"Mimi, *arrête*. No one wants to talk about weight during a feast. And don't forget Reine's a dancer. She must have spent the majority of her life in front of a mirror, she doesn't need *your* commentary."

"*Merci*, Charlie." Reine nodded his way. "But she's right, I've gone too far. I mean who wants a movement therapist with a belly? Today I had a pumpkin latte, pumpkin bread, pumpkin pie, and even half a pumpkin bar. This country is killing me. I feel awful and I can't eat one more bite."

"Well, on that note you missed a sumptuous pumpkin soup," Charlie chuckled. "In all seriousness that's a shame because *one*, you don't have a belly, and *two,* Henri has completely outdone himself." He cut a piece of iridescent fat off his steak and happily placed it in his mouth. *"Il faut se faire plaisir."*

"And that my friend, will be the quote you'll one day be remembered for," Reine said. "You put pleasure above all else."

Charlie smiled my way.

"Speaking of pleasure," Camille said slowly, "our darling *Henriette* found a way to get out of work, he's got an intern named Peter now *tu sais,* who does nearly everything for him—and I mean *everything*. Just pretend you don't know about it, we don't want him going off the deep end again, do we?" She flicked a vein in her arm.

"*Oh-là-là*, Mimi. Too far." Charlie's face tightened and he turned toward Hélène. She was talking to a grey bearded man and hadn't noticed.

Reine leaned into my ear to whisper, "Henri used to be a big name chef in Paris but got in some huge fight with the restaurant's owners, lost his job, and got addicted to heroin. But he went through rehab and when he got out he happened to meet Jean-Paul, that board member over there with the green bowtie. Jean-Paul offered Henri a job that same night and Henri decided to move here. He calls it his nonreligious born-again moment."

"*Simone, ma petite*," Camille said. Her freckled face distorted from the candle's flame. "Look how well you fit in with us. Maybe we'll be a panoply at last."

* * *

Throughout dinner I observed the board members, Professor in particular. It was impossible not to be struck by her curvaceous body in that shimmering dress. She had a rosy hue in her cheeks tonight and several times I heard her laugh from three tables over. But she was not the only one in the spotlight. I was introduced formally to the entire party as the newest recipient of the Anne Boucher scholarship. There was a round of applause and the snap, snap, snapping of photos as the other students whispered to one another, Jackie their ringleader. We then had our pictures taken for The French House's annual roster and were lectured to regarding the upcoming public dinner, the pressure the House was under to be perfect before the Centennial Fête, the French government's involvement, the big funders, the media. Jean-Paul, the same board member who'd hired Henri, made a curiously worded speech about what had "happened in the past" and how we'd best ensure it "not happen again" if we were to continue, a euphemism-loaded discourse, which elicited many side conversations. I supposed it was about Anne-Marie Fisker. When he finished his diatribe, he raised his flute for a toast.

"You drink first," someone called out. "So we know it's not poison!"

"Well, if that wasn't inappropriate," Reine mumbled.

"What was that about?" I whispered.

"A reference to Boucher. That's how she killed her lover."

I sipped champagne to mask my reaction, thinking about what Bertrand had said. That Professor's hometown experienced a mass poisoning. Maybe instead of letting my experience with her unfold naturally, it would be better to look her up, see what else I found.

* * *

Camille insisted that our group walk through Vilas Park to the Arboretum. "Like we did last year," she looked at me to clarify. We were still energized from all the wine and espresso, and the musty autumn air at this late hour was a shock of reality. Camille led the way, which was to say she aimlessly ambled along the campus streets. We certainly made a bizarre troupe in our cocktail attire, finally reaching an unmarked route in the woods.

"This path makes me feel as though the Headless Horseman will come galloping past at any second," Camille said. She had a distinctive way of generating excitement without so much as a smidgen's change in tone. She was shuffling through leaves, and I only now noticed she'd swapped her black satin heels for a pair of heavy navy and tan duckboots. Her flowing dress juxtaposed with these clunky rainboots like something from a whimsical photoshoot. "Ichabod Crane was my lover in a past life," she added.

"Yeah, who wasn't?" Reine teased.

"We used to make out—there, right there." Camille pointed to a spot on the path and Charlie pressed down on Camille's bun like it was a button.

"That's to say you made out with a pumpkin head, you realize that *non*?" Reine said.

"*Oh là là ma petite*. Crane wasn't the headless horseman in Irving's story. You'd better drop a dance class and enroll in American literature next semester."

"I've read Humpty Dumpty," Reine said nudging Charlie. "Surely that's American."

"Close enough." Charlie laughed. "But you should talk, Mimi. If I recall, Ichabod was an ugly son of a bitch."

An owl hooted. Camille twitched her head to the side and the moon washed her milky skin with a luminescent sheen. "You know, my English tutor read me every nursery rhyme when I was a girl. *Peter, Peter, pumpkin-eater. Had a wife and couldn't keep her. He put her in a pumpkin shell. And there he kept her very well.*"

Reine stopped walking. "Jesus, Peter was an asshole."

"Actually, *mon lion,* Peter was a murderer." Camille plucked a leaf and blew it to the ground. "He killed his wife and hid her body in the pumpkin."

* * *

The farther we walked down the path, the taller the trees became, as if we'd devoured Alice's cakes and were growing smaller by the minute. I swore I saw a glowing Cheshire cat leering at me from a tree branch, until I pinched my eyes shut and counted to ten to make it go away. It was one of those synaptic slips that only went away with my pills, but then again, so did a lot of things.

We rounded our way toward the glistening lake, a half moon's reflection rolling over the waves. Sitting in a pile of leaves I worried about Professor's dress. I certainly did not want to be Maupassant's Mathilde—borrowing and losing—or in my case, ruining a beautiful dress and having to spend the rest of my life working to replace it.

"A group as small as three can technically form a coven. Therefore, we were equipped last year, Reine, Charlie and I. Others have come and gone of course, but life usually brings it back to three," Camille said, spreading the pleats of her taffeta dress, the same color as her autumn auburn hair.

"But the more the merrier," she added in English, "Or so the saying goes." Her eyes gleamed and she gave me a little smirk.

"Forgive Camille, she has a flair for the dark side," Reine said, pulling an orange leaf apart with surgical precision.

"Always has too, as long as I can remember." Charlie said with a lighter tone than Reine.

"I've only been back one day and already I find everything so utterly—boring. I think we ought to have a little more fun, don't you?" She dipped her neck back to face the moonlight, but quickly snapped my way, her eyes hidden from the glare of her glasses. "What do you think, Simone, *mon trésor*? I'd love your opinion."

"My opinion on what?"

"Yes, what is it exactly that you have in mind?" Charlie gripped her shoulder, forcing her to look at him. She pushed him away only to lean forward and reclaim their proximity.

"Anne the Butcher," she said in one flat note.

"What about her?"

"We test her."

"Maybe there's someone else we can test," I said trying to sound indifferent.

Camille looked my way and heaved a sigh. "No, it can only be Boucher." She swatted at the strands of hair streaming across her face from the wind. "If my thesis is to be the least bit credible, I need to know how exactly she got Anne-Marie Fisker to go on a killing spree. Did she use the power of suggestion alone or was there another force behind it? I have to find out."

"You're jealous of Boucher's power, aren't you?" Reine said, looking at me then mouthing crazy. My shoulders dropped, I nodded.

"I'm not jealous, I'm obsessed. Damn that woman." She stood up and whipped around, her taffeta swirls draping behind when she stopped dramatically, arm stretched high above reaching for the moon.

"Camille," I paused and cleared my throat, "how did you get my mother's copy of her book?"

She lowered her arm and placed her hand on her hip. "*Bon,* I've had it for some time now. I found it in the House library. We have several copies of Boucher's book, of course, but I liked that there was a name written in that one so I took it." She smiled. "When I got your pre-course introductory letter I thought, *quelle coïncidence!* I've found there's an odd amount of coincidences when it comes to Boucher."

"Did she really poison her lover?" I asked, chiding myself for continuing to push the topic.

"Arsenic soup, was that it?" Charlie said. "How very old world."

Camille turned toward me. "Yes, she really did poison him."

"How do you know?" I asked.

"*Professore* Miloa, that ancient Italian Studies Professor with the three-piece suits and the tortoiseshell cane."

"He told you?" Reine asked. Camille nodded. "That was tacky of him."

"He didn't tell me what *kind* of poison she used, mind you."

"Thank God for that."

"Why'd she do it?" I asked.

"Because he refused to leave his wife for her. Even after she tried to lure him from his wife with all her money. He still said no! Shortly after..." Her eyes went wide and she stumbled. She mocked shock, bringing her hands to her lips and pretending to choke. She took a few unbalanced steps backwards, gasped and fell to the ground. Her body shook and she released two croaking sounds until she stopped moving completely. An Oscar-worthy performance of death by poison. Charlie slow-clapped.

"We would have no French House if it weren't for her," Reine said, ignoring Camille's performance. Camille jerked on the ground, one last jolt of life. "She donated so much money to the House, which I suppose does afford her the right to haunt it. I think she did it so that she would never stoop so low again."

We sat quietly for a moment and I took the chance to process this new information, to mourn the revelation that Professor wasn't perfect. Then again, I knew better than to believe everything I heard.

"Her lover was an Arab, you know," Camille said, sitting up and brushing the leaves off her dress.

"My God, Camille what year is it?" Reine said.

"*Bof*, someone else in the House is too, that's my point."

"*Enough*!" Charlie shouted. All three of our heads turned his direction. Reine and I with wide eyes, while Camille laughed, a sound akin to a violin going from a low to high chord. Maybe musicians ended up sounding like their instrument in the same way pet owners eventually looked like their pets.

"Just drop it, Mimi," said Charlie with a gravelly voice.

Camille sat into the tufts of leaves. The light shifted and I saw her eyes behind her glasses. She closed them and her eyelids fluttered in thought but then a blast of icy wind tore off the lake, blew our hair, and churned more leaves in the air. Camille rose and twirled with them, and when she stopped, she pointed to us the way a witch might, with a curved finger and menacing regard.

"If we can survive until Halloween, what shall we do? Something scandalous." She went up on one toe and spun like a deranged ballerina wearing duckboots.

"Sur*vive*?" Reine said incredulously.

"Yes—as in The French House. As in our group. All of it. Then what shall we do? Drink one another's blood?"

"I refuse to catch whatever it is you have, Camille so you can count me out."

"You won't be able to stop yourself and you know it, my little witch." Camille said to Reine.

"Vampires drink blood, not witches." Reine shook her head.

I definitely understood Professor's reason for concern, and yet their mischief was charming. I wanted to be a part of their group as much as I wanted Professor on my side.

“I’ll take a test to prove I’m clean. But consider this,” Camille said. “In *Les Liaisons Dangereuses* Laclos says we mustn’t over-indulge in those we want to keep around forever, and look at us all. We wear each other like jackets in a brutal winter. Consequently we’re plummeting toward explosion.” She clapped her hands, “So if we survive one another this semester, and if I’m able to prove my thesis, I will bring us all to Paris to dine at La Tour d’Argent in celebration, on my dime over Thanksgiving break. Charlie and I will be going home for the break anyway and we’ve convinced Reine to join, so that just leaves…” She looked at me. As it was, I would be in Paris over Thanksgiving for the wine expo.

“I’ll be there,” I said.

She smoothed her dress. “Good.”

The sky opened then, and rain fell, cold and relentless.

* * *

There are now two timers set on my days at The French House: Papa’s and Camille’s, I wrote in the margin of Professor’s book. I didn’t understand why Professor threatened Camille so. To be sure, Anne Boucher was bizarre. But I got the feeling she truly cared. Cared about me, about us, and the House. Which is why several weeks later, I first thought the note on my pillow was from her.

Chapter 15

Bertrand and I rushed to Maman and Papa, prying our little fingers over their arms and trying to untangle them.

"Please stop it!"

"Let go!"

"Maman, why are you doing this! Put the knife down!"

"Lisette—*arrête*!"

"Maman—be careful!"

Chapter 16

Be careful. A two-word note left on my pillow, its own handwriting careful, as if someone had taken time with each letter. Beautiful swirls, exquisitely feminine, yet not the same as Camille's handwriting—that much I knew from her summer letters. Nor was it Professor's.

I didn't like the message any more than the idea someone had been in my room when I wasn't. After three short weeks I had taken ownership of it, especially given I had no roommate. I'd brought enough from home to create my own space, a shelf worth of books, a quilt made by my grandmother, even a couple tinctures Papa recommended each cold season, Echinacea and garlic. On the white wainscoted walls, I hung a picture of the vineyard and a copy of Maman's photo from *Saveur*. There were two beds but I slept in the one closest to the window and its lovely lake view.

I opened my dresser drawer, not to put the clothes away rather to find the bedroom key Henri gave me after I signed my resident agreement. There it was in the first drawer, still in the cream envelope with my agreement copy, cold and heavy. I left my room and turned it until the lock clicked.

* * *

The TA in my business development class gave us the last half of class to discuss our final project, which was to rebrand an existing product. He'd assigned me to work with two guys, Jerry and Dan who always referred to class as *biz dev*. Like most days, today they were both wearing gingham shirts though Jerry's was navy and Dan's pink. Jerry nodded at me as I sat, and they continued heatedly discussing the upcoming football game against Ohio State, "We need to cream those mother fuckers." I tuned them out and flipped the *be careful* note in my hand over and over.

"Hold up, let's ask Simone," said Jerry. "You have any ideas which product we should pick to rebrand?"

Dan was eyeing my note and finally pointed at it. "Is that French? Or Spanish?"

"It's French—*I'm* French."

"Oh my God, you live in that French House, don't you? I saw you coming out of there one day."

"I do."

"No shit! That place is freaky. I'm like *dying* to get inside, but your damn Centennial party tickets sold out frickin' immediately. What's it like in there?"

"Yeah, why don't you guys come out to party with the rest of us?" asked Dan pushing his chair back and resting his foot on his knee. He licked his finger and wiped a scuff from his shiny tassel Dockers.

To keep from meeting people like you.

"Dude, we should totally go with a French product," said Jerry. "Or like rebrand something with a French spin. My sister has all these books on how do things like a French person. Raise Your Kids Like a French Person or something like that."

"I've seen that, there's a ton of versions."

"Eat Steak Frites but Don't Gain Weight, Like a French Person."

"Wipe Your Ass with Chanel Scented Toilet Paper, Like a French Person."

"Know when to stop—like a French person," I said.

Dan guffawed. Jerry nodded.

"You're good."

"Yeah but *no*—wait, what product should we choose?"

I folded the note and put it in my pocket. "Wine."

* * *

I left class feeling brazen. I was fine living away from Papa and Bertrand, and above all, off my pills. I'd settled into a comfortable pattern with Charlie, Reine, and even Camille. Aside from our other classes, the four of us stayed together starting with breakfast. Camille with her hard-boiled egg followed by a plate of cornichons, Reine's *pain aux chocolat,* Charlie's bowl of yogurt, and my plain croissant. Throughout dinner we poured infinite amounts of wine (Wisconsin law allows minors to drink so long as a guardian is present, and apparently the term guardian is quite loose). After dinner we prepared digestifs and lounged by the fireplace, or when it was warm enough, went to the terrace to listen to Camille play her violin. I usually fell asleep, her music like a spell. I'd later wake to find I'd been carried to the sofa closest to the fireplace; apparently Charlie never dared bring me to my bedroom and I vowed to wake the next time he picked me up, desperate not to miss such an intimate moment.

But now my mind went back to the note. Who was trying to warn me to "be careful," and was I really surprised? I'd been blinding myself to the imperfections and warning signs I should have recognized with ingénue hope of claiming utopia. There was no debate needed, The French House was far from perfect. The more I chipped away at what I wanted to believe a masterpiece, the more I worried I'd come across something else. My concerns ranged from the awful mass murder, Henri's rough history and exorbitant spending, Hessa not fitting in, and Camille—just Camille. I loved her in my own way; she was like the mean version of Bertrand.

I harbored these concerns yet continuously told myself it was fine—because what was my other option, to return to the vineyard? No. I would remain in the simulation. I would find the theme between the three works Professor assigned. I would keep tabs on Camille. And I would save The French House.

* * *

On my way home from business development I swiped my hand along the statue's bronze foot. Dark storm clouds hovered over the lake but did nothing to deter the Thirsty Thursday crowd, bass thumped from nearby houses, the street filled with intermittent shouts and laughter. I entered the front door and hung my jacket. The house smelled like gingerbread and I traced its wafts to the dining room, stopping at the kitchen's swing doors where I heard Henri and Peter's voices. Lately Henri had been asking me about the wine I committed Duchamps Winery to donating for the fête and I assured him someone would call soon. I had yet to ask Papa, afraid he'd think I was pushing my limits by moving here, leaving Bertrand and him on their own, becoming involved in the business. But the fête was already four weeks away and I'd have to ask soon.

Jackie's friends Tim and Kate sat at a dining room table. Before them were papers from a recent French Lit assignment, covered in red ink. Camille's handwriting.

"She's such a pompous bitch," Tim whispered to Kate.

To my disappointment, Professor had not lectured in French Lit since the first week of class. She left it all to Camille. She would sit in the corner watching her TA, and when Camille discussed portions from *Les Liaisons Dangereuses*, Professor would hold my gaze with a sly grin and a nod, and I'd be so thrown I forgot what passage Camille had just referenced. Charlie, who always sat on the end of the front row, never wrote a thing, so there was no use asking him for help—not that I'd want him to know I was having silent exchanges with Professor across the room. But it didn't matter as I knew the material inside and out. What was elusive to me was Professor's riddle—the connecting theme of the three works—and in the end I wanted to figure it out on my own. I fantasized of the day I'd arrive in her office and say, "I solved it."

Tim and Kate noticed me hovering. They twisted their heads around.

"Hey," I said, "Why don't you ask Camille if you can rewrite the paper?" I hoped it to come off as a coy suggestion à la Professor. "Ask her what she was looking for?"

"Oh gee, thanks for the *tip*, Simone." Kate rolled her eyes.

"The problem is, she was looking for native level grammar structure, which *we* obviously don't have. Now, if you'll excuse us." Tim said, and they turned around.

I wasn't put off, and I would keep trying. I'd have to keep rereading Professor's book until I mastered the art of suggestion.

Through the French doors I saw Reine dancing on the terrace. She was wearing a dark brown ivy cap, pale pink leotard with long sleeves, and newsboy pants with suspenders. I went outside and walked to the far end of the terrace, placed my hands along the cold iron railing. The storm clouds had traveled halfway across the lake by now, and had rainy blue wisps trailing them like a comet's tail.

"*Bonjour*," Reine said finishing her eight-count. She lifted her ivy cap to wipe her sweaty forehead then grabbed a water bottle and sipped. "I'm choreographing a dance to engage sensory sensitive women."

"It looked beautiful."

"It looked beautiful, but—"

"What?"

"You look totally preoccupied, what's going on?"

I took the "be careful" note out of my pocket and handed it to her. "This. Do you recognize the writing?"

She shook her head. "No, where's it from?"

"Someone left it on my pillow this morning."

She chewed her thumbnail. "That's—*odd*."

A rush of cool wind came off the lake and I tucked my hair under my scarf to keep it from blowing in my face.

"Reine, what else happened in this House, since Anne-Marie Fisker?"

Her mouth swiveled from side to side setting off her dimple. She gripped the railing, leaned back and stretched her calves. "*Bref*," she said, "Fisker caused a turning point. Before that—*tragedy* it was extremely competitive for the French and Francophones to get a full room and board scholarship. But after it, no French person wanted to study or live at the House. Which is why now, the House practically begs French natives to come, and will accept just about anyone."

I've gone from one group of Misfits to another, I thought. What had prompted Reine herself to come here? I didn't ask. I wasn't sure I wanted to shatter the image I had of her as an exotic sophisticate. But she must have read my mind because she went on to say, "I came here because I don't want to turn out like my mother."

She leaned to the side to look beyond me. Someone had opened the kitchen window and the gingerbread's spicy scent drifted out.

"Oh man, I need some of that. Besides," she held up her palm, "it's starting to rain."

I followed her inside. Henri's intern Peter brought the freshly sliced bread to the buffet table then quickly returned to the kitchen. Reine grabbed a steaming piece and bit into it, holding her palm under her chin to catch crumbs. "*Mm*, first mention of my mother already and I'm stress eating. Take some of this stuff, it's delicious."

"I'm not hungry."

"Neither am I, that's my problem." She dabbed her mouth with the back of her hand. "Anyway, I know for you it probably sounds shameful to say something like that about my mother." She lowered her bread and ran her tongue over her teeth. "But my mom used to tell me that I was cursed to turn out like her no matter what—that it's mother-daughter destiny. And a curse doesn't have to be black magic, Simone, it can be a thought that haunts you to subconsciously fall into patterns that lead you to your greatest fears. That's why I came here, I needed a *totally* new environment. Because I can't turn out like my mother." She took another bite. "Or we'd all be in danger."

"Oh come on, you're going to leave me hanging there?"

Reine finished chewing. "If I give you the whole story I'll eat that entire loaf. What I will tell you is about the girl from Monaco living here last year, supposedly a quasi-royal—she got expelled for in-house arson. You know that closed off room a few doors down from yours? That one. Henri keeps saying it's closed for restoration and I don't know about you, but I've never heard anything hinting that they're fixing it. They probably can't afford to." She pursed her lips. "This House has loads of stories. You'll learn more over time."

I'd heard a few already. Last week a fraternity guy asked me which one of us was the "witch girl," because he'd earn bonus points for "banging her." Then of course, there was the rumor that Professor almost got fired for sleeping with students. This one from Jerry in *biz dev* so I didn't put much stock into it, even though Professor was awfully—*seductive.*

Camille came through the front door and strutted our way, wearing her fluorescent yellow running jacket and black running tights, her hands in knit gloves cut off at the knuckle. Her cheeks were flushed and her hair frizzed. I went running with her whenever my schedule allowed as I missed the physical activity now that I no longer worked on the vineyard, and Camille knew the best paths in the wooded Arboretum.

"*Mes belles*," she said, scowling at Reine's gingerbread. I smelled the outdoors on her as she kissed my cheeks. "I can't tell you how much I'd rather hang out with you, but I have to change clothes and meet a study group at that curry joint on State Street." She tugged off her gloves. "Whenever I leave that place my skin smells good enough to eat—but not in a good way. What's so wrong with a café? I'll be desperate for my bath as soon as I get back." She swiveled on her heels and went upstairs.

Camille made quite the production with her baths. She only took one when everyone was out of the bathroom, though she usually wanted Reine or me—or the both of us to keep her company. Her ritual consisted of twenty or so sedentary minutes in the claw-foot's baby blue waters, slouched over her bony knees, long arms wrapped around her legs. Her hair curled in the damp, droplets dribbling down her pale freckled back, arched so that I saw each rung of her spine like bumpy golf balls lined in a row. She'd pull in deep breaths, pooling a few fingers in the water by her side and mindlessly watching the ripples. I'd wait for her to speak, eventually she would, whether it was to dissect Camus, or to ask Reine to tell her more about life in Gabon. It was Reine's stories about Africa I liked best.

Now Camille descended the stairs in a slow crisscross, she'd changed into an oversized tan sweater with maroon leather pants. Her style was like an haute couture take on the burlap sack. Oversized beige or brown sweaters over earth toned leggings, velvet or leather pants—never jeans.

She opened the disguised wall closet door by the mustard-colored chesterfield chaise, and grabbed the only shoes she ever wore when not running, her navy and tan duckboots. She slipped them on and joined us, her boots squelching on the herringbone. "Why didn't you warn me Mousey Girl was home. You'd have thought I was in a ski mask and holding a knife the way she jolted when I came in."

"Stop calling her Mousey Girl. Her name is Hessa."

"Ugh, you don't know her like I do, Reine." Camille pulled her glasses off and wiped them with her sweater. "*I know, I know*, she looks shy and twittering, but she's not to be trusted—under any circumstance."

"And why is that?"

"I don't have time to get into it. Are you coming or not, don't you have dance soon?" Camille made her way back to the door. She stepped on one of her untied laces and nearly tripped. Reine grabbed her bag and the two headed out.

It was the perfect time to talk to Hessa.

I knocked on the door to the room she shared with Camille, one I never went into because Camille always came to mine. As I stood outside the door waiting, Jackie walked past me and to the bathroom muttering something incomprehensible under her breath.

Hessa opened the door. "Simone, *bonjour.* Camille's not here."

"I know, I came to see you."

She blinked twice then stepped back and displayed her arm as welcome.

"What is it?"

"Oh, just wanted to chat. I'm trying to find the connecting theme across the three books we were assigned in French Lit," I said. "And I'm kind of lost."

"Well then that makes two of us."

"Look," I said, digging into my sack, my orange pill bottle falling out to my embarrassment. I quickly stuffed it back inside and instead grabbed Professor's book and held it out to Hessa. "You should read this, Boucher wrote it. It's fascinating. You can borrow it for a couple of days, just um, ignore my little notes in the margins." I smiled conspiratorially, I hoped.

She reached for the book and rubbed her hand across the title. "The power of suggestion," she said, her voice smooth and ripe, crisper than her usual whispers. That book just gets us in trouble."

"You've read it?"

"We all have, Simone. Every girl who has lived in The French House has read this book."

"What did you make of it?"

She looked past me and sat on her bed, the book still in her grip. "My mother thinks The French House is a girl's only residence. Not like she'd ever be able to afford to leave Paris to visit me and find out."

She blinked long and heavy. "She's spends most of her time visiting my brother in prison—"

"You're from Paris?"

"Yes, I'm here on the Anne Boucher scholarship. Apparently, they were so desperate for native French speakers they stooped to recruiting in my neighborhood."

"What do you mean?"

"I'm from the ninety-third district."

"I don't know that neighborhood."

"Yeah, you wouldn't—you *shouldn't.* It's an immigrant's slum full of crime and murder—no chance for escape. I don't know if they recruited there because they can't entice French people to live here anymore, or if it they're testing something again and would feel better doing it on poor Muslims."

"Testing?"

"Yeah, testing—experimenting. I overheard Henri on the phone one night. From what I gathered, The French House was once more than a simulation for studying in France. The residents were guinea pigs—for what I don't know, and I never asked. Of course, I didn't know any of this at the time I learned about the House and I'm sure it wouldn't have made any difference in my decision. I was so desperate to get out. I saw the scholarship as my lottery ticket and I came to America hoping to live the dream. When I discovered Boucher's book I thought it was the key to it all, I needed to empower myself so that I would never end up back in my neighborhood—or like my brother. So I stopped wearing my hijab for a while and tried to fit in. I basically became a new person. I used the book to empower myself and it was incredible—at first."

"What happened?"

She smoothed the pink blanket at the end of her bed. "Simone, some things—some people are better left alone."

"What things?" I asked. "Which people?"

"Those we put on a pedestal, for one." She licked her lips and looked away.

"But who—"

She shook her head. "Don't make a fool of yourself the way I did, that's what I'm trying to say. Keep the line where it should be between Professor and student."

"What happened?"

She opened her mouth to speak but stopped herself.

"Just tell me," I pressed.

She looked down. "I was an idiot, Simone. I dishonored my religion, my family and myself. Using all of those *damned* lessons. I slept with—" she stopped herself, her face melting into her palms.

"Did you sleep with Professor?"

She wiped her cheeks. "Boucher had it wrong, we don't need to empower ourselves, we need to learn how to restrain ourselves. The book is dangerous, as is this house, and I plan to leave. I'm going to go back home. Maybe I can make a difference there, maybe I can help people from my neighborhood." She pushed herself off the bed and stood. "So don't worry about making friends with me, I won't be here long."

"But Hessa," I paused, seeing the image of Professor's eyes roaming my body the night she dressed me in her gown. "Did you—"

"Yes," she said, her eyes pinching shut. "We slept together. And it was—there was—*nothing* better. But now—" She opened her eyes. "Now I'm paying the price. The price of playing with the devil. And if you follow my footsteps, you will too."

Chapter 17

Maman's body became ash. Aunt Violette said she preferred to think of the ash as energy. She smelled exactly like Maman. I closed my eyes and pressed my face into her warm back, inhaled as much as my lungs would hold.

"Try to sleep, sweetie," she whispered.

"Why, because then I'll see Maman?"

She turned around. The mattress dipped and the springs squeaked, just like it did when Maman had slept in my bed.

"What do you mean by that, Simone?" She brushed my hair to the side.

"Someone told me Maman was sleeping—forever."

"Oh, *les américains*." Aunt Violette groaned. In the pale light I saw her blink several times. "My sister, your Maman is—not *sleeping*. She's dead. And we don't know what happens to the soul." She pointed to my forehead, then to my heart. "After one has died. But we can hope that Maman went somewhere beautiful. And that we'll see her again. Maman wouldn't want you to worry about that, but to worry about yourself instead, okay?"

I rested my head into her neck. "I worry about Bertrand and Papa."

She kissed my forehead. "Yes, of course you do. You're just like your mother." She shifted onto her back, looked up at the ceiling. "I was trying to get your mom to worry more about herself."

"Lately Maman wanted me to find some papers for her—in Papa's lab."

"What kind of papers?"

"I don't really know. Papers about something bad."

Aunt Violette pushed herself up to sit. "Like what?"

"I'm not sure. But Papa keeps the room locked and he doesn't let me in anymore. The only reason I used to go was to make tea with him—for Maman."

"Okay. We'll think of a way to get in. We'll find whatever it was she was looking for." Aunt Violette squeezed me into her body and we held each other crying until I opened my eyes to the sun and heard birds singing, happy for morning because they didn't know any better.

* * *

Bertrand and I sat on the stools at the kitchen island, the golden croissants in front of us untouched.

"I looked a hundred times," I heard Aunt Violette saying harshly to Papa. They'd been going at it in the living room all morning. "Simone doesn't have a black dress. Tell me, when was the last time you saw your wife wear black?"

"So what do you suggest, a rainbow colored dress!"

"It doesn't fucking matter what she wears," Aunt Violette said. "This day will be the worst day of her life no matter what!"

Bertrand slumped over and put his head in his hands. He was only four years old. I rubbed his back. "Should we go in there?" he whispered.

I shushed him. "Not yet, I want to listen."

"I don't believe your story," Aunt Vi went on. "Your father, bless his soul, he loved Lisette. He wouldn't write you out of your inheritance over what she did—which was *fucking* brilliant and you know it. Thankfully your brother kept all of it!"

"Violette?" It was Mamie's voice. She and Grandpère had slept in Bertrand's room and Bertrand had slept with Papa. We'd been so excited about the reunion, about the full house. It had felt wonderful to be together again until we remembered why they were here.

"Maman," said Aunt Violette, "I'm sorry we were shouting, we're just—"

"*Oui, je sais,*" Mamie's voice, soothing as I remembered it. "We all are." I heard steps on the creaking floor. "Now answer Violette's question.

What really happened? You didn't lose the winery over what she did, did you? All of the questions I had then are resurfacing. What happened!"

"Everyone needs to calm down," said Papa. "I'll make some tea."

"Tea?" Aunte Violette spat. "I don't want any fucking tea, I want my sister back! You drove her to this—you!"

I hopped off my stool and rushed to the archway that divided the kitchen from the living room. I didn't recognize Papa at first. He was wearing a suit. Aunt Vi wasn't close to ready, she was in a white lace slip, and one side of her black hair in rollers, the other loose.

"Tea would help though, right Aunt Vi?" I said.

She retracted a bit then nodded. She understood. "Yes, yes of course. Where do you keep the tealeaves again, Guy?"

"You need to understand that your sister was unwell, Vi," said Papa, ignoring Vi's question.

"She was nothing of the sort, you *monster*!"

Mamie rushed over and covered my ears with her frail hands. Her gardenia scent rushed up my nose as she led me back to the kitchen making *shhh* sounds. I pushed her hands away and peered around her waist. Papa rushed through the kitchen and out the door.

"Papa, wait!" I ran to the screen door to see him flailing around outside. He kicked a pot of red petunias over then stomped his foot onto the yellow ceramic planter until it shattered into pieces. Then he crumpled, laying in the dirt. He covered his face and cried like a baby.

I gripped the door handle but changed my mind and ran back to Mamie and Violette. They were embraced in a hug, crying.

"Why'd you call Papa a monster?"

Violette let go of Mamie and crouched over me; a roller tumbled out of her hair and onto the floor. "Because I'm upset, I'm sorry Simone. Come on, let's go upstairs and get you dressed."

"I'm upset too!" I ran to the buffet table and swiped my arm across its length. I knocked over a glass lamp. It crushed to pieces like the ceramic pot next to Papa outside, and just like all the vases—and mirrors—and candles—and picture frames Maman had broken since we moved here. Maybe if I acted like them, people would stop treating me like a baby. I kicked a chunk of broken glass across the floor before I pounded up the staircase.

Chapter 18

The door to Professor's office was ajar but she was not inside. On her desk, next to the butterfly glass paperweight was a small, ripped page from a book. I checked the corridor, Professor Miloa, the Italian Studies professor, was a dozen feet away in a tweed three-piece talking to a girl with a ponytail. I pulled the door to Professor's office shut without clicking it completely and stepped closer to read the ripped paper. It was a quote from *Les Liaisons Dangereuses*: "The hope of vengeance soothes my soul."

Was it an idea for an upcoming lecture topic, or had someone else left her the note?

Like Hessa.

* * *

I pocketed the paper and left her office. Based on what Hessa said about Professor, I understood why she'd leave a cruel note behind. But I was more concerned about Hessa leaving the House; I had to persuade her to stay. If one person left, surely more would follow suit.

I dug my phone out of my bag and speed dialed home.

"Bertrand. Tell me more about Pont Saint Esprit."

"Oh, so *now* you're interested in conspiracy theories?" Based on the time and the background noise I knew he was in the high school hallway, heading to his next class.

"Supposedly my Professor poisoned someone. Just tell me what you know about her hometown."

"Poisoned someone? God I'm jealous of you," Bertrand said. "Living in a beautiful drama-filled home, full of people who speak French and poison others." He laughed. "You want to know the most exciting thing that happened here? Yesterday while Papa and I were eating dinner—*buttered noodles* in case you're wondering, two mice got caught in our traps and squeaked so much I lost my appetite. I asked Papa to bring them outside, and he said he would *after* dinner. I went to bed hungry."

"Oh God, I'm sorry, Bertrand—"

"No, no, I didn't mean to make you feel guilty, you always do anyway. When are you coming home? You owe a visit to your aurologist, you know."

"Yes, doctor, you're right. You still don't know what's different about my aura?"

"Come home and maybe I'll figure it out."

"I will, I'm sorry, Bertrand. I miss you a lot too."

"Don't worry, I'm doing fine, I spend most of my time with the Misfits Sam and Kip. But back to your question, the Pont Saint Esprit poisonings. It was a really big deal, and affected over two hundred people. They blamed it on a bakery, said it was from tainted bread. Some fungus that made people go crazy before dying. Conspiracies came about that it was the CIA testing a chemical behavior program because it happened right around the time they bought psychoactive drugs from Sandoz Laboratories in Basel."

"That's insane. Our government testing chemicals on French people?" I laughed. "Come on, Bertrand."

"Testing programs like these go on all the time. In the thirties impoverished African American men with syphilis were denied treatment for the government scientists to examine the effects. All of them died, *obviously*. Then in the forties prisoners were unknowingly injected with malaria so the effects could be properly analyzed. Poor neighborhoods were subjected to radiation—"

"Bertrand, even if this is true, all this stuff happened a million years ago."

"Not really, they were testing measles vaccines on poor Hispanic and black babies in Los Angeles in the nineties."

"According to whom?"

"My favorite—"

"Podcast," I finished for him.

"Voilà."

"Must be credible. And how about the mass poisoning in Pont Saint Esprit, when did that supposedly happen?

"The Cold War era."

"Doesn't add up. My Professor wouldn't have been alive yet—plus two-hundred people would have been a bit extreme even for a woman they call the devil."

"Maybe her parents were killed and she's seeking vengeance."

"Drop it," I said, pushing the door to the outside. "The whole thing is ludicrous. I won't think about it again."

It was colder than it had been on my way here. I ducked my head low and rushed back to the House to talk to Henri. But when I got there Peter told me he'd stepped out and wouldn't be back until dinner so I camped out in the dining room to reread *Les Liaisons Dangereuses.*

Soon enough the other residents made their way downstairs and to the dining room, talking about their day, finding their seats, and pouring wine. As Reine, Camille, and Charlie made their way to our table I decided I wouldn't tell them what Hessa told me. At least not yet.

Hessa was the last to come to dinner. She smiled timidly my way then sat. Camille noticed.

"Making friends with The Mouse?"

"I feel bad for her is all."

"Our Simone has such a big heart, *non*?"

"Have you guys seen Henri?" I asked. Peter had prepared the buffet then disappeared into the kitchen.

"I have not," Charlie said.

"Guys, who's that?" Reine nodded toward a mustachioed board member I remembered from the banquet. He was dressed exquisitely, a purple and magenta paisley *pochette* in his navy sport jacket.

"It's Richard," Charlie said cutting his *lapin à la cocotte* with such concentration I knew he was done with the subject.

"I am not a crook," Camille quoted in English.

"I didn't know Nixon had such thick French accent." Reine's dimple showed, she was trying not to laugh.

"That explains why *Henriette*'s missing."

"How so?" I asked.

"They had quite the bad breakup from what I understand."

Richard noticed our attention and came to our table.

"*Bonsoir, mes amis.*" He lifted his wine glass with a quick gesture of cheers. "Tell me," he paused to scratch his mustache, "do you ever sit with the others?"

Without hesitation Camille said, "No, we do not."

Charlie kicked her under the table. Richard frowned and stood tall. "I'm sure you're aware that defeats the whole purpose of this place. You'd better start or I know of one particular donor who will certainly find other causes for her money. And if that happens, then—"

"Then what?" said Camille, narrowing her eyes.

"Then you should have your bags packed."

He walked away and for once we spent the rest of evening in awkward silence. Was he referring to Boucher? She never came to our dinners, and maybe she'd sent she him to check on us.

When the others retreated to the salon after dinner I again sought Henri. I found him taking what he thought was one of his secretive smoke breaks on the terrace. Upon noticing me he put it out but I told him to do as he pleased. He ran this house and had every right. With fumbling hands he lit another, and said he was stressed about Richard showing up, about the upcoming Centennial Fête, and about money.

"Richard will single handedly ensure this place shuts down if you guys don't start comingling. We have to be on our best behavior at the Centennial, prove we're different now. That we're unaffected."

A car alarm went off somewhere in the distance. "Unaffected how? From Anne-Marie Fisker's murders?"

"Yes, partially because of that—and some other stuff in our—*history*." He took two desperate inhalations from his cigarette.

"Like testing."

"What do you mean?"

"You tell me, Henri. That's what I heard. That this place was used for research."

"That was ages ago. Just some stupid thing to get grant money, and money we got—but these days grants are hard to come by and we're sinking, Simone." He looked down. "This place is everything to me. I'm not sure I would make it," he subtly shook his head, "out there." His blue eyes moved toward the lake.

"We need to do more to unite everyone," I said. "I remember this activity we did in middle school. It's silly but it will help break the ice. You give everyone a piece of paper and ask them to write the name of a famous person on it. You mix up the cards and people wear them on their heads. They have to mingle and ask questions to learn who they are."

"*J'adore cette idée*! Let's try it tomorrow after dinner." Henri lifted his shoulders and took an affected drag, blowing a puff into the indigo sky. For a pulse I saw the Cheshire cat in the smoke and closed my eyes only to see an x-ray version of it.

"You know Charlie should be the one to come up with an idea like this," Henri said, breaking apart my vision. "Let me ask you…he hasn't done anything, I don't know, that's worried you?"

"Charlie? Like what?"

"I don't know. I mean—you'd know if—he had." He took a final inhalation from his cigarette, exhaled and stubbed it out. "Forget it, I worry too much. I overthink things."

"That's usually my job." I said, thinking that now I had that much more to worry about.

* * *

The next night Henri announced that we had an activity planned winking at me as he said it. I nodded back. There was a collective moaning and groaning but I knew everyone would comply. As our house guardian, Henri never asked much of us.

"Now," said Henri, "I've placed paper crowns and cards along with markers at your tables. Write a famous person's name on the card. I'll collect them and mix them up. You'll wear the names on your crowns without seeing who you are—you'll have to mingle—and ask for details until you guess correctly."

"For the love," huffed Camille, tugging on her big brown sweater.

"It'll be fun," I said. She slumped into her chair.

"*Allez*!" Henri shouted, "Write down your person."

I was pleased to see that everyone was writing. Jackie pondered for a moment then dipped her head and blocked others from seeing what she wrote with her hand. Next to her Tim pretended to steal a look then focused on Hessa at the table next to him.

Henri collected the cards with a smile and asked Jackie and another girl who sat closest to where he stood, to help him redistribute them. Jackie didn't look at me when she handed me the facedown card. I quickly clipped it to my crown. She handed one to Charlie next, saying in a condescending voice, "Here ya go, *Prof*." She'd been calling him this ever since the day he pretended to be the professor, in fact all from her clan called him Prof, and he stood straighter whenever they did. I was surprised he hadn't commandeered another class as if it were his own.

Reine giggled as she arranged her card and crown. Even Charlie was smiling. In fact, everyone was. But I veered away from my group and into the salon—determined to set an example and speak to as many people as possible; everyone had already started playing.

"Am I still alive?"

"Am I blonde?"

"Was I in a recent film?"

In the corner of the salon Jackie whispered something to Tim and they laughed. Kate joined them.

"Who did this? *Who* wrote this?" Henri shouted walking toward Hessa. Written in all capital letters on her card: WHORE. Henri snatched it off Hessa's head and held it up with trembling hands. "Who wrote it?"

I looked at Jackie. "You did this, didn't you?"

"Why are you accusing me, I distributed the cards at random!"

"She's accusing you because *that* word on *her* head is too big a coincidence." Camille said.

"Camille, *mon dieu*," said Charlie. "Let's be professional."

Henri flapped the card back in forth against his fingers, his face reddening as the rest of us stood around him in pathetic torpor. "Who wrote this? Come clean—right now!"

"Fine, I wrote it," Camille said as naturally as if only greeting us. "I meant to write Madame du Barry, but I guess my mind slipped." She shrugged and looked at Charlie, "I should have been more *professional.* She turned to Hessa. "I'm very sor—" Before she finished Hessa lunged at her. Wrapping her hands around Camille's throat, strangling her. Camille fell down trying to wrestle her off. Her glasses slipped off and I heard them crunch underneath Hessa's knee. They knocked two dining chairs over and rolled around the burgundy Turkish rug, Hessa on top. Charlie dove in next, trying to separate them, Henri joining in.

By the time they wrenched Hessa's hands from Camille's throat it looked as though red-hot coals had been laid upon it. Her glasses were cracked, her hair kinked in every direction. She didn't say a word. She patted her hair and went upstairs to the very room she and Hessa shared. Hessa took off toward the terrace and Henri chased her, "Hessa, *Hessa*!"

Charlie scratched his head, walked to the closet for his coat, opened the main door, and nodded at Reine and me before leaving—where, I had no idea.

"*Vous êtes insupportables*! Get over yourselves!" Jackie shouted at Reine and me. "Stop torturing us! Thanks to Camille, most of us are failing Lit—you should see the comments she writes on our papers! Stop treating us like idiots!"

"Jackie," said Tim, grabbing her arm. She shook him off.

"The way you take over the salon every night like it's yours! Like the rest of us should go back to our peasant quarters—leaving you to sprawl about the room like the gluttons you are. Your ridiculous fireside chats and bottomless digestifs!"

"Jackie—"

"And you, Simone. You're just like Hessa, and the exact same thing will happen to you as it did with her, and you know what? You can't get away with that twice, you guys will self-destruct in no time—"

"Jackie!" Tim shouted.

"What is that supposed to mean?" I asked but my voice was lost in the fray.

"Jackie!"

"What!"

"Camille didn't do it…she's not the one who wrote 'whore,'" said Tim.

Jackie shook her head like she didn't believe it, or maybe didn't want to lose her momentum.

"I was sitting behind Hessa and I looked at what she'd written on her card." Tim held his palms out. "Hessa was the one who wrote it."

Jackie looked as confused by this news as I must have. I turned around and rushed upstairs to find Camille. The sound of running water led me to the bathroom and there she was, sitting hunched over in the clawfoot tub.

"Why'd you say you did it?" I asked her. "I know you didn't write 'whore.'"

Camille took in a deep breath as she massaged her throat and looked up at me. "Someone needed to. I know the game was your idea, *mon lion*. Your attempt to unite us. I thought if I took the blame maybe it would still turn out okay."

"Except you made it worse when you said it was too big a coincidence—Hessa and the word 'whore.'"

"No one's perfect." She made a yawning like motion and winced. "That came out without my thinking."

"How'd you know the game was my idea?"

She dipped her head underwater then resurfaced abruptly. Water spilled over the ledge of the claw foot tub and wet my feet. "Believe me, if someone is going to try to manipulate the behavior in this house, I'm going to find out about it." She tipped her head to the side to drain water from her ear. "What about you, how did you know I didn't write it?"

"Because someone saw Hessa do it. She kept her own damn card. She did it to herself."

"I told you she's not to be trusted," Camille said standing, her long skeletal and freckled body before me. I handed her a towel. She buried her face in it then looked at me closely. "I love you for trying to do what you did. You're painfully sweet—and while I may not show my emotions all the time, you should know that I care about you immensely. But you need to free your mind, Simone. Stop worrying so much about others. Live like Meursault in *L'étranger,* separate yourself from the past, separate yourself from anything that slows you down in the present." She reached for her white waffle press robe and enveloped herself inside it.

"Reciting your lectures at this hour?"

"Better for retention."

"And Meursault as a role model?" I said following her. She walked not to her room, but to mine. I grabbed the key from my pocket and let her in.

"I'm not talking about his actions, just his mind. He was free. He didn't care. Didn't let things bother him. He—" she paused, heaved in a deep breath, sat on my bed. Without her glasses, her hazel eyes looked washed out, looking past me, past anything. Her freckles like the stars seen clearly from the vineyard on a cloudless night. She motioned for me to sit in front of her so she could braid my hair. She pressed her hands into my scalp and separated three sections of hair to crisscross.

"Meursault lived in the moment, truly lived in the moment," she went on. "He was able to kill someone, to be convicted, and not let it ruin him. I think that's the true test, *non*?"

"Test?"

"*Écoutes mon lion*, I'm only saying that you need to let go, stop being so uptight. What I'm really saying here is—do it already. Fuck Charlie."

"What?"

"Oh please, Simone, don't pretend around me. It's what you want. All you have to do is give him the key to your bedroom, you're the only one in The French House without a roommate. The key will serve as a silent invitation." She ran her hand along my scalp, smoothing my hair. "And you'll lose the naivety that's holding you down. I know that's what you want. I'm only trying to help." Her fidgety hands braided the last inch of my hair, twisting the hair tie around the end vigorously and pulling so hard I yanked my head back.

"Ow,"

"*Désolée.*" She tossed my braid like it was a rope thrown from the House's turret window, it landed on my chest. She leaned into me from behind, her lips on my ear. "Do it Simone, *libère-toi…tu serai libérée.*"

Free myself.

* * *

I lay in bed with my eyes open repeating her words in my head until I switched on my lamp and grabbed Boucher's book.

In it wrote the word that bothered me most on the first page I landed:

Libérée.

Chapter 19

By the time Papa found me leaning against the birch tree in the forest behind the vineyard, it was completely dark. My face was puffy, and my ears rang from crying so hard. It had been a difficult week. Some were easier than others, Dr. Landau, the school psychologist frequently reminded Bertrand and me. Without taking her eyes off of her needlework, she'd tell me it was okay to have a bad day or a bad week. I didn't tell her that ever since Maman died I was having a bad life. A bad day would have been great. That would mean I might again have a good one.

"Come back tomorrow and tell me one good thing," Dr. Landau had said before I left her office for our set hour. "I know you can find something."

Papa scooped me into his arms, wiped my tears and sang an old French song inches from my ear as he walked me down the hill and back into our house. It was windy and the leaves sizzled like onions in a frying pan. The first step for so many of Maman's recipes.

Inside our house the popping fire kept the living room toasty. Shadows danced on the walls. Bertrand sat in Maman's favorite chair, curled up and sipping tea. He looked completely out of it, his stooped head and his lips parted like he was dumb. He was having a bad life too.

My muscles were sore from shaking. It had become very cold in the forest but it was the frozen feeling I wanted. It numbed me—it numbed everything. But Papa had rescued me yet again, and his calming, bitter tea would transport me the same way the cold did. As I sipped, he would tell me stories about Maman and eventually I would calm down. This was our routine. He wrestled me out of my stiff jacket, mittens, and hat, tugged my wet socks off and held my pruney feet in his big warm hands to restart the circulation, then set me in front of the fireplace opposite Bertrand with a quilt.

"Now close your eyes and relax." I did. Soon the fire wrapped me in its red arms, tickled my neck with long fingers. From its embrace I opened my eyes, focused on the rug between Bertrand and me until its shapes moved and pulsed. Distantly I heard Papa's voice speaking of Maman as I drifted away.

I had no idea how long we were downstairs listening to his stories but eventually Papa put me to bed. As soon as he left I heard a knock on my bedroom window—*dum dum dah-dum dum.* I peeled the covers back and tiptoed to the window. There was a black shadow on the other side. I slowly pulled the curtains aside—"Maman!"

She was perched in the tree, finger to her mouth. "Shh."

I pushed the window up and Maman climbed inside.

"We're going back to France, Simone. You, me and Bertrand."

* * *

I reported to Dr. Landau's office early the next day. Mug of coffee in hand she welcomed me and asked if I'd come up with something good to tell her.

"I did," I said with a smile. "But it's a secret." Dr. Landau nodded patient as ever. She wasn't going to push me, and that's what made me decide she was worthy of knowing, worthy of my confession. "I saw Maman last night. She's not dead, Dr. Landau, she just wants Papa to think that she is."

Chapter 20

"*Mon Dieu*, the air smells good out here." Camille popped out of my truck the second I parked. She'd overdone it, wrapped herself in a thick cream scarf and tan wool jacket, a hat and gloves chopped off at the fingertips to showcase her black painted nails.

Per my suggestion we'd come to my favorite pumpkin patch, I hoped a little outdoor time would calm us all. It was the perfect day, the sun bright as an orange in a bowl of blueberries. I took off my scarf as we marched across pumpkin fields. Reine was going on about the bakery we'd passed at the main barn and how she wanted a fresh cup of apple cider and a slice of pumpkin pie.

"Reine, *mon chou*, you definitely don't need any pastries," Camille said from across several rows of pumpkins, "No one likes a fat girl." She put her hands on her hips.

"Camille." I stopped walking.

"All I'm saying is that Reine would look like a model if she lost a little weight." Camille explained in her even tone. I didn't know if her inclemency stemmed from obliviousness or if she was seeking provocation.

"Stop ordering us around like you're our mother," I said.

"Ah yes, you probably don't remember what that feels like."

"Ladies, *laisse-tomber*!" Charlie clapped twice. "We came here for pumpkins not cat fights. Go pick one."

Reine quickly led me away, toward a row of pumpkins tangled to one another like a chain gang. She reached over to squeeze my hand and asked if I was okay. I told her I was, though I wasn't sure that was the exact truth. I asked her the same.

"I'm fine, I'm used to it, and I know she cares about me—she loves me. She loves us all."

I believed this too. When Reine came down with an ear infection last week Camille transformed into a matronly nurse and stayed by Reine's bedside, took her temperature each hour, read *Candide* aloud, and pet Reine's head as though she were a baby. She was so caring I'd briefly thought I wouldn't mind being sick myself. Her attention on Reine so fully the only time she interacted with me, or Charlie was via perfunctory delegations: *ask Henri to make soup, grab an ice pack, pick up Reine's prescription from the pharmacy on State Street.*

"She shouldn't take antibiotics," I'd told her standing in Reine's bedroom doorway. Camille was on the edge of Reine's bed folding a blanket for the second time. "They'll only weaken her immune system by killing off her good bacteria."

"Well, Geneviève was big into antibiotics."

"Who's Geneviève?"

Reine, who lay in bed with a blue cold pack on her ear, signaled for me to drop it, waving her hand under her chin.

Camille stopped folding. "My...mother."

"Oh, well I've got a garlic tincture you can drop into her ear to kill the infection, and I'll go buy some honeycomb. She should eat a few chunks morning and night, it's antimicrobial."

"*Incroyable*, Simone," said Reine. "And here I thought Camille was wrong to get off the pre-med track."

"*You* were pre-med?"

"Surprised?" Camille fanned the blanket and started folding it again.

"She must have met someone inspiring enough to swap to French Lit instead."

Camille stood and leaned over Reine. "My little witch. Feeling better then?" She scuffed her feet as she walked me to the door, put her hand on my lower back. "Shall we buy the honeycomb?"

* * *

In the pumpkin patch now Reine removed her black fur bolero and slung it over her forearm. "It's you we've been worried about. We were just talking about it the other night."

"Me?" I said. "Talking about what? And where was I during this?"

"Oh I don't know, with Henri maybe? You're so sweet, always helping him clean. But anyway, we went to a coffee shop—"

"You left the House without me?"

"Simone relax, it wasn't a calculated decision to leave you behind, we just wanted to talk about—"

"*Me*." I finished for her.

"Well, we've been concerned, you know, like are you doing okay living away from your father—"

"What?"

"It was Charlie to bring it up, he's always talking about you. He's smitten so you'd better watch it around him. Don't tempt him…just don't go there."

I rubbed my lips together to keep from smiling. "What makes you think that?"

She kicked the hay at her feet then lifted her Mary Jane shoe to examine how much mud was stuck to it. "Only the sappy way he looks at you. He and every other guy, I should say."

"People look at me because I'm awkward. I was made aware of that very early on."

"No, Simone, people look at you because you're gorgeous. And if your classmates didn't like you it was precisely for that reason. Your aloofness to this fact is half your charm. Add your absurd amount of French lit knowledge to the equation and Charlie becomes helpless."

I turned around to see where Charlie was, determine how likely it was he might overhear. He'd gone the other direction and was watching a hawk soar across the cobalt sky. Not far from him Camille crouched down pretending to inspect an oblong pumpkin with wart-like bumps, her eyes glued to Charlie.

"He's like putty every time you two talk Balzac or Stendhal, even Camille can't keep up—it's driving her a little crazy."

"Yet you brought all this up to say you're worried about me—or that Charlie is?"

Reine clicked her tongue. "Yes, we are—he is. It's about your—behavior. We've heard you talking to yourself and talking about things that don't always make that much sense, to be honest."

"Oh that," I said, thinking of my full orange pill bottle. I'd completely forgotten I used to talk to myself. How humiliating. What did my old psychologist used to say about it? I had no idea. I looked again at Charlie—to think he had seen me behaving like this and hadn't even confronted me personally. What else had I done off my pills that he may have seen?

What else would I do?

Chapter 21

Dr. Landau looked like she was afraid of me. She was sitting at her desk mid-needlepoint wearing a thick black turtleneck with beige make-up smears on its neckline. I thought she'd be happy upon hearing my good news.

"I shouldn't have told you about my mother."

"No, I'm glad you did. Have a seat." She put her needlepoint aside and pulled closer to her desk. I stayed by the door. "Simone, you didn't see her. Your mother is no longer here, and we need to work through that."

"You're horrible!" I said dropping my schoolbooks to the floor. "You told me to find something good and I did. She was there! She's alive!" I turned around but her hands were on me instantly, easing me back to her plaid couch. I writhed in her grip, trying to escape. She aided me to a sitting position and asked me in her soothing voice to explain everything that had happened last night. Maybe she was just confused. I told her where I'd found Maman, and how she wanted us to escape to France.

"Okay, Simone. Now close your eyes and take three deep breaths."

I didn't want to close my eyes. I knew what I'd see. Instead, I looked around her office, my eyes landing on a vase of fresh roses. Good for her. Her life was fine. Rosy. Next to the vase was a framed photo of a golden retriever.

"Go on, Simone. Close your eyes and reset."

I crossed my arms and smashed my back against her sofa. "Fine." As soon as I closed my eyes I screamed. Dr. Landau embraced me and I told her what I saw. What I always saw when I closed my eyes. An x-ray version of the world covered in bright splatter paint. The colors formed meaningless shapes at first, but then they transformed into a black figure. Usually when I opened my eyes it went away. Sometimes it didn't.

She returned to her desk, chewing on her lip, jotting notes. "You don't need to go back to class today, Simone. You can rest here, or I can call your father and you can go home early."

"Papa's busy."

"Isn't there anyone else? Like maybe someone who comes around the house to help?"

"I do it all."

"You cook and clean?" she said in a teasing voice. Adults always thought they were so funny, like they were figuring things out so much faster than us.

"Last night I made an omelet and boiled potatoes. And I didn't need *any* help, and yes, I turned the burner off when I was done. Dr. Landau, I'm not like most kids."

She frowned. "You're not, no." She moved her hair behind her ears and sighed. "Listen, I want to talk to your dad about coming to see me in Madison. My husband found a job and we're moving back soon. But I'm going to open a practice out of our home, and I think it's really important that I still see you. There's so much to work through." She kept talking but I tuned her out and looked at the door to her office. The doorknob turned and someone pushed it open.

"Aunt Violette! You're here!" I ran into her arms.

"I'll get you out of here," she said. "We'll go find Maman."

Dr. Landau stood, gripping her notebook and pen, and took a tentative step toward Aunt Vi and me.

"Simone, do you see your Aunt Violette right now?"

"Of course," I said, "don't you?"

Chapter 22

On the way back from the patch I kept my eye on Camille through the rearview mirror. My truck was rattling louder than usual, weighed down from the pumpkins we loaded in the truck bed.

That night we ate dinner in silence. I spent my time observing either Hessa who sat alone in the corner, or Jackie, who sat with Tim, Kate and a few others, talking loudly with her mouth full of steak about a final project for her anthropology course.

Immediately after the *gâteau basque* dessert and coffee, Camille declared her need for a bath "all that time in the country," and headed upstairs with Reine. With her usual spot next to Charlie on the green velvet sofa left vacant, I claimed it for myself. Maybe it was that extra glass of wine I'd had, or what Reine said when were in the pumpkin patch. Or that I'd sat so close to Charlie that our thighs touched. His eyes moved from the page in his book to our legs and then back again. He didn't retract an inch.

"Charlie," I said, though it came out as a whisper. His eyebrows lifted to indicate that he'd heard me and that I should elaborate, but his eyes remained fixed on his book, André Gide's *The Counterfeiters*.

"I had a dream about you last night." This fell in line with the lessons in Professor's book, in that you can architect your desire by planting suggestions in another person's mind.

"Mm?" he asked, his eyes were moving along the lines of his novel. I paused, thinking about the art of pacing. *Purposeful silence is far more powerful than words. Resist the temptation to explain your every thought.*

Think of your communication as your best set of China, offer it on special occasions and only to those worthy.

He closed the book with a soft swoosh and looked at me. "What was the dream about?"

I looked around the room again. I knew no one was within eavesdropping distance, but I wanted to place a suggestion in his mind, that I wasn't comfortable sharing the contents of the lurid dream around others.

"Simone?" He was impatient. "What about?"

"Charlie, I don't know if I should tell you about it," I paused, my lips parting. I licked them.

"Why not?" he asked, his voice louder. His cheeks were rosy. He placed the book to his side and faced me fully, leaning in.

"Not here."

"Where?" he asked and leaned closer still. This was my moment. He'd follow me upstairs, or outside to the black woods, to a hallway closet for all it mattered, but instead I dug my bedroom key out from my pocket, reached for his hand and placed it in his palm.

"What's this?" he said, his face mischievous. He knew very well what it was.

"A suggestion."

He smiled.

* * *

The only light in my bedroom came from the window, the moon was nearly full and reflected off the lake.

His soft hands cupped my face. "*Tu es merveilleuse*," he whispered, his thumbs gently moved along my cheeks, his nose touching mine. "I've been waiting."

I brushed my lips against his neck and delicately kissed along his hairline, then tilted my head and planted my lips on his to taste the cinnamon and clove of his mouth. He pulled me closer and my face buried against his unshaven cheeks as I tasted more of him, while his hands moved from my face to my shoulders then worked their way down my sides and stopped at my waist. He slipped his right hand under my shirt, and brushed his fingers back and forth against my bare skin before edging them under my bra strap. My stomach trembled. How was I to stay in control? He knew what he was doing and I wanted all of it. I'd be his servant.

He pulled back, pressed his lips against my cheek. "Simone, you said the key was a suggestion."

I swallowed. "Yeah?"

"Do you really care about me or are you experimenting with Professor's book?"

"Why? Did Hessa show you my copy?" I pictured all the notes I'd written about him in my book which, despite her saying she had no need for it, she had in fact taken it from me.

"Hessa?" Charlie said, taking a full step back. "Simone—please don't tell me you've talked to Hessa about all this. What are you trying to do to me?"

I shook my head, bewildered. "I haven't the faintest idea."

Charlie's eyes closed. "God, what am I doing?" he muttered. "Don't tell anyone about this, *please* Simone."

"Charlie," I said, chastising myself over the whine in my voice. "I thought we both wanted this."

"Trust me when I say I do—and that I really care about you. But we can't."

He walked out of my room and I was too dumbfounded to do anything about it. I'd lost control. I'd failed. Professor never would have.

I slammed onto my bed, my body still tingling from what he'd awakened. I hadn't sobbed in ages; my prescription hadn't allowed emotion of that level and now I questioned if I still knew how. It was building in my gut, ready to geyser up and burst out my mouth like a broken dam. I counted to ten repeatedly, faster and faster, hoping sleep would find me a willing victim, until someone cracked my door open in the tar-black night. The figure paused at the doorway without saying a word. Charlie still had my bedroom key, and pathetically I wished he had returned to apologize and start over, to lay his body over mine, but it was Camille's rosewater face wash I smelled as a lanky presence hovered over me in the dark, hands reaching toward my naked throat. I scrambled out of bed, grabbed her arms in the dark.

"Jesus Christ!" Camille said, shaking me off. "I was just coming in to close your window, *ma petite*. I felt a draft underneath your door."

"I want it open."

"*Mon lion* let's close it—"

"Get out of my room, Camille. Right now."

"Oh my!" she faked excitement. "I love this side of you." She leant in and kissed my sweaty forehead. "*Fais des beaux rêves*."

Beautiful dreams I did not make. Rather I suffered a nightmare in which Camille had slashed my wrists and stood at my bedside with a sneer as I bled out. When I woke with a jolt, my wrists were hot and itchy.

* * *

"She's usually back by now," Reine said, standing to return her espresso cup and crumb-covered breakfast plate to the kitchen. Across from me Charlie stared into his untouched yogurt. We hadn't spoken all morning.

A roaring wind gushed in from the front door. It was Camille. She walked to the dining room, her fluorescent yellow windbreaker crinkling with each step. Her nose was running, and her cheeks were red from the wind. She filled a small plate with cornichons.

"You get a late start or something? We've got to get going," Reine said, grabbing her black Longchamps bag.

Charlie returned his bowl and mug to the kitchen.

"Said the student to the teacher." Camille bit into a cornichon. "Anyway I'm sorry I ran longer than usual. It's amazing how energized you feel after a night of fucking." She set the plate down, stretched her arms into the air and rotated her torso as though she were starring in her own exercise video.

"*Salope*." Reine laughed. "Faking a sore throat last night then running off, who is he?"

My instincts triggered. I don't know what did it, the silence, a look, her aura?

"Nothing like the safe and familiar." She nodded toward Charlie who was obliviously walking back to our table.

Sweat beaded my upper lip. I pushed Charlie's shoulders. "How could you?"

His face pedaled through a range of emotions until his mouth pulled down as he realized what we were talking about. "*Shh*, lower your voices." He pressed the air as if tamping down its volume. "Let me explain, but not here, let's go outside."

"*Oh. Mon. Dieu*," Camille said, disregarding Charlie. "*C'est quoi ce bordel*? What is going on here, *mon chou*?"

"Nothing." I ran onto the terrace. A cool rain pelleted my cheeks and I wheezed for a breath.

"Simone!" Reine rushed after me, her long black beaded necklace flying behind her shoulder. Camille quickly stepped onto the terrace behind her, dragging a reluctant Charlie.

"Don't tell me I'm the second course." Camille looked between us.

"You're not, he wouldn't sleep with me." I turned to Charlie "Why her?" I asked with what gravelly voice I found, trying to swallow through my tight throat as Reine pulled me into a protective hug. I kept my eyes on him, desperate he'd come up with something to erase this, or at the very least explain it. His eyes watered, but he didn't say a thing.

"You see what's going on here, don't you?" Camille said, her hair sprawled wildly in the wind so that she looked like Medusa. "It's her, it's Anne the Butcher and her damn book planting ideas in everyone's head. She's going to break up our coven."

"Stop with the coven references!" Reine threw her hands in the air.

Camille laughed. "I know you have a hard time with that particular word."

Reine flicked her off.

"Trust me, this is Boucher's fault." Camille turned to face me. "You've taken oh-so many notes in her book, *ma petite*."

I wanted to push her over the ledge of the terrace and watch her drown in the lake. Her milky skin sinking into the green murk. "Did Hessa show it to you?"

Camille shook her head. "Oh Simone, she didn't need to show me anything."

"But you," I said carefully. "You were the one who gave me the book. And you were the one who told me to sleep with Charlie."

"What?" Charlie asked, simultaneously to Camille's, "No I didn't."

"*Ça suffit*!" Reine shouted. "Camille, drop it, Anne Boucher and her damned book are not manipulating us. You are!" She pointed at Camille.

"Ohh," Camille groaned, slumping over as if she'd been kicked in the stomach. "Spare me, *ma petite sorcière*." She turned and took a few steps away but paused to hold her hand up in the air, pointer finger to the sky, ever the flair for drama. She whipped around, her hair spewing again in every direction and said in English, "You ain't seen nothing yet."

Chapter 23

Dr. Landau said Aunt Violette wasn't there, that I was "seeing things" and we needed to figure out why. I had an outburst Maman would have been ashamed of, I told Dr. Landau that I hated her and left school early. Never again would I confess my secrets.

Violette rode the bus with me and told me not to worry. That grown-ups were idiots. When we got home she helped me search the woods for Maman but we didn't find her and by the time it was completely dark, I lost Aunt Violette, too.

Now the sun was rising, a big yellow balloon teasing its way up from behind the blue hills. I rushed back to the house and tiptoed around the first floor but didn't see Papa or Bertrand. Last night's teapot was still out and liquid sloshed inside. I poured myself what was left not caring it was cold, then crept upstairs to wash up and get ready for school. I didn't want Papa to find out I had slept in the forest again.

* * *

At school I couldn't concentrate on what Miss Kemp was saying; all I did was try to keep my eyes open. Shapes and colors blended like the spinning color wheel in art class that showed us how red and blue made purple. It was disorienting but when I closed my eyes my desk became a canoe that wobbled away from shore—and everyone else.

"Simone?" Miss Kemp said.

I opened my eyes, apologized. She was passing out thick sheets of construction paper and colored feathers. The other students opened their desks and pulled out their craft boxes. Libby, the girl next to me, traced her hand with her fingers spread apart, onto the paper. Then rubbed a glue stick over it and stuck the feathers on top. I guess it was supposed to be a turkey. I stared into the brown paper on the desk before me. The fibers within it looked like stringy hair. I held it up and took a closer look, scratched at it, tried to pull the fibers free until they moved aside to reveal a face. There was a person stuck in the paper!

"Shh, I'll save you," I told it. "I'll save you."

"Oh my God, you're crazy," said Libby.

But Libby looked like a Picasso, her right eye was much higher than the other. I'd never realized how deformed she was.

"You're crazy," she hissed again.

I took out my scissors. Instead of cutting out my turkey, I jabbed them into her hand.

Chapter 24

I woke up feeling indifferent, I stood and stretched then pushed aside the curtains to look out at the lake gleaming under the morning sun before I remembered: Charlie slept with Camille.

I dug, rather feverishly, around my backpack in search of my tincture. I knew it was nearly gone if not completely out, but I had no idea how else to deal with the pain, the stab in the back—the rejection. I didn't feel the tincture bottle inside rather a notebook's cold spirals. It was the old unicorn notebook I'd found in Papa's lab weeks ago; I'd completely forgotten about it. I pulled it out and flipped through the pages of my childish script, stopping when I spotted a page with a recipe.

Gentle Sedative Tea

5 grams dried chamomile
3 grams dried rhodiola rosea
Lactuca virosa?

I wasted no time and took the recipe to an herbal shop I'd serendipitously passed on State Street yesterday when skipping calculus. I had a coffee nearby as I waited for it to open and as soon as I noticed a redhead flip the *closed* sign to *open*, I rushed over. It was dim and dusty in the store, the air already heavy with incense, and bizarre ambient music playing. I passed salt lamps, Freyja warrior goddess candles, a section called Wicca 101, and essential oils until I finally found their dried herbs.

There was no problem locating the first two ingredients, but I'd have to ask the redhead shopkeeper for help with the third.

"*Lactuca Virosa*...wild lettuce," she said dubiously. "Are you sure you want that? It's pretty strong—it's an opiate for Christ's sake."

"An opiate?"

"Don't worry I'm not judging, I've tried everything." She laughed to herself and turned around, her gold bracelets jangling as she opened and closed a few drawers before presenting me with a small bag. She put it on a scale, removed some dried herb crumbs, and handed it to me through the smoke trailing from a patchouli incense stick. "You'll definitely get some sleep with this stuff."

I paid, thanked her and left. I decided I'd take my calming tincture by day and Maman's old sedative recipe by night as means of controlling my stress. I leaned against the shop's brick exterior and grabbed the tincture. Not much remained. I didn't care, I needed it now. I squeezed a few drops into my water. A girl in a yellow Ralph Lauren sweater eyed me suspiciously as she passed, and I dropped an extra for good measure.

* * *

I was feeling faint by the time I got to The French House, my elevated nerves and adrenaline had been taking their toll. I'd skipped all my classes and spent much of the day staring into the lake and was only now feeling hungry, yet when I saw Professor I decided to skip dinner and speak to her instead. She slipped through the door quietly, so unlike the usual entrance she made—a parting of the seas, a blinding white light—that I had to do a double take to ensure that it was truly her. She walked across the foyer, her bright, red-gloved hand beckoning me to follow and I did so eagerly, like a child chasing a balloon. She entered the office near the English phone booth and sat behind the desk.

"I sensed something was not right, not just because you weren't in class, but in the behavior of—the *others*." Her head dipped slightly in the direction of the dining room.

Tonight would not find me brushing my teeth next to Reine, or attending to Camille as she bathed. And though I despised Charlie now, I ached for him to stand behind me and give my shoulders a squeeze, whisper in my ear as he had a week ago, *you're so much more than you know*. Despite it all I wanted to return to my yearning him instead of wanting him to hurt—wanting him dead.

As for Camille, we were done. I didn't see how I would forgive her for setting me up like that. Pushing me into Charlie's arms only to sleep with him herself. Was it about humiliating me or winning him?

Feeling Professor's eyes on mine, I shifted in my seat unsure of what to say, moving my long black hair to cover as much as myself as possible, my cloak of comfort. Thinking about what Hessa had told me about their…*liaison*…I felt especially exposed.

"Simone, you must retain your optimism. Your childish optimism." Her face was so still it was as if the words reached my mind telepathically and again I was dizzy.

"I'm not really helping you with what you'd asked, am I?" I leaned into the chair. "I'm not strong enough to influence Camille, it's more the other way around."

Professor laughed, looking beautiful and threatening at the same time. The lights flickered. "Simone, you're wrong about that. You're influencing her in just the way I'd hoped."

My skin prickled. "I'm not your puppet."

"No, you're not." She replied quickly enough that I believed her. "Simone, perhaps it would be good for you to return home. Reunite with your father and spend some time in the countryside. With your Misfits."

I sighed, inhaling a whiff of her crème brûlée perfume. "Yes, I'll go home tomorrow. I can help my father pick mushrooms. We always do this time of year."

"That sounds lovely." She rubbed her hands together like she was applying lotion, focused on picture on the desk. The photo was of Henri with his arms around two board members, Richard and Jean-Paul, all of them with wide smiles in front of a Christmas tree. What was her life like outside of the university and the House? I pictured her in a dark home along the lake, pouring herself a glass of wine, staring listlessly out the window.

"Would—you like to join me, tomorrow on the vineyard?"

She quickly looked up. "I would *love* to."

"Okay…great."

We settled on the time and I retreated upstairs, stopping mid-step when it occurred to me that I'd never told Professor about the Misfits.

* * *

I unlocked my bedroom door and immediately heard Camille's violin through my open window. A frenzied, chaotic tune. I peered out to see her silhouette on the terrace working the bow up and down the strings like a madwoman in the moonlight. I leaned my forehead against the screen's mesh and imagined puncturing through it and falling out, landing on Camille with a splat.

"What are you trying to do?" I whispered. She turned around as if she'd heard me, her neck craning toward my window. I quickly backed up and shut it despite my desperate need for air and waited for her concerto to start again. It never did and it wasn't long before I recognized her knock on my door.

Hearing what she had to say was better than listening to my thoughts, so I labored out of bed and opened the door enough to see her. She had changed into her blue pajamas with white trim and her hair was down and brushed smooth. She was again sans glasses as she had yet to replace the pair that broke during her fight with Hessa. Without them her eyes were beady and unfocused.

"I am sorry, Simone," she said, enunciating each word so precisely it was like coming from a robot. She lingered in the doorway gauging my reaction, rather than barging in the way she normally would have. A small concession.

"Say what you want to say." I opened the door enough for her to slip past.

She strode in and perched onto the end of my bed, crossing her long skinny legs and sinking down, the smell of her expensive rosewater soap drifting my way. I too sat on the bed and waited to hear her out. I planned, ultimately, to make amends, make her think that she remained in control of me, of our group. But although I may have lost to her once, Camille had underestimated me. It wouldn't happen again.

"If you're only interested in jumping off the virgin wagon, I can help you."

"What makes you think—?"

"Simone, don't crack me up this late at night."

"*Bon*, brand me with a giant V then."

"You're not a *voleuse*, so I won't do that. *Tu sais*, that makes me think of Jeanne de Valois. When that bitch was to be branded with a V on each shoulder as punishment from the Affair of the Necklace, she moved at the last second causing the scorching hot brand to instead sear her breast." She laughed in her snarky way.

I didn't respond. I wanted her to leave. She studied my face, giving nothing away in her own. Finally, a slight tick, noticeable enough to know she was bothered by something.

"He adores you."

I shook my head. "Right, that's why he slept with you and not me."

"Exactly, I was a just a body. But he respects you, and he's saving himself."

"*C'est pas vrai*—"

"Simone, I've known him my whole life. I know how he feels before he does. It's you he wants, and that's what makes me the idiot here." Her face transformed by a veil of sadness. What she said next came out so quietly it was virtually inaudible and yet I knew what I heard. "I've loved him since I was a child."

"Then tell him," I said unsure why, especially when all I wanted to hear was why she thought he loved me.

Her eyes watered but she blinked heavily, and no tears released. "Oh, he knows." She got up from my bed, walked in her usual way, a directionless circle around the room dragging her hand on my dresser, the curtains, the windowsill. At the door she paused. "It's okay. You can't control everyone, you know? I thought coming here might change things. Now I realize that the only reason one ever leaves home is to escape, and I'm no different. You can't reinvent yourself without first coming to terms with yourself."

"What do you need to come to terms with?"

She made her way back to the bed and sat. She smoothed her hand over the quilt on my bed. "When I was in fifth grade, my teacher assigned this awful family tree project. It came just a few months after my parents told me I was adopted," she paused and her lips tugged up, forming what I assumed was her strange attempt at a smile. "All the kids were so excited about it. There was this girl, Fatima, she was totally sure her history would lead to Marie-Antoinette until some boy pointed out that nowhere in her tree was any Austrian lineage whatsoever." She licked her lips and rubbed her right eye like a baby. "I never showed my parents the assignment. What was the point? It was the first time—the *only* time I blew off a school assignment. Actually, I failed it. It's kind of funny when you think about it, failing a fifth-grade project, the French schooling system's not quite the gold-star-everyone's-a-winner system they have here, *hein*?" She smiled again. "That same year a different girl in my class, Laure was her name, lost her mother. Someone appeared at the door and called her name in the middle of class, asked her to come see the principal. We knew it was bad. Turned out it was her worst nightmare, everyone felt so sorry for her, myself included. Teachers went out of their way for her with everything, to get her to the front of the lunch line, to give her the best seats in class, and talked about her like she was an angel even though she was never that nice to begin with. But after her mom died she could do no wrong and I actually grew *jealous* of her—it's awful I know, and it was brief, but there it was—jealousy. I was going through this phase, trying to come to terms with what I'd learned, blaming my adopted parents for everything wrong in my life even though they were the only family I ever knew and I loved them—I still do—and they love me. But that didn't mean much then. Not after learning my birth mother abandoned me. Left me at a hospital without so much as a note. To this day I have no clue who she is or why she did it. Was she too young? Was she a prostitute?" Camille shrugged. "By high school I decided I didn't need to know and put all my energy into school. But then, this past summer, when I read your introductory letter I remembered that girl, Laure, whose mother died. You wrote such beautiful things about your mother, credited your knowledge of literature to her and all my old questions popped up again: why do *I* love literature? Why do *I* need glasses? Does my mother hate sweets like I do? Does she eat cornichons for breakfast?" Camille tugged a hangnail on her ring finger. "Your mother may have died but at least you know which of her traits you inherited. You have something you recognize." She lifted her chin and her face twitched. "So you see, I'm an easy one aren't I? My raison d'être is to prove I'm worthy of love and at the same time I tell myself I don't care about love."

I appreciated her honesty, but it was all the more reason why she shouldn't have said what she said about my not remembering what it was like to have a mother. Plus, she was wrong to assume. If she had only asked, I'd have told her I didn't truly know what I inherited from my mother aside from looks—though lately I'd come to worry I'd also inherited Maman's mental instability.

"That's awful, Camille. I'm sorry."

Camille held her finger up as if she were the warning mother, the very thing neither of us had. "Don't empathize. It will only make me feel worse." She looked past me, shaking her head, mouth tight. Her eyes pivoted back to mine and she softly gripped my hand. "I only ever told one other person that, Simone, but I trust you."

* * *

After Camille left I mixed the herbs I'd bought at the shop to create the sedative tea from my childhood recipe. It felt like minutes after I finished the mug that I fell asleep—without once analyzing the day's conversations in my head. It must have been eight o'clock in the morning when I woke and I felt good. Until, once again, I remembered what Charlie had done. *Fuck.* I got out of bed, put three tincture drops into my water, and drank it in one go.

At breakfast, I perked up with every person that entered the dining room. But he never came and I struggled to pay attention to Reine. She was comparing ballet to tribal dance, claiming ballet was so disciplined it led to rigidity, while tribal dance was so freeing it released. Under normal circumstances I would have been interested but it was as if the fog hovering over the lake had permeated my mind.

"Simone, are you feeling okay?" she asked. "You look totally out of it."

"Me? Yeah, I'm fine. Probably just need to eat something." I quickly finished half of my croissant then went back upstairs to get ready to meet Professor.

Chapter 25

I didn't mean to stab Libby. At least I don't think I did. But Miss Kemp didn't care to hear what I had to say. She rushed me to Principal Mueller's office, sat me on a chair across from the secretary and told me to wait there, that she had to get back to the classroom.

"Duchamps," said the prune-faced secretary. I didn't bother to correct her pronunciation. She licked her finger and drummed through the files inside her desk. "I can probably find your daddy at the winery, huh?"

"Yeah." Through the window behind her I saw the older kids playing at recess.

She snorted, held the paper she'd pulled to her small eyes, and dialed. "Oh hi there, Mrs. Kaiser. It's Nancy over at Longfellow Elementary, yeah—no, no Jackie's fine. It's about Simone. Can you find her dad and tell him to get over here as soon as he can?" She hung up, looking at me with narrowed eyes. "He'll be here soon, hon."

My unicorn notebook poked my side. I removed it from my sweater pocket and flipped it open looking for a distraction from her mean glare and stinky perfume. I opened to the lesson Papa had given me over the weekend. *Mushrooms*, I'd written. *Amanita muscaria*—next to this I'd drawn a crazy face. "These mushrooms are easy to avoid," Papa had said. "Because they're easy to recognize." I told him they looked like the kind a fairy would lounge on. They had bright red umbrella caps and were speckled with white polka dots, perfect little toadstools.

"They're not edible because they'll make you feel funny."

The line below I'd written, *Amanita phalloides*. Next to this I'd drawn a face with X's for eyes.

"Phalloides," I said sounding it out in syllables, "That's hard to say."

"You can blame a Frenchman for naming it. Sébastian Vaillant—a botanist from the eighteenth century."

"Phalloides…what's it mean?"

I could have sworn Papa blushed as he quickly Papa grumbled. "It um, it describes the shape."

"Can you make tea from it?"

Papa's brows lowered until his eyes became slits. "Absolutely not. This mushroom—above all others you must avoid. Draw a picture of it, do what you need to remember that if you eat this one, it will kill you."

Chapter 26

I worried Professor might have dropped the idea of mushroom hunting with me, but sure enough there she was, waiting by my truck at the time we'd set. I tuned into a jazz station and drove the curving highway to the vineyard internally planning how to ask her about her affair with Hessa.

Upon arrival Professor hopped out and turned herself in a three-sixty. "So this is where you're from."

The clouds hung low, whirling across the bluff like pink meringue and bringing with them a drop in temperature. The fall was proving to be what Papa's almanac had predicted. The winds turned from cheek-slapping cold to skinny-dipping warm with the snap of a finger. Already thunder was gurgling one hill over, only about a fifteen-minute walk away.

Papa and Bertrand weren't in the main building or the house so I led Professor to the hills. She declined my offer to wear a fluorescent orange vest over her jacket, so I opted for a silly orange hat myself, to be safe. Gun season didn't officially open for a couple of weeks, but bow season was active and there were always several unlawful hunters out early. Enthusiastic and drunk—Sam's dad being one of them—they were ready to aim and fire at anything moving in the brush. Sam's dad had a deer stand at the top of the bluff, right where our property lines met, and last week Bertrand told me Sam's dad had just shot and killed a deer that was eating our grapes. When Papa heard the rifle he ran outside and shot back. "It was disorienting," Bertrand said. "Papa said he was trying to kill the deer but to my ears it was like he was shooting at Sam's dad."

* * *

The temperature dropped even more so with our first step into the forest and I saw my breath. The lighting was dim except for a few sunny spears that cut through the canopy of leaves. Though it was difficult to see, the effect was breathtaking, it looked as though we were walking under a canopy of honeycomb. I was rattling off mushroom facts, where to look (near trees), what to avoid (anything with white gills, bright red tops, or rings around the stem), how we sautéed them (in a vat of butter), and boasted of monster-sized finds from the past the way guys in my high school bragged about the bucks they'd shot.

"What's the difference between the good and the bad? Can you tell?" Professor asked.

"Of course—"

"Show me the poisonous ones," she said standing in a lance of light that made her look white as a marbled masterpiece.

"What is it with you and poison? Did you poison your lover?"

She smiled. "I don't talk about my past. Why should I? We must live in the present."

That's what Camille had just said.

"Have you thought more about the theme between the three works I've assigned?"

Live in the now. The true test.

"I have." I frowned. "But I haven't solved it yet."

"You will." Her eyes narrowed.

"Professor, what happened with you and Hessa? Or the girl from Monaco, the one who set fire to her bedroom last year? And—Anne-Marie Fisker."

"Like I said, I don't speak of my past. I came for a lesson in mushroom hunting. Now show me the poisonous ones."

I looked in the direction of my stone home. It was awfully far away.

"Show me, Simone."

I felt a cold tingle on my neck. We were already out here, what else was I to do?

"There are different degrees of poisonous mushrooms, Professor."

"But of course. Poison is such a metaphoric word." She blinked long, heavy. "Go on, what do you have here?"

"Some that will trick you and tease you—psilocybin semilanceata, amanita muscaria and psilocybin cubenis."

"Magic mushrooms," she said. "You have *those*?"

I gauged whether they were visible from where we stood. "Yes, the cubenis type grow over there by our compost pile." I pointed to the edge of the woods. "We use the manure from my neighbor's farm to grow it as they thrive on it—gross, I know." A part of me wanted to tell her that Jackie used to sneak on our land to steal mushrooms back in high school, but I didn't want to be a snitch.

"Interesting," she said ducking below a spiked branch, and standing tall on the other side. "What are the others—the darker degrees on the scale of poison?" she asked, stepping ahead a few paces. There was no mud on her boots and yet the black earth clung to mine and weighed me down.

"Some will make you sick. And some will kill you. But I get the feeling you already know that."

A long lightning bolt zapped across the sky and illuminated the forest. Then, thunder crashed so loudly I jumped. The storm was directly overhead now, we needed to keep moving, but Professor asked me to explain what happened if you ate a poisonous mushroom as if we had all the time in the world. As if this was the most normal topic in the world.

"They cause kidney and liver failure, blood clots, too…your organs shut down." Another lightning bolt split the sky in half.

"And do you have those here?"

I stepped away from her once more, scanning the woods until my eyes landed on the mushroom, the bad mushroom, the white angel. The death cap.

"It's there," I said. "*Amanita phalloides*."

"That translates to phallus-shaped," Professor said amused. She turned to see where I was pointing. There was no question why it was named this.

"Professor, let's go."

"You should pick some," she said. "Bring them back."

I stared at her for so long she disintegrated into the landscape for a blink and I was dizzy. Refusing to entertain her insanity, I walked toward the house quickly, stepping this way and that to avoid fallen trees, low hanging boughs, and slippery green rocks underneath the sky's lightning throbs. I thought of Camille, her story about making out with Ichabod Crane in the forest, Charlie and his warm hands on my face. Reine and her high-pitched giggles. Thought of the night we walked in the forest weeks ago dressed in our gowns. I imagined the trees coming to life, the branches transforming to arms, lanky brittle-thin hands clutching my shoulders and pulling me in, sucking me into their dewy hard bodies and whispering to me. Giving in to them until they told me to let go. *L'appel du vide.*

Chapter 27

The secretary cleared her throat and I put my unicorn notebook away. The names of herbs and mushrooms repeating in my head: *amanita muscaria, amanita phalloides*. Images of dancing red and white speckled mushrooms flashed like a strobe light.

"Simone, are you all right?"

Maman was standing behind the secretary.

"You get three chances to seduce," I told Maman. I wanted her to know I remembered her saying this even though it was slipping away with each day.

"What in God's name are you talking about?" asked the wrinkly secretary. "You're not going to the nurse's room if that's what you're trying to pull, missy." She dragged me into the principal's office.

Papa arrived moments later in his work clothes. He'd probably come straight from the vineyard and would certainly be angry that we had bothered him. He shook Principal Mueller's hand and sat across from him. I looked at the painting on the wall to my left. It was an oil canvas of the woods in autumn. In it sat a fox that was looking right at me. Principal Mueller edged into his chair and folded his hairy hands together. He sighed.

"Mr. Duchamps," he said, "you really need to bring Simone in to see someone about—this."

"What do you mean?" Papa growled the English words out like a bear awaking from winter.

Mr. Mueller shook his head and looked out the window. "I can't pretend to know what you—or she, is going through, but it's okay to seek help. It's too much to deal with on your own. Simone has become—"

"Become what?" Papa said very low, his most serious tone. I looked at the fox. It smiled at me then jumped out of the painting. I reached for it and fell, smashing onto the floor. The fox walked out the open door, his bushy maroon tail swishing. His head jerked back as he passed the cranky secretary. He must have thought she smelled bad, too. I changed my focus to the silver specks on the lime-colored linoleum, laid my cheek against the cold floor. It felt good.

"Jesus," Principal Mueller said very quietly. "Look at her, she needs help." He picked up his phone and dialed a couple of numbers: beep boop beep: "Dr. Landau—can you come down here?"

Dr. Landau shook hands with Papa then looked at me and said, "Hi Simone." I remained on the floor connecting linoleum specks with my finger. I never wanted to speak to Dr. Landau again. I focused on the floor.

"Orion's belt," I said pointing at three silver dots. "And that one's Venus—it's brighter than the others."

"Simone," Papa said.

"You see what I mean?"

"What is she talking about?"

"We were hoping you'd tell us."

Their voices sounded funny, deep and long like when you talked through an old paper towel roll.

"I agree with Principal Mueller that Simone needs help," Dr. Landau said. "She doesn't exactly have friends to turn to here at the school aside from her brother, and with such a tragic event, I think—"

"You're being awfully diplomatic, Dr.," said Principal Mueller. "The fact of the matter is that Simone has become violent, the other students are scared of her—and if I'm not mistaken, some teachers are, too."

"We're worried about her. Many of her behaviors fall into line with what you'd expect—lashing out, confusion, anger, emotional dissonance—but it's still concerning. "It's a form of post-traumatic stress induced psychosis," she said.

"Psychosis?"

"Yes, that's why she's seeing things. But I assure you it's normal—well, not normal, but you know what I mean. It's a symptom of PTSD—a treatable symptom. As long as she's on medication, she'll stop with the temper tantrums and hallucinations."

"And if she's not?" asked Principal Mueller.

"Well, she gouged a girl in the hand with a pair of scissors already. I really don't want to know what she might do next."

"Gouged?" said Papa.

"Yes, she stabbed another girl in the hand today. I mean, it wasn't serious, the students only have very dull scissors, but it's the intention that's worrying. From what I understand she was quite deliberate about it."

"Stabbed?" said Papa. He didn't understand this word any more than gouged.

"Yes, stabbed," said Dr. Landau. "Look, you don't have to answer this now, but does Simone know the details about how her mother, um, died?"

"Enough," Papa boomed. The room shook. He stood and picked me up. "She knows what she needs to know, and it is not a topic for you to bring over."

"Bring up." I corrected him. They both looked at me. "And stab," I told Papa, "means *poignarder*."

Papa's face crumpled. "Did you—do that? Did you—stab her with the scissors?" he asked in French.

I looked at him. "*Oui*."

Chapter 28

The scissors in my hands had edges like freshly sharpened ice skate blades. I leaned to the side so that my hair draped down then clipped off a wide section. The long black strands coiled around my foot like a snake. When Reine had first asked me what I'd dress as for Halloween, I hadn't a clue. I'd only chosen to be Amélie yesterday when I caught myself making a wide-eyed grimace in the mirror like Audrey Tatou had for the movie poster. There was no way to fake Amélie's bob, so I cut until my neck was bare and the air prickled my skin. Next, I cut the labels off the lingerie I bought on an afternoon I'd gone to State Street for a coffee but ventured into a boutique instead.

I changed into a red dress and looked in the mirror once more, appraised my short black locks and tight red dress. I was missing one thing: red lipstick. I swiped it on and smacked my lips together. *Ready.*

I was the first downstairs and admired our work. We'd spent the afternoon decorating for the Centennial Fête, though a professional crew had also been brought in. The French House glistened, everything polished to perfection; blue, white, and red balloons at every turn; cocktail tables, exotic flower arrangements, a red carpet. The lawn had been raked clean of all errant leaves, there were French flags hanging at every turn, and a banner splayed between the two maples trees: *100 ans! Vive La Maison Française*!

We sat in a mandatory meeting led by the board about how we should conduct ourselves with the attendees, studied their names and titles and the PR-approved statements to make regarding The French House. Strangely,

Professor had not come. At the end of the meeting we were asked to refrain from going out for Halloween festivities, and instead to stay in and rest. The room's energy implied that no one would oblige. Camille had already decided that we would party outside of the House. For the first time.

Charlie, Camille, and Reine weren't downstairs but from the salon window I saw them by the statue. I assumed to avoid Jackie, Tim, and Kate who were laughing obnoxiously in their skeleton pajamas in the dining room. I closed the main door behind me and joined my group. Charlie was dressed as Voltaire though he had yet to commit to the powdery white wig he held in his hands. When he caught sight of me he shook his head and mouthed "stunning." Just like that, everything he had done to hurt me faded into the night.

"Remember what I said, Simone. Don't go there." Reine said, but it was hard to take her seriously speaking through a dress, disguised as Marie-Antoinette's pale blue gown with decapitated neckline. Or Camille for that matter, as the queen's executioner in all black, a bald cap on her head, stuffing in her stomach to make her burly and engorged, and shoulder pads to give her the broadness of a man unashamed to slay the beloved *Autrichienne*. Her look was somewhat ruined by the glasses she wore around her neck. A pair she'd recently bought to replace the pair that broke during her brawl with Hessa. I'd never seen her wear them around her neck. Was she copying Professor or did she simply not want to wear them with her costume?

A guy in a hockey mask brushed past me and banged my shoulder.

"Sorry, babe!" he stopped in front of the statue and pretended to dry hump it, but given its height it was more accurate to say he was humping the base. A guy in blue scrubs and a comically small plastic stethoscope filmed him with his phone.

Their toga-clad buddy then caught up. "Well if it isn't the ol' French club?" As he got closer I saw his white toga sheet was striped with grey plaid. Very authentic.

"*Voulez-vous couchez avec moi, ce soir?*" The Jason guy sang through his hockey mask.

"*Avec toi, non merci,*" said Camille turning her back to them. "*Mes amours*, let us experience the outside world." She threw her prop spiked flail into the air and led the way down a soggy leaf-littered street, where we joined hundreds of costumed revelers.

We strutted and swayed along the streets, all of us merry from the bottles of *Philtre d'Amour* I'd brought from home, and the pleasure of being out like this together again, which we hadn't done since the night of the banquet. After a few blocks Charlie grabbed my elbow and slowed his pace until he stopped completely and faced me.

"Simone, what I did was unforgiveable. And I don't mean that in the sense that you'll never forgive me. By now I know you well enough to understand you will, because you're that kind of person. But I won't forgive myself. I've gone over my actions and tried to psychoanalyze why I did it, and to be honest they're embarrassingly simple. I wanted to be with you that night—as I do every night, but it wasn't the right time. So instead of being a man, I was a baby in search of getting my needs met wherever I could."

"I get it, and I'd rather move on." Maybe I was too optimistic or maybe it was true, but I saw honesty in his eyes.

He ran his fingers through my hair, just a quick swipe and his hand was out and I reached for a lock that was no longer there.

"Your haircut is bold. And so is this." He inspected my arrowhead necklace. "It's sharp."

"My mother found this arrowhead. It's a weapon."

"No," he whispered, pointing to my heart. "That is."

I gave him a look. "That's cheesy."

He jutted his lower lip in a pout and shrugged one shoulder. "I suppose that's because I live in Wisconsin now."

* * *

People, so many people, houses thick with them like paste, like bubbles, all of them trying to get out or in or who knew where. Blue, red, yellow bobbing lanterns and colors and pastel shades, and beer cans and sticky feet and ear-splitting bass, laughter and shrieks, skeletons and phantoms and witches and whores. Seconds and minutes spun 'round and 'round on the carousel of night, ignited to fire by those zippy shots of emerald absinthe. The colorful trees like tufted layers, cancan dancers lifting hoop skirts and swaying their red ruffles before us, candy colors weaving up and down with their high kicks. Was I bathing in the clouds or were we swinging on wreathes? Did I spin like a debutante and dance like a strip tease? Screaming into the night and begging it for more, twirling and skipping and childishly splashing about the piles of leaves, as though they were bathtubs to soak in, and fall in, and drown.

* * *

After we'd had our fill of roaming campus and absorbing the Halloween energy we returned to the House through the front door. The still silence was disorienting after hours in the loud streets. Reine must have felt the same way, she laughed.

"*Shhh*," Camille hissed. "We can't let Henri find out we're awake. Come on, follow me." She slipped off her duckboots and lightly scaled the stairs to the attic on the fourth floor. Charlie was swearing under his breath, asking himself what he was doing, saying something about going home, his steps heavy and wavering. Twice I grabbed his arm to steady myself, my vision blurry.

The light coming from the attic's dormer windows was just enough to make out a slew of cardboard boxes labeled in black marker. Camille tore into one of them.

"*Mon dieu*." She yanked a Ouija board out of a box labeled *miscellaneous*. "Has to be *Henriette*'s, *non*?" She blew the game box's dust. "We'll summon Anne-Marie with it! But first we have to find her photo—just remember her actual name was Maria Fisker."

It was absurd, pathetic even, and I'm sure Charlie and Reine felt the same way. Yet there we were, fingering our way through cardboard boxes with years written across them in streaky black marker (1970 – 1979 and so on and so forth) looking for The French House photo composite from the years Anne-Marie—or Maria lived here.

"Here, try these," Camille said slurring, handing me a few frames.

I scanned the photos and names. All those smiling people raked my nerves. Young and eager, ready to live their time at The French House only to disappear into the world. Then of course there was the realization that one day my photo would be here too, in a cardboard box in the attic.

The board members' names were listed on the bottom of the rosters and my eyes stopped on a familiar one. Hal Green. But before I could make sense of what that meant, Camille shouted.

"I found it!" She shoved a frame in my hand and pointed to the photo. I had to blink out the dust and take a closer look. There she was, Maria Fisker, murderess. She had a nose far too large for her face, thin lips, and stringy light brown hair she'd tried to style into waves. Once again at the bottom was Hal Green's name. Maybe it wasn't that strange that our vineyard's former proprietor had been a board member. He owned a winery and this was The French House. But then there was that tourist's comment about Hal in the CIA, doing covert research.

Camille snatched the frame out of my hands and broke my thoughts. Standing, she wiped her glasses on her black executioner's pants and slid them on. "It is time to summon the deceased!"

We followed Camille downstairs, out the door, and walked in the cold all the way back to the lake. Under the moon we huddled into a circle, our fingers lined atop the Ouija Board's planchette. I was nauseous and confused, desperate to go back home. Camille sensed as much and whispered to me that we'd return soon. I looked at game board's device, waiting for it to move, stupid as it was, and focused on Camille's black fingernails.

The lapping sounds of lake waves vibrated us into a rhythmic lull, our shoulders helplessly swaying into one another as Camille called out, "Anne-Marie Fisker I call unto thee, answer my questions whatever they may be!"

"Do you seriously have to rhyme, Mimi?"

"Oh come on, Chuck." Camille seized Charlie's shoulder, pulling him tighter into our circle. "Inspired by the butcher, you killed and you gave in, share with us the reasons for your sin! Now you'll tell us who is next, who will suffer from your hex?"

The plastic oval moved, our cold fingers along with it, and our eyes following as it darted about the board spelling out: R.E.I.N.E. Immediately Reine let go of the pointer and stood.

"Fuck you, Camille."

"Me?" Camille still hovered over the device, offering an innocent grin. "This is the voice of Anne-Marie Fisker!"

"No," Reine warned. She brushed herself off and took a few steps back.

"Reine, *ma coquine*," Camille resituated in the grass and tilted her strange, costumed baldhead to the side. "Don't do this now, we made it this far and therefore we must drink one another's blood."

"*T'es folle.*" I said, "You've gone too far, Camille. I won't let you harass her this way. You're sick, let it go."

Charlie stood too and gripped his bad knee. "Simone is right, *Mimi.* We've had enough."

"We're just having fun," Camille said. "Drink some more, and perhaps you'll all remember how." Like a kid unwilling to quit her favorite game, she repositioned her fingers on the Ouija Board's planchette.

"No, Camille, we're going back to the House." I linked my arm in Reine's, Charlie into her other arm and off we went, leaving Camille with her board, her bald head a sphere of light as if the moon's own reflection, alone and resolute in the black night.

* * *

Reine did not say a word as we returned to The French House. Charlie and I tucked her into bed, her roommate already asleep, breathing heavily behind us. I moved strands of Reine's hair to the side and kissed her cheeks.

As I was about to pull away, she clasped my arm, her fingernails digging into my skin, and pulled me close. "Camille is right," she whispered. "There's something evil in me, Simone."

"Reine, you're drunk, and she's just trying to unnerve you. Nothing new," I said, tightening her covers. "Get some sleep."

* * *

Charlie and I returned through the main floor and went to the salon where a dying fire crackled. Charlie leaned against the velvet sofa and rotated his knee.

"It's so hot in here," I said watching him move. "Let's go back outside."

We were alone and it was time. He followed me out of the house where I paused at the statue to grab Charlie's hand. I moved it underneath my dress so he would feel the lace that covered my willing body.

He said we shouldn't do it here, not at The French House. He'd find a hotel he said, then led me down the crowded streets.

* * *

Finally confronted with a dark and still room, a quiet so vast I worried my stomach would growl or that my breath would betray me, it occurred to me that to regain power I needed not Professor's advice, but Bertrand's. I tied a piece of cloth around Charlie's eyes to blindfold him, leaving his hands to blindly discover. What he touched brought him so much pleasure he moaned and gasped as though thrown into freezing waters, followed by the fireplace's flames, his torso contorting as he ran his hands over my naked body, while I discovered each groove of his skin, touching like an experimental child, kissing and licking and surprising him—pleasing him to the point of panting my name twenty times in a row. Finally he took from me what I'd been guarding for far too long, and by doing so brought me to a place that was both petrifying and fantastical, my brain visiting faraway memories as my nerve endings popped. Charlie and I shook and clenched and shouted as we sweat like laborers under a soaring sun—until our work was done and I crawled into his embrace, pinching my eyes shut while he released the black blindfold from around his wet head.

* * *

It was just when sleep had opened its arms that a shrill penetrated our dark room. Charlie jumped then leaned over to pick up a white techy gadget. I'd never seen him use his phone before.

"Yeah?" a breathy grunt, "right now?" his weary eyes rolled to the side to find mine. "It's Camille," he said, rustling the sheets. "She needs to tell you something."

I held the phone to my ear gingerly as though it might bite. Camille told me I was a fool to have left, that the "show was about to begin." There was something strange about her voice.

"What show? You're crazy, it's what—one in the morning?"

"What show?" She mocked me. "My thesis. I'm about to test my theory and you cannot miss it. Reine and I will wait for you. You must be a part of it."

I hung up and reached for my clothes.

"You're leaving?" Charlie asked.

"I have to."

"But—stay with me. I'm serious, Simone—this is love. Not just lust."

I paused, my dress halfway over my head and repeated his words in my mind—had he truly said that? I didn't have time to digest it, I pulled my dress down and grabbed my shoes off the floor. "I have to stop her."

"Stop who—Camille? From doing what?"

I realized what it was about Camille's voice. It was rushed. She was never rushed. "I don't have time to explain, Charlie."

I left the room and ran to the elevators. The red ticker above indicated it was on the fifth floor, I was on the second. Charlie called my name as I went into the stairwell. The light flickered and the steps were dusty, I scaled them, coughing. I came out near the first-floor bathroom and ran past the front desk and out the automatic doors. The cold cement shocked my feet. I hobbled putting my heels on and took off for the House. Costumed partiers crowded the streets, coming in and out of focus like a nightmare, laughing clowns, skeletons and witches, voices rising and falling, my vision blurrier than earlier.

* * *

Back at The French House I pushed my house key into the front door and turned the lock. *To live happy, live hidden.* The House was as quiet as we'd left it. The Modigliani nude shone in the light from the dimmed hanging lantern. The salon's fire was but a few sparks from completely dying.

"Camille?" I whispered harshly. Nothing. "Camille!" I said in full voice.

I checked the dining room, the office, the library, the solarium, even the coat closet. No one. I went upstairs and toward her room but stopped short when I got to my bedroom. There was a note taped to the door. Try as I might, I couldn't read it, my vision was so damn blurry it was as if the letters were dancing. I yanked the note off and put it in my pocket. Then, I knocked on Camille's door but there was no answer.

"Camille!" Nothing. I knocked again. "Hessa?" Nothing. She wasn't in the bathroom so I went to the attic. Not there. I returned to my room and unlocked the door. I needed to calm down and think. I looked for my tincture. It wasn't in my backpack and it wasn't in the dresser drawer. I took the sedative tea sachet I'd made with the herbs I bought at the shop on State Street and returned to the main floor for hot water, knowing it was a stupid idea and would probably put me to sleep, but I needed something to help me think. Where did they go? Back to the lake? I again called for Camille in the dining room. No one was there. My heart pounded like the treble and bass throbbing from the lame frat guy who patrolled campus in his Camero with tinted windows. *Thum. Thum. Thum.*

I filled a kettle and fired up the stove, plopped the sachet in a teacup, seeped it for a minute or two and drank it quickly, pouring more water for a second cup. It warmed me, but I was dizzier than before.

"Camille?" I opened the French doors to the terrace and stepped out. Moonlight spilled over my face. The wind hissed. No one was there. I closed the door. I took the note from my pocket hoping I'd be able to read it now—and sure enough I could: *Simone, your brother called and was adamant he leave you this message: your aura looks like a Pollock.*

Book II

L'étranger

Chapter 1

November 1, 2022, Day of the Dead

I remembered blood on my hands. I remembered crying.

Papa was taking every highway curve to Madison like he was testing his truck's turning radius. The air was thick like a greenhouse. I was sweating and smelled repulsive.

"Where's your—*house*?"

"The French House?" I said weakly, what else? I think up until now, I imagined going to the police station. Pictured sitting in a windowless room across from a haggard looking detective with an unlit cigarette dangling from his mouth. A double mirror on the wall.

"Turn left there," I said. *Dead End.* "It's there—by all those people."

The banner, the balloons, the fanfare. I'd forgotten today was the Centennial Fête. I'd forgotten nearly everything—except the blood on my hands. It wasn't on my hands when I woke in the forest, I must have washed it off, but when? Before I drove home? Were my bloody prints on my truck—around the House? I wiped my eyebrows they were soaked in sweat.

The House was marked off with yellow police tape. It was something you'd expect to drive by and gawk at, not a place your presence was requested. Students watched from the sidewalk, some of them crying, others speculating with big hand motions, *What the hell happened?* There were two media vans parked in front, and a blonde journalist in a stiff blue pantsuit stood and faced a camera explaining the scene, whatever it was—I wasn't sure I wanted to know. And yet I had to. There were two policemen in uniform, and a man in dark jeans and a black fleece zip-up standing around one of the maple trees near the front door, all of them focused on the ground. I didn't have a good glimpse of what was there.

"I spoke to your French Lit Professor last week," Papa said as he killed the engine.

"About what?" I asked, disturbed Professor hadn't mentioned this to me. When and why had she called him?

"Are you struggling, Simone?" This question was beyond inappropriate given that Hessa had died.

How do I know it's Hessa?

"With your classes, with keeping up?" I scanned the lawn for Hessa, my breath short. Why Hessa?

Because I saw her. Pictured it all. Hessa in the clawfoot tub on the second floor. Dying.

She wasn't one of the students the lawn.

More gawkers arrived including two girls and a guy with skeleton-painted faces for *Dia de los Muertos*. I scanned the lawn again. There were a handful of people in their forties and fifties assumingly in town for the Centennial, they had French flags pinned to their lapels and I didn't recognize them as board members. A brunette in a long wool jacket and high black pumps covered her face with her hands. She lowered them to reveal her red lips, which twisted down, horrified like she'd purposefully drawn a frown with the lipstick.

"Simone," Papa urged.

"I'm doing fine. I may have skipped a few classes but I'm fine. Stop," I shook my head, "stop talking to my professor." I assessed the lawn again. I needed to find Charlie, Camille, Reine—and most importantly, Hessa.

"Your Professor is the one to have called me." He zipped his coat and forced a sigh.

"What is it you're trying to say?"

"*Ce que je veux dire*, Simone, is that I really need your help. The wine expo in Paris is a matter of weeks away, and we haven't even discussed what we'll do. You promised you'd help and yet you haven't even begun. But I let you be, I didn't interfere with your new life. I allowed you to move here—and now what?"

My hand clutched the door handle so hard it risked snapping off. I counted to ten in my head the way I did with Camille. "*Tu rigoles*, Papa. Someone died, this is not about you or the fucking expo."

"Not anymore it's not, not since the police called to speak with you. What the hell did you do, Simone?"

"Nothing—I didn't *do* anything!" I opened the truck door with an aggressive swing and stopped myself just short of slamming it, too awestruck by what I saw to maintain any strength.

The word *Libérée* had been spray-painted in cursive on a French flag flapping beside one of the maples. Below the tree, though there wasn't a body, yellow police tape staked out a rectangle shape to mark the place of death. The juxtaposition was sickening, all the balloons and French flags, the flapping banner amongst crying students and police tape. Acid bubbled up my throat and I covered my mouth.

I crossed the street and stepped onto the lawn. I heard students talking about Hessa in their broken French; that they'd remain in-language now was baffling. I strained to overhear against the wind. What about Hessa? Was she missing? Was she the body slumped in the claw foot tub I remembered standing over—if that memory was real of course. I tried to relax my face as the other residents watched me, nodding as though it was about time the police found had me.

"What's the deal with this thing?" A man with a badge on his coat motioned toward the statue. It was the guy in the black fleece and dark jeans I'd seen by the—sectioned off rectangle. "I hear you rub it for luck."

I itched my nose. The air smelled like burning leaves. "What's going on here?" I asked him. Responding to a question with a question was one of Professor's tricks, and I knew I needed all of them today. Lessons from her book swam across my addled mind.

The book.

Puitan. I'd written that very word: *libérée* inside Boucher's book. I had to get inside and hide the thing.

One side of the guy's cheek pulled back like a trigger, making a snapping sound. "Well, that's what we're trying to figure out," he said, taking a step closer. "Simone, is it?"

"How do you know who I am?"

"You fit the description."

My right knee buckled and I widened my stance.

"I'm Detective Adam Chris," he reached out his hand, "I've got to ask you a few questions. Why don't we have a little walk this way."

He led me away from the statue and to the side of the House where the wind was twice as vengeful, no barrier between the lake and us. It whipped up frothy fish-smelling spurts. I felt far removed from all the people on the lawn. Papa, too. He stood on the sidewalk by the truck watching.

"So, Simone—"

"Are you really a detective?"

"Why? Because I look young? I get that all the time. And you look like—God, what's that French movie?" He laughed, then said, "It's the only one I've seen. With that girl."

"Amélie?"

He clapped his hands. "Yep, that's it. Your accent's not as strong as the rest of them— you are one of them, aren't you?"

I pulled my scarf up hoping to disappear. Every time I blinked I saw Hessa in the tub. Slumped. Blue. Dead. I knew it was something I should probably tell the detective. But then, how did she get from the tub to the lawn? My memory was wrong. I was just hungover and delirious.

"One of whom?" I stalled.

"One of the French kids. Look, it doesn't take a genius to figure out there's a bit of a rift between the native speaking clan and the non-natives—which I learned today are called frank files."

"You mean Francophiles."

"Oh, is that it? So, anyway—where'd you spend the night last night, Miss Duchamps?"

"Last night," I mumbled. My eyes landed on The French House. What had we been doing in the bathroom? What had Hessa said about Charlie? Why did I remember *violently* pushing someone?

"You implying you stayed here?" The detective asked in a conversational tone, like we were chatting just for the fun of it. I nodded. "Oh? I had been told otherwise. I'd been told you were here, but left in a rush."

"By whom?" I asked, my eyes shifting to the residents on the lawn. Where the hell were Charlie, Camille, Reine—or Hessa?

The detective shrugged and told me it didn't matter. Didn't matter? Of course he knew it did, didn't he? I tilted my head back, eyes pointing toward the tempered sky. I closed them and pushed away the bizarre flashback of Hessa in the claw foot. I needed a moment to think about what it was that was going on here, how I was involved, and how I should respond. No matter how he sounded, how friendly and welcoming, I had to remember that my answers were lining up either against me or for me.

"I left for a hotel around—eleven. Then went to my Papa's house."

"Okay, okay," he jotted in his notepad. The left side of his face washed in the sunlight streaming through a hole in the grey clouds. He had reddish blonde stubble, the same color as the leaves, not quite yellow, not quite red. Did he investigate deaths frequently? Was this morning mundane for Detective Chris or big news?

When he looked up from his notepad he asked me what my relationship with the other residents in The French House was like.

"There are really only a few people I talk to," I said as slowly as Camille might have.

"Who are they?" the detective asked, his voice still friendly. "These few people you talk to?"

"Charlie and Camille and Reine."

"Reine. How do you spell that?"

I pictured our fingers on the Ouija's planchette as they spelled out her name. R.E.I.N.E. Did he really need to know this for his notes? He wrote something else down and I looked past him to the lawn where I saw Jackie, Kate, and Tim. No Hessa. No Charlie, Camille, or Reine.

"Detective, what happened?" I asked. "Who died?"

He clicked his pen, lowered his notepad. "Hessa Mifsud. She was found deceased right over there, under that tree and the flag with the spray-paint on it. Your house chef—*Henri* discovered her around six this morning." He rolled his tongue on the r in Henri. "Are you okay?"

I was slouched over as though catching my breath. The acid crept higher into my throat.

"Simone?"

I straightened my posture. "Yeah, yeah, I'm fine." I wiped a tear; my eyes were watering from the wind rather than emotion. I was too sick to feel anything. Too lost to register how bad this was. My thoughts darted like minnows, too slippery to catch. Too small to matter.

"Let me ask you, Simone. What does lib-er-ray mean to you?"

Chapter 2

"Simone!" It was Jackie, leaves hissing behind her like rattlesnakes. She looked bad. Like she was still in zombie costume all smeared mascara and a tangled mess of overly highlighted curls.

"I saw you with Hessa last night," she said, walking our way. She was carrying something that looked like Professor's book. "Wondering where your army is, *hein*? You can't operate on your own, none of you. I doubt you did last night either." Her raccoon eyes narrowed. "What did you guys do to her, Simone?"

"Thank you, Jackie." Detective Adam Chris said with his one-sided smile. I didn't know if it was pompous or genuine. I turned around to see Papa, he stood against his truck watching, scratching his cheek, his arm, the back of his head.

"If you have more questions or thoughts, you can direct them my way."

"Maybe you should see this," Jackie said, holding up the book. "It's by Anne Boucher, it's Simone's copy."

My stomach concaved.

"Hessa was reading it last night in the salon. I thought it was sad, like it's Halloween you know, and the only thing Hessa has to do is stay home reading Boucher's book?" She dramatized a teary sniffle. "It was still on the coffee table when I got home and I like, grabbed it. I was gonna return it to her, but it has Simone's name in it."

Et voilà. Ça y est.

"Is it your copy?" The Detective asked as if he were only interested in borrowing it.

"If it has my name in it, then yes I suppose it is," I said. "I lent it to Hessa the other day. How nice of Jackie to return it," I glared at her.

The detective put on a pair of latex gloves and pulled out a plastic bag. I guess we were already at that point.

"The page of interest is bookmarked," Jackie said impatiently, her jaw going slack like she was waiting for him to arrest me right then and there. I knew instantly she was referring to the word *libérée* I'd scrawled in a moment of hope.

"All right, thanks again, Jackie. I'll have a look, okay? You have my card."

"Understood," Jackie said like she was doing us both a favor.

He paged through the book with his glove-covered fingers too quickly to read anything. A loose sheet flew out and the detective swatted at it, missing as if it was sucked into windy curlicues and then zigzagged down and into his palm as though magnetized. It was the syllabus for Fundamentals of French Literature's Euphemisms for Society. My blood smeared across it from when I'd cut my finger with my arrowhead. He quickly put the book in his plastic bag but gripped the syllabus so hard it crinkled around his thumb.

"Who were you with last night, Simone? I need to know."

"Like an alibi?" I said with a cringe, eyes on the paper.

"It would help."

"I was with Charlie."

"Derosiers?"

I nodded, still fixated on the syllabus in his hand. The pieces coming together, the Rorschach splotches rendering clear. "Are you familiar with *L'étranger*?"

"Say what?"

"*L'étranger*," I repeated, "by Camus."

"See, you're much smarter than I am. Try to help me with plain and simple English," he said, trying to remain playful.

"I'm just thinking if you look up Camus, look up *L'étranger*, it may help to understand this."

"What's *this*?"

This was a flagrant copycat, a Muslim killed. Leading up to it an obvious match to *Les Liaisons Dangereuses*, our group entangled in love triangles. But what about the third act? *La Vénus d'Ille*. An unsolved murder blamed on a statue-come-to-life. He'd think I was insane. But if I were right in my thinking, it may actually prove I wasn't. My head wobbled back and forth, like our backyard tire swing metronoming in the breeze. "This," I said looking back at the spray-painted flag, "is a puzzle."

Professor's simulation, her game—*her test*.

Chapter 3

The detective told me I was free to go. *For the moment.* I crossed the street toward Papa, who was still leaning against his truck. He looked me up and down.

"Well, are you in the clear?" he asked.

"In the *clear*?"

He took keys from his pocket and walked to the driver side door.

"You know, Papa, the right thing to do here would be to give me a hug, make sure I'm okay." I joined him on the other side of the truck.

He unlatched the door. "Let's go home."

"*Non*," I paused and thought of Professor's book, what she would say to get what she wanted. "I'll catch up with you soon, I need to make sure everyone here is okay, so I can focus on my plan for the expo."

He thought about it for a moment, then wished me luck and started the car. He drove away but slammed on the breaks mid-intersection. He'd blown the stop sign. A guy in a Tesla leaned out of his window and called Papa a piece of shit. When he was out of sight I set off to Professor's office.

* * *

"I know what you're doing," I said, standing in Professor's doorway. I'd been surprised to find her here, and yet it was just like her to be so unperturbed. Like she had that first day, she sat in front of the diamond embossed windows, both hands placed atop her desk. It was dark. There were no rays of sun on this side of the building, and yet she hadn't lit her small green lamp, leaving the walnut bookshelves in black shadows.

"*Ma belle, viens ici*, you must be so shaken."

"Professor—"

"Anne, call me Anne."

"What are you trying to prove?"

She motioned that I should come further inside. I did. This was the woman who had mastered manipulation and in that moment I was her willing servant. *Just like Anne-Marie?* It occurred to me that if we were all disciples of her book then we were all trialing her lessons whether subconsciously or not. Who then, came out the victor? Surely she always would, the source of the knowledge, the skeleton key to our mere copies.

She stood and cupped my head in her hands, pulling me into her bosom where the invitation of crème brûlée was so strong that I realized I was salivating. She stroked my head, then clasped my shoulders to push me back and study my face.

"*La pauvre*, are you okay?" She motioned toward the chair across from her desk and I sat.

"What happened between you and Anne-Marie Fisker—and then Hessa?"

"Mm," her hum and its crystal bowl resonance. She eased herself back into the chocolate leather chair and pouted. "What happened was tragic." She flipped her palm to face the ceiling, a gesture of indifference.

"Before that."

The little light coming through her window shifted, and the room darkened even more. Her eyes changed from green to slate and green again, like the glimmering algae on Lake Mendota.

"We're the connecting theme to the works you assigned, aren't we? What is it—you wanted to see how closely life might mimic the readings? Well then congratulations: sexual triangles—check, a murdered Muslim—check, an unsolved death—the connector? The French House, your sick simulation. What are you testing? Your power?"

She smiled so entrancingly I forgot what else I intended to say. I nearly apologized for my tone but closed my eyes and saw Hessa again. The anger resurfaced. I leaned into her desk, pushed her butterfly paperweight forward. "You either set this up or you killed her. It's one or the other and I refuse to take the blame."

"You want to play with fire, Simone? I'm the one who got you in the House." She batted her lashes.

"Are you blackmailing me? Hessa is dead and I won't let you get away with any of this."

"Are you absolutely sure you're innocent, Simone? You remember what happened last night?"

"I—"

"You should go."

I agreed. She'd stumped me and I didn't want to lose the battle any more than I already had. I needed to find my friends. Needed to find my missing memories.

I stepped out of her office and she said, "We should have clearance to return to the House very soon and I've asked Henri to prepare a special dinner, it will be good for us all to reclaim some normalcy."

Normalcy. I shook my head thinking of what Charlie had said once, another lifetime ago, when we were sitting on the terrace, the lake's winds on our faces and our mouths full of macarons. He'd said that when Camille played her violin things felt normal. I wished I knew what normal was.

I walked into the hall. *Speak of the devil.* "Charlie." My breath caught on his name.

"Come," he said, heading toward the door, his body disappearing into the corridor's shadows. "Let's go get a coffee."

I wondered but didn't ask, why he'd come to see Professor.

Chapter 4

As we were leaving Professor's office, Charlie suggested that we not talk about what happened until morning. I disagreed. I didn't want the memories to fade. I asked him where he went last night after I left the hotel, what time he learned about Hessa, and what the detective asked him.

"I don't even know." His fingers moved along the back of my neck. "I'm just so tired." His hand dropped to my lower back as he ushered me into a hotel on Carroll Street.

"Relax in the lobby, I'll check us in."

"*Relax?*"

"Well, you know what I mean."

Actually, I didn't. But I sat and waited for him on a beige armchair in front of a gas fire anyway. There was a stack of books on the table to my side and I grabbed one: *Great Expectations.* I tried to open it but it was glued shut, a fake.

I'd written *libérée* in Boucher's book and given it to Hessa. Was there significance there? Jackie turned in my book to the detective. Had she found what I'd written and pre-meditated a way to tag me to the murder, just short of writing my name on the tree? But then, why? Why would she kill Hessa? Camille disliked and distrusted Hessa, and she was the one to suggest I liberate myself. Was this some theme of hers? Part of her thesis? Was she working with Professor or maybe against her, to see who was more powerful?

Charlie returned waving a plastic key card. He put it in his pocket then helped himself to coffee at the buffet table, stirred in two sugars. "Want one?" I shook my head. He walked toward the elevator. Its doors opened and Charlie got in. They closed halfway but he held his arm out to stop them.

"*Simone.*"

I put the book down and joined him.

* * *

Charlie fell asleep immediately after sex, apparently his equivalent to sedative tea. I drifted in and out of dreams, chasing the scenes that dangled in my mind like sparkling lights, but as soon as I got close they flickered and went dark. Hessa in the tub. My hands covered in blood. Pushing someone—Camille? The digital clock said ten past two. Charlie's arm was draped heavily over my chest. I carefully moved it to the pillow, then slithered out of bed and into the bathroom. I arched over the toilet to dry heave until my stomach muscles were sore.

Sun poured into the room around seven but did nothing to rouse Charlie. I noisily paced beside him. I took a shower. I paced some more. I studied a tear in the duvet where gauzy white material oozed out and if I stared long enough it looked like a screaming face.

Charlie woke around nine and pulled himself to a slumped position at the edge of the bed. He covered his face with his hands and through them told me that French Lit was "obviously" cancelled but that I should get ready and head to campus to act normal. I wanted to punch him.

"Normal?" Nothing in my life had ever been normal and after what had just happened, it was asinine to even suggest it.

"We'll talk later," he said walking to the bathroom.

"No, we should talk now," I said gripping the door so he couldn't shut it.

"I'm going to take a shower, Simone."

"What is wrong with you?"

"Me?" He tried to shut the bathroom door again.

"I need to know what happened."

"As do I," he said. "I'm sorry." He adopted a more coaxing tone. "I'm beyond stressed."

"And I'm not? Why are you avoiding this conversation? What is it you don't want to talk about? What happened on Halloween—or *us*?" The second the word us came out I regretted it. Even without experience I knew this teeny tiny word weighed eternally on a man.

He leaned against the door looking defeated, exhausted. "Why am I doing this, it's like I want to sabotage myself. Clearly I have zero restraint. When I'm with you I can't stop myself. Simone," he ran his fingers down my short black bob, "you make me powerless."

I appraised his eyes until I felt like I was having an out of body experience, watching from above. I stepped back and sat on the bed. He said I made him powerless, did that suggest one's empowerment rendered others powerless? Of course it did. Life boiled down to a billion exchanges, all of them little games, all of them producing a winner and a loser.

"Simone, you're without a doubt the most beautiful and intelligent woman I've ever come across. And yet—you need help as much as I do. *Je m'inquiète pour toi.*"

"Ah yes, you're worried about me. Reine told me."

"Look, I don't know how to help you because ultimately, I need help, too." His face was red, his veins bulging and for a second I was frightened until a tear fell down his cheek. I stood and reached for him but he gently pushed me back. "I need to get ready and get out of here. Go to the Union, we can pretend to run into each other there. No one can see us leave the hotel together."

I stood before him unknowing how to respond until the anger got the best of me and I left the hotel room with a door slam. A housekeeper scowled my way but I brushed past her, descended to the ground floor, and walked through the lobby with my head down.

* * *

At the Union Terrace I stood at the edge of the water watching foamy waves lap up the manmade shore. Behind me students sat at the yellow, green, and orange tables with coffee or beer studying, laughing, living. Charlie showed up not long after he said he would, calling my name like an actor and giving me not even the assumed cheek kisses, but a pat on the back. After having penetrated my body, maybe even my soul, twice—three times last night, such detachment made me want to spit on him. What kind of woman was I? Clearly not the empowered seductress Professor wanted me to be. Nor the woman in the Renoir.

I recognized a few students picking up from the table next to where we stood. They were in my psychology class. I checked my watch.

"I've gotta go."

"But I just got here. I thought you wanted to—"

"You know what?" I patted his back. "I gave you an opportunity to talk, *my friend*—and you didn't. I'm going to class."

"Simone!' he called, as I walked to psych.

* * *

I sat in the back row of auditorium for psychology intending to doze, the fatigue weighing on my eyelids. But when the TA began lecturing about involuntary memory and one of my favorite authors, Marcel Proust, I couldn't help but fully dial in—I even corrected the TA after he mispronounced the title of Proust's novel.

"Simone Duchamps," he said. "You're French, right?"

Students from the other rows turned to look at me and I could have sworn I heard whispers about The French House and Hessa. A few students pulled their phones out, looking at me, and then again at their phones, typing, as if I were already in some line-up they'd found online.

"Do you know anything about Proust's novel and involuntary memory?" the TA went on.

"I do," I said, grabbing my arrowhead and organizing my thoughts. I closed my eyes only to find a glowing Cheshire cat. I opened them and spoke clearly, my voice strong and firm. "In *La Recherche du Temps Perdu*, Proust defined involuntary memories through his narrator, who had consumed a tea-soaked *petite madeleine* and the scent and taste sparked an influx of childhood memories, memories which in all probability would have remained hidden in his mind if it were not for the familiar taste of the tea and cake. They were the trigger, and he referred to them as a potion working its magic. He described involuntary memories so well that many now refer to them as Proustian memories."

The TA took his hands out of his faded jean pockets and he clapped a few times. "*Merci*," he said. "That was—pretty much perfect." He took a sip from the water glass siting on the dais and looked up. "The thing about these types of memories—why they hit us so quickly, is that the olfactory sense, which is directly linked to our sense of taste, has the power to transport us to a memory in a way sounds, sights, and words cannot. In fact, once you begin discussing a memory, it risks drifting away and spinning into something else entirely. Scent is the most reliable memory road, the surest path. Our olfactory system works directly with the hippocampus and amygdala, whereas our other senses require neural transport via our synapses, and that can mean disruption, even distortion along the way. In short, scent is the wormhole of the mind."

His words brought me back to Charlie's refusal to talk—maybe he was right not to. Maybe to remember, I'd have to put myself back in the situation from Halloween night.

On my way out of class, the TA chased after me calling my name. I turned around and waited for him to catch up. He stopped before me, pushing his elbow-patched blazer sleeves up and digging his hands into his jean pockets.

"Yes?"

"I just wanted to say that you captured Proustian memory impeccably." He took a pair of fifties-era black-rimmed glasses from his pocket and slid them up his nose. "You want to go get a coffee? I've never had the chance to discuss Proust with a French person."

"Now?"

"This isn't a romantic invitation or anything like that, I mean, God, I'm your teaching assistant." He pushed his glasses up but they were already as far as they'd go. "We couldn't um . . . do *that*."

"Do what?"

His cheeks flushed. "Nothing, nothing."

I thought of the quote I found on Professor's desk about vengeance soothing. It made more sense than ever. I imagined myself taking this cute young guy out and parading him in front of Charlie, the two of us laughing in one another's company as though we had never had a better time, his hand circling my waist, Charlie sick with jealousy, then stealing me away. It was abhorrent to even think this now. Trite. Pathetic. I wanted to hate Charlie, but I kept remembering the warm feeling I had when he said he loved me, and it was this that made me powerless.

"Let me buy you a coffee."

"After everything that just happened I shouldn't."

"Do you live in The French House, Simone?" I nodded. "I'm an idiot. I'm sorry—about what happened. God that place is—"

"Is what?"

He shrugged his shoulder. "I'll tell you over coffee."

I grabbed his wrist, "I can't wait that long. I have a feeling you have something interesting to say, I can see it in your eyes, and maybe it would help."

He studied me, his mouth edging into a nervous smile. "It's just a rumor."

"That's okay, I want to know."

He nodded. "People say The French House used to be the subject of mind control research—our own psych department was involved. A couple professors in the seventies who teamed up with a former CIA agent."

I shook my head, then nodded, like a bobble head. "What was the agent's name?"

"I don't have a clue, like I said, it's a rumor. Are you okay? You look kinda pale."

"I'm fine," I lied. My head was hot, my body cold. "Tell me the rest."

His face tensed. He opened his mouth and closed it. "Supposedly, this guy had been involved in Project MKUltra, some program where they practiced mind control, and despite the fact the program had long since ended and he wasn't even active with the CIA anymore, he kept on with his own research and used The French House as a test, a test to see how easy it would be to pit two cultures against one another."

"My God."

"That's really all I know. Maybe it's psych department urban legend, maybe not—"

"Carter!" A man slapped his—*Carter's* back. A burly guy with Einstein like hair appropriately sporting a black tie covered in $E = mc^{2.}$ "We still going to Michelangelo's for a coffee?"

"Ah, yes of course." Carter's lips pulled back. "Sorry, Simone."

"It's no problem, I have to go anyway."

Go back to the vineyard and talk to Papa about Hal Green.

Chapter 5

I sped to the vineyard. Most days the ride blurred into highway hypnosis. Now my mind was acute and loud. How would I confront Papa? Did he know about Hal Green's past?

I pushed my truck from seventy, to eighty and only let up when my truck started to rattle at eighty-five miles per hour. The last thing I needed was my truck falling to pieces.

I parked by the main building. It was only three forty-five but so cloudy it looked like the sun had already set. I ran to the vineyard expecting Papa to be there. Instead, Carol was leading a tour group. She startled and whipped her hand to her heart.

"Simone, you scared me."

A few heads peered around to see me.

"Sorry…carry on!"

"Simone!" Sam's voice called from the top of the hill.

I ran up so fast my quads burned. Sam, Kip and Bertrand were sitting around a pile of Junior Mints, licorice, Crunch Bars and Reese's Peanut Butter Cups, the close-to-expiring goods Sam sometimes brought after her shift collecting tickets at the movie theater.

"Where's Papa?"

"At Schneller's," Bertrand said chewing licorice, "claimed he couldn't find a decent wrench. What's wrong, why are you home?"

I sat down. The grass was wet. The sky was clearing, and a dotting of clouds lay over the valley making everything violet.

Kip passed me a Crunch bar.

"Twice now I've heard twice that Hal Green used to be in the CIA. My psych TA said he was a part of MKUltra."

"Seriously?" Bertrand unwrapped his licorice.

"What's MKUltra?"

"It was a CIA program at the most classified level—*hence* the 'ultra,'" said Bertrand.

Kip rolled his eyes. "Silly me, everyone knows that."

"And the MK?"

"Mind Kontrolle, a German spin because most of the scientists involved in the program were former Nazis."

"*Nazis?*"

"Yeah, but the program was instigated by the Cold War. Americans thought the Soviets and North Koreans had access to—get this, a *truth serum*. MKUltra's purpose was to master mind control and brainwashing tactics that would get enemies to admit things, stuff like that. They used electroshock therapy, ritual abuse, LSD and psilocybin on their test subjects. Anything to alter the mind and make one more susceptible to messaging."

I picked a handful of grass and flicked the wet blades away with my finger. "Did they ever test people at universities?"

Bertrand yanked another bite of red licorice. "Oh yeah, loads. They were involved with over forty universities if I remember right. Hospitals too—and prisons. They drugged subjects unwittingly, and others volunteered. But they failed to control the outcomes, there was so much unknown about these drugs and the right dosages, and people died. There's not a ton of evidence about any of it. During the Watergate era the CIA director had all the files destroyed. So what's the point of all this, you think Hal Green actually used to be a part of it?"

"Yeah, I do. And I think he tested people in The French House, he may have driven a girl so mad that she—murdered seven people."

"What?" Bertrand lowered his licorice. "You didn't tell me—" he paused and turned his head. "Papa's home."

I stood. The clouds were gone now, replaced by a gigantic black cloud. From the bottom of the hill gravel crunched.

"I gotta talk to him." I ran down the hill, zigzagging to lessen my speed and stop myself from barreling down like a log.

Papa was already inside pouring himself a glass of water from the tap at the kitchen sink.

"What are you doing here?"

"I need to talk to you about some things—Hal Green."

His eyebrows lowered; he took a sip of water. "I don't have time." He set the glass down. "I need to rouse a yeast. I have a stuck fermentation, among other problems."

I followed him outside. Carol and the tour group were now at the winery's main entrance and Papa rushed through a side door.

"Simone?" Carol called, "You want to say hi? This gentleman—sorry what's your name again, Jim? Jim from Lacrosse remembers reading about your mother, and he wants to meet you."

"I'm sorry, I can't right now." I rushed through the main building's side door but it was too late; Papa's lab was locked. I knocked. "Papa, are you in there?" Nothing. I pounded until my fist hurt. "Papa!"

"Simone, not now." His voice was growly, resolute. Enough to send me back to the house.

Earlier I hadn't realized how dirty it was. Dishes crowded the sink, moldy bread sat on the counter. There was unopened mail on every surface, boot prints throughout the kitchen. Empty brandy glasses in the salon. The result of my not living here.

The Misfits came in via the screen door, still talking about MKUltra. Something about the CIA sending prostitutes with LSD laced lipstick to kiss Fidel Castro to get him susceptible to mind control.

"Bertrand, Maman was looking for papers in Papa's office. What if it had something to do with this?"

"I highly doubt it. Anything she was doing then doesn't have merit. She was going crazy…at the end."

"Maybe, but I also found a letter Maman wrote to Aunt Violette and never sent. She said Uncle Guillaume had something that would save her. What if Papa was involved in this research somehow and…and he was going to be found out and we were going to lose the vineyard, so Maman sent Guillaume proof that the unethical research was all Hal's fault and not Papa's."

"Whoa, Simone. Do you hear yourself? You're making no sense. Please don't crazy, too. I need you."

"I don't know," I said. "There's a connection between Hal, my Professor, and the problems at The French House. The question is whether or not Papa was tangled into it."

Or me.

* * *

I banged the lab door again at four, five, and six. I told Papa I'd make dinner. I asked him what he wanted. No answer. I went back to the kitchen and opened a bottle of 2013 *Philtre de Courage* and walked uphill to the same spot as earlier. I tugged from the bottle, happy for the warm feeling the wine brought my belly. Had I truly been brainwashed, coerced—controlled?

I stumbled down the hill around ten. Papa was still in his lab, Bertrand at Kip's. I was exhausted and went to bed. At two in the morning I woke up sweaty and nervous. I swore I heard someone banging on the front door and something told me it was the police. But when I peered outside there was no one there, a lone floodlight shone over the empty gravel drive.

The next time I woke I thought I heard the phone ringing. I opened my eyes to see the sun was up. It wasn't my imagination this time; the phone was definitely ringing. I rushed downstairs to answer.

"*Mon lion.*"

"Camille. How'd you get this number?"

"Paranoid, *ma petite*? Henri gave it to me. You weren't answering your mobile and we needed to find you to tell you to come back. Hessa's funeral is today. Can you give us a ride? It would be nice to go together."

"Oh," I said, looking out the window. Soon tourists would prance about the vineyard, learn about wine and buy silly t-shirts unknowing, and uncaring that Hessa was gone. "I'll head in soon."

I went back upstairs and searched for the tincture in my bag but it wasn't there. In all likelihood it was in my bedroom at the French House. This was not the time to skip a dose. Not when I'd have to withstand Hessa's funeral—and Camille. *Unless*—I opened my pill bottle and shook out a little yellow oval into my palm. I brought it halfway to my mouth then chucked it in the garbage. Wasn't my pill a form of mind control?

The only black garment I found in my closet was a long sleeve black shirt with white stripes. I'd brought most of my clothes to The French House, not that I owned much black to begin with. The only true black garment was the transparent dress I'd worn at the banquet. I made note to return it later.

I took a black sweater from Bertrand's closet and paired it with black tights and a green skirt that hit mid-shin. Acceptable? I had no clue.

* * *

I pulled up the dead-end street to The French House. My group was waiting for me by the statue, Reine and Charlie wearing all black, Camille in a long tan wool coat. Like last time, Charlie sat in the passenger seat but I avoided looking or speaking to him. In the backseat, Reine stared straight ahead, her face still, her body jittering.

"You okay, Reine?" She didn't respond.

"She's fine, *mon lion*, let's get going. We don't want to be late."

It started raining so hard it looked like we were driving through a car wash.

"*Mes amis,* can you believe Hessa's family overrode the police?"

"What do you mean?" said Charlie.

"There was no autopsy, that's what I mean."

Camille explained that Hessa's death had been officially ruled a suicide. I should have felt relieved. Relieved no one had taken the act upon himself and relieved I was no longer a suspect. But I knew there was more to it. Hessa's family didn't support the suicide ruling either, nor did the media (according to Camille), but perhaps it still trumped having their daughter's body torn up in an autopsy—a violation of their religious beliefs, or proving without question that she'd been drinking (Camille claimed Hessa was a closeted alcoholic despite that I'd never once seen her drink wine at dinner), and that she wasn't a virgin.

"Wouldn't they rather know exactly how she died than to follow a custom?" Charlie asked quietly. His normally regal posture was slumped and he was leaning his head against the window.

Reine remained mute, her eyes so unfocused they looked like musty grapes. I turned the wipers on a higher level. I struggled to see the car in front of me and gently pumped the brakes, listening carefully to their every word and hoping one of them would offer a clue as to whether or not they'd been involved with Hessa's death in any way.

"There must have been some back and forth about the autopsy between Hessa's family and the police, since today it's three days postmortem." Camille went on. "According to their tradition the timer's up and she has to be buried today."

Charlie's jawbone flashed. "That's enough, Mimi."

"I guess some charities pitched in to fly her mother in," Camille went on as though not hearing him. "God, can you imagine? The woman got off a trans-Atlantic flight, was probably harassed in customs, and then had to rush into town to shroud and bathe her dead daughter. But, I did hear that a bunch of local Islamic women stepped in to help her."

"Camille Cloutier," Charlie said, "We've got more than enough information, please be quiet the rest of the way there."

Camille remained unruffled, and appeared disturbingly well rested, her eyes were clear, her skin shiny and hydrated. She looked like a politician's wife with her tan wool jacket, pearl earrings, and baby blue cashmere scarf draped around her long neck. That is, until she arranged her scarf like a hijab, posing in the visor mirror as though no one else was watching. But I caught her eye. She knew I was.

* * *

The lull of the Salat al-Janazah was otherworldly, the cyclical nature of unending prayer inspiring a faint back and forth sway. The mosque's activity room was packed and I was ever the outsider.

. . . *Allahu Akbar* . . .

Not that Charlie, Reine, or Camille looked any more comfortable, or the other residents from The French House for that matter, all of us stiff, subtly glancing this way and that all seemingly in hope of a cultural clue as to how to act.

. . . *Allahu Akbar* . . .

I searched the room for Professor. She wasn't here. Not that I knew what that meant either way.

. . . *Allahu Akbar* . . .

When the prayers changed slightly I looked down, focusing on my knees, my black tights, and counted to one hundred over and over again.

Un, deux, trois, quatre . . . allahu akbar . . . quatre cinq six sept huit . . . Allahumma Salli.

* * *

Outside the mosque, news crews dotted the streets, spinning their webs for the camera. Camille informed us that Hessa's story had gained momentum. Without a major event to report on in recent weeks, the media had put all their energy into this one—reinventing it no less. No matter the suicide ruling, they claimed we were making a statement against Islam as some sort of counterterrorism. That we had poisoned an innocent girl, left her for the public to see, and mocked her religion with the word *libérée*, as if to imply she had been freed from her religion now that she was dead. It was amazing how quickly my quiet world had changed, how fast stories snowballed.

We filed out of the mosque to find no sign of the morning's downpour except for a few fat puddles, the world shiny and new, worms retreating to the earth and ions clinging to the air. The news crews descended on us, ladies with bug eyes and glowing white teeth holding out microphones and addressing us, disturbingly, by name. It was a windless afternoon and the air smelled of bonfires.

Reine looked to be in shock and hadn't yet said a word. While we rushed to my truck, I linked my arm in hers hoping to offer her silent comfort, but she shook me away and stopped in her tracks. "I must talk to—the detective. Don't wait for me."

Camille, Charlie and I watched as she staggered toward Adam Chris, calling his name and waving, her grey scarf fluttering behind her. He stopped walking, turned, and shooed away several reporters. They spoke, though we couldn't hear them.

"What is she doing?" Charlie mumbled.

"*Mais c'est très intéressant.*"

Reine's voice was louder now, but I still didn't make out what she was saying. She threw her arms in the air and the detective reached forward, stopping just short of touching her, clearly trying to calm her down.

"Maybe we should go over there," I said.

"*Bah, non,*" Camille said. "She's a big girl, let her work this out herself. This is what I've been waiting for."

Chapter 6

Driving back to The French House with only Charlie and Camille, I regretted leaving Reine. I hated to think about her taking a cab home, silly, I know, and Camille ensured me that Reine was "a big girl" and could work things out for herself.

It was unlikely to find parking near the House at this hour, so I took the first spot I found two streets out. Charlie, Camille and I walked back to the House in silence.

"*Mon dieu*, what is all this?" Camille said crossing the intersection to our dead-end street. She wiped her glasses then swatted at her hair, which was blowing this way and that in the wind.

There were people on the lawn—*again*. Some held candles, others held signs.

Charlie tore a taped sheet of paper off a streetlight. "*Shut down The French House!*" He crumpled it.

As we got closer, I read the students' signs: *Je suis Hessa*, Go back home! and *Liberté, Egalité, Fraternité.*

"Stop," Camille said. "I want to hear what's going on." We were directly in front of the statue and House but across the street, next to an older couple who both wore red and black checkered fleece vests.

"It was emblematic against Islam," said the man. "A way of saying that the only way to free her from her oppressive religion was through death."

"The French people did it. I just know it. Things are terrible in France right now, and they're mirroring it." the woman added.

"According to whom?" Camille interrupted them. Her accent gave her away, and the woman blushed.

"I saw, um, a special about it."

"Ah yes, television." Camille nodded. "You can always trust it." She brushed past them and to the House in the straightest line I'd ever seen her walk. Charlie and I followed. The people on the lawn were chanting in a way that made me think of buzzing insects.

"Charles Derosiers!" A guy shouted. "Charles!"

We ran the rest of the way up the cobblestone walkway. Camille took her key out and fumbled to unlock the door. I focused on the fire in the gas lamp hanging over us. *To live happy, live hidden.*

This time it was a woman's voice that shouted for Charlie.

"What do they want with you?" I asked harshly.

"I have no idea." He hastily grabbed the key from Camille who was still struggling with the key, and opened the door. We rushed inside and I slammed my back against it as it closed, as if we'd outrun the monster on the other side.

"Why are they making her death a religious affair?"

"Oh, *mon lion.*" Camille tugged off her duckboots. "It's become a religious affair because the media are idiots. And those believing what they say, are idiots. And idiots order the idiots to report such things to the idiots so that all idiots remain fearful idiots living in the dark. Don't be an idiot." She walked across the foyer to the salon and slumped onto a green velvet sofa.

"I'm going to go out the back," Charlie said in a low tone so that only I would hear him. "I can't make the meeting but meet me at the Campus Inn at seven."

"What meeting?"

"With Henri. Seven o'clock, okay?" he said kissing my cheeks goodbye.

* * *

The meeting turned out to be a collaboration between Henri and a local officer named Ron, a husky man with a shiny bald head. They advised us to ignore the protesters and recommended we travel in groups whenever we left the House. But all I could wonder was whether or not we were safer inside or out?

Ron also suggested we refuse to speak to the media. There was a news van outside again, most likely covering the protesters. "They'll take your words out of context," Ron said rubbing the back of his head. "They'll use you for their story."

Apparently, Jackie didn't care. After the meeting she went to the coat closet, slipped on her long black leather jacket and purposefully sought the blonde journalist on the lawn. Camille and I watched from the salon window. Camille's eyes were wide behind her glasses; she was like a girl on her first trip to the ballet.

"What do you think she's saying?"

"She's publicly blaming us, *ma minette.* She's saying it's our fault."

"How do you know?"

"*Please.* I just know." She stood abruptly and rolled her neck around. "I need a drink—actually I need to be—*complètement bourré.*" She meandered away but I stayed by the window. The statue stood over everyone with her all-knowing air.

Camille returned holding an opened bottle of wine and drank from it like it was her post-run water bottle. She wiped her lips with the back of her hand and sank back onto the sofa. "I'm going to watch this *show* until I pass out." She flicked her head toward the lawn.

It was my chance to leave. "I don't feel well," I said. She didn't react so I slipped away and went out the terrace door. The lake was rough, and it was so windy a cyclone of yellow and red leaves were twirling across the balcony. I half ran, half walked across campus, past State Street and to a seedier part of town for the Campus Inn.

* * *

In a nondescript room Charlie scooped me into his arms. My questions disintegrated. We undressed so quickly we hadn't even closed the door all the way, but Charlie jogged back, kicked it shut and returned to me. Why did tragedy inspire the animal in us? Because it made us forget. And forget I did, for pulsing, throbbing minutes, hours. By the time he was done, I lay sated, like a girl who'd given up midway through her snow angel.

"All my life I've felt like an actor," Charlie said rolling onto his side to face me. He traced my curves with his finger. "For as long as I can remember I've made the faces I thought appropriate for my close-up, adjusting the level of drama as I saw fit. I even apply a soundtrack—that's to say that in my head I'm adding music to life's most intense moments." His eyes moved around the room in thought, stopping at a point on the ceiling and squinting. "It's not that I'm insincere, I'm not really sure what it is. Maybe I'm trying to deliver the performance I presume others expect of me. Or I'm simply trying to make life more beautiful." His eyes shifted back to mine.

"Maybe we're all acting."

"Are you?"

I looked away, my body aching, tired. I didn't know how to answer his question and inevitably thought of Reine telling me they'd seen me talking to myself. What was I saying and to whom?

"I'm not making sense, am I?" he said.

"No, I just—I guess I'm not sure I know myself well enough to answer that yet."

"Then what's the first answer that comes to your head?"

"That I exist because I think."

He grinned—and if I were to bet my life I'd say it was his true smile not an actor's.

"Descartes." He gently tugged my nipple and winked. "You're quoting things now, what does that mean? You don't believe me."

"Believe what? In your existence or what you're saying?"

He fell to his back and exhaled, focused again on the ceiling or beyond, and I lost him. Maybe he was waiting for his director's cue, the next lines. I too rolled over, the desk lamp's light transforming my nakedness into cool marble, or a body atop a cold slab in the morgue.

"Charlie. What did we do?"

After a moment his face turned my way slightly as though he'd just become aware of my presence. A smile forming, he reached between my thighs, "You want to do it again?"

I halted his hand. "I'm talking about the night Hessa died. What did we do to her?"

He looked annoyed. "Why do you imply that we were involved?"

"Because I can see her there—Hessa. I think I remember."

"Maybe you should…" he paused, propped onto his elbows, a few abdominal muscles flexing and flashing. He looked over to me, brows knitted, "…talk to the others about it, because I told you, I don't know anything."

"Just tell me anything you remember." I touched his arm hoping to gently encourage him but it flexed harder, hot and tight. "Please, Charlie."

He sighed, pulling the sheet to cover his naked body and rolling onto his back again. "I remember you running back to The French House, that's about it."

"You didn't follow me there? I thought you were getting dressed when I dashed out." You also told me you loved me. Are you going to say it again, or was it only one of your lines?

"Well," he said, not meeting my eyes. "I started to, but—"

"But what?"

"But I stopped—because I'd run into someone I know, *Detective*."

"How long was I inside?"

"I don't know." He cupped his hands behind his head. "I didn't make it all the way to the House. Not that I'd give a reliable account anyway. Five minutes might have been five hours. All that wine, time was completely distorted."

"What if it was all a set-up."

"What are you talking about?

"Did you know The French House used to be used for mind control experiments? Maybe they're doing it again."

"*Oh là là,* what are you doing, Simone? Hessa ended her life. No one else was involved." He grabbed my arm and pulled me into his body so that I was flat alongside him. Trying to ignore the fear in my heart, I savored his closeness, the very thing I longed for every night I lay in bed without him. But I remembered standing over Hessa' blue and lifeless body in the claw foot tub of the second-floor bathroom just off Reine's room. I heard Reine's nervous giggle and Camille's drone rising and rising and rising, until the sound of Charlie's phone ringing stopped my memories flowing down stream. It was enough to freeze my blood. Had we brought her downstairs to the tree and written *libérée* on the flag? Was it possible to black something like that out? The opiate tea I'd consumed suggested it was possible, and of course, my memories hadn't been reliable since Maman left us. On top of it, if Professor were truly capable of mind control, who knew how many of us she'd implicated?

"Hello?" Charlie held his phone tightly against his ear. "Don't call Simone's father," he said. I lifted my head from his arm's embrace and flashed my eyes at him. "I'll tell her," he continued. "No, I'm not with her—yeah, something like that."

"What was that about?"

He clicked off and turned to face me, his eyes weary. "That was detective Adam Chris and he's—*bon*, he's requested us back to the station for questioning."

"Why?" I sat up, pulling my knees in the same way Camille did during late hours in the bath.

"Because Reine confessed."

Chapter 7

The police station smelled like old fries and disinfectant. Sitting in the waiting room I asked Charlie over and again why he thought Reine had confessed—and to what? That she killed Hessa? That she was involved—and if she had been, I must have been too. But Charlie wasn't concerned and assured me everything was "just a mix-up," that we'd be free to go home soon.

A lady came through a door just beyond the front desk. She had grey hair but a young face and was eating a hamburger. She wiped her mouth and said, "Miss Duchamps, we'll take you back first." I followed her but paused to look over my shoulder at the door. Charlie was sitting with his legs crossed and had begun paging through *Self* magazine.

Detective Chris had his own office however the walls were glass. There were files covering his desk and a framed photograph of what I assumed were his parents, his mother with striking rhubarb colored hair. He had yet to shave and his eyes were mottled with thin red webs, but even so he was a good-looking guy.

"Is Reine okay?" I asked.

He finished whatever he was writing, tic-tac-toe for all I knew, probably a delay tactic intended to make me nervous.

"Depends on how you define 'okay.'" He looked up. "Thanks for coming in."

"What did she tell you?"

He tapped his pen on the table. "Oh come on, you must know the drill. I'm the one asking the questions."

"Whatever she told you, whatever she may have done—I think she was forced to do."

"By whom?" His smile faded.

I should tell him, I knew that. I rubbed my lips together.

Tell him.

I focused on the ceiling corner. Was I being videotaped? Did they have to ask for my permission? I didn't see any lights flashing. Only a spider web.

"Simone, I asked you to come in because Reine told us concerning details about the night of October thirty first. She said that you all were involved in some—and I quote, 'black magic.' Is that what would have 'forced' her?"

"No—"

"Because you can imagine what the media would do with that one. You'd be an anti-Islamic terrorist and a witch."

"I don't care about the media and besides, we played with a Ouija Board on Halloween, you can't say that's black magic, can you?"

"Fine, let's go back to what you told me earlier, about the book *L'étranger* by Albert Camus?" He moved a white coffee mug aside and shuffled a few papers on his desk.

"Your pronunciation has improved tenfold."

"*Merci beaucoup*." He looked up. "It's because I looked into *L'étranger*. So the protagonist kills an Arab."

"Voilà."

"In the book it felt as though Meursault killed the Arab quite haphazardly, wouldn't you say? I didn't quite see the point."

"That *was* the point."

He raised his brows, interested.

"And what about the other book, *Dangerous Liaisons*? Tell me, how long have you had a sexual relationship with your Professor?"

I jerked my head back and nearly laughed. "What?"

"You heard me. Are you sexually involved—"

"No."

Tell him.

I closed my eyes. I saw Hessa's bloody body slumped in the tub and I opened them quickly. Adam Chris grabbed a glass of water on his desk and pounded a few gulps, still watching me, his Adam's apple bobbling. He set the glass down with a thud.

"And *libérée.* The word you wrote in your book. Isolated just like it was when spray-painted. What does that word represent to you—why was it written above Hessa? Or on the French flag? Because she was Muslim?"

"I don't know. I don't think so."

"Could it have to do with sexual freedom, maybe? Your little dangerous liaisons?"

"I—"

"Like losing your virginity, couldn't that refer to it? *Libérée, libertine*—same thing?"

"I don't think I should answer any more questions." I stood, clumsily pushing my chair into the front of his desk and tightening my scarf just short of choking myself. Maybe this was where he'd stop me, tell me I wasn't allowed to leave.

"If you say so. I'll walk you out."

I took a few steps then stopped. "Detective, Hessa slept with Professor."

"Are you sure?"

"She told me so."

"Which professor? Just so we're clear."

"Our French Lit professor, who else? Listen, that's who you should focus on; I think this is bigger than just Hessa."

"What do you mean by that?"

"I'm not sure yet." He concentrated on the floor, his forehead tight in thought. I wanted to tell him. Tell about Hal Green and MKUltra. About Professor and her mind-control. But I needed more details. I'd once confessed seeing my Aunt Violette to Dr. Landau and it had ended disastrously—she thought I was crazy. I couldn't afford for the detective to think the same thing if I was way off base now.

"When did Hessa and your Professor sleep together, do you know? Several times or only once?" He looked up. "Who approached whom?"

"It must have been some time last year. The rest I just don't know."

"Okay," he said, nodding, eyes pensive. "Simone. What did you mean that if Reine was involved, she was forced? Who forced her?"

"I was just thinking out loud."

"Yeah but that's not the average thought. Not the average guess."

"Well, I'm not exactly average."

He picked something from his eye, a lash he then blew. "Simone, before you go, answer this. Do—do you think it's possible that Reine confessed to something she didn't do? That she wasn't forced to do anything rather that she's fabricating memories? Or protecting someone?"

Was he implying that she was protecting me? What about Professor?

He walked me back into the waiting room where Charlie's magazine sat alone on a chair. He opened the door to the outside, I guess I wouldn't stick around for Charlie. As I stepped out the sunlight harassed my dilated pupils and the crisp air froze my cheeks. I put on my red gloves and remembered what Reine had once said, *A curse doesn't have to be black magic, Simone, it can be a thought that haunts you to subconsciously fall into patterns that lead you to your greatest fears.*

"I don't know if Reine is protecting someone," I finally responded. "We'd had a fair amount to drink. So I'm sure her memory isn't perfect."

"The human memory is a funny thing. Have you heard of conversion disorder?" he asked. It sounded familiar. Had we talked about that in psych? I pictured the TA talking about it in his faded jeans and blazer with elbow patches. Did conversion disorder have anything to do with mind control?

"It used to be called hysterical blindness, but that's kind of an outdated term now. It's when there is no physical reason for the blindness, rather the brain has turned off the sense as a way of protecting itself."

What would Bertrand think of that. "Why do you bring that up?"

He shrugged and gave me his lopsided smile. "Just thinking out loud."

I tilted my head. "Yeah, but that's not the average thought. Not the average guess."

"Oh man, I walked myself right into that one." He slowly nodded. Solemn. "Well, Simone thanks for coming in." He took on a distanced, professional tone.

I was walking away when he said, "You know, the mind is a funny thing and it's hard for me to do my job when—"

"When what?" I said and turned.

"Oh, I don't know. Listen, Simone, just call me if you think of something that might help. It can be anything…seriously *anything*… that strikes you as abnormal."

Adam Chris didn't realize I was probably the worst judge in the world as to what classified as abnormal.

I walked off but was unable to stop myself from turning around for one last look at him. Wanting to know for certain if he was watching me. Watching me he was. He pulled out his phone and made a call. He didn't believe me.

Chapter 8

I paced outside the police station for twenty minutes waiting for Charlie. I called and texted but he didn't respond. So be it. I'd see him tonight at The French House for the first dinner since—Hessa died.

I decided to call Dr. Landau. I didn't remember the last time I used her phone number and debated with each ring whether or not to hang up, telling myself it probably wasn't even hers anymore. When she answered hello, I moved the phone away from my ear but brought it back just as quickly.

"Dr. Landau?"

"Yes?"

"It's Simone Duchamps."

There was a silence. Did she even remember? A decade has passed since we last saw each other.

"Simone!" she finally said. "I think you owe me a visit."

"I'm sure I do. But right now I'm hoping I can ask you something quickly."

"Of course."

"How powerful is the mind," I paused and swallowed to slow myself down. "When it comes to protecting itself?

"Limitless. What makes you ask that?"

"You know, just going through my memories."

"I'm not sure if you'll ever completely reorganize your memories again, Simone. But you can make peace with that. Like I said, this is better to speak about in person. You really should come in. We can talk about it."

"I will," I said. In the background I heard a dog barking. I tried to picture Dr. Landau, who worked from her home office ever since leaving the school. I envisioned a dim room full of plaid and leather chaises, a golden retriever waiting at the door wanting to go out to the rose garden. What kind of patients saw her there? How normal was I compared to them? I didn't want to know so instead I got to the point, "Do you know anything about mind control experiments happening at the University of Wisconsin? In the seventies."

The dog barked again, and I heard a door open and click shut. "What's this all about?"

"MKUltra? Have you heard of it?"

"What have you got your head wrapped around? Why this?"

"I know it sounds crazy, trust me. But I think my residence hall was once a part of mind control tests. And I think the experiments are still taking place and may even have to do with a recent death."

"*That* place? I saw it on the news—they're calling it counter terrorism."

"I know but they're wrong."

"Why is that?"

"I think it's my professor who's running the experiments now. She and her TA. Whether or not other departments are involved, I have no idea. But at some point they were, along with an ex-CIA agent who once worked with MKUltra and who I believe used the House to test mind control techniques."

"Christ," she said breathily.

"You believe me?"

There was a long pause.

"I do. My mentor was involved in MKUltra research so how can I not?"

"Who?"

"Carl Rogers. The man behind person-centered therapy—what I base my own therapy on. I don't know if he did anything unethical, I never read anything indicating that, but I know that during his years at the University of Wisconsin he accepted a lot of money from the MKUltra's board of Human Ecology."

"Can I ask you one more thing, Dr. Landau?"

"Like I said, anything—anytime."

"Can the mind erase?"

From her end of the line papers were shuffled. "Yes, Simone. The mind swipes memories that cause terror. Sometimes those memories are impossible to resuscitate. But the mind is equally susceptible to suggestion. Tell a witness they saw something they didn't actually see and nine times out of ten they'll believe you; they'll recount the planted details themselves later as if they were theirs all along. On top of that, they'll even add their own colorful additions. Our memories are malleable and each time we take one out it becomes open for editing and stored slightly differently than it was originally. It's this trait that makes us adaptable but it's also dangerous. There have been studies that proved we can convince someone they committed a crime they didn't commit. So you see, the mind erases just as well as it creates."

* * *

It was The French House's *l'heure du dîner,* our first dinner back, and the chandeliers emitted their same warm glow, the floors were more freshly polished than perhaps ever before, and the smell of tarragon and butter, baking bread, and breathing wines infused the home with welcome. A goddamn charade.

I hung my jacket in the closet and rushed to the kitchen to find Henri. Pots and pans bubbled on the stove and perfumed the air with red wine and beef: *boeuf bourguignon.*

"Where's Henri?" I asked Peter who was flicking sizzling onions in a sauté pan, but then I smelled it. Faint but sure, cigarette smoke from just outside the open window.

Henri was huddled in the corner on the terrace, cigarette in hand. He wore his chef's white uniform without the hat and acknowledged me with a quick nod.

"*Ça va?*"

"Mind control experiments," I said quietly.

He lifted his cigarette an inch to his lips and kept it hovering there.

"In this House."

He pulled in a drag. "It was a long time ago."

"Was it?"

Cigarette in hand he scratched between his brows with his thumb. I heard the French doors open and close behind me.

"Henri, Simone," Jackie greeted us coolly. She had gone extra lengths to avoid me since the day she'd given Detective Chris my book, or maybe vice versa.

Henri stubbed his cigarette on the iron railing then flicked it into the trees beyond.

"Sorry to interrupt, Henri, but I want to make sure you remember my new dietary restrictions?"

"Of course, Jackie. Vegan, right?"

"Since when?" I said.

"Since," she paused to sigh. "Since Hessa. I'm just so upset all the time. The last thing my stomach needs is a pile of cow."

Henri's eyes moved toward the heavens. He lit another cigarette. I didn't know if Jackie lacked the vocabulary for what she wanted to say or if that was what she had intended. Henri again squeezed the bridge of his nose; he must have had a hell of a headache.

"And also out of respect."

"For?"

She brushed her hair to the side. "Hessa."

"But Hessa wasn't a vegan."

"My God, Simone, do we have to keep dragging this conversation on? I mean, in light of it all, I don't need to be eating and drinking like your table of gluttons. I'm trying to find peace, center myself instead of going on like nothing happened, partying it up at dinner. But you guys go ahead—more for you!"

During her rant Henri had sucked down a second cigarette, put it out and sneaked inside.

I retreated to my glutton's table, my whole body on edge. Camille was the first to sit, pulling out the chair she always claimed, reaching for the decanter of wine and dumping a heavy red glug in her glass. She nearly returned the decanter to its place on the table before looking at me and holding it back up as a question.

Reluctantly I said, "Please." She filled mine carelessly to the rim. Charlie slowly lowered into his chair and motioned toward the wine. Camille filled his glass and he subtly raised it, murmuring, "Santé," always one to adhere to etiquette, but this nonchalance made me cringe.

"Guess what?" Camille said, drumming her fingers on the table. Her nails no longer painted black, they were now shiny and clear in a French manicure. "Reine reached out for legal help. Her father is flying in from Gabon."

When neither of us reacted Camille resituated herself irritably. "You don't know about her past, do you?" she said looking at me. She was right. Reine was always asking about my family life, my studies, my dreams. Come to think about it, she'd evaded all of my questions and I'd never pushed her. Not even after her weird comment about her mother. I'd spent more time asking her about Charlie.

"Reine comes from a family of witches."

"Oh come on—"

"It's true, remember all those horrific murders in Libreville a while back?"

"I barely recall my own past, so no."

"Well," Camille said pleased, "at the time Reine's father worked for the ALCR, the Association against Ritual Crimes, and while he was investigating a brutal and satanic ritualistic killing of a young girl in Libreville, he found himself confronted with the most horrific thing imaginable. His wife was involved in the killing; she thought herself a witch of sorts. What's worse is that when Reine's mother's ties to the satanic cult surfaced, she claimed it was deeply embedded in their family history and pleaded with Reine to carry it on, said it was her duty. That it was inevitable. So you see—she's always been a ticking time bomb."

I stared at her waiting for her to say more. So this was why Reine was always bothered when Camille made crass references to witches, and most of all, why Reine wanted to be nothing like her mother.

"You're suggesting Reine killed—?"

"The Mouse."

"Hessa," I corrected her. "Why can't you say her name?"

"Ladies," Charlie said quietly.

"Oh la-de-dah, respect for the dead." Camille lifted her wine glass.

Two tables over Jackie gave me a pursed lipped *told you so* look.

"Who did it?" I whispered. "I have a feeling you know."

"Guys—please." Charlie's tone turned angry.

"I believe we all do, actually," Camille mocked my whispered voice, then leaned into her chair and smoothed her potato sack of a sweater.

Henri came out of the kitchen and clanged his knife against his water glass, calling the room's attention, and standing in his tall white chef's hat. We turned to face him; Camille's eyes hot on my back.

Henri wiped his free hand on his pants and spoke of Hessa and the joyous young woman she was, the future that was taken from her. He said she had loved to read and write poetry. That she dreamed of learning to play the flute. That she had recently changed her major to social work, and that she had intended to return to Paris and help the youth in her neighborhood. With that I wrapped my arms around my stomach and swallowed what felt like a razor blade grating against my pink throat. I hadn't made enough of an effort to speak to Hessa; to know her or be her friend, and now it was too late. She would never become a flautist. She would never help anyone back home. Instead, those from her home would speak of her as a tale of warning. I clutched my arrowhead, said a few words to Maman. Aloud? I wasn't sure.

"It's their fault," someone exclaimed.

Everyone in the dining room turned our way.

"It's true," said Jackie. "They tormented Hessa."

"They never talk to the rest of us," said another.

"We're not here to assign blame," Henri said, spreading his arms wide as if he was a conductor trying to calm an orchestra.

Kate popped out of her seat, "Fault or not, this house is messed up. We moved here because it was supposed to be our chance to study French as if we were there. The moment we step through that door—" she pointed to the entrance, "—it would be like we were entering a new country. We'd be in France. But this simulation's not working. We're all trying so hard to be French and the actual French people alienate us," she said, as others nodded and mumbled in accord.

"I'd say you just captured the real France perfectly," said Camille. "Stop romanticizing it. You're in love with the language, the Eiffel Tower, the chocolate-fucking-crepes. The reality is actually much closer to what's happening in this House than you realize, in fact, it's pretty damned spot on."

"Well then I don't want to be French anymore!"

"Holy stereotyping," Camille murmured.

"Look what happens when you try to be like them—to fit in with them—you die."

"Translation, they kill you," someone added, I didn't know who.

"Camille and Simone, you were with Reine that night," Jackie said, slamming her palm against the dining table. It wobbled in reaction, momentarily snuffing the candle flames. "What'd you do to her?"

"*Calmez-vous*," Henri pleaded.

"This is hilarious," Camille said under her breath, a devilish smile tugging the edges of her lips. She took a laborious inhalation into her wine glass followed by a composed sip.

"We can host a separate meeting on house dynamics," Henri said, more forcefully this time. "Now is not the time."

"Isn't it?" said the first girl who had spoken. "If someone in this house is capable of…of—"

"Of what?" Camille asked.

The girl sat back down and looked away, blowing out a heavy puff of air that fluttered her bangs.

"My parents don't want me to live here anymore," Tim added.

"They're going to shut down The French House and even if they don't, we're going to lose our funding. I'd say we ought to talk about it as soon as possible," Jackie said.

"*Je sais, je sais.*" Henri's face was now red as my Pinot Noir. "We will, just let me," he shook his head as if to finish his sentence, but instead passed a stack of papers to circulate from table to table.

"It's your fault," Jackie said looking at me.

"Enough," said Henri.

"She's crazy. She once stabbed a girl at our school!"

Charlie turned to me, and Camille let out one dry, *oh*.

"Let me get through this—for Hessa. I'll set up a forum, but right now we're going to continue this dinner in peace for her. No more blaming. No more shouting. No more hate."

This earned sneers and more whispers, but the declarations ceased and the papers were passed: photocopies of a handwritten poem by Hessa. Henri had wanted us all to read it in unison but given the energy in the room I found it inappropriate. A girl passed a few sheets to our table, refusing to make eye contact with me. I grabbed them, passed the rest to Charlie and then looked down at the photocopy, at the feminine curls of penmanship. I'd seen this writing before. *Be careful.*

Chapter 9

A bright white light blared through the salon windows. It refracted across the floor and walls, transforming the room into a massive cubist painting. Through the window I saw a newscaster's van and journalist reporting behind camera. Either nothing notable was happening in Madison or they thought we'd act again soon and wanted to be there to catch us.

Despite everything we found ourselves playing our normal roles in the salon after dinner with poire eau de vie. In no way did I think it appropriate but was too frightened to sit in my room alone. Most other residents had already left the first floor, making sure we heard their low-voiced, cowardly accusations before walking upstairs to continue their discussions behind closed doors. Only Jackie, Kate, and Tim remained in the dining room, watching us like amateur spies.

Camille lay on her belly covering the length of the green velvet sofa closest to the fireplace, her legs pedaling back and forth like she was at a slumber party painting her nails. Charlie and I sat on the adjacent sofa. Missing of course was Reine, in the wingback she usually claimed.

"What are we doing?" I asked.

"We're enjoying a fire, *mon chou*, and one another's company."

"I'm going to call Adam Chris." I stood to add weight to my words. "I can't take it anymore."

Camille propped herself to a sitting position and pushed her glasses up her nose. "I wouldn't do that if I were you."

"Why the hell not?"

"Are you trying to implicate yourself?"

"Was I involved?" I asked, my voice loud enough to be heard from the dining room where Jackie and her friends stopped what they were doing, their saucers and cups clanging, and listened.

"You truly don't remember, do you?"

"No, I don't. I don't remember anything other than you coercing us to taunt Reine!" I reached for the first thing I found, fury sizzling my blood. I hurled a small vase from the bookshelf across the room. It shattered into a thousand iridescent shavings. "*T'es une chienne*, Camille! A true bitch! You don't get to con—"

"*Poète maudit*!" Camille said with a laugh, glancing at the broken glass before looking back at me with a smile. "I'm going to jot that Parnassian absurdity down." I watched as she did, she actually wrote it down, or wrote something in her journal. Charlie's eyes were wide as he stood.

I tried to compose my breath and ignore the comments about me coming from the dining room. But I was sick of holding everything in. "I know what's going on here. We're an experiment in this House. A control experiment—just like it was in the past."

"Simone," Charlie interrupted.

"Are you behind it, too?"

"Behind what?" I ignored him and turned again to Camille. "Did you prove what you had intended for your thesis?"

Camille's tongue twiddled around her mouth as though trying to free something stuck in a tooth. "I did."

Charlie turned to Camille, and slumped. "Jesus, what did you do?"

"You mean what did *we* do?"

"Oh my God," Charlie mumbled.

"Enough!" I screamed.

"Shhh, *Calmes-toi, mon amour*," Charlie whispered, grabbing my arms, pressing his finger to my mouth.

"You're worried they'll overhear what Simone's saying?" Camille huffed. "Maybe you should be more concerned about calling her *your love*."

"Why am I even here, I need to go home." Charlie said more to himself than either of us. He walked quickly to the coat closet despite his slight limp and got dressed in a rush. He finished tying a knot in his scarf and rubbed his hands over the span of his face.

"Where are you going?"

"I just told you, I'm going home, Simone."

"But you live here." I protested, grabbing his warm hands.

"With how much I've been hanging out here you'd think I did and," he took his hands out of my grip, "I'm going to get in so much trouble. *Je suis foutu.*"

"Trouble for what?" I asked, but I was already losing him. He bent forward and kissed my cheeks as though I were any old acquaintance, though it was better than the slap on the back he'd given me the other day. He opened the door and left without looking at me again. When it shut I leaned my head against the thick wood, closed my eyes. The image of Hessa in the tub ticked its way across the Milky Way behind my lids.

I waited too long to chase after him and by the time I made it outside, Charlie was nowhere to be found. Did he really not live in The French House?

The street was empty, eerily empty for this neighborhood. No protesters, no dogs barking, no joggers, no sirens, no distant conversations, no wind. Even the leaves were dead still, and all of the news vans gone. The only movement came from the lake, black and white capped waves under an oddly bright Venus. Yet I sensed someone watching me.

"Hello?" I wrapped my sweater tightly around me. "Charlie?" I thought I saw a shimmer of movement under the closest streetlamp, just at the edge of its golden triangle.

"Charlie?" I called again, but there was no one there. Except the one that always was. The statue.

"Who killed Hessa," I said to the bronze goddess. I swore she smiled at me.

* * *

I called Papa in the morning. I told him I'd come home later to make dinner and discuss the plan for expo in Paris. It was bait.

Papa was walking around the vineyard when I pulled up. I suggested we forage mushrooms for dinner and he followed my lead. On the dome of the hill, his breath was heavy, and I realized I was walking too quickly for him. I didn't allow him a break and instead picked up my pace as I entered the woods.

"Why is it that the poisonous are thriving so much?" My eyes locked onto a patch of *amanita phalloides*.

"It's the wet fall," said Papa catching up.

"Is that it?" I said before we went our own ways, gathering handfuls of nonpoisonous mushrooms before meeting again, inspecting one another's finds and returning home.

In the kitchen I sautéed our collection in a golden bath of butter and garlic and slopped them on crusty bread. The perfect snack to chase with a bottle of robust wine. I brought the toast to the table and set it in front of Papa, its aroma spiraling before him.

"Hal Green," I said.

Reaching for a mushroom garlic toast, he paused, and I noted a scarcely noticeable twitch and a wiggle of the ears, like a horse sensing danger.

"What do you know about him?"

"Not much," he said quickly.

"You worked with him for a whole year, you must know he was in the CIA."

"He didn't speak French and I spoke only a few English words. Our exchanges were limited to gestures and wine-related techniques. I have no idea…" he looked down "if he used to work in the government, why are you asking me this again?"

I folded my arms, kept my eyes glued to him.

He set his toast on his plate. "You've stopped taking your pills, haven't you? Your mind's on fire the way it once was—you're focusing on matters that have nothing to do with your reality."

"And what's my reality?"

"A brother and father who love you more than you grasp and who need you. I'm worried sick about the current vintage, about Bertrand getting through high school, and questioning why the hell the police want to speak to my daughter—meanwhile you're musing about the man who ran the vineyard before me."

It wasn't the time to voice my opinion, that I thought the two were connected. If he wasn't going to tell me—or perhaps he truly didn't know, I didn't need to waste my time pushing when I had other questions. Plus, it occurred to me how to finally get into Papa's lab. I'd ask Bertrand to do it when we were in Paris. I knew Papa kept the key hidden under a rock just outside, I'd watched him the last time I was home, I just never managed to get in there when he wasn't there or with me. I would ask Dr. Landau to help Bertrand with the search and reading of anything they might find. Whether or not she'd be up for the clandestine task was to be determined, but I had inkling her curiosity would overtake her ethics.

"So what's this idea of yours?" Papa asked. For a moment I thought he'd read my mind, understood my devious plan to search his lab. Then I remembered why I had come. To tell Papa my idea for the expo.

"Oh, that, I'll explain."

We transitioned from the old barn door dining table to the three-season porch. Every window displayed cerise leaves falling to the ground. "It's for the expo in Paris," I said. "But it's also for my class, my business development class. We've been assigned to create a plan to develop or rebrand a product—basically the same task the expo contest gave us." He took a sip of wine then analyzed its color in the rosy light streaming through the window.

"I know I'm an old-fashioned man but I don't think our wine needs to be rebranded."

"I know but—"

"My brother on the other hand would disagree," he interrupted, flinching slightly as he said the word brother. I knew that Papa feared my uncle Guillaume, who he claimed was the showy, creative one in their family, would unleash a brilliant plan at the expo. That he would bring Papa's family's winery to its glory. He'd reminded me several times again that if I cared anything for him then I shouldn't speak to my Uncle—the vengeful liar. He'd crossed our family and didn't deserve our time—I assume it went back to his affair with Maman. I agreed to Papa's request, but I had lied.

"But to your point," Papa went on, "that is what the expo asked of us."

"Exactly, and so my thought is this. All of our wines are marketed to people seeking help, *non*? Love potions, courage potions, those are our best sellers."

"Right," Papa concurred, eyes still on his wine.

"We need to unveil a polar opposite," I said, pausing to take a sip of the potion myself, to slow myself down. I thought about Professor's book and mastering pauses, controlling your speed of delivery to lure your target in.

My lapse caused Papa to shift to the edge of his seat, holding his wine glass so tightly it might shatter. "L'appel du Vide," I said. "The opposite of a potion—it's the wine calling *you*."

He grinned, the wrinkles at each corner of his eyes crinkling like tinfoil. "And to empty it no less."

Then. A crash.

Glass raining down.

"*Mon Dieu*!" I took cover. My first instinct. Was it an explosion?

"*Les cons*!" Papa shouted, bursting out of his chair and hurrying to his gun chest. He ripped his hunting rifle out, loaded it and opened the door, his feet crunching over glass.

"*Mais, qu'est-ce qui ce passe*?" I asked, still covering my head but daring to look around. There was a jagged hole in the window, a rock on the floor.

"*Reste-là*, Simone!" Papa barged out the door and fired a few shots into the air. They echoed into the sky. Geese honked. Wind blew. Papa returned to the porch and shut the door. What was the point, now that our window had a giant hole in it?

He set his gun down.

"We're not safe here," I said quietly. I remained crumpled on the floor. "We should call the police."

"Huh," Papa groaned. "They won't help us. And I'm not worried about cowards who throw rocks. Hicks from town using what you got involved with as an excuse to start this up again."

"Again?"

Papa sighed. "It used to happen when we first moved here. They'd throw eggs at our house, spray-painted *Go back home* a couple times. That one they did last week. I washed it off."

"Someone spray-painted here last week?"

"We're fine, Simone." He sat back into his chair and moved his hands through his black hair, which had turned far more silver than I remembered it. "As for your idea—" he closed his eyes, "that's the same sort of brilliance your mother had."

* * *

I decided to stay overnight at home. I was shaken, afraid to leave Papa and Bertrand there, not that I offered any protection. Maybe I was just as afraid to return to The French House.

I wanted to go upstairs and take a long hot shower. It was the only relaxing activity I could think of aside from drinking Papa's calming tea. I hadn't asked him for it in years, but tonight I begged for a cup before heading upstairs.

"Tea?" he looked at me, surprised. "How about a good glass of port instead? I'll get our twenty year out."

I brought my glass of port upstairs and turned on the faucet in the glass-enclosed shower. Nothing. I wiggled it. Nothing. Bertrand used the one downstairs, it was bigger and easier for him, and without my using this one, the mineral build-up must have clogged it.

I sat on the clawfoot's lip and sighed. I hated baths especially now, given the bizarre glimpses I recalled of Hessa in the one at The French House, but I filled it anyway.

It had been a bad idea.

Memories came on fast, the light reeling on the other side of my lids like a film. I had been there with Hessa.

I remembered.

Chapter 10

Thick blood, so thick it nearly curdled, chugged out of Hessa's wounds. I pressed my hands to the gashes knowing it was too late. Her life slipping out with the blood, eyes clicking from full tank to empty. I heard myself screaming, and my scream echoed in The French House's tiled bathroom, which tilted and rocked like a funhouse—"Help!" I pleaded, but there was no one. My words echoed over and over, losing all meaning.

In some ways this memory was a relief. I had tried to save Hessa's life. But how and why had I been there with her—and what happened before I tried to save her? What led her there? Had I been drugged? Brainwashed? Had Professor controlled my mind and made me do it? Or was it Camille? How did Hessa end up downstairs and outside? Had we carried her there—of this I had no memory.

Dr. Landau said the brain was capable of erasing memories deemed too terrifying.

* * *

It took an entire night of tossing and turning agony and three glasses of port but I'd made my decision come morning. I would tell Det. Chris what I remembered. There was no other way to go on.

I left my cell phone in The French House and would have to use the house line in the kitchen to call the detective. Bertrand and Papa were sitting around the island drinking coffee. I had no idea how long they'd stay there and refused to wait any longer—I had to get on with it. I said a quick goodbye and took off. But Bertrand followed, his light footsteps on the gravel behind me.

I turned around. "What?"

"Who is it that you need to call so badly?"

"What do you mean?"

"Oh come on, you stutter stepped around the phone several times. It was obvious." His voice cracked.

I was sad too. Sad that I didn't tell him, that I was drifting away. And yet for once I didn't need his advice. I knew he'd try to stop me if I were to tell him the truth, even if knowing in his heart it was the right thing to do, he would protect me until the end. But I had to confess what I remembered, tell the detective I'd seen Hessa die. Maybe it would help. Maybe I had played a part. "Bertrand, I'll fill you in later. But I have to go now."

"What is going on with you?"

I looked to the grey sky trying to prevent tears. "That's what I'm trying to figure out. I promise I'll fill you in later."

Before he said anything else I got in my truck and put her in reverse.

* * *

I called the detective from my bedroom in The French House; he told me to meet him at the Union Terrace.

"Wear a hat to avoid attention."

It was a warm afternoon for November. I didn't wear a hat but carried a sweater with me as I walked between the colorful tables. Students sat with pitchers of golden beer and foamy filled cups alongside platters of *bratwurst mit sauerkraut*. There was a jazz band setting up on the little stage nearby, a young group with loose fitting clothing and oversized winter hats. They played a catchy melody and I was thankful for the distraction.

I found Det. Chris sitting at an orange table facing the lake, tapping his foot. He wore the same black fleece as he had been the previous times we met. He had finally shaved, and his face looked boyish, soapy clean. The red webs no longer dominated his eyes and his periwinkle irises gleamed.

"I'm supposed to go to Paris soon," I said pulling out a chair.

"Never been." He dipped his head hello. "What's it like?"

"I don't remember. I was four the last time I was there." I looked at the calm water, small silver ripples was all it mustered on this windless afternoon. "But I guess what I'm asking for is, permission to go."

"Why would you need that?"

I shook my head and frowned. Let the music whorl around me for a few chorus lines.

"Simone," he said softly.

"I remember."

He nodded like he knew. Like he knew that eventually I would remember and that I was involved. I told him about the bloody bathtub. About the bleeding wrists. About Hessa's long-gone stare into oblivion. How I'd screamed for help and how I didn't know how I'd gotten there or why. I didn't know if she'd killed herself by slitting her wrists—or if we'd assisted or forced her. I'd drunk too much and the night was a mosaic of fractured memories.

I refused to go on without admitting my memory. I potentially owed Hessa Mifsud a lifetime of penitence.

Det. Chris did not respond right away. He chewed over my words with his pink bubblegum. Around us the happy students drank, shouted and flirted, danced and slammed beers, and high fived. They lived lives foreign to me. But I had been so happy in The French House for that short time, had found a place where I was challenged, inspired. The bickering and the tension were beautiful in their own way, a part of the thread that had bound us to one another.

What I had admitted hurt. But it felt good, too. What we call *la douleur exquise*. "Detective Chris," I said. "Do we need to go to the station for my statement?"

He looked down, rapped his fingers on the table a couple of times. "I tell you what," he finally said. "This case keeps getting more and more peculiar." He looked away from me and to the lake. For the first time all day I saw the wind's gentle whirr as it fluttered his hair. "While I know there is more to this story, and I'm damn determined to find out what it is, you're not a suspect, and you're free to go to Paris."

I shook my head. It was like a doctor refusing to admit what you were so certain you were sick with. "After everything I've just told you, how can I not be?"

"Because…" he picked a scab on his hand, then looked at me and put his hand behind his back. "We've got enough evidence to tell us what really happened."

"And what is that? Was it Professor? Did you figure out the simulation?"

"I can't say anything else. Besides, we're supposed to lay off the case."

"Because the CIA?"

He frowned. "Why would the *CIA* pressure us to lay off the case?"

"Because it trails back to their experiments." I put my head in my hands. It was throbbing. Was this the end of the line? The case would go unsolved like that in *La Vênus d'Ille*. Just as Professor wanted. I looked back at the detective. I knew he had something else to add.

"What?"

"No, I—"

"Tell me. Please."

His mouth was tight. "You really need to find your missing memories, Simone. Because," he sucked in his lips, "I keep having a nightmare about you. In it, you didn't kill Hessa rather you killed someone else, and I can't figure out who."

Book III

La Vénus d'Ille

Chapter 1
Paris

November 2022

Papa was grumbling as we boarded the Roissybus at Charles de Gaulle Airport. Something about how he's always hated Paris. He sounded like a caricature of a countryman, the typical Gaulois from the vineyard hills, twitching in reaction to the sounds and lights, the hordes of people, and the pace of the city. Additionally, the expo had him more anxiety ridden than I'd ever seen. He mumbled the tag lines I'd given him, perhaps imagining being forced to interact with journalists at our booth.

Unlike Papa, I was in love with Paris. The City of Lights and its golden halo, the beautiful people, the smell of steak frites, the endless bistro tables dotting the sidewalks. I wanted to get lost in every arrondissement and never find my way out. To live as though everything that happened was but a bad dream, start over here. It was not an option, at least not until I helped Reine, and the only way to do that was to prove Professor was manipulating us, using us as guinea pigs in her mind control research. I was relying on Bertrand and Dr. Landau to find incriminating documents in Papa's lab.

* * *

We found our hotel on a side street near Les Halles. The entrance cleared only a foot above Papa's head, and the lobby or lack thereof, made the last cheap place where Charlie and I stayed look like the Sofitel. It must have rained before we landed, dirty footprints covered the lobby's beige tiled floor. Two small wood chairs were pushed against a wall next to a shelf of tourist brochures. The check-in was more of a small window. From somewhere behind it a man was having a heated phone conversation, shouting with a thick accent about dirty thieves.

Papa dinged the bell. I was sorry I was leaving him alone at a time like this and lying to him on top of it all. I'd told him I would stay with Camille because she was my "best friend." I certainly didn't want him to know I was staying with Charlie.

The day before we departed Charlie had brought me to a cozy restaurant on the Capitol Square, apologized for his behavior, and begged me to stay with him in Paris. Over coffee and dessert, his hand running up my leg underneath the table, I'd agreed. I cursed myself for not being stronger, for remaining so hopelessly optimistic. I knew it would be far more heroic to tell him to forget he ever knew me, but the look in his eyes still made me relentless with desire.

We walked down a dim corridor and Papa inserted the key into his hotel room door. The room was dark and smelled of years' worth of cigarette smoke wrapped into stale cushions. I pulled the shades on the window to the side to reveal a view of a brick wall. No reason to linger.

I freshened up in the bathroom then Papa and I agreed to meet at the expo tomorrow three hours before it opened. I didn't have time to go to Charlie's to change and shower as originally planned if I were to make it to dinner with Camille and Charlie on time. And I certainly didn't want to miss a second: Camille had promised to tell us all about her thesis at dinner, at La Tour d'Argent.

I texted Charlie. He told me to bring my suitcase to the restaurant and he'd have his driver pick it up and return it to his parent's flat. I changed in a bathroom on the ground floor, applied my lipstick, and asked the front desk clerk to call me a taxi.

* * *

The view of Notre Dame against Paris' pink sky was type of place I imagined marriage proposals to take place as a little girl, or maybe the backdrop in a Madeline book.

"Vos amis, Mademoiselle," the maître presented Charlie and Camille with a slight bow, they were mid-discussion but Charlie noticed me first, ticked his head to the side and Camille quickly turned to see me. They stood to kiss my cheeks. Camille in a shapeless velvet eggplant dress that hit just below her knees. She was alarmingly elegant sans duckboots and in five inch black heels. Charlie wore a maroon velvet smoking jacket and black bowtie. I wished I'd had time to prepare at his parents' apartment before dinner if only to break the foreignness of seeing them in their full splendor, glammed up in a manner they hadn't been since the banquet. Charlie assured me his family's driver was already en route to retrieve my suitcase.

A green bottle of Dom Perignon reclined in a sweating wine stand next to the table. Camille motioned to a waiter to fill my flute. Charlie concentrated on his cufflinks, twirling and reclasping. As the waiter poured my champagne he informed me that my meal had already been ordered.

Camille raised her flute and we toasted. The champagne tasted like pears and brioche.

"Notre Dame's buttresses, they look like Clydesdale legs, don't they?"

"Oh, *ma coquine*, let's not bore ourselves trying to describe the view."

"*D'accord*."

"Let's talk about something more interesting, shall we? Our interrogations. You know, the way the Detective went on about you throughout my interrogation I thought," she sniffed. "Well I thought maybe you two..." she twirled her finger in the air as if it clearly finished her sentence.

Two lines between Charlie's eyebrows deepened. Beyond him my attention pulled to a woman a few tables away—Professor. *Is that you?* I scrutinized the figure until Charlie and Camille turned to follow my gaze, distracting me enough to lose her. The woman stood and walked off, a glittery emerald dress disappearing behind a server hoisting a large tray.

"Looking for the detective, *mon chou*?"

"No, I'm not, and you're really reaching here, so why don't we talk about whatever it is that you want to talk about. I don't know what you're implying about Detective Chris."

"Oh!" Camille laughed, touching her clavicle softly with her hand. I sat still waiting for her to get to her point.

Our waiter presented us each with *soupe glacée*. Camille continued after he walked away.

"You gave Mousey Girl—"

"Hessa," I corrected.

She blinked, long and heavy. "Of course, *Hessa*. You gave her your book by Anne the Butcher, didn't you? Do you think that book had anything to do with her death?"

I shook my head and looked at Charlie. By the resigned face he made I knew he was in no mood to play referee.

"What the fuck are you getting at?"

Camille looked around, playing mortified. "Shh, *ma minette*, we're not at McDonald's. Now think about my question with a different angle and you can figure it all out, I know you can. The book. The lesson. Hessa."

"Please, Camille, just tell us—tell me," I lowered my spoon, "I'm sick of all of these riddles." I saw Camille raise an eyebrow at Charlie, but she let me go on. "We owe our thoughts to helping Reine and if incapable of that then let's discuss the weather or even the view." I extended my hand toward Notre Dame. Beyond it, the Conciergerie. I pictured Marie Antoinette there when it served as a prison, frail and emotionally destroyed, waiting her day at the scaffold.

"What I'll tell you is this," Camille said, "The last time I went in, I stole a report from Chris's desk."

"You what?" said Charlie.

"The idiot went to the bathroom and I grabbed a snapshot of it on my phone. They weren't exactly running a tight ship over there. The report was from the chem and tox labs. Results from Hessa's skin, hair, and clothing fibers. One stood out above all others. A toxin known as *amanita*—"

"*Puitan*," I whispered.

"What," Charlie said. "What is *amanita*...?"

"*Amanita phalloides*," I said, "is a deadly mushroom. So that's how she died? She was poisoned?" Then why did I remember blood?

"Why should we believe you, Mimi?"

"Because I leaked the official document to the press this morning," Camille shrugged. "It's public knowledge by now. Even CNN mentioned it—that's a television station by the way, I know both of you are so out of touch, that that one may have eluded you."

"Jesus, of course you ordered us the *vol-au-vent aux champignons*."

Camille ignored him. "Our little media darling, Jackie, already commented on the news. She told them that she grew up near you. And that everyone in your town knows you have poisonous mushrooms on your land. To make matters worse, she too leaked a document."

"What document?"

"Document is the wrong word, it was more of a kid's notebook—the name 'Simone' sprawled childishly across it, underneath a unicorn. Like a recipe book and it had an awful lot of information about mushrooms."

"She went through my things?"

"That's what you're concerned about?"

Charlie pulled out his phone and by the looks of it, started his own search.

"What?" I asked him. "What does it say."

"What doesn't it say?" Camille said. "You know how small-minded people are, Simone. They love to rally in times like these, share an opinion, earn a spotlight. It seems everyone in your town has something they want to add about you, your family—and your instability. Hashtag Psycho Simone."

"She framed me," I said. I didn't mean Jackie, she may have found my old unicorn notebook but this was beyond that. This was Professor's work, and I would need Dr. Landau and Bertrand to find something in Papa's lab linking her to Hal Green and his sick experiments. Given the time it was now, it was likely they were going through his lab at this very moment. They'd told me they would email any updates they had.

"Framed you, *hein*?" Camille said. "Can you prove it?"

"Enough, Camille," Charlie said sternly. "Let's change the subject."

"Should not the paying party drive the conversation?"

"*Oh là là* how bourgeois of you to have to remind us that you're paying," Charlie said, "We're not at McDonald's." He imitated her voice.

That stopped Camille for a moment or two, as she calculated her next move.

"What's he like," she asked after her pause. "In bed." She nodded toward Charlie but held my eye. Charlie and I both deflated visibly enough to send the waiter our way to ask if we needed anything. After he ambled off Camille returned to her quipping. "I was always rather fond of his skills." She exaggerated a tongue roll, causing Charlie to clatter his spoon against his plate loudly enough to cause a few looks to sneer our way. He grabbed Camille's wrist tightly as warning. She smiled.

I ignored them, my mind still reeling over Professor. Hessa had said that she was paying the price of sleeping with the devil. What happened after their affair? I remembered seeing Hessa leave Professor's office that first day I went there, she'd run off crying. But Charlie too, had been in Professor's office and he had followed her. Did he know her secret? Was he a part of it—yet another triangle?

"Charlie," I said.

"Let me guess," Camille interrupted me, her hazel eyes widening behind her thick glasses. "Charlie told you he's falling in love with you. That it's love, not lust."

Instinctively I pushed my chair back and stood, placing my napkin on my plate. "*Bonne soirée*," I said to them both, already making my way to the coat closet.

"Simone," Charlie called, but I did not turn around. I didn't want to see the looks the other patrons were giving us as Charlie's hands grabbed my elbows.

"Simone, listen to me, I never told her that. Those words were for you and only you." He pulled my arm. I told him his recycled *bon mots* were of no interest to me and walked out of La Tour d'Argent.

* * *

Tears rolled down my cheeks as I walked along the Seine. Boat after boat passed, the famous *bateaux mouches*, each one packed with happy couples holding selfie-sticks and clicking shots of themselves to immortalize their Parisian river ride. I walked on and the more distance I created the more I felt—*libérée*.

And yet how free was I after what Camille had said? It was possible the police were at our property now, collecting samples of our mushrooms to link me to Hessa's death. The detective said in his dream I killed someone else—who? The only death I'd experienced in my life was Maman's and I had nothing to do with it. Right?

I sat on the quay and looked into the shiny waters, knowing the night would stretch long and taffy thin with my torment. A part of me hoped the detective would be waiting for me at the wine expo come morning, cuff me, and bring me home. And yet something told me it wouldn't be Adam Chris I'd see there, it would be the woman shadowing me all this time. The woman controlling my mind. Professor.

Chapter 2

Paris had yet to fully rise at seven a.m., the freshly washed sidewalks were empty. I passed Église Saint Eustache then walked down rue Montorgeuil and all its charming restaurants and traiteurs. The smell of rising croissants from the corner patisseries filled the air. I was headed for the textiles district where immigrant workers busily escorted their shiny naked mannequins down the cobblestone streets and into couture workshops. When I sensed the dummies' black eyes on mine I couldn't shake the feeling that it was Professor on my trail.

There was a bell labeled "Derosiers" on the first floor. I would make it quick—all I wanted from the visit was access to a computer and my suitcase. No words, no fights, nothing more. I wasn't upset with Charlie. I didn't think that the man to deflower me would end up being the love of my life. This was my fault. I was the true idiot. I missed Bertrand. I missed Sam, Kip, and our easy walks in the forest. I guess that's what we call, *nostalgie de la boue.*

Another resident arrived to the Derosiers building, eyed me suspiciously, and buzzed herself in. She carried a bag of piping hot croissants in a dainty crumpled sack, their buttery aroma making me salivate as she pranced in front of me. I mumbled "Derosiers" and she reluctantly allowed me inside. Perhaps Charlie's parents took in enigmatic visitors like me frequently. Though I certainly did not embody the image of the girl you'd hope your son would bring home, showing up in the morning wearing last night's red cocktail dress. Social media's favorite new pyscho.

Chez Derosiers was very different than I'd pictured it. It was a stark comparison to Charlie's style. Charlie embodied the past, with his berets and corduroys. In contrast, his parents' taste was mod-minimalist. He had warned me how despite their age they thought they were the coolest couple to grace Parisian streets, that they were hipsters at heart, wore JC de Castelbajac every day, and ate sushi for breakfast as they went on about the importance of an alkaline diet. Cement floors sprawled from room to room, smooth and slippery. Giant silver lamps hung from the ceiling, their bulbs subtly changing from rosy pink to baby blue. The tables were all empty except for a glass paperweight on one. I had walked closer to have a look, surprised by its familiarity. It was the same exotic butterfly paperweight as the one on Professor's desk. Perhaps Charlie bought it for her. *Overthinking, Simone*, I heard Dr. Landau's raspy voice.

Charlie embraced me upon arrival but I pushed him away. All I wanted was my bag, and then to return to my father's sad hotel, shower and rush to the expo. Charlie's mother joined him. She wore an oversized fluorescent green sweater that drowned her petite frame along with leather leggings. She placed a hand on his back, smoothed his hair. I had a feeling her doting was constant, as Charlie didn't seem to register it at all.

"Simone Duchamps," she said stepping toward me. In her voice I heard Charlie's. Smooth as cinnamon, warm and spicy. She must have been at least a decade older than Papa, possibly more. I'd place her around sixty-five—a very glamorous sixty-five. Maybe Charlie was her miracle boy.

"I'm so sorry to intrude on your morning this way," I said, thinking about Professor's book: Do not apologize for hackneyed occurrences. By doing so you empower others and lower your stature.

"Charlie's been worried about you," she said, blinking her hazel eyes, just like Charlie's.

"We had a little spat," I said, patting down my hair. "I thought it best to gather my thoughts and have Paris as my night's companion."

"Oh!" Madame Derosiers boomed. "I love this girl. I wish I was more like you!" She pointed at me and twitched her head around looking for Monsieur Derosiers. As if cued he entered, in a black button-up chemise and lavender trousers. Unlike Madame, he looked nothing like Charlie: slick black hair, blue eyes, and a tan, leathery face.

"Please, join us for breakfast." It was then I noticed the chopsticks in his hand and had to stifle a laugh.

"Thanks," I said quietly. "First though, would you mind if I checked my email? Do you have a computer?" Per usual, my phone had died.

Charlie's mother laughed. "We do happen to have a computer," she said winking. "Follow me."

Charlie followed too but I whispered to him to wait for me elsewhere. He sulked off, his mother leaving soon after. I entered the University of Wisconsin webmail server. There were emails from Jerry and Dan but I didn't read them. The one email I feared would be in my inbox was, indeed, there.

Chapter 3

The Detective's email was vague. All he asked for was my return date. Maybe he would be waiting for me at customs in the airport.

I wrote him back and reminded him to focus on Professor. "The House is a simulation," I wrote, "and has been for a long time—a simulation for something sinister and evil, an experiment."

What kind of idiots were he and his team that they weren't already all over this? Idiots, idiots, the world was full of them, as Camille had said. Maybe he was an idiot, I probably was too, but I hoped he'd take me seriously. He did, after all, look into the theme of the three books Professor assigned us. But why didn't he link the clear connection back to her as the master architect? Enough evidence was probably in her office alone, like the ripped page from *Les Liaisons Dangereuses* I'd found on her desk, with quotes about vengeance. Could he search her office without her consent? Or sample mushrooms on my land without Papa's and mine? I was about to log out of my email when a new message popped up.

On November 26, 2022, at 10:20 A.M. From Agatha Landau info@landaupsychiatry.net

> *Simone,*
>
> *Read the attached and call as soon as you can. Your father's lab was overflowing with Hal Green's documents. All of them behind that shelf you suspected. I sent only one. Your brother said you'd probably find this*

one most interesting. The rest we'll discuss when you're back.

- Dr. L

My hands started shaking, my heart ricocheting. I had no idea when I'd get the chance to check my email again. There was a printer next to the computer. I printed out the document, deleted the email, and logged out of my email. Charlie's mom was humming a cheery tune, steps away from the door, back to check on me. I rattled my fingers on the printer as it whirred.

"Simone?"

I ripped the first page out of the printer.

Madame Derosiers stepped in the room. She looked at the paper in my hand, then at the other one making its way out of the printer.

"I have finals when I get back," I said. "Last minute studying."

"I don't miss those days for a minute. Come." I stuffed the papers in my bag. "I can take that for you." She reached for my bag and reluctantly I let her grab it. She escorted me to the dining table, hanging my purse on a hook in the hallway.

The Derosiers' dining table was a preposterously large white circle surrounded by black blobs, which served as chairs. They were backless and rounded, and I sat on one gingerly, like the thing might scurry away. In the middle of the table a tray of elaborate maki and nigiri glistened. Madame passed me an iridescent blue clay plate with two sections, along with a pair of beautiful chopsticks. I'd only ever used the splintered wooden disposables from Sushi Express on State Street. I struggled to bring an oversized tuna roll into my mouth.

"Charlie says you're just a freshman," Madame prompted, as a glob of wasabi struck the back of my tongue. My eyes welled and my nose ran in compliment.

"Simone," Madame said, her formerly line-free face creasing. She took me to a washroom, a sort of cement box with a bizarre square toilet and lighting so dark it would pass for a nightclub. All I wanted to do was grab my bag from the hook, leave the Derosiers residence and find somewhere quiet to read the document Dr. Landau had sent.

"Maybe you'd feel better after a shower?" Madame suggested scrutinizing my coif. She tugged open a drawer from a steel cabinet at her side and took out a plush gray washcloth and a metallic tube of emollient cream. She wet the towel and dabbed the lotion onto it, then wiped my face as though I were her four-year-old covered in ice cream.

"You're quite the tigress by the way, so much younger than my boy and yet look at you, you've got him completely wrapped around your finger from what I can gather." She stood back, dropped the towel in the sink, and crossed her arms, observing me like a painting she admired. She must have loved Pollack.

"I'm not that much younger," I said, turning to look at myself in the mirror, which glowed with an eerie purple light. Seeing my reflection proved that with one clean swipe she'd managed to remove all of my make-up. I again looked ingénue and fresh, my skin supple. With the nakedness of my face perhaps I looked younger than I was.

"Darling, you're quite a bit younger than my Charlie."

"I'm nineteen," I said, meeting her eyes through the mirror where she stood behind me. Did she think I was a freshman in high school? "I'm nineteen."

"That's adorable. *N'inquiètez pas*, I don't judge. You clearly put a spell on my Charlie, so whatever makes him happy. I know it's a risk, but as long as you're both discreet." She turned around to open a disguised cupboard door and handed me the larger version of the plush gray towel.

"All I ask is that you take good care of my darling boy. Ever since his knee injury, he's been a bit—needy. Can you imagine, though? He lost his dream. Now this drama at your university, my poor boy." She held my eyes for an elongated moment, then pressed her finger into small silver button causing a rain shower to spill down from the ceiling at my side. There was no shower curtain or even glass partition. Did she expect me to undress in front of her the way Professor had? No, she slipped out of the bathroom and left me to my own devices.

Droplets coursed over my weary body, wiping away the Parisian night. As I soaped myself, I questioned what she meant that I was "quite a bit younger." It was then I noticed the bathroom door slightly cracked open and Charlie's wild eyes watching me.

I stepped out of the shower, careful not to slip as my wet feet squelched across the cement floor. Water dripped from my hair, my nose, my shoulders, my breasts, and Charlie studied every drop. He smiled his wide, lecture hall performance smile. I shut the door in his face.

Chapter 4

There she was. Professor. At the Centre Pompidou for the wine expo. No longer in the glittery gown as at the restaurant last night, but in a chic black wrap dress and red heels, and already inside the museum while I remained in line at registration, squirming like a toddler in fear of losing her as I waited for a slow-moving man with binoculars for glasses to create my vendor ID.

By the time I received my badge and entered the vast museum I'd lost her. But I kept my eyes alert and it helped me spot the *L'appel du Vide* banner above our booth. Jerry and Dan were more artistic than I'd given them credit for. Jerry dappled in photography and had asked to photograph me for the wine's label. He suggested I wear a long flowing white dress "like a ghost's". We went to the Arboretum, not far from the spot I'd spent with my group the night of the banquet. The photo we chose was black and white, my side profile at the edge of a pier, the still lake and forest beyond. Dan had cut multiple slits into my dress and in the photo they fanned about in every direction. Jerry doctored the image so that it was hazy and Dan provided the artistic font.

"Where have you been?" Papa's face was taut. In a scratchy voice I replied, "*partout*". The last twenty-four hours in Paris may as well have been a year. "Why don't you start by having a quick look around," he suggested. "Scope the competition and report back."

I knew this to mean: spy on Guillaume, see if his is better than ours. All I wanted to do was read the document from Dr. Landau but sensing Papa's eyes I went off for my search.

There were over a hundred booths but I spotted Guillaume's rather quickly. It was hard to miss my own last name: Chateau Duchamps, written on a purple banner above his booth. What might have been. Would he recognize me? Did he know I was coming—that Papa and I had entered the expo? Hanging above his booth was a bizarre art installation, a group of mannequins that reminded me of those getting strolled about naked in Le Sentier neighborhood. These mannequins however were suspended from various levels, some upside down, others right side up, all of their soulless black eyes surveying the crowd of eager winemakers. Some, I noticed, had deformities—an extra hand, a third eye. Others had rashes grafted onto their plastic skin, or odd patches of hair. Dangling beside them were several deformed fish, a two-headed cow, and a wine glass filled with fluorescent green liquid.

I picked up a pamphlet and learned that it was supposed to represent chemical farming, the horrors derived from genetically modifying crops and dousing them with pesticides and herbicides. The other scene represented the opposite: organic farming. In this scene was a blanket atop thick green grass where a happy mannequin couple lounged next to a quintessential picnic basket with red and white gingham lining. Spread before them was a delectable assortment of charcuterie, cheeses, and wine.

"*Alors, mademoiselle! Qu'en pensez vous?*"

The man was nearly identical to my father, the thick wave of black and gray hair, the fiery copper eyes, and yet he looked younger—quite a bit younger, despite that he was three or four years older than Papa as far as I knew. Perhaps he was less stressed, having had the family vineyard handed to him along with all of my grandparents' estate, not a penny of debt.

"Simone," he said, his face lighting with recognition. "*Mon Dieu*, you're the spitting image of your mother," he shook his head, and studied me so intensely I became uneasy. "There's not an ounce of your father in you." I wasn't sure if it was a dig against my father but I did love being compared to my mother. Bertrand and I both looked so much like her. It must have been difficult for my father to see us sometimes, only to be reminded of the woman who died too soon. And of course I couldn't help but wonder what Guillaume's relationship had been with Maman, if it was true they'd had an affair.

Guillaume walked around the other side of his booth and greeted me properly, kissing my cheeks and squeezing me tightly. I remained stiff as a board, his energy confusing me, the familiarity of it, the years passed, the moments gone and the chance to change that right here and now.

"*Et alors*, answer my question, what do you think?" He gestured toward his toxic mannequins, but I kept my eyes on the happy picnicking couple instead.

"Very clever," I said, a safe response.

He nodded. "And your unveiling, the *L'appel du Vide*, whose idea was it? Yours or his?" There was a twinkle in his eye that rang familiar. A twinkle that Papa had possessed once, too, so very long ago.

"It was mine. And some…friends'."

"*Bon*, now that I know the idea is yours, I can say well done. Our ideas are not so dissimilar." I did not see how they were similar in any way, shape, or form and my face must have shown it. "Polar opposites. We've both provided two contrasts. Our display of organic versus chemical, and you with your potions and call of the void antidotes. *C'est adorable*."

Adorable. Did no one take me seriously? Maybe he'd read my expression, because he took on a much more serious tone, leaning in so close to me that I faintly smelled cigar. "Listen, Simone, I imagine you don't know the reason for your father and I falling out. Just know this, the version you were told is the wrong one—"

"I'm here now," I interrupted him, "I want to know."

"Guillaume!" a woman called, a vixen in black dress, a mole above her lip.

"Duty calls," he said, leaning in and kissing my cheeks, "May the best man win!"

"Or woman."

"Don't forget what I said," he whispered. "Find me later."

"I absolutely will."

Chapter 5

Our booth remained busy from the moment the doors opened to hours after the supposed last call. I struggled to remain engaged but anxiously waited for a moment to sneak away, to read Dr. Landau's document then return to Guillaume's booth and ask for the full story.

"*J'adore ce concept*," one of the judges told me after sipping a rather large amount. "I'm going through a divorce and need the call of the void to tell me my next move." I instantly related to her, thinking of how I'd run out of La Tour d'Argent last night.

"Fucked our nanny," the judge went on, as if our wine was also a truth serum. She paged through our recommended pairings recipe book, experienced the scent box and told me about her soon-to-be ex-husband as though she were lying on the leather chaise in her psychotherapist's office.

"Simone," a voice in my ear, a warm hand on my back.

"Uncle Guillaume."

"Do you have a moment—the day is passing by. It is so great to see you, all grown up and," he shifted around and his eyes froze on Papa who was pouring a glass of wine for a judge. "Quickly, I don't want him to see us."

"Let's get a coffee?"

He ushered me away and to the coffee bar at the other side of the expo where he ordered us each a café au lait. We sat at a glossy blue table, each of us silently sipping until he spoke.

"Simone," he said, "is everything okay at home—are you okay? And Bertrand?"

I lowered my coffee. "Because of what happened at The French House?"

"No," he said looking confused, "I mean—in general."

"Papa can run a winery on his own even if he lost the one he was born into, if that's what you're asking."

"It's not, Simone."

I frowned. "What did my mother do that your father gave the entire vineyard to you and not Papa? Was it because she had an affair with you—I know she loved you; I found an old letter of hers."

Guillaume closed his eyes; his lids were thin and papery. His lips began to tremble and for the first time his face looked wrinkled and aged like Papa's.

"I don't know where to begin to make you understand how we got to this place." He rubbed his eyes and swallowed hard. "Let me start at a time before your mother came along. And to understand the dynamic you must know that your father and I had always been very competitive, over grades, our parents' praise, and of course over girls too. And I know that most brothers are but this was different. Our parents were a little loony themselves—why else would they name their second son the derivative of their firstborn's name? It's like they set Guy up to hate me—to forever try to knock me out of first place to claim it for himself. But anyway, let me take you to the summer after my last year of school when a family from Australia came to our small town—just a father and his daughter. He'd been struggling with his vineyard and wanted to study the vine-training system we used in Bordeaux. Your father and I were smitten with the girl—Cassie was her name. Perhaps your father more so than me, but he never was real smooth with the girls so he put all his time into creating a new vine-training system for Adam—Cassie's father, based on the maps Adam had given of his vineyard in Australia. I think he thought if he won over the dad he'd win over the girl. Months went by during which all of us spent a good amount of time together, and Cassie was a good girl, she didn't lure one of us over the other, we were, the three of us, best friends—as best you could be given the competition buzzing between us. Then one day I came across your father's old notebook, he always kept one around, was always taking impeccable notes and making the best observations. I looked inside and saw he'd designed an ingenious vine-training system for Adam, it was something new and yet I knew immediately it was going to work." Guillaume paused and shook his head. "Then I took it—and privately presented it to Adam as my own work. And God—things spiraled from there. We were having dinner, both our families together when Adam said I saved him with my design, that he'd take it back home next month to try. Guy knew immediately what I'd done and lunged over the dinner table to physically attack me. My father wouldn't have any of it and separated us after that. We were to work in different areas, go to church for different masses, and never come together not even at the dinner table—from then on our mother served an early supper for Guy and a late one for me." Guillaume sipped his coffee and looked past me. "It worked for a while. We lived our separate lives and then your father met your mother Lisette. They were married and had you and Bertrand and everything seemed good until—until the phone call."

"What phone call?"

"From Australia. It was Adam telling my dad how the vine-training system worked, that over the years it had completely transformed his vineyard, and that he'd told everyone about the genius Frenchman name Guillaume who designed it. Phone calls came after that, from newspapers, television stations, and before I could do anything to stop it, my name was published in industry magazines as the inventor of what was actually Guy's design—and they called it the Guillaume Method. It was too late to reverse, everyone assumed Guy and Guillaume were one and the same name anyway, and even if they didn't, there's already a vine-training system called the Guyot Method. To this day winemakers refer to the Guillaume Method and it was all your father's work. But back to that day when your father Guy found out he lost it. And it just so happened I was at one the village's summer parties, and that's where Guy found me and beat me to a pulp. Our parents heard about the commotion and rushed over to find Guy practically killing me." Guillaume looked into his coffee then took a last sip. "That night he ordered Guy to leave for a year—told him to work on another vineyard and come back a grown man or he'd lose his share of the family vineyard. But it was too late in the summer to find a decent internship at any respectful winery and I guess that's how your father ended up in Wisconsin—a place we'd never heard of and had to locate on a map."

"You never told your parents what you did?"

He shrugged. "Of course I did, and I apologized more times than I can count. I was a greedy eighteen-year-old who had acted like an ass. They didn't care about that. It was Guy they were mad at—they always put more pressure on him."

I pushed my coffee aside, unable to stomach any more stimulants. "When does my mother come in?"

"Right well, your father went to the States and while he was there your mother began to have concerns. Said his letters sounded strange. He kept asking her to send him old botany books our grandma used to keep and we were having a laugh over it, like what the hell was going on in the U.S.? Did they not even know what kinds of plants grew on their land—was it that unchartered? But he was jealous too—threatening your Mom not to talk to me, and I think that drew us closer. But nothing happened between us—not then at least." His cheeks flushed pink, and he looked away. "When your father returned he was different. Darker. Was it your culture that changed him? I don't know."

"My culture? I'm French, too, you know," I bristled at his finger pointing. "Maybe it was Hal Green, the winemaker in Wisconsin. What do you know of him?"

"Nothing really, I only know that when your father came back his interest in herbs had grown into an obsession—he tinkered with them constantly. And he'd become manipulative—about everything."

"If he's so manipulative then shouldn't he have been the one to end up with the entire vineyard—half of his birthright? You're the one who got it. Why? He said it was Maman's fault. What did she do? Or maybe I should ask what you did in order to win it all."

"Simone, this was all of your father's doing. He convinced our father to write me out of the will."

"Then why did you get the vineyard? And what did my mother do?"

"She did her job, that's all. It never had anything to do with her, he only convinced her to take the blame, the piece of shit coward that he is.

It was when I caught on to what he did that our father wrote him out of the will. I've still got your mother's work, and I'm keeping it for you and your brother. I didn't know how to get into contact with you to tell you. Your father would never let me through to you, I can't believe he came here. How'd you convince him? Never mind I don't need to know. What's important is that we find a way for you and Bertrand to get what your mother inadvertently left you. We need to do it without him knowing. He's evil, Simone."

It was my instinct to defend my father. And yet he'd cut me with an arrowhead, slapped me across the face. Still, I had forgiven him for these acts. He lost his wife, was now losing his daughter, and his son too, was growing up and leaving him alone and vulnerable.

"He's not evil," I said, and suddenly someone gripped my arm. *Papa.*

"I told you not to speak to him, Simone. He's a liar and a sick man." Papa shoved his pointer finger into Guillaume's chest and my uncle stumbled back. "Filling my daughter's head with lies? Haven't you taken enough from me?"

"You, *you*, it's always about *you*!" Guillaume shouted rebalancing. "What about your daughter? What about your dead wife!"

Everyone sitting at the petit café tables looked up. Papa pushed Guillaume. Guillaume waved his arms in a circle once before he fell and slid across the polished floors in theatrical fashion, his shiny black shoes in the air. He landed on his butt and then lay flat on his back and emitted a low moan.

Two men in security uniforms rushed to our side. They didn't care to hear the story and showed us to the door.

What had my mother inadvertently left me? What had she done—or made? I was still no closer to understanding what transpired to make Papa lose his share of the vineyard. Was I to stay in France and find out? Claim whatever it was my uncle was saving for me and Bertrand?

As the Pompidou's door closed, I saw Professor standing by the Stravinsky fountain, its bobbling skull just beyond her shoulder. Sun poured over the Marais, her hair, the bubbling water.

She waved and turned to walk away. Her magenta dress rippling behind.

"Professor—wait!"

"Simone, come on." Papa clutched my hand in a hot grasp and rushed me back to his smelly hotel room with its brick wall view. I told him I didn't feel well, then closed myself in the stale smoke infused bathroom to look at the document I printed. It was hard to read, a scanned image of Hal Green's cat scratches. But I was able to make out a name in his script: Anne-Marie Fisker.

Chapter 6
Scanned Document: Hal Green's Notes

Project: Danaus Plexippus

This project was created with the purpose and devotion of studying the effects of:

- *Substances that alter personality*
- *Substances that create temporary amnesia*
- *Long and short term hallucinatory effects*
- *Behavior control and manipulation, specifically creating distrust in another a person or group of persons*
- *National identity & ability to enhance or reconstruct it*

Test Subject: Maria Fisker

Upon first meeting the subject it was apparent she was enamored with French culture and loved living at The French House. We invited the subject to attend meetings under the pretense that she was helping the psychology department with research on premenstrual syndrome and in turn paid her a generous stipend.

Prior to each meeting, the subject was dosed with psychoactive drugs (various, see full list in appendix) via juice given to her in the waiting room. Using imagery, triggers, and the drugs' effects, we taught the subject to believe she was French and that her real name was Anne-Marie. She began to speak English with a French accent. We instructed her to associate only with native French, and to alienate the Americans in order to be safe. Flashing the Americans' photos we conditioned her with negative association. After two meetings she spoke of the American students with disgust and contempt. We then reversed the messaging asking her to turn on the French students, and identify only with the Americans, flashing imagery of them with negative association conditioning. She became hostile during these meetings, irritable, violent at times. She constantly scratched her arms, legs, torso, pulled her hair, or rubbed her bloodshot eyes. She spoke of the French students with loathing and thought they were mentally torturing her. She said she wanted to kill them.

Chapter 7

The U.S. customs agent at Chicago O'Hare stared at my passport photo as though something rang familiar. He asked question after question about what I'd been doing in France while those at the checkpoints to either side came and went with ease.

"You live on campus at the UW?" he asked.

Where was Papa? We were supposed to pass together as family but I lost track of him at the self-service check-in.

"Do you live on campus?" the man asked again, checking a screen to his side. "Ma'am?"

Finally, I spotted Papa, he was already on the other side, walking to the baggage carousel.

"Ma'am? Do you live on campus?"

"Yes. I live on campus."

The border agent smiled. "That's my alma mater," he said stamping my passport. "Go Badgers."

* * *

Detective Chris was not amongst the crowd at the arrival gate. Papa and I returned to his truck in the airport lot in silence. It was much colder than Paris and a light snow was falling. The city was loud, even this far from downtown, the constant roar of planes overhead, the highway's white noise, horns honking. So different from our quiet vineyard where the first crickets to chirp were as obvious as a fire alarm.

* * *

Three hours later we pulled into our long gravel drive. On the lawn someone had spray-painted a giant mushroom. Neither of us said a thing.

Our house was empty. Lonely. Bertrand was at school and Papa disappeared immediately to his lab. My stomach clenched. Would he notice his things moved? But I had to trust Dr. Landau and Bertrand. They'd have been meticulous, Dr. Landau's eyes and Bertrand's senses.

I walked to the sink to pour myself a glass of water. The answering machine was blinking red.

"Simone, it's Detective Adam Chris. Your email said you'd be home today. Can you call me when you get this? Or just come on over."

Come on over? This was the police station he was referring to. Was this how you invited an arrest? I looked at the clock. French Lit started soon. It was my last chance to confront Professor, this time with Hal's document. I grabbed my bag with the printout and sped to Madison.

* * *

Camille stood behind the desk in the front of the lecture hall, Professor nowhere to be found. Maybe she was still in France, but I hoped it was because they'd finally taken me seriously, figured it all out, and arrested her.

Camille checked the clock on the wall behind her. "*Qu'est-ce que c'est, le surnaturel?*" What is the supernatural? No one responded. Usually, I would have been the one to do so, but I was far too nervous to speak, my mind as jumbled as the contents in my suitcase. At the vineyard I'd discovered my once carefully folded jeans and t-shirts were in heaps. The only neat thing in the suitcase was the TSA's typed letter stating they'd searched my bag.

Camille paced the room twice and spoke, "In *La Vénus d'Ille*, is there a police procedural to find the killer? Does the bulk of the oeuvre treat the investigation of Alphonse's death?" She put her hands on her hips and waited. She got nothing. Only half of our class had shown up anyway, the rest probably still traveling from Thanksgiving break.

Camille clapped her hands. "Let me repeat the question. *Qu'est-ce que c'est, le surnaturel?* In *La Vénus d'Ille*, is there a police procedural to find the killer?" she asked louder. "The answer is no. But—is there any proof that Venus, the statue, had anything to do with Alphonse's death?" She again crossed to the other side of the lecture hall, the squish squash of her duckboots the only sound echoing in the vast space. "While the author strongly suggests that the statue—the Goddess—may have killed Alphonse in a jealous rage, having gone so far as to make love with him before doing so, he gives us no actual proof." She stopped walking and faced the room head on. "That, *mes amis*, is the definition of supernatural. When we're left never knowing the truth but offered a mystical way out."

I wrote this down verbatim to busy my jittery hands.

"Detective," she said, "you appear aporetic."

I dropped my pen and twisted around. There he was wearing his black fleece zip-up, chewing gum and smiling his lopsided smile. The wait was up.

Chapter 8

Camille smiled at the detective. "Let me clarify even more," she said. "The author of *La Vénus d'Ille* left it to us, and us alone to decide what really happened on that fateful night. And I find that rather beautiful. But for a detective, that must feel far too—open ended."

Camille ended her lecture with that. The few who had come filed out noisily, looking at the detective and back at me. They pulled their phones out and tapped away. One of them snapped a photo. Finally, the three of us were alone in the colossal hall. I asked Adam Chris why he was here. There was still a chance he'd come for Camille. But he replied that he'd come to see me.

"Why me?" I asked. "Why not her," I pointed to Camille. "And what about Anne Boucher—have you spoken to her at all?"

He shook his head, "I have not. Where can I find this Anne Boucher?"

"Why," Camille limply placed one hand onto her neck, "at The French House of course."

"She's there, right now?"

Camille smiled, moving her freckles into new formations. "She always is."

* * *

I followed Det. Chris to The French House, clingy as a shadow. Camille wanted to accompany us and grunted dramatically when a student who hadn't attended the lecture arrived at the last minute, pleading for her help with the final paper.

"Am I under arrest? Because honestly, I know Boucher did it. I really do," I said putting on my gloves. "What's more I have proof of what caused Anne-Marie Fisker to murder all those students years ago."

He walked briskly along the sidewalk toward the House. A light dusting of snowflakes dangled before us as if unsure whether or not to fall all the way to the ground.

"Let me show you," I said, digging for the papers in my bag.

He stopped walking but didn't face me, looked in the direction of the lake instead. "You're not under arrest, Simone. And I have no interest in going to The French House right now, I just wanted to speak to you alone. I came to see you because of your mother."

"My mother?" I too stopped walking, took my hand out of my bag and grabbed his arm, crossing some invisible line.

"How did she die, Simone?"

"A car accident. What's it to you?"

Snowflakes muddled his lashes and created zebra stripes. "I'm really sorry to be the one to tell you this, but that's not how she died."

At that moment, Jackie showed up. "What are you two doing here?" She wiped her nose. "I'd have figured you'd be heading home to pick up your lover, Simone." Her lip snarled into a nasty curl.

"What are you talking about?"

"Our Professor," she said in English glancing at the detective, "is headed to your house— to the vineyard. Wanted to pick mushrooms with your father apparently. Probably to kill him or Camille, or maybe even you. You guys are so fucked up."

There was no time to respond. No time to seek help. I ran toward my rusty pick-up. My flats slipped several times on the ice but I kept on. I had to get home, to stop Anne Boucher before she seduced my father's mind like she had me—or worse, killed him.

Chapter 9

I called for Papa as soon as I stepped foot inside. He calmly entered the kitchen, brandy at hand.

"Papa! Are you all right?" I asked. I was out of breath, my stomach puffing in and out.

"Why wouldn't I be?" He set his brandy down on the kitchen island and took a few hesitant steps toward me. "Simone—"

"I thought that…" I paused to catch my breath, "I thought my Professor had come—"

"I did come," said a cinnamon voice. Cinnamon with a hint of clove. He was so out of context inside my home that I laughed.

"Charlie, what on earth are you doing here? And where's Professor?"

"Simone, I *am* your professor." Charlie gave a sad smile.

I moaned like Professor—like Anne Boucher, widening my stance, afraid I'd lose balance, the unevenness of the floor mimicking a rocking ship at sea.

"I came to speak to your father because as you know, Simone," he paused, whipped his hands out of his pockets and flattened his palms together. "I've been quite worried about you. The way you've explained some of your memories and, well, I've seen you talking to yourself and, even—" he cleared his throat, "talking in your sleep. I asked the others about it and they've been worried, too—"

"Who are you, Charlie? Who are you—and where is Anne?"

Charlie winced, shifting his glance to Papa who only nodded in return.

"Where is Anne?" I asked again.

"Simone, this is why I've come to speak to your Papa, this is why I'm worried about you. You're having delusions. Your father mentioned that you stopped taking your medication." Charlie took a gentle step toward me and held his hands open and outward.

"Delusions," I forced a laugh. "I don't want to those pills—I don't need them! They make everything hazy." I glared at Charlie. "You of all people should understand that. Why are you here picking mushrooms? Are you looking for poison?" I took a step back feeling the house sway and teeter like a flashy carnival ride.

Charlie shook his head, his eyes widening and giving me the distinct feeling that he viewed me as completely crazy.

Papa motioned toward the kitchen table. There sat a woven basket stuffed with innocent ribbed mushrooms, the same kind we always picked and sautéed with golden butter and lavender-colored garlic to serve with crusty baguettes. If there were any ill intent—any intent to poison—it was certainly not on that table.

"Simone," Charlie said. "The report Camille leaked showed that Hessa had residue of *amanita muscaria*—not *amanita phalloides*."

"But she said—"

"No," Charlie said, "I remember, she said *amanita* and you finished for her. You're the one who suggested it was *phalloides*. I doubt Camille even knew the difference between that and *amanita muscaria*—not that I had a clue until I looked it up."

"That's a big difference," I said quietly, remembering that he was right. I had jumped the gun. I had said *phalloides*, not Camille. And I hadn't even bothered to check the document she leaked to see for myself.

"I called the detective when we got back. He wouldn't give me names, but he said half of The French House's residents had the same results in their blood work. Apparently a large group of them had decided to go for a *little trip* on Halloween night."

I remembered Jackie, Kate, and Tim laughing hysterically in the dining room that night, wearing skeleton pajamas. *They'd been high.*

"So it's not what killed Hessa?"

"They still won't say."

"You've been overthinking again, Simone. Making false connections." Papa held up my pill bottle, shook it. "You need to take these and rest."

He and Charlie walked to me with looks of pity on their faces, so exaggerated they may as well have been wearing tragic prosopon. A couple of chorus players in the Theater of Dionysius. Charlie closed in on me first. Like a frightened animal I burst into a run, my feet working faster than they ever had before. I sprinted out of the back door and into the forest, pumping up the muddy hill's incline in search of my own potion.

I knew where they were. They'd avoided the recent snow thanks to the few remaining leaves that hovered above them. My name echoed into the hills, a cinnamon calling and Papa's deep bellow. I launched into a feverous dig, dirt wedging underneath my fingernails. It was magic mushrooms I wanted. Maybe—just maybe—they'd help me see the whole picture and return my mind to Halloween night. Maybe I'd get closer to Hessa somehow—connect myself to her last moments. I yanked a few from their roots and pressed them into my mouth, chewing the way a cow might by tonguing them around and absorbing their dry earthiness. There was a distinct and disturbing taste to them—oddly familiar.

Snap!

Without the raspberry syrup it tasted exactly like the tea Papa used to give Bertrand and me when we were upset about Maman.

I looked at my hands.

They were a child's hands.

I was small again.

I was a child.

Chapter 10

Ce n'est qu'un cauchemar. I repeated this three times, batting away the wet hair swathed across my sweaty forehead. It's what Maman told me to do. It's only a nightmare. Papa called to me, alerted by my screaming. He told me to come downstairs, to have my calming tea.

Grabbing my stuffed lion Chou Chou I popped out of bed and followed the sound of Papa's voice. First, I would get Bertrand, I always did when I had a bad dream and it was time to take my tea. "Come with me," I said, "*Je fais des cauchemars*." Bertrand was groggy but he took my hand and followed me down the creaking wooden steps and toward the golden light coming from the kitchen where I already smelled it.

"I was looking for Maman," I told Papa, one hand gripping Bertrand's, the other gripping Chou Chou. "I had a dream that she died because I wasn't able to save her." I wanted to cry but I refused myself, hoping to be brave for Papa. His warm bear arms scooped me into his embrace and gently placed me onto a wooden kitchen chair. He slid an ivory teacup in front of me and blew over its steaming spirals.

"There, there," he said, "take small sips, it's still hot."

Then he stood straight again, folding his arms together and watching me, as if to ensure the tea worked to calm me from my nightmare state. Papa grabbed Bertrand next, placing him, too, onto a chair and pouring him his own tea, tapping three times in front of him to indicate it was there, and that it was hot. Bertrand nodded and fingered for the cup handle with one hand, the delicate ivory saucer with the other. He blew on the steam, like me, it was our ritual. Sometimes we blew so much that it would frustrate Papa and he would tell us to just go on and drink it already.

"In my dream Maman was taking a bath."

Papa held his finger over his mouth and made a long *shh* sound.

"Maman never took baths," he said. I smiled for I knew he was going to tell me more about her.

"She didn't?" I asked, a ploy to keep him on track.

"No, she hated baths."

"We hate baths, too!" Bertrand said. "I would rather smell like the forest all the time, every single day, than smell of soap!" I nudged him to be quiet, I wanted to hear more about Maman.

"Did she take showers?" I asked sipping my tea again; it was so bitter my tongue recoiled with each sip.

"Of course, my dear," Papa said in his storytelling voice.

"I don't know why I keep remembering her in the bathtub upstairs," I said as I grabbed Chou Chou from falling off the chair. "If she hated it so. Did she have to take a bath for punishment?" I asked, thinking of how Bertrand and I used to get in trouble if we didn't get into the bath fast enough on Sunday evenings, purposefully stretching out our bedtimes. We didn't take baths anymore though, Papa told us to shower.

"Memories can be a funny thing," Papa said, patting my shoulder. I nodded because I liked to show him that I was paying attention and understanding everything he told me. "Drink more tea and I will tell you about your mother, you'll remember again."

It always worked. Papa would tell Bertrand and I about our mother and, as we drank, we saw the images he described, as if Maman had come back to life and was dancing before us in colorful shapes and sounds.

"Simone? Simone?"

That voice.

"Simone, look at me!" Molasses. Anne Boucher. She sat on a fallen tree trunk, moonlight on her hair. "Simone, this is why your father gave you the tea."

I wasn't sure if she was really there or if I were hallucinating her.

"Papa gave us some sort of psilocybin tea. Or maybe he'd mixed it with *amanita muscaria*," I mumbled, my voice dissipating into night mist. "My mother was in the bathtub."

Professor nodded. "You remember now."

Chapter 11

I did remember. So vividly, the memories rushed onto me pent up and cascading. Wearing a white nightgown with yellow bows, I stood, my ear pressed against my bedroom door, clutching Chou Chou, struggling to hear Maman and Papa shouting in the living room. Earlier at supper Maman had taken a knife from the dinner table and attacked Papa. Bertrand and I intervened and grabbed them both until Maman gave up and retreated to her room. Papa put us to bed, and I thought we'd get through the night until their arguments woke me.

"How can you deny it, Guy? I saw the two of you together yesterday and I can't go on like this, I cannot be disrespected like this! I'm taking the kids back to France—and I'm taking this winery from you, too! It was paid for it with *my* parents' money—it was *my* ideas that made it a success—and look what you've done to thank me!"

A clanking sound. *What are they doing?*

"And it wasn't my fault you lost the vineyard!" Maman shouted. "You can't own up to whatever the true reason is. You can't even admit that this winery is successful because of me! You're too busy fucking every last woman who works here—you are a sick excuse for a man! What did you do to your father—tell me! Tell me!"

Another bang, like a pan hitting the wall. "Don't touch me—get your hands off of me!"

My stomach dropped. I rubbed my hands against the door. Should I go downstairs? Was she in trouble? Would I be in trouble if I went downstairs too?

"You're not going anywhere—"

"Stop—get off of me, Guy!"

"You're my wife and you *will* remain in this home!"

"To work as your slave while you humiliate me over and over again? I won't! I refuse to allow my children to see me so powerless, I'm taking them to France this week— you have no choice—I am *done*!" She laughed a scary laugh, "You're a pathetic, lying, violent, worthless nothing! I should have married your brother—and you know what? If you'd have had just a bit more class when you returned from the States from your deranged internship, maybe I wouldn't have finally fucked him!"

Maman's footsteps pounded up the staircase while I remained fixed, my ear planted against the door, my hands pressed onto it so hard I worried it might collapse, and then wouldn't I be in trouble! Papa would find me awake and intruding.

I heard Maman open the bathroom door next to my room. I moved my ear to the wall by my bed. The turning of the whiny faucet caused a flush of water to roar out. Maman always filled a bath when she was stressed. She would sprinkle drops from the lavender tincture Papa made into it, and say that it had a magic way of curing all anxieties. Some days she allowed me to sit in the bath with her. She would wash my hair as we made funny faces to each other with soap foaming on our cheeks.

I knew she was dipping herself into the tub now, and I was about to open the door to my room and go into the bathroom and ask her if she was all right when I heard Papa's footsteps coming up the staircase, heavy and determined. He opened the bathroom door. I again pressed my ear so hard against the wall it burned in response. I held my breath in order to hear.

"What are you—?"

Loud splashes came next, the kind that Bertrand and I made when we bathed together and tried to overtake one another's toys with a homemade rip tide. These sounds never came from the bathroom when Maman took a bath.

"What are you doing?" I strained to hear. Her voice was muffled, so muffled, and bubbling. My stomach pinched. I didn't care how much trouble I'd be in. I left my room, tiptoed to Bertrand's room to find that he was awake and also listening in.

"Come on," I beckoned.

"It's so dark." He rubbed his eyes. "I can hardly see a thing."

"We have to go into the bathroom, something's wrong with Maman, I think she's drowning!"

I twisted the knob to the bathroom door.

Red. So much red, red everywhere. Red water, red fountains. Red Maman. So much slippery shiny red. Maman in the tub, her wrists like the fountains spewing at Place de la Concorde.

"Maman!" I pressed my hands over her wounds. "I'll fix you!" I screamed. Behind me Bertrand stood motionless, eyes wide, and his mouth in an O shape. Just past him Papa stood in the same fashion, his hands covered in blood, Maman's shaving blade in his hand.

"Save Maman," I cried. "Save her!" She was going away, her eyes holding mine, fear-stricken and changing from bright to dull.

"Please save her!" I grabbed Papa's arm. He slashed me away, and I slipped onto the bloody floor like a newborn fawn, quickly scrambling back to Maman's side to hold her shredded arms.

"Maman? Maman?"

Her head lolled to the side of the tub. I was lightheaded. The bathroom spiraled. I threw up. The remnants of my stomach mixed into multi-colored lollipop swirls.

"Maman?" I whispered. She lay limp, her eyes as blank as Venus de Milo.

I remained at her side crying, begging, "Maman, are you there? Can you hear me?"

Maman.

Maman.

Maman.

It sounded like a siren.

Maman.

Maman.

Maman.

The way sirens sounded back home in France.

Pam-pom.
Pam-pom.
Pam-pom.
Maman.
Maman.
Maman.

Chapter 12

Memories rained down, fat drops forming a muddied puddle that started to clear. *Papa killed Maman.*

By now my feet had brought me to the next hill over, one covered with hunchback apple trees, their spines giving up over the weight of plump fruits hanging from cracking arms. I reached for a branch and reveled in the rough sandpaper against my palm, scraping it back and forth until my hand was raw. I plucked an apple from the tree, squinting my eyes in the direction of my home. Was Charlie in danger here with Papa, whose side he was on?

I used my boundless energy to run down the hill, the icy wind a reprieve against my hot face. My feet hit the gravel, stones splashing out with my footsteps *swish-crunch-swish.*

The kitchen and living room lights created a yellow glow in each window. I entered the kitchen determined and growling, imagining myself as a wolf with shears for teeth and volatile eyes.

"Papa!" I shouted.

Upon hearing my voice Papa stepped into the kitchen. I adopted a calm tone, the kind Professor Anne Boucher would have appreciated, a thick molasses tone, a tenor, "You murdered my mother. You slashed her wrists to make it appear a suicide. You told me she died in a car accident. You served Bertrand and me hallucinogenic mushroom tea to rebuild our memories while under the influence. You made us to believe in an alternate ending." *The power of suggestion.*

"That's enough!" Papa flung his arm against my face with such force that I flew to the side and crashed into the wall, a shelf of china plates fell on my head.

I got up so fast that Papa did not see it coming; in swift movements I grabbed a knife from the butcher-block drawer and wielded it toward him.

"You will not hurt another person in this house!" I held the blade under the light, its tip aimed toward Papa's face. He reached and grabbed it, twisting my arm around my back and holding it against my throat, so tight my shoulder pulsed in agony. I bent my knee so that my foot came up and into Papa's crotch with a strong blow. He groaned and fell over, the knife still in his hand but letting go enough for me to wriggle loose.

I ran out of the kitchen, out of the three-season porch to the outdoors, but already Papa was behind—his feet on the gravel, gaining on me. I needed to call for help—I'd run into the winery. I grabbed Papa's lab key from underneath the grey rock, entered the side door, passed the tour room and into Papa's lab. Dr. Landau had gone to lengths to return the scene to normal. I didn't know if she'd taken the moleskin notebook I remembered finding next to my unicorn one, but I quickly rummaged around to find it was there.

The side door closed with a bang. Papa would be here in seconds. I took the journal and ran to the fermentation room, then descended the spiral rod iron staircase to the lower level with the immense silver fermentation tanks. I slowed my breath as I flicked through Papa's leather-bound book, and held the book up to the fermentation tank's temperature control screen to read in the dim red light:

> *Amanita muscaria Tea - 3.5 ml/serving.*
> *Dry and mash mushrooms, boil 15 min.*
> *User becomes very susceptible/open-mind-*
> *ed to memory rewriting. Overdose causes*
> *hallucinations that last even after the tea's*
> *effects should have worn off. Paranoia,*
> *anxiety & violence when going over 4 ml/*
> *person. Measure dose with precision.*

The door creaked open. It was him. I dropped the notebook wincing as it hit the ground. Footsteps on the stairs. I retreated farther behind the tank—*cornered.* My arm hit a rung—the tank's ladder, it was my only choice and I climbed up. From the top of the tank I located Papa. He paused halfway to the tanks looking for me. I had to get to the metal walkway that hung around the perimeter. I hurled my body over the railing and ran to the door. Locked.

There was nowhere else to go but—around again? Back down? I jumped over the railing and again onto a fermentation tank. I hopped from one tank to the other; six tanks in total, the cement ground far below flashing my leap's reflection. Back to the tank with the ladder, I scaled it halfway and jumped the rest. I ran across the room, up the spiral staircase, and back outside. I ran and I ran and I ran up the purple hill until I got to the other side of the bluff.

"Sam!" I shouted, "Sam! Sam!"

Sam's house sat squashed at the bottom of the valley, the other side of this bluff. Smoke chugged from its chimney.

"Sam!" my voice echoed. I heard my name called back, her glorious trumpeting grunt calling my name and the tears fell. "Call 911 Sam! We have an emergency at my house!" I cried. "Call 911 right now!"

"Okay," her voice echoed. *My dear Sam.* I raced back down the hill. I'd trail the perimeter of the winery to determine where he'd gone, but I didn't make it there, I was grabbed from behind.

Chapter 13

"Charlie, what are you doing here?" I clasped his shoulder to find equilibrium.

"*Shh*, I never left—I told your father that I did, but instead I went out looking for you— but these woods go on forever."

"Charlie," I said, my eyes, my voice, everything welling up at the thought of saying what I had to say out loud. "He killed my mother."

Charlie wrapped his arms tightly around me, whispering, "I think I figured that out, too, after piecing together your memories and," he kissed my head, "after having a very odd conversation with your father."

Under the harvest moonlight a silhouette ran across the gravel. "Simone! Come here, let's talk this out." He still held the knife.

"Talk it out?" I shouted from halfway up the hill, "You're insane!"

He came after us. The knife held high like he was hunting a wild animal.

Charlie tugged my arm. We ran up the hill, his pace slower than mine given his bad knee. The branches, the leaves, the mud, the incline, the darkness—

Bam!

Everything went black. My stomach flew up and out of my head until our bodies slammed against dry earth. A slice of moonlight bladed down to where we lay sprawled. We'd fallen through one of the manholes and were deep inside the old cave now, the cave once built within the hill to store wine over a hundred years ago, the cave we allowed tourists to venture only a few steps into. *The cave where we sprinkled Maman's ashes.*

"Are you okay?" Charlie asked.

"I don't know," I said, trying to stand up but there was a crack and a slicing pain shot through my leg. "Charlie, I think my leg is broken." I held it together in a way that made it feel whole again.

"What about your knee?"

"Amazingly, it feels fine."

"Charlie…you lied to me? Are you really the French Lit professor?" The blackness wrapped around me as I waited for his response.

"Yes, Simone, I am." I heard him take in a deep breath. "I was confused at first, thought you were carrying out some elaborate game of pretend—until I realized you'd actually thought I was a student and Anne Boucher our professor. That's when I reached out to your father. I'm sorry."

"Simone." It was Professor. I saw her despite the darkness, saw her perfectly, her and her only. Her long waves of hair fell over the sparkly gown she'd worn at the Centennial Fête. A lone star in the black sky.

"You're not who I think you are."

Professor pouted. "Aren't I?"

"Why not?" Charlie said in a whisper. "You can't listen to everything Camille says."

"I am who I have always claimed to be."

"*Shh*, not you."

"Simone," Professor Anne Boucher purred. "You know the truth."

"Yes," I said, shutting my eyes. "I made you come to life so that I had someone to look up to," I said quietly, though my voice reverberated around the cave.

"What are you talking about, Simone?" Charlie asked.

Professor smiled. "I must say that you recreated me very close to how I was once upon a time. *C'est très impressionnant.*"

Her name I knew from the past. Buried memories from Maman talking about her, idolizing her, and reading her book to me. When I read Camille's pre-course letter her name had been reawakened and I decided to quit taking my pills in hopes that by returning to my more vibrant albeit somewhat delusional self, I'd impress her. Then, on my first day I drank Papa's mind-altering tea as given to me by Bertrand who was simply trying to help. By the time I got to campus my mind was on fire and would have done anything to give me what I'd been waiting for, the woman whose name conjured powerful associations from somewhere deep inside my mind.

And yet Camille had never implied Professor was still alive.

Before me a film roll played of all the moments I had shared with Professor, and I knew now that she was my invention, brought on by my lack of pills, my tincture, and my high hopes. That first lecture Charlie had introduced himself as the professor and yet I'd already fantasized her and empowered her to be real, convincing myself Charlie was only pretending to teach our class, a charming jokester. She didn't she tell me the House was short on mother tongue residents or about the Centennial Fête, I'd read it on the scholarship application form in her name I'd taken from the lecture hall's corridor after it fell in Charlie's wake. She hadn't asked me to watch over Camille; I'd already been concerned about Camille from the bizarre letter she'd sent inviting us on a journey to help complete her thesis. And Professor Anne Boucher hadn't lent me her dress on the night of the banquet, I'd found it myself in the arson-damaged room and it had most likely belonged to the girl from Monaco who'd been expelled. Any time anyone else mentioned Anne Boucher they spoke of her as a ghost, "haunting" our House, or as a legendary figure, and I'd refused to interpret their true meaning.

That first day I arrived on campus and parked near the statue whose blank, patina eyes beckoned me so, and rubbed it per some girl's advice. The inscription was no longer there but I knew whose name would be there if it was—*Anne Boucher*. The beautiful statue that captured the eyes of all who passed it, the goddess of the isle on campus.

La Vénus d'Ille.

Ever since quitting my pills my mind was reopening, reconnecting. My subconscious wanted Anne Boucher to be real to have that connection with my mother so badly, that my mind created her.

The mind erases just as well as it creates.

"You donated all of your money to The French House."

"I did," she agreed, her molasses voice drifting away.

"How did you die?" Though she was fading away, her image flimsy like a mirage over the desert, I saw her frown.

"What matters is that I keep coming back. Every time another one of you opens my book, hears my voice, enters my world..."

"Simone!"

"Who was that?" Charlie whispered.

"Simone!" *Papa.*

"I have to let you go," I told Professor. "It's time for you to go."

She smiled now, her big, beautiful mouth, her large white teeth, and her glittering green eyes. "I know."

"Simone," Charlie whispered, "I can't see you." He sounded disoriented, his voice shaky. I sensed Papa at the entrance of the cave.

Then, a new voice. "I won't let him touch you."

"Bertrand," I whispered. My brother had materialized in the darkness. I reached to find him, pulled him to me and collapsed my head into his embrace. "How did you know we were here?"

"I was at Kip's," he said, stepping back and gripping my arms. "When I got home to find the house empty, I called for you outside. I sensed you here."

"Simone!" Papa shouted from the cave's entrance. "You're confused! I'll show you—I'll explain!"

"Charlie," Bertrand whispered, "We have to stop him."

"I can't see anything," Charlie said.

"Neither can I," Bertrand said, holding back his frustration. "But we'll hear him, we'll know. When I pinch your arm you must reach for him—pin him down. Come on, we can't wait any longer. He's totally deranged and still has the knife."

Their steps sloshed away over the sandy dirt while Papa's came closer.

Please, Maman. Help them.

The darkness was so complete that closing my eyes and opening them made no difference at all. There was only one existence: blackness. It was the world Bertrand had known for so many years and because of that I knew he would find Papa; he would lead Charlie to him so that together they'd strike him down. The Blind man and the Lame.

A jumble of sounds. Slapping, wrestling, and screaming.

Too much chaos to decipher whose voice was whose, too much darkness to know how close or far away. I pulled myself forward into the fray, dragging my injured leg behind me. There were hands and legs everywhere, entangled in a knot, and then I was grabbed, hands clasping my throat, pinching—choking me.

I smelled Papa. Earth and fermented grapes. I imagined my nails as razors, cutting and cutting until his grip loosened enough for me to bite the soft web of his hand. I clamped down like an enraged great white shark, the taste of metallic iron wet on my lips. He shouted in pain and I slithered from his grip, sensing Charlie and Bertrand closing in on us, ready to overpower him. They held Papa down against the dirt ground, and I felt for his warm wide face in my hands, unmistakable. I yanked at my rope necklace, clutching the arrowhead and piercing it into Papa's cheek with a satisfying cut. He yowled but yielded to my carving. The letter "M." Fast, swift, and sweet.

* * *

"Hello! Hello? Simone Duchamps, are you in here?"

"Simone!" Another voice, my savior.

"Sam!" I called back, tears streaming down my dirt-caked face and neck.

Flashlights cut the black, round orbs shining like UFOs ready to spirit us away from this horrific scene. "Police!"

"Simone!" Sam cried making her way to me. "There's a detective here, he wants to talk to you. Are you going to be okay?" she asked, reaching out to caress my face the way a mother would, the same way I saw her mother do.

"I am," I said sinking my hands into the cave's dirt. Maman's ashes. "I am." I said again because it was good to hear out loud.

In that moment I sensed her. I sensed Maman and she was lavender and lovely and wouldn't you know—she smelled of crème brûlée.

Chapter 14

February 2023

I have come to have a whole new respect for Charlie and Kip for moving so quickly and remaining so positive despite their physical handicaps. This was my second round of crutches. I'd given up on them too early the first time and compromised my leg from healing fully—so here I was again. At least they provided a good excuse as to why I was late in meeting Detective Adam Chris at a coffee shop on State Street.

He sat in the corner with his head dipped into a book. Upon hearing the jingle from the bells on the door as I entered, he perked up and looked my way, folded the book he'd been reading and jogged over to help me.

"I'm fine, I'm fine," I insisted, though I was happy to have him escort me to a petite round table, pull out my chair, and set aside my crutches. I spied the cover of his book when he set it down.

"Camus, huh?"

"What can I say? I'm trying to become more cultured." His cheeks prickled with tiny pink roses. A waitress brought our coffees and we sipped for a moment in silence. The vibe of the café was dark and relaxed, a college kid strumming on his guitar in one corner and next to him, a girl warming up her vocals to perform for the few patrons dotted about the room.

My father was in jail and no bond was posted; they feared he'd flee to France. He'd stabbed Charlie, and his own son—and as for me, I'm not really sure what he had intended to do when he held my throat in his grip. What I would say in court one day, was that I witnessed him slice my mother's wrists and stand back to watch her die.

After sitting down and piecing things together with Reine, I was able to recall that upon return to The French House on Halloween night, I'd found Hessa in the bathroom crying. Camille and Reine were there too. Camille telling Hessa to leave this world, to free herself, because no one cared about her, and most of all, he didn't care and he never did. As Reine and I pulled on Camille's arms, trying to lead her out of the bathroom and away from Hessa, she shouted, "He only slept with you because I told him to—as a joke. You were a test to see how far Boucher's lessons on the power of suggestion go, and look what we learned, Boucher would be so proud! You turned your back on your religion and morals with only a few. Now empower yourself for good by ending it. *Sois libérée*!"

"I will be free," Hessa had said through tears. "When I kill myself."

I vaguely remembered pushing Camille at this point, telling her to stop, and trying to get past her to Hessa. But Camille clasped my wrists and came inches from my face. "Are you going to arrest me for making a suggestion?"

I escaped her grip and ran to my bedroom for my truck keys, then drove to Papa's, the familiar roads my saving grace given the state I was in. I woke in the forest beyond the vineyard, my mind blank. My brain, so trained by Papa to erase traumatic memories, was protecting me and of course, I'd consumed two cups of an opium-laced sedative tea.

When finally confronted by the police, Camille admitted that she'd later "suggested" to Reine that Hessa's death had been her fault, the fault of the evil that ran in her family. Reine, drunk and traumatized by the next morning's scene, listened to Camille's words like the loyal student and friend she was and turned herself in. She'd asked to be put away so she couldn't hurt anyone else. Adam Chris hadn't gotten very far with her after that. She wasn't able to provide any real details as to how Hessa died, and only languished in her self-made prison of guilt and shame and fear as the rest of us hurtled toward a climax I doubted even Camille had anticipated.

Ultimately, Hessa's end had come by her own hand. A fraternity boy came forward with a video from his phone. He'd noticed her spray-painting the flag that night and wanted to catch a French House kid debauching in public. When he heard that she'd died, he'd been afraid to come forward, to be labeled a terrorist for accusing the dead Muslim girl of a petty crime—most likely ignorant the significance of precisely what he'd captured. The film showed Hessa spray-painting the word *libérée*, but also, just as he was turning away in the darkness with his prize, you could barely make out her next gesture, which was to swallow back a handful of pills and lean against the maple to await her oblivion. She'd sat there until morning, observed by countless Halloween revelers and perceived as merely a drunken college girl, a passed-out student, steps from her own bed.

Eventually, the boy with the video did the right thing. He brought it to the police to show them her act of graffiti, and their investigators spotted her final act of defiance, the pills in her palm magnified and leaving no more doubt as to her intention. He liberated all of us, but I didn't even know his name.

With this out in the open, Tim from The French House had come forward too. By now the media no longer cared, they'd moved on cover a story about a local lottery winner. But what Tim said helped clear my conscious of any remaining doubt. He admitted that he and many of his friends in The French House had eaten "magic mushrooms" in hopes of a little Halloween fun. He said that even Hessa had tried them, but that she'd been so averse to the taste that she spat them back up. This explained the residue upon her clothes.

"When you told me that you remembered seeing Hessa in the bathtub, I knew something was seriously wrong. You were so hell bent on your memory that after some time I knew there was no way you were playing with me," Adam said, pausing to take a sip of his frothy latte. It must have been doused with caramel syrup because it smelled of crème brûlée and I faintly pictured Anne Boucher sliding into the chair next to us, flirting and analyzing my every last move. But she was gone, and my moves were fine without her.

"That's when you looked into my history," I nodded, "and learned about my mother's death, and realized I'd swapped the memories of two very traumatic events."

Maman's death had been officially booked a suicide years ago, slit wrists in a claw foot tub. Over time, Papa had led Bertrand and me to believe she'd died in a car accident, and that Bertrand had been in the car with her and that it was the accident, which caused him to go blind rather than the conversion disorder that caused it, from seeing such trauma at a young age. Over the years Papa erased our memories of Maman so much as taking baths, of her bleeding, of them fighting, and practically everything else in between. His mastery of the botanical world, his wizardry with plants and herbs, and the mind control techniques he'd learned while interning with Hal Green, allowed him to manipulate his own children into forgetting that he was a murderer. With the tea he was able to get our minds into a so-called alpha state, ripe for suggestion. Then he planted a new version of history into our minds. But I knew the truth now. No car. No suicide. No accident. My brother still blind, but from psychological trauma, maybe one day he would see again.

"But I was never prepared for..."

"The truth behind the experiments," I finished for him. He looked down.

"Yeah."

Dr. Landau, Bertrand and I had turned in all the documents found in Papa's lab. The police then conducted their own search and from what I understood, looked into the psych department as well. From there I hadn't had much of an update.

"Why wasn't it big news?" I asked. "I mean I know it happened ages ago but that's a gigantic story. An ex-CIA agent conducting totally unethical experiments on students—they drugged Maria Fisker, they brainwashed her. They turned her into a murderer." I wanted the world to know. Shouldn't Maria Fisker's name be cleared? And certainly her relatives should learn that she wasn't a psychotic murderesses rather a victim of horrific mind control research.

"You'd have served yourself better posting the documents online if you wanted the truth to come out," he said. "But you didn't hear that from me."

"You're saying it's been swept under the rug?"

"I wouldn't say that exactly, but it's no longer my business. I'm not important enough to deal with such matters, you know. I'm not exactly an 'ultra' level guy. You still want to be here with me?" He masked his smile with his coffee mug.

"I'll write Anne-Marie's family a letter and try to go see them. It's the least I can do."

We sat in silence for a while. I looked out the window, sipped my coffee.

"You want to know something really ironic?" Adam asked. "I've done a lot of research on mushrooms. Turns out psilocybin and muscaria have been proven to trigger the brain to grow new cells in the prefrontal cortex and help overcome frightening memories. They're no longer used for mind control purposes. They're now used to treat PTSD side effects like memory fragmentation, disassociation, and nightmares. Crazy, isn't it?"

"Ah, so you might also call it a Proustian memory." I sipped my tannic coffee and thought about Proust's tea-soaked madeleines sending him on a childhood memory escapade, the same way the taste of the mushrooms had for me.

"You think the doping caused your brother's synesthesia?"

I'd thought about this a lot lately. "Yes."

At least Bertrand had come away with something beautiful out of all his pain. I'd come to this conclusion on my own but I'd also asked Dr. Landau's opinion. After she got over the initial shock of learning that Papa had, time and again served us hallucinogenic tea to reshape our memories, she said it explained everything. My case finally made sense. She said that for an adult to undergo what we had, the brain would open up, mix and match ideas and senses, hallucinate. For a child's mind—and especially with multiple use, the effect would be ten times as strong. In other words, she explained, our brains' topography had changed forever. Rewired to make connections they normally would not, to see, feel, and experience imaginative ideas as if they were reality (in my case) or synesthetically (in Bertrand's.) We were a case study, she said, and I think she was already ideating a book. Or, as much as I hated the word now, a thesis.

I simply quoted Proust in response: "Neurosis has an absolute genius for malingering. There is no illness, which it cannot counterfeit perfectly. If it can deceive the doctor, how should it fail to deceive the patient?"

Steam spirals from the coffee, reminiscent of those from Papa's tea, whirled before us. The guitarist and singer began performing and the café lighting dimmed. A barista in all black traveled from table to table, lighting red votive candles.

"Are you still living at The French House?"

"No," I said and felt sentimental. If I squinted my eyes enough, maybe, just maybe the dancing candlelight transformed me back to our table and its rich linens and golden lighting, its cozy yet eerie ambiance.

"I live at home, at the winery. My uncle Guillaume is staying with my brother and me for a time, he's helping us take over the vineyard."

Learning from Uncle Guillaume was proving to be the best medicine for Bertrand and me. We'd never have known how much we would love making wine. Not just smelling and tasting it, providing tours of the vineyard, or coming up with catch phrases and marketing campaigns—but actually making it. Though I hadn't completely given up on marketing, I'd already convinced Uncle Guillaume to work on a new line: Misfit Wines.

Uncle Guillaume also helped me understand what happened in France, and why Papa lost the vineyard. It all started with our family winery's Centennial Fête—if I've learned anything, it's not to celebrate one hundred years.

My paternal grandfather asked Maman to create a special wine label for the party's wines. She loved this type of work and accepted it with pleasure, and decided on Venus as the theme for her art. Her work was displayed on wine labels and giant canvases at the Centennial Fête. A robust and sprawling nude Venus standing on a vagina disguised as a shell. It caused quite a stir amongst the prude religious folks. Many left hastily, saying they wanted nothing to do with a pagan party. At some point during the party my grandfather suffered a heart attack, Guillaume thinks instigated by Papa's arguing. Grandpère was rushed to the hospital and the party ended.

The next day Papa visited their father in the hospital. There, a nurse overheard him manipulating his father to leave the entire vineyard to him, spinning an elaborate story as to why it made sense to do so—and mentioned how Papa had kept serving him tea. Papa's tactics worked, my grandfather called his estate handler and updated his will. The nurse, who also overheard my grandfather's phone conversation, called my grandmother and Guillaume to tell them what happened. Papa had abused his own father's condition to write his brother out of his inheritance and by doing so, was then written out himself. Everyone had agreed that Papa was different when he returned from the States. He'd become extremely manipulative.

What they didn't know was that he'd learned from one of the best. He had helped Hal Green transform a winery pet-project for retirement, into a success. In turn, Hal had taught Papa the art of mind control. Papa's knowledge of herbs must have been glorious for a man like Hal, who had been one of the first people involved in MKUltra research, using psychoactive drugs to control behavior. Upon retirement the old man, who had become quite senile, hadn't gotten it out of his system and kept at it. He probably donated massive amounts of money to the university, as he had to The French House, for his crack at continued research.

As for Papa, to hide his devious behavior, he convinced Maman that it was her fault they'd lost the inheritance, their portion of the winery. That his father was so disgusted with her crass pagan label that it caused his heart attack, and that he'd decided to disown them. The sad reality, Guillaume said, was that their father had loved it, had loved everything Maman had ever done or created. But Maman believed Papa—for reasons we now know, and was humiliated.

"It's surprising your father didn't blame everything on me," Uncle Guillaume told me, "but now I suspect he was trying to rid your mother's memories of me as much as possible."

Without rights to the family vineyard or its home, Maman and Papa moved in with my maternal parents for three months during which she became a recluse, so embarrassed for the pain she believed she'd instigated. From what Guillaume knew, she was elated about the winery for sale in Wisconsin, a new opportunity, a chance to spread her creative flair in a whole new country.

But life in the States didn't turn out the way she'd hoped. Our family was less than welcome in town, Papa cheated on her, and culture shock wore her down. Papa told her that she was mentally unstable, and this too she believed as she sipped his tisane and fell victim over and again. Poor Guillaume said he'd never forgive himself for not having the courage to tell Maman the truth before they moved. He didn't know how sinister his own brother would become.

As for all the Centennial wine bottles and their racy Venus labels, they'd remained properly stored all this time in waiting for Bertrand and me to claim. My mother's drawing of Venus looked curiously similar to the image I'd created of Professor Anne Boucher. Guillaume shocked me with their worth, they were from an extraordinary vintage, and their special label only added to their value. I'd already reached out to Henri and begun planning a gala for late spring. A renaissance for The French House and an auction for some of these wines, which would surely raise enough to save the place I still loved and believed in.

"Taking over the vineyard—wow, that's ambitious," Adam said, shaking his head of strawberry blonde hair.

"Yeah, I've switched my major, too," I said. "Horticulture."

"I'm really happy for you, Simone." He raised his latte to me as if it was a flute of champagne and we were toasting to our good health.

"So what about Camille?"

"What about her," he said. But he knew what I meant. "We can't arrest her for suggesting Hessa kill herself; there's no evidence against her, other than what you and Reine said you overheard."

I looked down. Thinking about this always made me nauseous. Would Hessa have done it on her own? Was Camille's suggestion the tipping point? If so, then Camille had proven her thesis. She had tested the lessons in Boucher's book and ultimately proved that the power of suggestion was capable of causing one to dishonor a religion, to seduce, and ultimately to kill. Her victory had been a pyrrhic one, though. She'd lost the only meaningful relationships she had in her life. I knew deep down she cared about us, loved us in the only way she was capable, but that she was too broken to allow herself our friendship. She didn't believe she was worthy of love. And that which she wanted above anything else, Charlie, she'd pushed out of her life with her recklessness.

Reine told me that Charlie had promised to put in a word for Camille within university publishing circles, but that he banished her from ever working or living near him again. How did one banish in today's age, I'd asked Reine and she told me she didn't want to know. Said banishment may or may not include Paris, because Reine also said Charlie was torn between staying here and "fixing himself," or returning to Paris to start over. I wouldn't know. I hadn't spoken to him.

Whatever Camille may publish I had to admit I'd be interested to read it. Despite that her interpretation of Anne Boucher's lessons was the exact opposite of the author's intentions, at least if you were to ask me. Especially knowing what I did now that I took the time to read about the real Anne Boucher—in fact I'd insatiably read everything I found about her both online and in the library.

Anne Boucher's mother died in the mass-poisoning in Pont Saint Esprit. Bitter over what had happened, and determined to understand why, Anne moved to Paris when she was eighteen. A young woman with big ideas, she made her way up the ranks at the Sorbonne and in her free-minding circles, heard rumors about MKUltra and the CIA's potential involvement in her town's poisoning. She'd been one of the first to publicly blame the American government for testing chemicals on her hometown. To fuel her fire, it was during this time in Paris that one of the main chemists working on project MKUltra, had been accused of hanging around the City of Lights and poisoning an American artist with LSD at the Café de Flore. The man had soon thereafter gone insane and died. His family sued the government, but the case was closed and the news article about the matter was never published in the U.S. despite having been published in every other major international paper. This was one of several similar cases and after a while I had to stop researching; it made me stressed and I remained determined to work through my issues without pills or tinctures, something Dr. Landau was assisting me with.

As for Anne Boucher, she headed for the States to accept a position at the University of Wisconsin and became The French House's official "house mother." It was during her tenure at the UW where she developed the course "Fundamentals of French Literature's Euphemisms for Society." Whether or not the course had actually driven anyone to madness as Camille had once suggested, was undetermined. I think it was more to do with the book she authored around this time, *The Power of Suggestion: A Woman's Guide to Empowerment*. I now understood that she wrote the book as a response to the unethical mind control research she knew to be taking place. She wanted to prove how to manipulate minds with suggestions only—not with brainwashing tactics or LSD and the likes, and as she'd said in an interview I found, she wrote the book specifically for women as a dedication to her mother.

Additionally, I'd learned from digging in old archives that Anne Boucher was a whistleblower, calling out those she knew to be involved in unethical research. Because of this I questioned the way she'd died. Ironically, unlike what I'd believed for so long about my mother's death, Anne Boucher was killed in a car accident. Whether or not she was pushed off the road—I'd never know, but maybe I was turning into a conspiracy theorist myself. Then there was her lover. As rumor had it he was a married Algerian man named Mohamed, and he did die of food poisoning. I had to speculate on that one too. She'd been pointing fingers at people the entire time she was at the UW and was certain to have made quite a few enemies. Was this part of the reason why, shortly after she died, Hal Green turned to the House she ran, to use for his guinea pigs? Whose idea it had been to blame Professor's book for Fisker's killing spree and suicide? I had to assume it was one of those involved in Maria's mind control experiment as a way to shift blame and get back at the woman who had been against their research from the start.

Recently I'd reread Professor's book several times, each time finding new connections. God there were so many. Which of them was a response to the criminal research she knew to have taken place at the university? Which had a hidden meaning? I'd probably never really know, and I supposed as Reine had once said, each person interpreted the book in her own way, and used it for her own purposes. I truly missed Reine. She'd returned to Gabon saying maybe she'd try coming back to school again next year, and I really hoped she would.

"Simone, are you okay?" Adam Chris was watching me carefully.

"Yes...there's just so much to think about."

"May I ask you something personal?" He stirred his coffee. "The significance of..."

"The M on Papa's face," I finished for him.

He nodded.

"M for *meurtrie*r, murderer."

"Old world punishment?"

"I don't know how to explain it. He spent his whole life making me forget, and I want him to spend the rest of his—*remembering*."

"I'd say that explains it perfectly."

"Mm," I said, gripping my coffee and looking out the window, watching the clean and innocent snowflakes perform Swan Lake in the sky.

"And so what does Valentine's Day bring in the world of Simone Duchamps?"

It was a welcome change in subject. "A campaign launch party at the winery, the official release of our new label: L'appel du Vide." I smiled as I said this, feeling particularly proud of my wine label and brand creation, and closer to Maman for following in her footsteps.

"Your idea I presume?" he asked, scooting his chair in closer toward me.

"For the most part."

"And are you looking for the call of the void?" he asked, his periwinkle eyes wide open, full of energy.

"*Non*, it already came to me."

"I knew you'd say that," he said.

* * *

I left the café in contented spirits, which was a good thing. I needed all the positive energy I mustered to walk myself on those damn crutches all the way back to my truck in the wet snowfall, and atop the slick ice. Adam wanted to escort me but I didn't want him to know I'd driven here—I wasn't supposed to given the condition of my leg. More importantly, there was something I had to do first.

Everything was white now, the sky, the buildings, and the ground. The bleeding fall colors were a thing of the faraway past. I stopped in front of the columned limestone building for French Lit, and the romance language's staff offices. Where I used to sit inside, alone, and fabricate conversations with Anne Boucher. I never had retrieved my final assignment, a paper on our three readings that we'd had to turn in before the holiday break. Maybe I'd see Charlie inside, maybe I wouldn't. Maybe that was why I found myself hobbling into the building, or maybe I just wanted to see what I'd been graded.

But there he was, behind the desk and atop the chocolate-colored leather chair. The diamond embossed window behind him showcased the twirling dance of snowflakes, the wall of walnut shelves and first edition French books at his side. On his desk, the butterfly glass paperweight, the same one I'd seen in the Derosiers' Parisian flat. Probably a gift from his doting mother. I rapped on the half-open door. Charlie looked up and upon seeing me, reacted with a mélange of joy and surprise.

"I came for my paper."

"Oh, come on," he replied, standing and walking over to me, his cinnamon voice warm. We shared an awkward moment of confused *bises*. But what were we supposed to do—what were we, anymore?

"I really can't stay long," I said. We held each other's eyes for a moment, sharing so much without saying a word. The type of loaded silence I had so desired to achieve with him not long ago.

Charlie shuffled through some files in a drawer and plucked a paper out, handing it to me with a shy smile.

"Thanks Professor," I said.

"That's Charlie to you." He winked.

I placed my hands on the edge of his desk. "What was the thread? What connected the three works?"

Charlie's face fell as his eyes worked their way around the room, pausing on the shelf of old books. Finally, he said, "Nothing. It didn't mean anything—my question. There is no thread." He rubbed his hands over his eyes then through his hair. "I was taught in graduate school that if you ask your students to find a connection between disparate subjects, they'd find you more intelligent."

I shook my head and looked past him, into the diamond embossed windows. To think of how much thought I'd put into something so meaningless.

Everything about Charlie made sense in that moment, in my head the outlying dots connected.

"A long time ago you and Camille were seriously involved," I said, keeping my eyes on the snowflakes. "Then you ended it but remained friends. She followed you here, to the university to become your teaching assistant in hopes that someday you'd get back together again. Instead you slept with other girls, your students, and it killed her inside."

He tried to interrupt me, his face turning a fine shade of scarlet.

"And so Camille wanted to punish you for it. Wanted to get you fired. I'm right, aren't I?"

Charlie took in a deep breath.

"She left you a note once. 'The hope of vengeance soothes my soul.'"

"How did you—"

I interrupted him. "She encouraged Hessa to sleep with you, hoping to get you caught and lose your post—teach you a lesson—yet you somehow saved your job. I think you truly did care for Hessa, too, which made Camille hate her even more. You came to your senses though and ended it with her. But when I came along Camille found another chance. She knew that if I tried to conquer you as she suggested that you wouldn't be able to resist, because that's your weakness, isn't it, Monsieur Deroisers? That's your dirty past. Your haunting. You can't keep your hands off of pretty young things. You're so desperate to feel adored."

"Simone—"

"No, no," I held up my hand. He continued to explain himself, but I was already walking away. The cinnamon notes followed me with a new hint of desperation in their scent. He'd behaved enormously inappropriate as the real professor; it justified why I saw him as a fellow student in my version of reality.

* * *

I'd parked my old pick-up near the spot I had my first day on campus. Consequently, I had to walk past The French House, past its bare maples, its proud and boastful walkway, its welcoming whiff of fire crackling, of Henri's pastries rising in the oven, of delicious conversations in cozy corners throughout the House. I stopped at the statue. In the months I'd been gone, the base had been fixed, the inscription was now there:

Anne Boucher – Beloved Mother
of The French House

1936 – 1977

I traced her name with my finger. The bronze was icy cold in in the elements and a layer of snow lay atop her hair, hair that looked golden under the sun and mahogany in the shadows. The air held a hint of spring's embrace at the edge of winter's breath. Days were getting longer. Spring would soon find us, warm her bronze and ready her to shine. Then summer would shroud her with flowers until fall came again, and with it a whole new group of students for her to seduce. Leaning against her now, I unfolded my paper, which Charlie had graded with a big red "A" on top. I had found a theme between all three works, whether that meant anything or not. I proclaimed all three stories were about misfits. Misfits looking for significance in life, looking to belong.

When I looked up, I saw my mother. Standing at the other side of the statue, eyes locked on me. She dropped her purse. Her eyes, two planet earths, shiny and watering. Her face crumpled like a silk shirt as she opened her arms. But this wasn't my mother. I did not need my pills to know the difference.

Aunt Violette.

"What are you doing here?" I asked. My voice muffled in her thick black hair. Papa had cut her out of our lives, I realized now, even though he'd told us it had been the opposite. A taxi idled across the street.

Violette pulled away and caressed my face. "Guillaume reached out. He told me about your wine release party tonight."

"*C'est incroyable.* Grab your suitcase, you can ride with me."

She did as I said, beaming as her taxi drove off.

"Aunte Violette, how did you know I'd be here?"

She set her suitcase down and shook her head. "I didn't. But I was too impatient to see her," she nodded toward the statue, toward Anne Boucher.

"Anne Boucher? Why?"

"No, your mother." She loosened her sheer white scarf.

"Je suis tout à fait perdue, Aunte Violette."

"Yes, there's so much to say." She rubbed her hand across the base of the statue. "Your mother's ashes are here."

I shook my head. "But—"

"I'll tell you the condensed version now and anything else you want to know over time—because we've got that now."

She reached for me and I circled my arms around hers, leaned my head on her shoulder.

"Anne Boucher's book changed my life. It empowered me to leave our small hometown, go to Paris and study fashion. I've got my own label—or I did, I sold it. I'm retired now. Your mother," she paused, "she was impressed by the book, too."

"Yes, I can remember her reading it—it's still fuzzy but I remember."

"She wanted to empower herself to leave your father and return to France. Learn what really happened between he and his family, clear her name and her conscious."

A wind blew and Violette's green dress rustled. My black bob danced. We both looked up at Anne Boucher. She looked stoic and cold.

"My parents and I received half of your Maman's ashes. I laid them here. I thought in that way, Anne Boucher's lesson for your mother may somehow complete itself. To put a stop to your father's abuse."

"And so it was," I said.

"Yes, so it was." Violette grabbed my hand.

"I feel her energy here."

I looked at the base of the statue, where Violette had laid Maman's ashes so long ago. There, despite the light dusting of snow, tulips were crowning. When I looked back at the statue of Anne Boucher, she smiled.

Author's Note

There were several parts of this novel inspired by true events. Most notably, that The French House does exist at the University of Wisconsin, and that CIA MKUltra research took place at the University's psychology department. The two were never linked in any way, and all other coincidences or similarities end there. The truth is sometimes indeed stranger than fiction and the poisoning in Pont St. Espirit did indeed occur and may have been linked to the CIA.

The CIA's MKUltra program funded research at the University Wisconsin under the Society for the Investigation of Human Ecology. Carl Rogers, the famed psychologist, is one of many to have worked within the UW's research programs receiving grants by the Society, though I found nothing linking him to anything unethical. There was, however, a massive amount of depraved MKUltra research taking place in over forty universities across the country as well as hospitals and prisons, and with innocent civilians. Countless people were dosed with psychoactive drugs both voluntarily and unknowingly. Several deaths were attributed to the research, and some victims' families were awarded money by the government in settlements, others were not.

The real French House at the University of Wisconsin was created in 1918 to provide students with an immersive French language and cultural experience that few would have been able to afford at the time. In its first year, 21 American women and three French women made up the residents (making it an all-girls residence at that time). They lived across the street from what would one day become the current location of the French

House, in the Delta Upsilon fraternity, as most of the fraternity boys were away serving in the army. When the men returned, the French House's committee had to find a new location and The French House, Inc. was created selling stocks to earn money to buy a home. The following years would prove trying, the newly purchased home had countless problems, less and less students were enrolling in foreign language programs due to curricula changes, and of course the Great Depression didn't help. By 1933 The French House had severe debt. Thankfully, more glorious days came when the university agreed to pay the French students living in the French House (considering their native skills as a form of teaching in its own right) thus bringing a sort of renaissance complete with plenty of fetes and soirees. This era was short-lived however, because as the university grew, the chemistry building took over the block where the then French House was located. Fortunately, one of the stockholders, a woman by the name of Mrs. Slaughter, donated her home at the end of Frances Street (so fitting) at the edge of Lake Mendota (this is the only similarity between the fictional description of The French House and the actual one), and coincidentally across the street from its original location at the Delta Upsilon house (which still functions at that location today). Since that time, her Victorian home was demolished (too many repairs needed) and a new one was built in Frank Lloyd Wright's prairie style.

The winery where Simone and her family live was greatly inspired by Wollersheim Winery in my hometown of Prairie du Sac, Wisconsin. A Hungarian Count first built the winery and then went on to be a founding father for many more in the Napa Valley. The winery has an old wine-storing cave (which tourists can enter), though there are no manholes from the top of the bluff into which one could fall. Today a magnificent French-American family runs the winery, and their wines win international competitions time and again. That's where the similarities end, as they are the kindest people one could hope to meet in life and have nothing to do with the fictional (and very disturbed) family in this novel.

All references to research regarding memory, human testing, neuroplasticity, Jane Elliott's work, and the report that one can convince another they committed a crime (even murder) that never happened through the power of suggestion alone, are factual.

In 1951 a mass poisoning did take place in the small town of Pont Saint Esprit, France involving over 250 people, all of whom experienced psychotic episodes later linked to tainted rye bread. More than 50 of these people had to be interned in asylums. To this day, conspiracy exists that it was owed to a psychoactive chemical testing program run by the CIA's MKUltra program. The CIA had purchased psychoactive drugs from Sandoz Laboratory in Basel, Switzerland around the same time.

Finally, a note on mushrooms and psychedelics. I am an avid mushroom hunter as is my family (my uncle also runs a mushroom farm) and it brought me much joy to incorporate this hobby into the novel's plot. Identifying mushrooms can be tricky and picking wild mushrooms requires a lot of knowledge, cross-reference, and diligence, as there are many poisonous varieties, and like chameleons they tend to change with their environment to throw you off. The psilocybin variety are psychoactive, open memory, and make one susceptible to suggestion. The psilocybin class has also been proven to stimulate new brain cell growth and is continuously used in research as treatment for PTSD, depression, and OCD. This class is currently in the end phase of FDA approval to treat said conditions, and several states are predicted to legalize them. I should know—I am a journalist for psychedelic therapy and have had the honor of interviewing the field's top scientists; additionally, I am in the works of directing a documentary about it. My own experience with psychedelic therapy was life-changing, and I owe these plants, and this ancient medicinal knowledge, endless gratitude.

Acknowledgements

First and foremost, I want to thank Ian Graham Leask at Calumet Editions for always believing in me. We met at the UW Writer's Institute, and the moment I told him about my novel, he was sold. *Je vous remercie mille fois, mon très chèr ami.* I wrote this novel in 2016, then sat on it until the time was finally right. As for the UW Writer's Institute, it fed my writer's soul for over a decade and seeded beautiful memories while helping me grow: Laurie Scheer and Christopher Chambers, you are magic makers. To my editor Sarah Knight, I couldn't have dreamed up a better person to poke at this novel and I'm so honored to have worked with a legend in the literary world!

Dziękuję bardzo Maximilien and Mikołaj—my sons, and *mulţumesc fromos* to my partner Daniel for supporting me in everything I do.

To my early work beta readers, you are wondrous, and I am forever grateful: Jessica Cerepa, Joy Stoyanova, Timothy Young, John Wayne Pint, Danyelle Post, Mickey Johnson, Rey Castro, Donna Riethmiller, Amanda Hagerstrom, Richelle Smith, Keara Neifach, Nam Patel, Stephanie Naman, and Caitlin Leutwiler.

Finally, thank you to my family at large—you believe in me as an artist, and I can only wish all the world's artists feel the same love and support.

About the Author

Courtney Lochner holds degrees in French Literature and Communication Studies from Sorbonne Université and the University of Minnesota. A former professional dancer, she has lived throughout the world and worked as a ballet and hip-hop dance instructor in Rio de Janeiro, a camp counselor in the Pyrenees, and an English teacher in Prague. A travel writer and psychedelic therapy journalist, her fiction has been made into a film by Moxie Pictures in association with *Glamour Magazine*. Courtney is the co-founder of Cosmic Dust Films.

Made in the USA
Las Vegas, NV
11 October 2022